PRAISE FOR

Secrets of the Sands

". . . a lushly visual and highly detailed world of desert tribes, a language of beads, and a unique way of vi

--*Library Journal*

"intriguing . . . engaging."

--*Publishers Weekly*

"The final product put me in awe of where the world-building skills of Wisoker are at this early stage of her career . . . reminiscent of something out of an Ursula K. LeGuin novel in detail and complexity. Wisoker, like the best authors of this genre, has created a completely original society upon which to tell her story."

--*SF Site*

"*Secrets of the Sands*, the first novel of Leona Wisoker, is a truly amazing accomplishment. Restrained yet tense, compelling, intricate and imaginative, it contains so much of the everything lacking in most modern fantasy one can find oneself moved to tears when the pages finally run out. If all first novels were this good, no television would ever be turned on again."

--CJ Henderson, author of *Brooklyn Knight*

"Leona Wisoker is a gifted storyteller and in *Secrets of the Sands* she has succeeded in crafting a refreshingly unpredictable tale set in a stunningly rich and detailed world."

--Michael J. Sullivan, author of the Riyria Revelations series

"With a flair for evoking exotic locales and an eye for detail, Leona Wisoker has crafted a first novel peopled by characters who are more than they first seem. From the orphaned street-thief who possesses an uncanny ability to read situations and people, to the impetuous noblewoman thrust into a world of political intrigue, Wisoker weaves a colourful tapestry of desert tribes, honour, revenge, and an ancient, supernatural race."

--Janine Cross, author of the Dragon Temple Saga

". . . Wisoker makes a praiseworthy work when it comes to world building, creating with care and without haste a strong world, one piece at a time . . . another unique element of the story which . . . certainly will be developed more in the series' next novels."

--Dark Wolf's Fantasy Reviews

Secrets of the Sands

by

Leona Wisoker

First Trade Edition – published 2010
Printed in the United States and the United Kingdom

MERCURY RETROGRADE PRESS
227 Sandy Springs Place
Suite D374
Atlanta, Georgia 30328

www.MercuryRetrogradePress.com

ISBN 978-0-9819882-3-8
Library of Congress Control Number 2009-939060

Acknowledgments

I have so many people to thank; so many who believed in me when I didn't know how to believe in myself. Parents, grandparents, siblings, husband, stepdaughters, in-laws, and friends all served a vital role in the process; I am even grateful to many people who are no longer in my life, as they were, for good or ill, a critical part of moving me further along the path to where I am now. I suspect the full gratitude list would stretch for ten single-spaced pages, far more than I have room for here.

A few specific names rise to the extreme top of this long list, however: my mother, who showed me how to fight for myself and patiently put me back together over and over when I fell off the wall, scattering bits of yolk everywhere; my husband Earl, without whose unwavering emotional support, and willingness to cook dinner on occasion, I never would have completed this book, much less dared to try for a publishing contract; my cousin Rhoda, who remains an enduring source of dance, laughter, joy, and strength in my life; every single one of the beautiful folks at *Green Man Review*, who nudged my writing up several notches simply by allowing me into their company of merry jesters, wise men, and scholars; John Adcox, who unwittingly, with his seemingly limitless creativity and energy, kept my competitive spirit fired up during difficult moments; Patrick, whose deeply rooted strength and unwavering belief in me is a most precious bulwark in my life; Todd, without whose help I would still be smoking two packs a day, and who also showed me the way to a truce with my shadow-self; James Franchese, a high school English teacher I've unfortunately lost track of, for encouraging me to write, delivering much-needed reality checks, and pestering me about overdue homework assignments; Alan and Georgia, who were gracious enough to open their home and their hearts to me during a very chaotic period in my life; artist Ari Warner, whose hard work on the maps has brought a rough vision to vibrant life; my agent, Judith Bruni, who took a chance and opened the door for me; and my very own Blue Fairy, Barbara Friend Ish, who worked even greater magic than turning a wooden doll into a real boy: she turned a trembling newbie into a real author and a fuzzy fledgling of a novel into a soaring golden eagle.

Dedication

This book is dedicated to my grandmother, Martha Pfleger, who always urged me to write down my wild stories. This one's for you, Omama; I wish I could put this book in your hands and see your smile again.

Contents

Royal Library Map no. 123:
The Southlands and Southern Kingdom

Secrets of the Sands

Chapter One

Hee-ay, hee-ay: the cry of the water-seller in the broad and the narrow places; *shass-shass-shass*, the warning signal to clear a road for noble blood, be it one or many together. *Iiii, iii-sass, iii-sass*, the wailing of a merchant who protested his certain ruin—with overtones of castration—should he lower the price any further. To Idisio's sensitive ears, the cacophony wove a melodic pattern that steered him, unerringly, to the best possible target.

At the height of his madness, the previous king had issued a decree forbidding residents of Bright Bay to speak anything but the common northern tongue. Two months later he had died of less-than-natural causes. Whether that absurd law had been the final wring on a mad asp-jacau's tail would never be known; rumor said the new ruler, now six months on the throne, still worked day and night to untangle the mess left behind by his predecessor.

Idisio listened for more than words, in whatever language, as he worked his way through the cobbled, paved, and sand-gravel streets of Bright Bay. The most important sounds of the city had nothing to do with speech. The clink of a full purse at the side of a foolishly confident merchant meant meals for the next few nights. The solid crunch of guard boots nearby meant *seek cover*: although the worst had quickly been culled under the new regime, changes in permitted behavior were slow to filter to the street level. But hisses and whistles were more important than any of those. They served as coded warnings from the other thieves scattered throughout the city.

A strident whistle from a rooftop lookout could save Idisio's life: while no true organization of thieves existed in Bright Bay, no one thief could ever hope to keep track of all the powerful people who moved through this sprawling city. The open warning, given by those who knew to those who didn't, was a traditional obligation that only the most foolish newcomers to the trade ignored.

Idisio had grown up on these streets and survived the madness that had temporarily given Bright Bay the nickname "Blood Bay." Those thief-calls had saved his life many times, and he'd passed on as many warnings; but many thieves, along with nobles, commoners, and priests, had fallen during the last weeks of Mad Ninnic's reign. While the worst of the madness had passed, the streets would never be safe for Idisio unless he found a more respectable—and legal—trade.

He considered that as likely as an asp-jacau meowing.

As he slid between fat and thin, clean and unwashed, his breath clogged with the hot smell of a crowded southern city on a summer day. A light touch on a thick wallet bound at a man's side prompted a certainty: *gold*. Not the half-rounds he normally counted himself lucky to get, but uncut disks of gold: more than one, many more. Idisio always knew, just from a touch, if the purse held anything worth taking; other thieves, seeing him withdraw from a mark empty-handed, had learned to steer clear themselves.

Idisio decided that any man foolish enough to carry gold in an outside purse deserved to lose it all. He reached, fingertip-knives busy, and had three of the four strings cut before another breath had passed.

Too late, he heard the warning: *tee-tee-tee-awrk! tee-tee-tee-awrk!* The loud, insistent call resembled that of a common sea-bird, but that particular bird never strayed this far from the docks proper. One of the roof lookouts was sending an urgent, if belated, "stay-clear"; and with the intuition that had kept him alive so far, Idisio knew he was the one being warned.

He started to slide away into the crowd, but found his wrist gripped in the mark's hand, a larger and harder one than his own. He followed the line of the arm up. Dark, hawk-hard eyes glared at him from a narrow face containing a sharply hewn nose, bronze skin, and thin lips—reason enough for the tardy warning.

Old blood was in that face; desert blood, noble blood—definitely someone to stay well and truly away from. Idisio had never before been so stupid as to grab a purse without checking the appearance of the mark for danger signs first; but it only took one mistake, and this had been it.

"My lord," Idisio said, caught without escape. He reached for an excuse, an apology, anything that would loosen that deadly dangerous grip and give him just a moment to run like he'd never run in his life.

The grip tightened, grinding the bones of Idisio's wrist together; the very real prospect of death right here and now ran cold down his back.

The slender finger-blades fell from his hand, landing on the paving stones with a distant *clink*.

Something about the noble's touch sparked his erratic intuition: *He won't kill me*. The surety faded, though, when he looked up into the man's dark stare.

"Who sent you after me?" the noble demanded.

Idisio ran through a rapid list of names in his head, searching for one that might get the grip on his wrist released in a moment of fear. In the face of that desert-hot glare, he could only say, "Nobody, my lord." He wouldn't put his worst enemy in the path of that stare. And he didn't *have* any names that might rattle this man.

"Liar," the noble said, pulling Idisio a step closer, thin lips stretching back. "*Who?*"

"What's going on here?"

For the first time in his life, Idisio blessed the arrival of the white-robed guards. There were four in this patrol, all carrying the thick staves of their office. At their side, an asp-jacau, tall and narrow, raised its thin snout and sniffed at the air, head tilted to allow one pale blue eye to study him.

Idisio let out a gasping breath of relief. Asp-jacaus only went out with King's Guards. Even a southern noble had to respect *them*. But the man holding Idisio either didn't know that or didn't care.

"Just a pick-thief," he said briefly.

"We'll handle it." A guard's hand landed on Idisio's shoulder from behind, closing into a hard grip that pinched a tender spot; Idisio hissed and flinched. The fingers dug in deeper, and Idisio squirmed, praying he wasn't dealing with an unculled "Ninnic's Guard".

The noble didn't loosen his hold, either. "I claim justice-right."

"But—"

"I'm summoned to the king. Argue my right with the king. Argue the time with the tide that goes by. Let us pass!"

Idisio felt his bladder weaken, and clamped down just in time. He'd never had that extreme of a reaction before, but this mistake could cost his life.

Claiming justice-right marked the man as a full desert lord. *They* didn't consider themselves subject to *any* kingdom laws. Many of them offered no term of courtesy beyond "lord" to the king himself.

And he had heard that desert lords, when angry, took their price in blood . . . slowly. Idisio might be better off with a potentially sadistic guard after all.

But his odd intuition insisted: *He won't kill me. This is a good thing happening.*

Idisio wondered if he were losing his mind.

The guards gave way. The desert lord yanked Idisio forward. He trotted at the man's side, wrist bones no longer in danger of breaking but still held bruisingly tight.

"Give me no trouble," the noble said. "I'm not in the mood for it."

"You're hurting me," Idisio whined, deciding to give pathos a try, and dragged his step.

"I just saved you a notch on the ear at the least," the noble snapped, with no change in pressure. "You'll live through a bruise or two. Hurry up; I'll drag you if I have to."

Idisio matched the man's pace, feeling like a child against the noble's towering height and determined stride. He said, desperate now, "Nobody sent me, my lord. I swear."

"I'll ask of you later," the noble said ominously. His pace quickened yet again; Idisio jogged at his side and soon had no breath to protest further.

They swept through areas of increasing wealth, where Idisio had never dared move so openly. Plain clothes gave way to fine silks; brightly painted merchant stalls replaced worn storefronts. Horses stepped delicately through the corridors that opened for them in any crowd. Idisio even glimpsed the distinctive purple, gold, and black tabard of a King's Rider, honored emissary and royal news-bearer throughout the kingdom.

Spaces grew wider as they neared the palace grounds, the heart of Bright Bay. This area was no less sprawling than the rest of the city. It boasted seventeen gates into the grounds proper; at least fifteen noble families lived inside the miles of costly iron fence, along with enough merchants and storehouses to make the palace a small city in its own right.

The noble headed for the Crown Gate. Gold had been cast in great loops around the grim iron bars, decorated further with river-opal, diamonds, and bits of moon-shell—not particularly attractive, except to a thief skilled at prying gems from their settings. The guards protecting this gate stood sentry as much to keep that from happening as to ward against intrusion.

The noble went forward as if intending to simply walk right through the open gates, ignoring the guards and horizontally lowered pikes in his way. He stopped at the last second, the shaft of a pike almost touching his chest. Idisio, staggering at the jarring halt, bumped into the pole.

"I'm summoned to the king," the noble said, staring at the guards around him as if expecting them to bow on the spot.

"And this one?" The man wearing the white braid of command pointed at Idisio.

Idisio opened his mouth, hoping to get the guards to take him away from this madman. As his wrist bones tightened again, he abandoned the notion. He stood quietly, eyes downcast, gritting his teeth against the fire flowing from wrist to elbow to shoulder and neck. His hand began to go numb.

The grip loosened a little, just enough to allow prickling sensation to shoot through his hand.

"He's mine," the noble said briefly. "I'll speak for him."

A quick glance up showed the guards surveying him skeptically. He tried to look meek and innocent. Whether he succeeded or his captor's obvious status dominated, the guards finally stepped aside and allowed them through.

The pace resumed, Idisio jogging along beside the long-legged stride.

"You needn't hold me," he said, darting a quick glance up to the noble's stern face. "I couldn't get anywhere; I'd be grabbed right away if you weren't with me. I'll stay with you, lord. I swear."

The noble paused, considering. "Very well," he said at last, and let go. "Mind, if you try to run. . . ." He lifted a corner of his tunic to show a pair of long-handled throwing knives with hilts of solid ebony.

Any hopes Idisio had of escape failed immediately.

"Yes, my lord," he said humbly, his stomach once again queasy with fear. Only weapon-masters used ebony on their weapon hilts; this noble had to be one of the best knife throwers in or out of the kingdom to be carrying those at his side.

As blood rushed back into Idisio's hand, the pain increased. Cradling the hurt arm in the other hand, Idisio hurried obediently at the noble's side, trying not to moan in agony even as he gaped at the astounding sights unfolding around them.

They entered a wide space filled with flowerbeds and statues, fountains and benches where a strolling courtier might take his ease with his latest lady of favor. No smell of trash and marsh could be found here: instead, a faint breeze stirred up the scents of rosemary and roses, white-musk flowers and tall, red-flowering sage.

Idisio breathed deeply, overwhelmed; he'd never known such luxury. Knowing it now, he fiercely wanted it for himself. The thought of returning to the streets and lifting half-rounds from an unfortunate's purse seemed, suddenly, worthless as a worn wooden half-bit. And that damned intuition kept nagging: *This is a good thing happening. Stay with it.*

Maybe he wasn't losing his mind, after all. He started to sort through possible ways to stay in this magical place. Perhaps he could plead for a job, throw himself on the king's mercy. Was he really going to be in front of the king? His step slowed as that thought fell on him with the force of a fish-eagle's plunge. His knees wobbled, not wanting to carry him forward.

Even the noble's pace eased as they moved through the cloud of scent shaken loose by the light wind. Eventually he took a deep breath and resumed his quick stride, not looking back to see if Idisio followed.

Idisio hurried to keep up, trotting along at the man's side and keeping his eyes ahead as best he could. Moving too fast to properly focus on his surroundings, Idisio managed only a series of fleeting glimpses: silk curtains, elaborate tapestries, luxurious rugs, ornate chairs. He put a hand to his mouth, afraid he would start to drool with envy. They entered a series of hallways, turning this way and that, up and down short flights of stairs, until Idisio considered himself thoroughly and unusually lost.

Finally they stopped in front of a small grey door. Two guards with gold and silver braids looped on their sleeves watched as they approached, offering no challenge but also no welcome. The noble made a polite motion of greeting and stared at the door as if expecting it to be opened for him.

"Lord Cafad Scratha," he said briefly. "I'm expected."

"Yes," one of the guards said. "Go in."

Idisio's mouth dropped open. All tales he'd heard claimed Scratha Family had been wiped out almost twenty years ago; nobody knew why or by whom. Apparently one survivor hadn't been worth mentioning. A complete slaughter must have made for a more dramatic story.

Looking sour, Scratha pushed open the door. It swung noiselessly inward, and they walked into the king's presence.

Not into the throne room, as Idisio had expected, but a small apartment of sorts, filled with bright sunlight. Idisio glanced up, his jaw sagging once more. Thick panes of fine glass, some sand-cast, others clear, were set in the ceiling, arranged in an eight-pointed star pattern: the traditional king's symbol. The display of wealth and power made the Crown Gate look cheap.

"Lord Oruen," Scratha said.

Idisio brought his attention hastily down and sank to his knees in belated courtesy.

"Up," Scratha said. "This is an informal audience." His expression hardened as he looked back to the man across the room.

King Oruen stood easily as tall as Scratha and had the same eagle's nose, dark hair, and narrow build. His skin seemed a lighter shade of bronze, his eyes round where Scratha's held distinct angles. The royal robe hung neatly on a hook to one side; he wore a simple, if finely cut, outfit of blue and green cotton. If not for the robe and the "Lord Oruen" from Scratha, Idisio would have thought this man simply a high-ranking court official.

"Informal," the king agreed. His dark eyes studied Idisio for a moment. "Is this boy needed?"

Without thought intervening, before Scratha could answer, Idisio found intuition speaking for him. "I stay with my lord, Sire."

He couldn't believe he'd said it, but there it was, and now both men were staring at him. King Oruen's mouth quirked in what might have been amusement, while Scratha's expression could have melted sand into glass. Idisio swallowed hard and tried to look sure of himself.

"Very well," the king said, seeming to dismiss the matter.

With one last, ominous squint, Scratha let it go as well. Idisio realized he'd been holding his breath; he let it out as quietly as possible.

"Do you know what I've summoned you for, Cafad?"

"I imagine I've upset some petty courtier again." Scratha sounded indifferent, but his hands curled into fists.

"No," the king said. He looked at Idisio. "Do you like my solarium, boy?" He pointed to the glass overhead. "I saw you admiring it when you came in. It was Sessin Family's gift to me, marking their acceptance of me as the new king in Bright Bay. They tore down the existing roof and replaced it with that in less than a tenday."

Idisio glanced up again, then back to the king, confused.

"It's wonderful, Sire," he said. "It's a marvel."

"A marvel that could have been commonplace by now, if not for the Purge," the king said, his gaze on the glass star overhead. "A wonder that should have, would have been, if the madness hadn't destroyed hundreds of years of learning. Sessin now knows more about glasscraft than anyone north of the Horn. They're in an excellent position for trade, on that basis alone. Quite a lot of money in glass, as I understand it. Quite a lot of tax revenue potential for the city they choose to set up their main trade shops in. And do I need to note that this gift also marks Sessin Family as my *allies*? That's not something for a new king to take lightly, either." He didn't lower his gaze from the ceiling as he spoke.

Scratha's face was tight as his fisted hands. "This is about Nissa."

"*Lady* Nissa, of Sessin Family." The king at last turned his gaze back to Scratha. "She has some very livid bruises, Lord Scratha, and this isn't the time of year for long sleeves."

Cafad Scratha seemed to draw himself upright and compact, all at once.

The king said, "She claims you threw her into the street half-naked, bellowing that she was a whore."

"It's a good name," Scratha said. "She's Sessin."

"She admits she should have told you," the king said. "She was afraid of your obsession."

"*Obsession?*"

"That's what it's been named," the king said, "and I agree. The girl did nothing, by her account, that gave cause to humiliate her like that. Can you give a good reason?"

Scratha looked mutinous. "She's Sessin. I'll have nothing to do with that family."

"You're a fool." The king sat down with a heavy sigh. "I have to do something about this, Cafad. I won't alienate my strongest supporters for your pride."

"Your strongest supporters?" Scratha said, and while his volume stayed low, his tone was anything but mild. "Sessin's a family of cowards. Their *support* means nothing. Less than nothing. I wouldn't let one of their asp-jacaus near me, much less one of their women."

If there had been any point to running, Idisio would already have been edging towards the door. He stood very still and hoped they wouldn't notice his continuing presence.

"I *know* Sessin was involved in my family's destruction," Scratha said, "and gods save them when I find the proof to present to a desert court. And I will. I'll find it! And then you'll see—"

"Enough," the king said, raising a hand. "None of the desert families had anything to do with your family's slaughter. I won't believe such a thing, and neither should you. You're wasting your life on this. Find a good woman, of whatever family or line. Fill your fortress with the laughter of children instead of the wailing of ghosts."

Scratha stood mute and straight, a hard line to his jaw and a darkness in his eyes.

The king looked at that grim, silent refusal and slowly shook his head. "I had hoped to talk you into apologizing to Nissa. I see that won't happen."

"No, Lord Oruen," Scratha said. "That will never happen."

"Sessin isn't the only family you've upset lately, Cafad."

"That's desert lord business, Lord Oruen, and none of yours."

"You've brought your squabbles into Bright Bay, so it's now become my business," the king said just as sharply. He stood, and his tone changed to one of authority, one he might have used in front of a full audience in his throne room. "I have a task for you, Cafad Scratha."

Idisio could feel roses and silks rapidly fading beyond any chance of his reach. He'd be lucky to live out his life in a dungeon alongside the man he'd foolishly claimed as lord. Twice in one day, intuition had failed him, and each time more disastrously.

"The royal library has been decimated since the time of Initin the Red," the king went on. "I am of a mind to restock it. An accounting of the kingdom is sorely needed: history, current affairs, culture, religions, beliefs, and so on. Without such a guide, I'll be hard put to pull order from the chaos I've been left. You're a man of learning and intelligence; I place you in charge of compiling a modern history of this kingdom. I want tales of how the last two hundred years have affected the rest of the kingdom, especially the northern half."

Scratha opened his mouth to speak, eyes narrowing.

The king stopped him with another imperious gesture. "Arason is of special interest to me, but be very careful; they're a bit touchy at the moment."

The two men locked stares.

"This *task* of yours will take years, if I agree to do it," Scratha said. "If."

"You'll do this, Cafad Scratha," the king said. "Or lose your access to Bright Bay for the rest of your life."

Scratha stared, seeming more puzzled than angry, for another moment, then shrugged and gave a sharp nod. "I'll do the job."

The king smiled without joy and shook a small silver hand bell. At the faint tinkling sound, a servant stepped through a side door half-hidden behind draperies, and stood, attentive and silent, waiting instruction.

"Settle Lord Scratha and his servant in a guest room," the king directed. "When they're ready, take them to see the steward regarding supplies and two horses."

"I only need one horse, Lord Oruen," Scratha said stiffly.

"What about your servant? Is he to run at your stirrup? Take two, and a pack-mule if you need one."

Scratha turned a glare on Idisio.

"I don't know that I'll need a servant on this journey," he said after a moment, turning a markedly more polite glance to the king. "I'll move faster traveling alone, and I'm used to doing for myself. Taking this one on was . . . a whim. I'll find another place for him, before I leave."

Intuition prodding him hard, Idisio gave in, hoping for better results this time, and matched the desert lord's quick recovery with his own before the king could speak.

"My lord, I'm no whim. Just the other day you said you couldn't do without me! And I really don't know what I'd do without you."

"Take your servant along," the king ordered before Scratha could speak. "He'll come in handy, and he seems devoted to you: not something to toss aside lightly."

"Indeed," Scratha said.

Idisio shivered at the ice held in that single word, and wondered whether he'd made a very bad mistake after all.

The wall crashed up behind Idisio, and his breath thumped from his lungs at the impact. Idisio rolled away from Scratha's reaching hand and scrambled to his feet. Settling into a crouch, weight on his toes, he kept his eyes fixed on Scratha.

"Wait," he said, knowing it wouldn't do any good. "Wait, my lord, please. . . ."

The man fairly steamed with fury. Idisio didn't think Scratha would dare to kill him, since they both had the king's notice now, but he suspected a hefty helping of bruises for his insolence loomed in the near future.

Idisio let the plea hang in the air and watched with intense relief as the madness slowly faded from Scratha's eyes, leaving behind a simpler and safer version of that anger.

"I'll ask you again," Scratha said. "*Who sent you?*"

What the king had said helped Idisio understand the desert lord's obsession, but made a convincing reply no easier to craft.

"Nobody, my lord," Idisio said. "I'm just a simple street thief. I made a mistake, trying for your pocket."

"And as a *simple street thief* you nailed yourself to my side in front of the king?" Scratha demanded.

Idisio lifted his hands in a helpless gesture. "It's a better life than scrounging half-bits for a living, my lord; can you blame me for trying?"

"I don't believe you."

Idisio shrugged and straightened. "Will you take my service, my lord, or am I out on the streets again? If I go back on the street now, after walking into the palace by your side, I'll be dead by nightfall." An outright lie, which was dangerous with a desert lord; but it would resonate with the man's paranoid fears.

Scratha stared at him, anger easing further, and finally said, "Very well."

Idisio let out a very quiet sigh of relief through barely parted lips.

"Get your belongings, then, and meet me back here," Scratha said, turning away.

Idisio thought back over his small, carefully hidden cache of possessions; nothing there worth the trip to gather. A small dagger, a ragged shirt, a worn pair of sandals, a handful of coin that looked pitiful next to what he hoped to make now—if Scratha intended to pay him as a servant rather than use him as a slave. It seemed worth the risk.

"I have nothing to get, my lord."

"Sit quietly, then."

The noble knelt at a low wooden desk, pulled a quill, ink, and three pieces of parchment from the shallow drawers as though he'd known they were there, and began to write. Not being able to read, Idisio could only guess; one looked like a list, the other like a letter to someone. Judging by the frequent pauses, a good deal of thought was going into the writing of both. The third took less time.

Idisio sank to the floor while Scratha wrote, grateful for the chance to rest. His bare feet were scuffed and aching from walking over so much unaccustomed stone. He normally kept to the sand and dirt paths of the city, but almost all of the trip to and through the Palace had been on paved roads and along hard stone corridors.

"Here's your first task, then, *servant*," Scratha said at last, rolling up two of the papers, note inside the list, and fastening a silk ribbon tightly around them. The longer letter he folded and pushed to one side. "Go with that man waiting outside and take these to the steward. They're just supply lists and directions on what we'll need," he added, sounding impatient, as if Idisio had questioned him.

Idisio stood, feeling the weight on his feet as if he were made of lead more than flesh. "You're not going, my lord?"

"No. I have other . . . tasks to do."

The steward was a thin, sharp-faced man of no readily-apparent bloodline and a sour demeanor. He stared at Idisio as if examining a particularly nasty bug.

"Eh . . . the servant to Lord Scratha, *s'e*," the steward's secretary murmured, then withdrew hastily.

The disdain on the steward's face intensified.

"No surprise," he said, not standing, "that he'd take on such as you." He held out a thin-boned hand on which veins looped and sprawled prominently against paper-dry skin. "Give me the list, then, don't stand there like a fool."

Idisio stood silent, gaze on the floor, as the steward snapped the rolls open with quick gestures.

"I see," the steward said, his voice considerably colder than it had been. "Boy, look at me."

Idisio raised his gaze slowly.

"Do you know what this letter says, boy?"

"No, *s'e*. I can't read, and my lord said nothing of it."

"Kind of him, to send you with a handful of chaos and say nothing to you of it," the steward said. "Typical of him, in fact."

He leaned back in his chair and rubbed at his eyes, seeming exasperated.

"The man's got no idea of palace politics, none at all—and not much notion of how to play his own land's games, either. He said *nothing* of this to you? Are you lying to me, boy?"

"No, *s'e*, I wouldn't dare."

"I believe that, at least." The steward sighed and stood. "Come with me. I'll send a servant along with the supplies by the end of the day. No doubt your hasty young fool of a desert lord will want to leave first thing in the morning. Not that I said that, mind you," he added with a glare.

"No, *s'e*. *S'e*?" Idisio decided to chance his customary brashness. "What did the letter say?"

"Instructions to clean you up, and no surprise. You stink."

Cleaning him up, as it turned out, involved a thorough scrubbing by a fat old palace eunuch who only gave over the brush when Idisio threatened to shove it somewhere unpleasant, and only retreated farther than arm's length when satisfied that Idisio really would clean himself.

Idisio emerged feeling very raw and sour, especially when he found his old clothes gone. In their place lay the silks he'd wished for, spread out ruby and white on the wide clothes-stool, and a pair of dark soft-soled boots. He stared at them in dismay. The outfit might be suited to court, but certainly not the open road. He could imagine the state they'd be in after a tenday.

He suspected the steward of having a grim joke at his expense.

"S'ii," he started, turning to the eunuch to protest, but the man had slipped from the room already. There was nothing for it but to put the clothes on. Once dressed, Idisio stood very still, wide-eyed at how *smooth* the silk felt against scrubbed-raw skin. It felt like walking in a continual bath of cool water, and the way the fabric flowed over his body was heady and arousing. He swallowed hard and finally managed to subdue the reaction; it took him a bit longer to walk across the room and back without it recurring.

A long mirror leaned against one wall; he went to it hesitantly. He'd had a chance to look in burnished-metal mirrors, and once a real Sessin glass hand-mirror, but never his whole body at once.

Idisio knew he didn't qualify as handsome. He'd been laughed at and taunted by too many girls for that to be a hope. What stared back at him from the glass, however, wasn't as ugly as he'd expected.

He almost had the wide face of a born southerner, but free of dirt it showed a much lighter color than Lord Scratha's. His nose was far too snubbed to be true southerner, and his eyes, a clear bright grey, were unusually wide and round. His hair, washed, brushed, and tied back, turned out to be a fine shade of deep brown and as silky as the clothes he wore. His eyes shifted between grey-blue and grey-green as he studied himself, tilting his head this way and that. Standing straight in the fine new clothes, he could have passed for some noble's bastard down from the north.

Idisio hovered between shock and revelation: nobility weren't *born* looking one way and street-scum born another. They were all the same. Put a noble's son in rags and run him through the sand and dust of the back streets for a day, and he'd look like Idisio had that morning. Noble blood attracted girls. The way he looked now, maybe they wouldn't laugh at him any more.

It took him a while more to calm himself after *that* thought.

Finally, fairly sure he wouldn't embarrass himself, he took a guess at the door he thought opened to the hall and looked out. The eunuch sat on a wide stool just outside, and a guard stood to the other side of the door. They both glanced at him as he stepped out.

"Much better," the eunuch said, favoring Idisio with a faint smile.

The guard grunted, returned his attention to front, and said nothing.

"Sorry I took so long, *s'ii,*" Idisio said.

The eunuch's smile widened just a bit. "I understand," he said, standing. "Back in the room, boy. I've been asked to teach you some manners so you don't disgrace your lord at dinner tonight."

"At. . . ." Idisio stared, suddenly horror-struck at the implication. Needing manners, not disgracing his lord, meant he'd be at a formal dinner, a noble's dinner, more than likely with the king attending. The notion scared him silly. "At *dinner?*"

The guard made another small noise, his mouth twitching slightly in what might have been amusement or scorn.

"It would be rude beyond measure, as your lord is staying at the palace, not to join the king at table," the eunuch said calmly. "You have a bit over two hours left before the call. I expect I'll only need one."

"Nobody knows you as a street-rat," had been the eunuch's first piece of advice. "Don't act like one; nobody will peg you as one. Stand straight—that's it, like that—and say as little as you can. Better for people to think you slow or mute than to hear that gutter accent of yours."

Idisio stood silent at his lord's side for what seemed like hours in the before-dinner gathering, watching the nobility and their servants flow by like an unruly river. Scratha stayed still, not quite in a corner but with his back inches from a wall, and watched the proceedings with an expressionless face. He had dressed in sober clothes—black trousers and soft black boots, a dark grey tunic with a high collar. Idisio saw a thick silver band on his left thumb, stamped with what looked like a family crest, and a thin silver chain around his throat. His long dark hair was carefully pulled back and tied with a black leather thong.

In this crowd, all in silks and riotous colors, he stood out like an axeman at a wedding, and most people avoided him after a quick, uneasy glance his way. Idisio had the feeling that Scratha had aimed for exactly that effect.

Idisio's boots began to chafe. His legs hurt; his back and neck ached. He couldn't wait for this to be over. Servants didn't sit, the eunuch had told him. They stood at their lord or lady's side, hour after hour after hour, until the dinner ended. Only then, and only if they were lucky enough to have their lord's approval, could they go to the kitchen to scrabble over scraps.

Idisio had been unable to hide his dismay at that information. The eunuch had checked mid-sentence and given him a hard look.

"You haven't eaten yet today, have you, boy?" he demanded, then sent a servant for a plate of food. Crusty bread, still warm from the ovens, a wedge of fine white cheese, and thick slices of sand-pear; it had been a feast, and only the eunuch's restraining hand kept him from tearing into it like a hungry asp-jacau. Idisio's stomach still felt warm and full from that first lesson on eating in polite company.

Idisio looked over the before-dinner crowd with a rather benign feeling as a result, ignored his multiplying aches, and tried to see if his lord watched anyone in particular. He couldn't see any pattern, and his own gaze often wandered; a number of pretty girls were drifting around the room, most of them clad in thin silks and flowing gowns. The sight caught his breath hard in his chest. He looked at the ugliest old men in the room to calm himself.

"My lord," he said after a while, "may I ask a question?"

"What?"

"Why did the king say Arason is of special interest right now?"

"Ghost Lake," Scratha said, not looking down at him. "The people of Arason believe strange creatures live in the lake, creatures that come out and seduce unwary women. The children of such a union are supposed to have unusual powers, reading minds, seeing the future, and so on."

"Witches," Idisio said. Something about his lord's words sent a shiver up his back, as if there were more to the story. Seeing the future? *He won't kill me. This is a good thing happening. . . .* He blinked hard and tried not to think about whether his intuition could be considered witchcraft.

"Yes. The Church convinced Ninnic to investigate. Troops were sent to Arason to root out the witches. It got . . . ugly. Oruen called the troops back when he took the crown, but the damage will take generations to heal."

Arason is dangerous. Very, very dangerous. Idisio tried to quell the panic rising in his throat.

"Do we have to go there?" he husked.

Scratha made no reply beyond a faint smile.

They stood in silence for a time, watching the room; then the faintest of sighs came from Scratha, drawing Idisio's attention. His lord's expression had shifted from bland to stony.

"Damn," the noble said, just barely audible.

A tall, thin young man strode towards them, aristocratic jaw set hard and ugly. Idisio had seen him before, moving through uptown and downtown streets with no worry over safety: Pieas Sessin didn't need any thieves' warning passed before him to warrant caution.

Scratha shifted slightly, as if considering rapid evasion, then stilled and waited, expressionless again. Pieas came to a halt before them, fine dark brows drawn into a fierce scowl.

"You, Lord Scratha," he said. "I've words for you."

"Sessin," Scratha said, making the name sound like an insult. "I've none for you."

Pieas's dark face flushed further. "You dishonored my sister, Scratha."

People were beginning to turn and watch.

"Your sister?" Scratha said idly, watching the young man with the detached interest he might have shown an unusually colored rat.

"Have you forgotten her so quickly?" Pieas's hands were clenched now, his eyes narrow. "I shouldn't be surprised—"

Before he could say more, an older man with a similar face but broader build pushed through the gathering crowd and clamped a hand on his shoulder.

"Pieas," the new arrival said, and neither tone nor grip was gentle.

The rage in the young man's expression shifted to a sulky, resentful demeanor as he turned to look at the man, who Idisio felt sure had to be Pieas's father or uncle. Pieas opened his mouth to protest, but the words seemed to fade into silence under the man's hard stare. With a last, burning glare at Scratha, Pieas jerked away to stomp off into the crowd, which scattered like sand in a strong wind as he passed.

"My apologies, Lord Scratha," the man said, offering a shallow bow. "Pieas is a bit of a hothead, I'm afraid. I warned him to stay away from you, but he listens about as well as a deaf and blind asp-jacau."

Scratha returned the slight bow a bit stiffly, as if reluctant to offer any courtesy to the man, and said nothing.

"I don't know what happened with my sister's daughter," the man went on, lowering his voice and casting a quick glance at the dispersing crowd. "I do know the girl's done nothing but cry for the past few days. I believe she was actually quite fond of you, Lord Scratha."

Scratha's face twitched, brows and lips and eyes contracting for an instant, but he stayed silent, his gaze watchful and wary now.

The man, in turn, studied Scratha in silence for a few moments, then said, "I suppose I may as well be hanged for a turkey as for a leg. I've been troubled for years over the way my family treated you, but I couldn't go against my Head of Family—at least, that's how I saw it when I was younger. But I've grown up a bit since those days, and now I can say aloud what I should have said then: that I never agreed with Lord Arit's policy, and I am truly sorry about how Sessin has treated you, Lord Scratha." He kept his voice low, although to his credit he didn't glance to see who else might be hearing his words.

Scratha stood still in a way that reminded Idisio of a thunderstorm about to break.

"I'm afraid I haven't met you, Lord Sessin," he said at last.

"I'm Lord Eredion Sessin," the man said. "Sessin's resident ambassador to the northern court. When we last met, you were only ten. I'm not surprised you don't remember me; there was rather a lot going on at the time." He grinned, a bright flash of even teeth in a dark face. "I normally don't attend these dinners, but when I saw Pieas setting out with that look on his face, I came along to keep him in hand."

Scratha drew a deep breath and let it out slowly, staring at the man with a distant, thoughtful expression.

Eredion waited a moment longer, then said, "Don't think so harshly of all our family, Lord Scratha; some of us are actually human." He offered another shallow bow and smile, then took his leave, unruffled by Scratha's silence and brooding regard.

A rattling crash of hardwood sticks on wide, hollow metal tubes hanging near one of the wide entryways brought the crowd to hushed attention. Before the ringing tones had completely stilled, people began moving through the doorway into the huge dining hall beyond. Idisio obediently followed Scratha, took up a place behind his lord's chair, and tried not to look intimidated or overawed.

The gathering room had been large, but with all the people moving about Idisio hadn't noticed the size or grandeur so much. Once everyone had settled into their seats, the dining hall was revealed as even more tremendous. Incredible vaulted ceilings rose high overhead, painted with murals showing the triumphs and tragedies of past kings and queens. King Ayrq, the first ruler of Bright Bay, glowered down, unappetizingly, at the diners: a huge, fierce man towering over those around him, one booted foot on a large pile of skulls. Another mural showed a queen with long black hair unbound and flowing around her, beseeching the skies as if asking one of the old gods for aid, a child limp in her arms.

Idisio tried to keep his attention on his lord, but found it difficult. He'd never seen such vibrant artwork before, and certainly never on ceilings. He'd never been in a room lit by what must have been hundreds of fine candles, some of them taller than he could reach. More than candles brightened the room; several alcoves brimmed with with intense columns of light from some hidden source.

A hard nudge to the ribs from the boy standing beside him jolted Idisio into realizing he'd been gawking. Many of the other servants around the table openly grinned at him. He swallowed hard and stood a bit straighter, resolving to keep his mind on his job for the rest of the night.

Scratha said little, despite overtures from several people seated nearby; and the king, at the other end of the table, seemed to be ignoring the desert lord completely. Idisio had expected that Scratha, as a desert lord, would be sitting closer to the king's hand, but Scratha seemed oblivious to the unsubtle insult.

"My lord Scratha," said a thin young woman seated across from the desert lord.

She was dressed in what Idisio guessed to be the high fashion of the moment. It seemed to involve a tremendous amount of bright red chachad feathers and silver chains. Idisio thought it looked absurd, but the girl preened as if the feathers made her a firetail bird herself and fluttered her lashes at Scratha as she spoke.

"I'm Alyea Peysimun. Pleased to meet you. I understand you've not been seen at court for some time."

"True," Scratha said, not taking his attention from his food.

She waited, looking expectant; slow realization crept over her pert features like a growing storm cloud.

"Really," she said, no longer fluttering her lashes. "My lord Scratha, I had heard you were a man of few words; I see that's true as well."

He bit into a roasted chicken leg and said nothing. She raised an eyebrow and a shoulder at the same time and, her smile distinctly thinner, turned her attention to the people on her right.

"I don't blame you," said the thin man seated to Scratha's right, quietly, leaning over just a bit to keep the words private between them, "for not wasting words on her. She's a ninny."

Scratha spared the man a brief, dark stare before taking another bite of the chicken leg.

"Chicken," the man went on amiably, ignoring the lack of response. His voice acquired a conversational level. "I don't care for it much. I will say this for Ninnic; he knew how to set a table. Gerho at every meal, prepared in every imaginable way. Grilled, steamed, braised, fried; oh, that man knew good food, or at least his chefs did. Oruen's no gourmet." He flicked a finger at the plate in front of him. "Good enough," he noted with a shrug, "but I do miss gerho."

Idisio repressed a shudder. Marsh lizard had always been the food of last desperation for him, but all he had ever sampled was the stringy version available to anyone with the skill to set a small trap. Still, that was the first kind word he'd ever heard about the previous king. *He served good lizard*: what an epitaph for a mad ruler. Idisio held back a snort of nervous laughter.

"Do you like a properly cooked platter of gerho, my lord?" the man asked against Scratha's continuing silence.

"Yes."

Icy premonition scrabbled like a wet rat down Idisio's back: *Gerho. Something about gerho . . . is that going to be important?* He grimaced and pushed the uneasy worry to the back of his mind. He was having more intuitive flashes today than he'd experienced in the past four tendays, and he didn't care for it one bit.

"It's a shame for the merchants that King Oruen can't stand it," the man rattled on. "I understand some of them are rather put out financially; the market held quite favorable just before Ninnic had his unfortunate accident."

Idisio held his face as expressionless as possible. So that pleasantry covered Ninnic's death among the nobility? An unfortunate accident? The streets called it murder, and born of treason, but always in the tones of fact, not complaint. *Nobody* sane honestly missed Ninnic. Oruen had been marked as a hero the day he took the throne, from the lowest gutter to the highest table in the city.

The talkative man rattled on for a few moments about gerho prices, market collapses, and despairing merchants. "There's one man in particular, invested too heavily, been haunting the palace trying to convince the king to change his mind. I believe he's only just left a few days ago. Lashnar . . . yes, Asti Lashnar, that's his name. Have you ever met him?"

Scratha dropped the bare bone on his platter and reached for a piece of bread from the basket in front of him. He made no reply.

The man sighed. "Lord Scratha," he said, "you really ought to learn at least the basics of social convention, you know."

Scratha set the bread on his plate and turned his gaze to the man beside him. "Why? It's all chattering nonsense. I won't waste my breath on it."

"Suit yourself," the thin man said, and turned his attention to people who were interested in chattering nonsense.

By the time the last platter of desert-honey pastries had been cleared from the table, the afternoon snack seemed like days ago. Idisio found himself impatient to get to the kitchen and grab the remaining scraps of the glorious dishes he'd been seeing and smelling all evening.

But with a motion of his hand, Scratha called his attention.

"Stay with me," the noble said when Idisio bent to see what his lord wanted. The king rose to take his leave, and the whole room stood, everyone bowing deeply. As the nobles drifted to the surrounding gardens and social-rooms, Scratha laid a hand on Idisio's shoulder and steered him in a different direction.

They walked through hallways and around corners, turning this way and that, seeming to go in circles, until Idisio once again conceded himself lost. At last he saw a familiar portrait. Confirming his guess, they paused before an unremarkable grey door.

"Yes, you're expected," one of the guards said, deadpan, and once again they walked through the door into the presence of King Oruen.

The royal robes of public appearance were draped almost carelessly over the back of the king's chair. The king, now simply a thin, gangly man in breeches and tunic, half-slouched in his chair, looked up as they entered and pointed silently to seats. Without protest this time, Scratha sank into one and motioned Idisio into another.

"Lord Oruen," Scratha said. "Once again, I am here at your summons."

"And once again," the king said, "I'm holding back an urge to throttle you, Cafad." He held up a sheet of parchment that showed signs of having been crumpled and carefully smoothed back out. "What are you trying to do to me?"

"You benefit from this arrangement, Lord Oruen."

The king looked at the letter again, shaking his head slowly. "The desert families will have a collective stroke when they hear of this."

"Let them twitch," Scratha said. "Your steward already has a brief version of the letter in your hand. No doubt he'll spread the word before the news loses its value."

The king's gaze sharpened into a glare.

"You're a fool," he said, then: "No, you're not. You've made it impossible for me to refuse. Nobody will believe that I turned this offer down. *Damn* you, Cafad!"

Scratha's only answer was a shrug, hands spread wide.

"What did you put in the steward's note?" the king demanded.

"That I ceded you stewardship of my lands while I am working off your displeasure," Scratha said, emotionless. "Nothing more. The name change I put to you alone."

Idisio tried not to choke audibly. A *desert lord* was giving a *northern king* authority over his entire holding? *Collective stroke* would be a mild reaction, under Idisio's admittedly limited understanding of southern politics. And as much, if not more, ire would be directed at the king for accepting as at Scratha for offering such a thing.

But the king was right: nobody would believe he had turned down such an opportunity.

The king stared at Scratha for a while, fingers nervously working the edges of the note in his hand as if he longed to rip it to bits.

"Very well, then," he said at last. "I accept. I'll guard your lands from intrusion while you're gone. You do realize the implications of your offer?"

"I do."

"As for the name change—are you sure you want to do that?"

"I can't very well collect history, observe culture, and send useful reports if the people I speak to are busy fawning on or fearing me as a desert lord," Scratha said. "It'll be hard enough, in the northlands, for me to pass at all without being attacked. I'll probably be relying on my servant in some areas."

Idisio did choke this time. Up to this moment, he hadn't considered anything of his role beyond a hazy supposition that he'd be tending to Scratha's horse, cooking him supper, mending and cleaning his clothes. Not that he knew how to do any of those things, but he'd figured it would all be easy enough to pick up along the way.

His strangling noise drew a brief, amused glance from the king. "I see you haven't mentioned that idea to your servant yet."

"There hasn't been time," Scratha said.

"At least you took time to clean him up before dinner. I'm grateful for that. And I hope you've also taken the time to caution your young thief against stealing anything while on palace grounds."

In the following silence, Idisio could feel all color draining from his face, and Scratha looked completely at a loss for words.

The king managed a tired smile. "I'd be a fool if I didn't inquire about a servant that looked as if he'd been picked up straight from the dustier streets of Bright Bay just before arriving—especially as you've never taken a servant before, Cafad. I thought you understood by now that I'm not a fool."

"Indeed," Scratha said. "My apologies, Lord Oruen. I seem to have forgotten."

"You're not the only one that forgets." The king sighed. "Why, if I may ask, that choice of name?"

"Gerau was my *s'enetan*'s name," Scratha said.

The king nodded. "Honoring your grandfather's memory, I can understand," he said. "And— forgive me—*sa'adenit*? I know you're no fool yourself, but don't you mean *s'e deaneat*, son of a desert family?"

Scratha looked grim. "I said what I meant."

"There aren't many who understand the old languages anymore," the king said. "Most people won't know what you mean."

"All the better," Scratha said. "Anyone who understands that word is dangerous."

Idisio had held his silence for too long. Questions were crowding in his throat, becoming painful. He burst out, "My lord, Sire—what does it mean?"

"Ah," the king said, smiling again as his gaze shifted to Idisio. "This one, at least, is safely ignorant, if there is any such thing."

Scratha shook his head, brooding, and said nothing.

"What does it mean?" Idisio repeated.

The king answered, as Scratha sat silent. "It translates to 'Blood on the Sand.' The *sa'a* at the beginning marks it as matrilineal, where a line run by male parentage would call it *se'edenit*. It comes from an old verse. I learned it as a child, but I probably received a poor translation. Here's best I can recall." He began to chant in a hoarse voice:

When the desert sleeps
It does not forget its secrets
It does not forgive the blood
The blood that was shed without cause.
Stone grows cold and flowers close
But the desert remembers the warmth of life
The warmth of the blood as it fell to the sand.
The blood on the sand may disappear
But the desert does not forgive the death.
With the sun's awakening the blood flows fresh
And the killer is damned by the desert
Because the desert does not forget
And the desert will never forgive.

The king paused, then repeated softly, "'The desert will never forgive.' That verse always gave me chills."

Idisio nodded fervently in agreement, goose bumps running up and down his spine.

"That *was* a poor translation," Scratha said. He had crossed his arms during the recital, and still looked distinctly displeased. "It's much longer than that, and more explicit. Northerns like to water everything down. But that version serves the point."

"It's a call for vengeance," the king said quietly, his gaze fixed on the desert lord. "A thoroughly ugly call, at that, when it's translated without what you call 'watering down' the words."

"I will find the hand behind my family's slaughter," Scratha said, equally soft and calm, but madness flickered in his eyes again. "I will have their blood in equal measure. Never think I'm giving that up, however far you send me. Who knows, maybe the northlands will have clues I couldn't find in the south. Stranger things have happened in this world."

The king opened his mouth, checked, then sighed. "King's Researcher Gerau Sa'adenit it is, then. I really hope you've thought this out, Cafad."

"I have," Scratha said, and stood. With two long steps he loomed over the king; then he knelt and held out his hand, palm up, offering a heavy silver ring with what looked like a family sigil stamped on the face.

Oruen stared at it for a moment, as if the desert lord were offering poison; then he reached out and picked the ring gingerly from Scratha's palm. "I'll tell people you've gone to the Stone Islands," he said, not taking his gaze from the ring. "At least I can give you that much protection against gossip."

"As you wish," the desert lord said, sounding supremely indifferent, then stood, retreating as swiftly as he had advanced. "May we retire, Lord Oruen?"

The king waved a weary assent, sinking further into his chair. The last glance Idisio had of the king showed a deeply worried expression and a note once again crumpled between royal hands.

They didn't return to their room, as Idisio had expected. Instead, his lord guided him through another seemingly endless march. They turned and twisted through various hallways, climbing a shallow flight of steps and then descending, several changes of direction later, a rather longer set of stairs.

The air grew noticeably damp, and Idisio put his arm over his nose to ward against the increasing tang of mold and mildew. The space between the guttering wall sconces grew until islands of light lay ahead and behind while they walked in darkness. The hallway narrowed, too; eventually Idisio could put his hands out to either side and feel the walls. And then the passage tightened further, until he could extend no more than elbows.

Finally there were no more torches ahead: only cold, unbroken silence and empty, dark, stinking air.

"My lord?" Idisio ventured, voice just above a whisper, hoping his growing panic wouldn't show in the low tone. This place felt *foul;* although no smell of blood or refuse registered in his nose, an itching nausea seemed to lurk in the very air.

Something bad *happened here. Lots of bad things.*

Idisio felt as though the dead crowded close, their slimy hands caressing his arms and back and legs.

The noble made a low shushing noise and went on, his feet making no noise on the pitted rock that had long ago replaced smooth stone underfoot. Idisio drew breath, cursing himself for a fool, and followed, one hand out to avoid running into his lord from behind.

And then something *stirred*, something deep and wild and formless; there came a shriek that had no sound and a moment of grey eyes staring desperately into his own. Scratha's hand, latching onto his wrist, jerked him back to the moment and almost brought the held scream from Idisio's throat. With a faint whimper, he followed the man's tug to the left.

To Idisio's intense relief, the feeling of foulness faded with each step they took. Scratha walked behind him from that point on, steering with one hand on Idisio's shoulder. Every so often Scratha tugged him to a brief halt, nudged a little faster, or turned this way or that, all in complete darkness. At times Scratha reached to touch, push, or pull something hidden, provoking muted clicks or distant grinding noises.

The floor finally sloped sharply upwards, and the air freshened, feathering Idisio's hair. The darkness became that of an open, cloudy sky on a moonless night.

"Wait here," Scratha said in a low voice, and slipped back into the passage.

Idisio stood still, trembling with relief, and stretched his arms out full in all directions, just to prove to himself that he could. Returning, Scratha made an odd noise that might have been amusement and nudged Idisio's shoulder.

"Come on. We've a walk yet."

Idisio couldn't hold back a groan. More walking sounded as welcome as an asp-kiss.

"Where are we going, my lord?"

"We're leaving. I've arranged everything to be left at a safe spot not far from here. And don't call me *Lord* any more. I'm Gerau Sa'adenit, Master Gerau to you, now."

"What happened to first thing in the morning?" Idisio muttered.

Behind them, the Bright Bay Watch-Tower bells sounded the midnight hour. Idisio cast an aggrieved glare towards the sound and stomped after his new master.

Chapter Two

In her dreams, Alyea danced.

Not the stately movements of the court waltzes and pavanes, not even the wilder peasant dances she'd secretly attended from time to time. She could find a partner for those anytime she liked, these days.

But her dreams had long been the only place she could safely dance *aqeyva*, the only place it was safe to hate the *s'iopes*—the priests of the Northern Church. Even now, as the city slowly settled back into unaccustomed sanity, she found herself reluctant to find another teacher and take up the training that had ended, once before, in such bloody horror.

Her feet slid across the sand and chalky grit which Ethu insisted on scattering over his training floor. Sweet strain shook through her muscles as she leaned forward on her right leg, lifting the left high, higher, and up! above her head, fingers brushing the ground—not into a flip, not this time, although she'd mastered that long ago—and back down, turning, drawing in close, closer, and straightening to stand solidly on both callused feet again.

The calluses were the despair of Alyea's maids. She wouldn't let them smooth her feet; she liked the feel of rough skin scraping against stone and grit. She smiled, sliding the hardened heel of one foot up against the calf of the other, just to feel the difference in texture—and the dream changed.

She was back at *that day*, in the public square, tied to a chest-high post, sweat stinging the cuts and bruises from her training sessions: wrists bound to a hook near groin level, the bindings forcing her shoulders forward and down, arms wrapped around the post in an obscene parody of an embrace. Two s'iopes in brown and white linen garments tied Ethu to a post beside her.

"No tears," Ethu hissed.

Alyea's stomach turned over. A scream wanted to emerge from her mouth, but her throat refused to make a sound. This was a dream: she had to escape it; but events moved on inexorably.

A gold-robed s'iope stepped in front of her: Rosin Weatherweaver, the head of the Bright Bay Northern Church, faithful advisor to King Ninnic and a thoroughly evil bastard all around. His eyes glittered as he intoned her crimes: "You come before us accused of heresy against the gods, rebellion against not only the gods but their earthly representatives and the king himself; you have performed acts forbidden to women, committed sacrilege in the sight of gods and men alike. . . ."

It went on for some time. Weatherweaver repeated the offenses in several different ways, managing to make it sound as though she had committed an entire host of depravities. The crowd seemed to breathe as one, a slavering entity intent on blood and tears; among them, her mother swayed, white-faced and horrified, more afraid and ashamed than Alyea would ever be.

Weatherweaver's voice rolled on, seemingly unstoppable. "—deceit against your guardians, sacrilege against the laws of gods and men—"

Sweat slicking what clothes they'd left her, sand grating under her bare feet, Alyea wished he'd just get it over with already.

At last he came to his offer:

"Publicly repent your sin and swear devotion to the Four Gods undying, or to go into death a heretic, casting your family into shame for ten generations to come. And if you choose heresy your family will be given punishment as well, to ensure the lesson is never lost."

Her mother moaned, face whiter than bleached sand, and sagged in the grip of the two s'iopes holding her.

Alyea opened her mouth, but before she could make a sound, Weatherweaver snatched two whips from one of the nearby s'iopes and leapt to stand behind her.

The first blow shredded her breath and her voice; the second and third loosed her bladder and bowels, a small humiliation in the face of the moment. But she didn't scream. She didn't cry. She hung on to Ethu's command like a lifeline, determined not to give them the satisfaction.

A long, awful pause; she began to draw in breath to speak, but just as her lips moved to form a word the fourth blow came, driving all thought and courage from her mind. She crumbled, unable to stand another stroke. Forcing breath, forcing words, she husked, "No more. Please. Repent. I repent."

Weatherweaver came around to stand before her, leering as he leaned forward.

"What's that?" he whispered. His eyes glittered. "You want your mother to go through this too?" The whips in his hands dripped with her blood.

Her mother swayed, face even whiter than before, and let out another low moan.

"Repent," she tried to scream; it came out as a hoarse croak, but loud enough, thankfully, for nearby ears to hear.

"Louder," demanded a lesser s'iope; Alyea noticed, with surprising clarity, that the priest's hands had crumpled sweaty wrinkles into the front of his formerly immaculate brown and white shirt. Weatherweaver shot him a hard glare, then straightened, his expression sour and disappointed, as the junior priest repeated, his own volume rising defiantly, "Say it louder, so all can hear."

"Repent. I repent." She didn't—couldn't stand to—look at Ethu as she spoke. "I repent my sins. I swear undying devotion. I swear."

They made her repeat it again, and once more, each time louder, until her voice finally gave out.

"Enough," the junior s'iope said at last, casting a nervous glance at Rosin Weatherweaver's glowering expression. "We accept your repentance. Now—"

Weatherweaver's eyes brightened. "Five more, I think," he purred. "To make sure she doesn't forget."

"I don't think that's—" the other s'iope began, but Weatherweaver was already moving.

Alyea lost track of sound. She drifted through a white, orange, and yellow tunnel of agony, hanging on to Ethu's command with everything she had. *No tears*. It was all she had left.

At last her bonds loosed and hands tugged her to stand in front of Ethu.

Weatherweaver loomed up in her peripheral vision, a wild gleam in his eyes, whips still in his hands. "Your words have condemned this man as guilty," he declared loudly. Then, lowering his voice, he added in her ear, "Persuade him to repent. Death can be fast for him if he repents."

She stared at Ethu. He looked back at her, eyes blacker than black and face stony as a mountain. He said only, "No tears."

That moment was the closest she came to losing control.

Ethu looked straight at Rosin Weatherweaver and told him to do something anatomically impossible and thoroughly obscene, elaborating loudly on that theme even as the blows began.

Alyea woke screaming, as she always did, the image of Ethu's bulging eyes and bloody, bitten lips seared into her mind. He hadn't screamed, not once; not when they threw buckets of salt water over him, not even when bone began to show through the cuts on his back.

She shook in the darkness, bathed in sweat but freezing with remembered terror, and nobody came to comfort her.

Scarcely any s'iopes remained in Bright Bay. Alyea had made Oruen promise to get rid of every single one if he gained the throne, and he'd held to his word. Most had left months ago, trundling out the eastern gates in fours and eights and sixteens: headed east to Salt Road or north through the Great Forest, returning to their legally acknowledged holdings. One small, stubborn band of holdouts had built a group of cottages at the western edge of the city, and for some reason Oruen allowed them that space; but they kept to themselves, and Alyea was content to let them be if they stayed out of her sight.

The Audience Hall in which the priests had dispensed their notion of justice through a mad, puppet king had been destroyed, and a new one was being built. But more petitioners filled the ballroom that served as temporary Audience Hall than ever before: an untidy line of supplicants, ranging from rich to poor, mostly southern but quite a few from north of the Great Forest. Today there was even a desert lord. Not as unusual as it had been under Ninnic, but still rare enough to send an excited buzz through the court and prompt everyone to crowd in, just a little, to hear the conversation.

Curious to see if it was Lord Scratha—the man could chill a fire to ice in seconds, and an audience between him and Oruen would be something to see—Alyea pushed and slid though the crowd, gathering more than a few sharp glares along the way, until she could see the desert lord clearly.

From where she stood, his back was to her, and his voice didn't sound familiar. She leaned to one side as a large woman, shifting restlessly, moved into her line of sight. There was no visible insignia on the desert lord's clothing of blue and sand-tan, but those weren't Scratha colors in any case. A wide, beaded band covered the man's right forearm from the wrist nearly to the elbow, but he stood too far away for Alyea to make out any distinct patterns or colors.

Alyea heard the Hall steward begin to announce someone's arrival just as the large woman stepped directly back and stumbled against her. In the resulting fuss of sharp words and apologies, she lost her chance to hear the identity of the new arrival. It had to be someone important, or the steward wouldn't have bothered calling out the name; and the reaction of the crowd around her suggested it wasn't someone particularly well liked.

She managed to catch a glimpse of the desert lord; he had turned to look towards the approaching newcomer. Even seeing his face clearly, she couldn't place him, but the man striding towards the throne was much younger—and she recognized him instantly: Pieas Sessin.

Alyea would never forget his face pressed close, his breath foul with wine and drugs; would never forget the pain, never forgive the humiliation which had led, in the end, to Ethu's death. Not that Pieas Sessin likely knew about that, or even cared.

Nausea thickened her throat, along with a wild desire to call out his crimes; but she couldn't do it. Not in front of Oruen. Never in front of Oruen. She'd promised herself that much, long ago.

As Pieas passed, arrogant in emerald green and sand-tan, the normal low chatter of the Audience Hall ceased completely. Even the most witless courtiers edged away as he passed. In the complete stillness of the room, his voice carried clearly:

"*S'a-ke* Eredion," Pieas said, cold and deliberate, using the familiar *mother's-brother* rather than the formal *s'a-ketan*; a subtle insult all its own in this highly formal setting. "You neglected to inform me you had secured an appointment with the king."

Turning, he added, "Lord Oruen," while dropping a just-adequate bow to the man on the throne. "I offer my apologies for my late arrival. Please continue."

He straightened further, tucking his strong hands behind his back, then stood silent, poised like a desert hawk about to plunge. His arms, neck, and ears were all completely bare of ornamentation: another insult, implying that Oruen wasn't important enough to warrant such a display.

Eredion Sessin took a deep breath. "As I was saying, Lord Oruen—" The desert lord's clear voice carried in the continued stillness. "The next shipment of glass is well on its way to being completed."

That *wasn't*, Alyea knew after a swift examination of Oruen's face, what they had been discussing before Pieas swept into the room. Nice try, but it wouldn't hold; too many others had heard the discussion and not all of them could hide their surprise.

Pieas turned his head, his sharp eyes obviously picking up the slight start here and twitch there that spoke volumes about the lie presented.

"*S'a-ketan*," he said, the formal term now even more of an insult, somehow, than the informal had been moments ago. "Surely we aren't wasting our lord's time with servant's talk? I had thought we asked for this audience to press our complaint against Scratha."

Eredion's chin lowered, and his shoulders rounded forward as he turned a stare that could have melted glass on his nephew. "Surely you don't intend to tell me what I may and may not discuss, *s'ai-keia*." While his tone stayed mild, the threat—underlined by a word one would use to a sister's son still in drooling infancy—was unmistakable.

"Of course not, *s'a-ketan*," Pieas said humbly, apparently backing down, to the extent of physically retreating a step. "Please forgive me."

But the damage had been done. Complaint against Scratha? Those words had exploded a susurrus of murmurs across the room. Alyea dearly wished she'd arrived sooner, secured a better view, caught even a bit of the earlier conversation. They'd probably been discussing, in careful, sideways terms, the very thing on which Pieas had demanded public attention.

Eredion Sessin looked ready to take the man to pieces with his bare hands.

Oruen shook his head slowly. "I assume this is about Nissa? If so, I should tell you that I spoke to your sister before she left for Sessin. I also summoned Lord Scratha. And I have already settled the matter to my own satisfaction. Lord Eredion, just before you arrived, *had* agreed to wait on a more private audience to discuss it further, later in the day. You may attend that discussion, if you wish." His flat stare dared Pieas to protest further.

"Yes, Lord Oruen," Pieas said. Alyea thought some of the humility in his voice might be real this time; the man looked badly rattled.

Eredion spoke, his voice and hands tight: "We beg your leave to withdraw, Lord Oruen."

At Oruen's weary nod, Eredion dropped a deep and profoundly apologetic bow, gripped his nephew's elbow in what looked to be an iron hold, and hustled him from the room.

Intrigued, hoping to see Pieas receive a serious scolding, Alyea wormed her way back through the crowd and followed them. She slipped into the secret passageways and, undetected, watched them from hidden posts as they returned to their rooms.

Their private quarters were one of the few with multiple watch-holes, but only one other watcher was in place when Alyea arrived. She recognized the lean face and dark eyes of a man who had seen, if reports were true, three kings come and go. Not that Ninnic and Mezarak had lasted their full natural lifespans; but still, it spoke of capability. She didn't know his true name. The Hidden Cadre left all prior identity behind when they entered royal service. His call-name was a word from the old language: *micru*, the black and tan-banded viper that moved faster than thought and could kill a healthy draft-horse.

Micru gave her a swift and disinterested glance as she slid into the spying area, then put a finger over his mouth in a wordless warning: *be silent and you may stay.* She nodded, agreeing, and peered through one of the spyholes. She found the two men speaking quietly, not shouting as she would have expected. Even with her good hearing, she had to strain for their words.

For a long, annoying time, she caught only a fragment or an occasional word, not enough to make out what they were discussing. A glance at Micru showed him sitting perfectly still, intent, eyes half-closed as he listened. Alyea guessed he could read lips, and wished she had been able to pick up that skill; but her feeble attempts at it had always been disastrous.

After a while, Pieas stormed out of the room. Micru didn't move, his attention fixed on Eredion; she stayed, wondering what he was watching for now. It finally occurred to her that he'd be sitting here for hours; Micru was posted to watch the room, not Pieas.

She was being an idiot, and her presence was useless. No matter how adept she was at sneaking through secret passages and moving quietly, she was no palace spy and never would be.

The admission galled.

So did Micru's brief, amused glance as she slid past him on her way out of the passage.

Just tired enough to want to avoid chance encounters with ambitious nobles and courtiers, Alyea chose a little-used passage back to her rooms. While her family had a small estate within the Seventeen Gates, Oruen had set aside a small suite of rooms for Alyea within the palace itself, and she stayed there more often than not. Her mother never complained, more than content that her only daughter should remain as close as possible to the king. Alyea had given up trying to convince her mother that Oruen would never offer marriage. Once that woman got an idea, a mountain of sand couldn't smother it.

Swinging around a corner, she stopped, startled.

Alyea didn't know all the servants, but she did recognize the simple ruby-and-silver ring visible on this girl's right hand as she struggled with the man pinning her against the wall. Along with the long dark hair and a scar on the back of the girl's right hand, it served as positive identification: Alyea had given that ring to her favorite maid before dismissing her years ago.

Alyea pulled the man away and shoved him staggering sideways before he had time to react to her presence.

"Stand off, *s'e*!" she barked.

"How dare you!" he shouted simultaneously, catching himself against the wall.

The man out of the way for the moment, Alyea turned to the servant girl. "Wian, are you hurt?"

A livid bruise shadowed the side of Wian's face, and her simple servant's dress was in disarray. "I'll survive, my lady," she said, sagging back against the wall with one hand to her throat. "Thank you."

"How *dare* you!" the man raged, straightening and advancing a step; and at last the voice registered as familiar.

Alyea turned to stare at the man. Pieas Sessin—again! For a moment she didn't know what to say, and Pieas seemed to be searching for a suitably harsh reprimand. He obviously didn't recognize her; just as well.

"How dare you?" Pieas repeated, moving another stride closer. "This is none of your concern!"

"She's not willing, so it certainly is my concern." Her anger, now back in full force, burst loose. "You have no right to take any servant inside the Seventeen Gates against her will!"

"She's willing enough to have lured me here," Pieas said, arrogant in certainty. "Any cry of rape would be a lie; she almost dragged me with her."

Alyea stared at the man in disbelief. She didn't need Wian's pale, frantic head-shake to know Pieas lied. "And the bruise?" she demanded. "And her struggle to be free? Do you take me for a complete fool?"

"She only fought when she heard your step," he said smoothly. "And the bruise was there before she flung herself at me. She can't cry rape just because she's embarrassed at being caught!"

"She doesn't need to; I know her, and you, and *I* call it rape. Stay away from her and the other servants, or I'll see you barred from setting foot inside the Gates."

"You have no such authority," he said, laughing at her now. "Cry all you want. I'll let the little whore go; there are others more interesting." He turned to leave.

"You're a fine champion for your sister, Pieas Sessin," she snapped.

He stopped and turned with shocking speed and grace, looming over her before she had time to draw a breath. "Don't you dare compare my sister to some palace whore!"

"Wian isn't a whore," Alyea said, "and neither was I."

"What, you've known me as well?" he asked, almost laughing again, then stopped, searching her face more carefully. A faint frown creased his forehead, and he began to speak.

She cut him off. "Go away, get out of the Palace, Pieas, before I call the guards to escort you out!"

His frown shifted to a sneer. "Go on, call them! They can't touch me. Desert Family immunity, in case you've forgotten your lessons." He cast the maid a thoughtful glance that sent ice down Alyea's back, and sauntered away, whistling loudly.

"Gods," Alyea muttered. She turned quickly to her former servant. Wian had sunk to the floor, head on her knees, breathing in great, wobbly gasps. "Wian, come, let's get you back to Lady Arnil's."

"I didn't encourage him," Wian said shakily, "I swear, I didn't. He followed me all evening, and I was trying to avoid him, I know his kind, I know that look, and I thought I was safe, cutting down this hallway, and didn't know he followed me. . . ."

She started to cry, shivering, her eyes wide and dilated with shock.

"Hush, Wian," Alyea said, gathering the terrified girl into a tight hug before tugging her back to her feet. "I know. Believe me, I know."

"Pieas Sessin?" Lady Arnil shook her head. "No, I don't think I've heard of him before."

Lady Arnil, Alyea thought, lived a sheltered and deliberately ignorant life; her home just barely qualified as within Bright Bay boundaries. Her late husband had kept his frail wife there for the same reason Alyea originally sent Wian to the lady: as protection against the gross excesses of the last king.

While she'd dismissed all her servants after Ethu's death, convinced one of them had betrayed her to Rosin Weatherweaver, she'd done her best to arrange good homes for all of them. Wian, her most devoted servant, she'd been extra careful to place in a safe spot, far from danger. She hadn't known, at the time, Lady Arnil's temperament: arrogant, selfish, and even more obsessed with status and propriety than Alyea's own mother. A safe home for Wian, yes; but not, unfortunately, a kind one.

But Alyea didn't say any of that aloud. What she did say, after a carefully measured breath for patience, was: "He's an unkind person, my lady. And Wian's run across his worst side. She's in danger."

"How can that be?" The woman squinted at Alyea, seeming honestly puzzled. "We'll simply keep her within the house until he leaves Bright Bay. For that matter, what in the world were you doing in the palace, Wian? You weren't given leave to go anywhere—"

Afraid of the conversation sidetracking, Alyea didn't wait for an answer. "My lady, Wian's in danger so long as she stays in the city. I suggest sending her away until Pieas has had enough time to forget about this incident."

"This incident," Lady Arnil repeated, and peered shortsightedly at the silent maid standing beside Alyea. "You say this man trapped you in a back hallway of the palace—"

"Time is short," Alyea said, her patience thinning. "Take my word for it, Lady Arnil. You *have* to send her away to a place Pieas has no influence—"

"Don't you tell me what I must do," Lady Arnil said, her tone sharpening. "You're barely above a girl yourself!"

"I'm sorry, my lady," Alyea said quickly. "I misspoke—"

"Indeed you did," Lady Arnil said stiffly, and stood. "You may go, young lady. Wian will stay here, and stay within the house walls for a while; that may teach her a lesson about wandering about without permission."

"But, my lady—"

"You may *go*."

Seeing no point in further arguing, Alyea grimaced and turned to leave. She paused to embrace Wian on her way out, and whispered: "I'll find a way to get you out of the city, if you want."

"It's all right," Wian murmured. "I'm honored by your care, my lady, but I'll do as Lady Arnil says. I'm sure she's right. I'll be safe here."

Alyea shook her head, but under Lady Arnil's fierce glare had no room for protest. "Take care of yourself," she said at normal volume, and left feeling that she had betrayed Wian's trust.

By the time she got back to the palace, the hallways had grown relatively quiet with the advancing night hours. She paused at the passage leading to her rooms. She badly wanted a long, hot soak in a lavender-scented tub, and a light platter of fruit. Her stomach rumbled and her legs ached from the long walk, but the desire to talk to Oruen about the gross injustice of Pieas's behavior being protected by diplomatic immunity was too strong. She hurried onward.

Rounding a corner, she almost ran into a servant; he reached to tug anxiously at her sleeve as she detoured around him.

"Lady," he said. "Lady Alyea? The King calls you to attend him. A conference, he said, and for you to hurry."

Alyea stopped on the spot, staring at the servant: he was buck-toothed and gangly, his face heavily scarred with adolescent acne. He showed only relief at having found her.

"A conference?"

"That's what he said, Lady, and for you to hurry."

Conferences involved more than two people. "Do you know who else is with him?"

"The lords Sessin, I think."

"Thank you," she said, dismissing him. He scurried away, and she paused for a moment's thought before continuing. Pieas must have run straight to Oruen to complain, no doubt twisting the matter to her disadvantage. Her step quickened along with her temper. She vowed that by the time she was done, Pieas would be lucky to walk out unbruised himself.

The guards at the small grey door nodded silently and opened the door without even the flicker of a smile. The room beyond was quiet as she stepped through; she heard the door snick softly shut behind her. She paused a moment, studying the two Sessins—who were, as she'd expected, sitting stiff and grim on padded chairs across from the king.

With a few long strides, she covered more than half the distance to Oruen's chair. "My lord King Oruen," she said, dropped to one knee, then rose. She kept her gaze directly on his face, her expression carefully inquiring. "You sent for me?"

His dark eyes narrowed. She could see him considering both her formal address in what he referred to as his "casual room" and her ostentatious indifference to Pieas and Eredion.

Offended anger nearly steamed from the two to her left. Sessin Family always had been rigid sticklers for propriety, and her refusal to greet them directly qualified as insulting by even the loosest standard.

"I did," Oruen said at last, and pointed to a chair. "Sit, please, Alyea."

She held back a smile at having gotten away with the insult and sank into a chair, keeping Eredion between herself and Pieas.

"Pieas and Eredion Sessin, Alyea Peysimun," Oruen said, making the introductions with a sweeping gesture.

Alyea looked to the two Sessins and inclined her head graciously. Pieas's smile was strained and his glare murderous, while to her surprise Eredion actually seemed amused. Could a Sessin have a true sense of humor, to the extent of laughing at himself and his own kin? *The sea,* Alyea thought, *may be about to swallow us all.*

The king settled into the wide, thick-armed chair he favored, and studied them all for a moment. "Alyea," he said finally, "you've heard of Cafad Scratha?"

She blinked at him, caught off guard. Then she remembered the earlier court audience and cursed herself for a fool; this meeting had nothing to do with herself or Wian. "Of course."

Eredion's smile faded. "Lord Oruen, I don't understand the need for her presence."

"You will in a moment," Oruen said, relaxed and sure of himself now. "Alyea, as you may have heard by now, Pieas brought up a formal complaint against Scratha in my court this afternoon."

Alyea nodded without speaking, tilting her head, expression politely curious.

"And if you heard of the complaint, you likely heard the cause," the king prompted.

"Scratha offered insult of some sort to Pieas's sister, Nissa," Alyea said.

"This is a desert family matter," Pieas said sharply. Eredion's hand clamped down on the young man's arm, warning; the younger Sessin now wore a thin bracelet of gold and green beads on his left arm, arranged asymmetrically on fine silver wire. She squinted at the pattern, unsure what it meant.

"As is my right," Pieas continued as if his uncle hadn't moved, "I ask that she be removed as having no bearing on the matter at hand. Whatever you called her to . . . *discuss*. . . . "

Eredion removed his hand as abruptly as he had moved it before, expression suddenly stony. Alyea's ears burned at the crude implication.

"—Can surely be done later, after *our* business is concluded."

Eredion reached out, not even looking, and flicked Pieas's thin bracelet hard, as though to draw attention to it. Glass beads clicked and bumped against each other. Pieas turned a hard glare on Eredion; his elder ignored him, while the king's eyes narrowed briefly.

"Lord Eredion?" Oruen said, apparently choosing to ignore the insult himself. "You're a full desert lord, and the right he refers to is your prerogative, not his."

Pieas's scowl deepened. He covered the bracelet with his other hand and sat back into his chair, chin to chest, glaring sideways at his uncle.

"I have no objection to the girl staying," Eredion said. "I trust your word that she's important to this discussion."

"Thank you," Oruen said, not looking at Pieas. "The incident between

Lady Nissa of Sessin and Lord Cafad Scratha was serious, differences in telling aside. But in the end, Nissa chose not to press charges against Scratha. She considered it an unfortunate mix-up of identity and communication."

"In other words," Lord Eredion said, "she damn well should have told him who she was. She knew he hated our family."

Oruen nodded. "She admitted that herself, yes. All she wanted was her apology conveyed, and she hoped for a similar response from Scratha. But Scratha refused his part. Since I had to do *something*, I gave him a choice of punishments." He stared at his linked hands for a moment, brooding, then went on: "He chose temporary banishment to the Stone Islands, and voluntarily gave me control of *his* lands—"

Pieas was abruptly on his feet. Eredion made no move to stop him; his own mouth hung slightly open in astonishment.

"—in order to be sure, under desert law, that he will have them when he returns. Alyea will be leading my embassy to hold Scratha Fortress until I release Cafad Scratha from his penance."

"You cannot banish a properly named desert lord!" Pieas snapped. "Or take his lands under your hand!"

"He chose both," Oruen said. "He offered his lands, and chose his banishment, freely, rather than offer apology to Nissa. I found it a suitable and legal arrangement."

Alyea drew a long breath, rapidly fitting together implications. In essence, she'd just been handed control of a desert fortress, as representative of the king. Depending on how this fell out, she could find herself ranked as a desert lord, with the king's backing: an absolutely unheard-of situation—

Which also might just place her *above* Pieas Sessin in rank. She fought against a wide grin.

"Under desert law," Eredion said slowly, "the lord of a fortress has the right to abdicate his lands in a manner of his choosing, but that has not been done in hundreds of years, and never to a northern king. The last case was of Wiyric of Tehay Family, who gave over his lands to F'Heing in payment of a monstrous gambling debt, went with his entire family to the deep sands in shame, and never returned. The Stone Islands is not the place of shame for the desert families. It is not the right place to have sent Lord Scratha."

"If you like," Oruen said amiably, "I will certainly summon Scratha back, and send him to the deep sands to die; but his offer of stewardship was voluntary and unprompted in any way—and so, under desert law, holds regardless of Lord Scratha's punishment. If he dies, then the crown will hold his lands: not only for a short time, but forever. I thought this the better way, given the relatively small offense involved."

Eredion let out a harsh breath, clearly startled. "You are right, Lord Oruen."

"Right?" Pieas blazed. "*Right?* How can you say that? No desert Family has ever handed authority to any king!"

"We have no choice," Eredion said. "Lord Scratha is within his rights, and Lord Oruen is entitled to accept the freely made offer."

"We can call for a Conclave," Pieas said.

"Feel free," Oruen said calmly.

"Pieas," Eredion said, sounding exasperated, "a Conclave isn't a simple matter—"

"But the decision of a Conclave is binding even on a king, isn't it? I demand a Conclave!"

Oruen smiled, unruffled. "You can't make that demand, Pieas," he said. "Even Eredion can't. Only the head of a desert Family can call for a Conclave. You'll have to travel back to Sessin Fortress and convince Lord Antouin Sessin yourself."

Eredion snapped, "Pieas, sit *down*. *Stay* down. And *shut up*."

His nephew, mouth folding into sulky lines, sank back to perch tautly on the edge of the plush chair. Alyea rubbed at her nose to hide a grin at Pieas's discomfort; a stern eyebrow quirk from Oruen settled her down.

The elder Sessin drew a long breath and said, more quietly, "This situation requires a good amount of thought. May we have a day to consider, and gain audience to discuss this further tomorrow evening?"

"Certainly," Oruen said. "We would all be the better for some rest."

Alyea made a quick decision; whatever might happen tomorrow, she didn't want to lose the chance she had right now. It was too good to let go. She stood.

"My lord King," she said, hands clasped tightly behind her back, "I have a complaint of my own to press, one of a sensitive nature best discussed in the privacy of this room."

By the look he gave her, he'd desperately wanted to retire to sleep and wasn't at all pleased at the delay. "It has bearing on Sessin Family?" he asked warily.

"It has bearing on Pieas Sessin," she said.

"Lies!" Pieas cried, coming up out of his chair again; this time Eredion reached out and hauled him back down. "Lord Oruen, she offers only lies!"

"Without even knowing what she has to say?" the king inquired. "Let her speak before you cast doubt on her word, Pieas."

Alyea took a deep breath. "I think you know my maid, Wian; you recommended her to my service some years ago," she said, a blatant lie that Oruen had the wisdom not to challenge openly, although his expression warned her not to push further. She explained about the encounter, careful to stick to absolute truth from that point on. "I am dismayed, sire," she finished, "that desert immunity is being so abused as to allow rape in the very palace halls."

Eredion's expression bore the dark ferocity of a thundercloud now; his stare at Pieas made the young man squirm in deep discomfort.

"It's a lie," Pieas said, sounding much less confident now. "The servant girl is just a whore. She insisted on dragging me into a deserted hallway."

"I will speak for her honor," Alyea said. "The king knows her and will speak for her honor as well. Are you calling us both liars, then?"

One of Oruen's eyebrows cocked, just a little, signaling strong displeasure at that maneuver.

Stuck, Pieas looked to Eredion. "I swear to you, I never asked for more than the girl was willing to give. Any marks are those of passion, not struggle."

"I would have an easier time believing you," Eredion rumbled, "if this was the first such complaint, Pieas."

"No complaint of rape has ever been proven against me," Pieas said. A shadow of panic lurked beneath the bluster.

"You've never had noble accusers before," Eredion said. "It's far easier to believe a commoner or servant is out to wrench a handful of gold from us; but if Lord Oruen himself can speak to this girl's character. . . ."

Oruen's eyes narrowed. Afraid he was about to choose sides—and not hers—Alyea took a deep breath and, for Wian's sake, broke her promise to herself.

"I'll do more than speak to Wian's character. I present my own. Some years ago, Pieas took me by surprise as I walked in the town, and the bruises he left took days to fade." And before the bruises had faded, Ethu had begun training her to make sure that such a thing never happened again; but she left that part silent.

The king's eyebrows came down into a sharp frown.

"I *do* recall those bruises," Oruen said. "You wouldn't tell me where they came from."

She tried not to flinch from his stare. "There was nothing you could do. He was in Ninnic's favor, and my family wasn't."

There might have been the faintest flicker in his eyes, a hint of something she'd thought long gone; her heart turned over in her chest. A moment later Oruen's expression flattened again, and she looked away, jaw tight, and cursed herself for hoping.

"Are you claiming that Pieas raped you, Lady?" Eredion demanded.

"I am," she said clearly, then took a gamble. "And I also ask for blood-right, which I will stand to myself." It *sounded* impressive, and she was fairly sure that blood-right was just a first-blood duel; but as soon as she'd said it a bad feeling began to churn in her stomach.

Eredion studied her with narrowed eyes, calculating; and Pieas's grey face slowly regained its color and creased into an arrogant smile. "Blood-right under kingdom law, or under desert law?" Eredion said at last, cautiously.

"Kingdom," Oruen said before Alyea could even open her mouth. Just as well; she hadn't been sure of the difference. "I'm sure Alyea wants no part of a desert holding beyond what she's already being granted."

She nodded, agreeing fervently, glad he'd answered for her.

Eredion visibly relaxed. Pieas sneered.

"You have nothing to worry about, *s'a-ketan*," the younger Sessin said. "She has no skill at arms."

Eredion turned a black glare on his sister's son. "And how would you know that?"

Pieas scrambled to repair his mistake; before he managed two words, Eredion lifted a hand to cut him off.

"Lord Oruen," the elder Sessin said, directing a sober glance to the king, "if you're minded to allow this challenge, I'll stand on my authority as a lord of Sessin Family and permit it as well. I have to warn you both, in fairness, that I know Pieas as a skilled fighter with an unfortunate lack of scruples. I have little doubt as to the outcome."

"I can't refuse her choice," Oruen said dryly. "She knows what she's doing."

"What about your placement of her as embassy head to Scratha fortress?" Eredion said suddenly. "That's a binding she'd be abandoning if she fell in challenge. That makes her choice illegal; she has to call a champion to represent her." He looked deeply relieved at the thought.

Alyea kept her expression still with an effort. Fall in challenge? That didn't sound like a first-blood duel. Her hands tightened into fists.

"Unfortunately," Oruen said, "she hasn't been sworn to that yet; you yourself asked for a delay." He rubbed wearily at his eyes, and shot a sharp glance at Alyea.

The elder Sessin turned a bleak stare on Pieas. "You've been a concern to me for years, Pieas," he said. "I've seen you get away with more than your due, and walk proud in the company of madmen and murderers your father would have shunned. I'm at the end of my tolerance for you. If she falls, I will claim my own right as lord of Sessin, and challenge you myself."

Pieas stared at his uncle as if he couldn't believe his ears. "You would betray me like that?"

"You've already betrayed Sessin," Eredion said roughly. "From Water's End to Bright Bay, good people turn away to avoid your path, while disgraceful men steer straight for you. You're putting a reputation to our name that we don't want and can't afford. I've tried to warn you, and you've refused to listen, so you have three choices. Kill Lady Alyea, and face me after. Submit yourself to Lord Oruen's punishment instead of taking up the challenge. Or run disowned into the deep desert, to make your own way as you will."

Alyea stood frozen and trying to look placid; she hadn't expected such violent support from the elder Sessin, and the words *kill Lady Alyea* had locked her throat with horror. *Not* a first-blood duel, then. How could she have been so stupid?

The terrified look on Pieas's face suggested he wouldn't dare to go up against Eredion; two options remained. Which would prove more distasteful to him she couldn't guess.

The younger man's jaw worked for a moment; then he said, hoarsely, "I'd like a day to consider. May we . . . continue this along with the other discussion tomorrow night?"

"Certainly," Oruen agreed, seeming relieved. The two Sessins departed, Eredion's hand clamped firmly on the younger man's shoulder.

"Wait a bit," Oruen said as the door closed again. "Let them get some distance before you leave."

"I had no intention of tagging their heels." Alyea sat on the arm of a chair, studying the man across from her intently. "You look tired."

"I am," Oruen said, slumping back into the cushions of his chair and rubbing his dark eyes. "Gods, I'm tired. I begin to think I made a serious mistake, accepting this crown."

Alyea said nothing. He wasn't about to abandon the throne, after all he'd gone through to place his rear end on it.

"Are you planning on your aqeyva training being enough to beat Pieas with?" Oruen said after a while. "Because you're an idiot if that's all you're counting on. Eredion's right; Pieas is a nasty piece of work."

She shook her head, unwilling to admit the extent of her mistake. Even if blood-right had meant a simple duel, the move had been pure madness, more bluff than anything else, now that she thought back on it. What had she wanted?

For Oruen to stop her. For him to say—

—oh, gods, was she still that mad about him? He'd made it clear . . . or had he?

She couldn't resist finding out if that flicker of emotion, when he'd heard of Pieas's attack on her, had been real or imagined. "Why did you choose me for this?"

He had closed his eyes while she brooded; he opened them now and smiled. "Why not you?"

"I'm only eighteen," she said as emotionlessly as she could. "You have men and women in your service with the dignity of age and the wisdom of years who could handle this much better. Just because you seduced me once is no reason to give me important assignments like this one. Or do you want me out from nearby, to avoid the reminder?"

His smile hadn't faded; he watched her with a fond, if exhausted, expression. "You're a relative unknown, where those more seasoned diplomats already have reputations and enemies among the desert Families. You also have no taint of having been under Ninnic's service, which in itself will ease tempers along the way."

"I can't be the only one like that," she said, hoping her expression didn't betray the sinking feeling in her stomach. He'd carefully ignored the unsubtle prompt. "And I'm certainly not the most diplomatic envoy you have to hand."

"You're the only one I trust," he told her. "Young, yes, but you're sharp, and you've proven your loyalty beyond any question. This position requires a tremendous amount of trust. Diplomacy you can learn. And a rough edge can be a help, sometimes, with the desert lords."

She frowned at him. "Most girls my age are married already, with a child on their hip."

"You've often said that idea bores you to screaming," he countered. "Has that changed? I could find you a good husband within a day."

"No," she said. "It still bores me." She grinned at him, finding her resentment suddenly sloughing off like water over hard ground. She'd been a fool to hope anything had changed. "All right, I'll do it."

"Thank you," he said. "Now, I need some sleep. We'll meet here again an hour after tomorrow's dinner ends."

By the end of the next day, rumor had already flown round the palace: Pieas Sessin had departed without a word in the middle of the night.

"It's true," Eredion said, his face dark with anger, when presented with the question that evening after dinner. Alyea had arrived moments before the desert lord. "He's taken his horse, and those of his belongings that travel comfortably. I did not give him leave to go."

"Where is he headed?" the king asked, his own expression hard.

"I don't know," Eredion said. "I can't believe he'd be so foolish as to make his way back to the desert. I've sent a messenger-bird to Water's End, and to Sessin Family Fortress, warning them to hold him against my return if he shows up there."

Oruen rubbed at his eyes briefly. "You must have some guess as to where he would go."

"You likely have the same guess," Eredion said. "The Stone Islands, to hunt Scratha."

The king seemed unsurprised by the thought, and not particularly worried.

"Yes," he said. "I've sent word to the dock captains already to watch for him, and messenger-birds to the coastal villages nearby. If Pieas tries to catch passage on a ship to the Stone Islands, we may not be able to stop him, but we'll know about it within a day."

Eredion turned to Alyea. "I offer my apologies, and offer my services as some compensation. If you need anything, now or any day in the future, call on me. I'll do what I can to help."

"Thank you," she said, startled. "That's a generous offer."

He displayed another brief, intense smile. "I know. I'm counting on you not to abuse it."

"I won't," she said, at the same time Oruen said: "She won't, Eredion."

They all laughed, the tension easing, and leaned back in their chairs.

"Let's have some wine," Oruen suggested. "I'd like to hear your thoughts, Eredion, on the posting I'm proposing to give to Alyea. You have experience she lacks, and she's doubtless interested in your advice."

"She won't take advantage, maybe," Eredion said wryly, "but you're transparent, Lord Oruen."

"The desert Families keep themselves very private," Oruen said with a shrug. "Do you blame me for being curious?"

"No," Eredion said. "Not really. A good king should take every chance to learn about his people and allies, and I think you're the first good king this palace has seen for far too long."

"Thank you," Oruen said, sounding deeply flattered. "More wine?"

"Now you're trying to get me drunk so I'll spill Family secrets," Eredion laughed, and held out his glass. "You'll find it harder than you think."

Oruen just smiled.

Chapter Three

Idisio quickly decided that learning to ride a horse would always be one of his least favorite memories. If, of course, he lived through it; after the fourth time the horse threw him, that began to seem highly unlikely. Either the falls would break something vital, the horse would step on something critical, or Scratha would lose the remnants of a short temper and throttle him.

"I should have stayed on the streets," Idisio muttered, glaring nose to nose with his horse. It stared back with deceptively sleepy eyes.

"I should have left you there," Scratha said. He rubbed at his eyes, glanced around, and turned his horse away from the road at a sharp angle. "Lead the horse," he called back over his shoulder.

Idisio slogged over loose, sandy ground, walking-weed hitching at his ankles and legs. He spared a moment's weary gratitude that his master had allowed the time to change into more suitable traveling clothes before the disastrous riding lessons began. The sturdy linen of his new outfit had held up well so far, although Idisio suspected he'd be spending hours picking out the tiny green seeds.

If, of course, they ever got around to resting. Idisio stumbled, legs threatening to give way under him. It occurred to him, through a grey haze, that he wouldn't be standing, let alone walking, much longer.

"Sit down before you fall over," Scratha said at last. "I'll come back for you." He took the reins from Idisio's hand. Not caring whether he fell in the middle of a patch of walking-weed or blood ants, Idisio felt the ground come up under his body and was aware of nothing more for a while.

When his eyes were willing to open again, he found Scratha carrying him, cradling him like a child. Idisio mumbled incoherent protest, ashamed.

"Quiet," Scratha said, astonishingly gentle, and Idisio's eyelids, like undeniable, heavy weights, slid closed again.

The next time he woke, accumulated aches and bruises hammered at Idisio before his eyes were fully open. The smell of smoke came next, and the unmistakable aroma of food; Idisio's stomach woke with a loud growl at that. A woman laughed nearby.

Idisio struggled to sit up and focus sleep-bleared vision. Scratha knelt beside him.

"Don't get up," Scratha said. "Your feet are wrapped. I'll bring you some food, if you're of a mind to eat."

Idisio nodded, and the woman laughed again. Blinking past Scratha, Idisio saw an old woman sitting cross-legged by a low table; her hair was pure white, her face lined and weathered like a thick log after a sandstorm. With no stiffness to her movements, she reached to scoop food from a wooden platter into a wide-mouthed wooden bowl, then turned a sharp, bright glance his way.

Fine, wide glass windows spilled light across the plain wooden floors and low, desert-style furniture. Large, colorful sitting cushions surrounded the table; the old woman sat on a deep purple one, and Idisio had been laid out on a wide bench covered with several more. Tall, glazed earthenware vases stood around the room: some as tall as Idisio, and all with dried or fresh flowers in them. A squat cookstove hulked against one wall, large enough to give heat to the room in cold weather; shelves nearby held jars of vegetables, meats, jams, and jellies. *Glass* jars, and well-made; this woman had to be as wealthy as a desert lord herself, to have so many fine things.

"What's your name, boy?" the woman asked as Scratha squatted beside Idisio again, bowl of food in hand.

"Idisio," he said, taking the bowl from his master. A hunk of fresh bread, a pile of folded eggs speckled with green and red herbs, and a thick wedge of sourfruit; the food from the palace kitchen seemed to have been years ago. Idisio tore through the food, casting aside all his lessons on manners, slowed only by gulps from the mug of cool water his master held out to him. The eggs were just cool enough to pick up without scorching his fingers, the sourfruit sun-warmed and fresher than any he'd ever tasted before; he wiped juice and crumbs from his chin, surprised to find the bowl empty, and looked up to see two amused faces watching him.

"He's a boy still, Cafad," the woman said. "Give me that bowl again. He'll need more than that."

Idisio almost dropped the bowl as Scratha reached for it; the desert lord grabbed it, his expression souring, and said, "Yes. She knows who I am and the truth of the situation."

"I know *your* understanding of the situation," the woman corrected, a touch sharply; her smile took some of the sting out of the words. "Give me the bowl already."

She filled the bowl twice more before Idisio motioned that he'd had enough.

"I thank you, my lady." Idisio wiped at his face again and burped. "That was marvelous."

"You're welcome, Idisio," she said. "And you needn't call me *lady*. I left that word behind me long ago. Azni will do fine."

Now that his stomach had been filled, other pains, along with his bladder, began to command his attention again, even as Scratha asked, "How do you feel, boy?"

"He hurts everywhere," the woman said before Idisio could answer, "and he thinks you're a damned fool for dragging him all over until his feet are blistered."

"No," Idisio said quickly, afraid of looking as if he agreed, "I mean, I hurt, but I . . . I don't think you're a fool, my lo . . . Master." Or should it be 'my lord', since the woman knew Scratha's true identity? He couldn't decide, but as neither Scratha nor the strange woman seemed offended, he let it pass without further attempt at correction.

"Well, you ought to," the old woman said. "Because he *is* a fool for it."

"All right," Scratha said sourly, reaching for a pail of water, a cloth, and a small jar that were all on the floor nearby. "Let be already."

"I'll knock it in until I think you're actually listening," she replied. "We haven't got there yet."

Trying to divert the conversation and ease the dangerous tension hardening his master's jaw, Idisio said, "Where are we?"

Scratha reached out and flipped the blanket back from Idisio's feet, which were wrapped in linen bandages.

"We're in Azni's home," he said unhelpfully, and began to unwind the wrappings. For all his rough temper, he kept his movements gentle and careful.

Azni snorted. "About six miles northeast of Bright Bay is the right answer, and little enough to give at that."

"You value your privacy," Scratha said.

The wrappings dropped in a pile to one side. Holding Idisio's ankle, Scratha raised the foot slightly, squinting as he examined it. With his free hand he dropped the piece of cloth into the pail of water, pulled it out, and squeezed. Water dribbled back into the pail; the sound reminded Idisio of his increasingly full bladder.

"The boy's not about to lead a horde of murderers to my home," Azni retorted.

Scratha made a face and began dabbing at Idisio's foot with the damp cloth. Idisio tensed, expecting it to hurt, but felt only a faint tickling as his lord wiped away a layer of salve. Twice he hissed as the tickling shot into a sharp burning sensation; each time Scratha nodded without looking up.

"No," Scratha muttered under his breath as he worked, "I'm the only one likely to do that."

Azni showed sharp hearing for her age; she said, in a much gentler voice, "You haven't yet, Cafad, and I don't expect you will."

The previous layer of salve wiped away, Scratha spread more over two small spots at the edges of Idisio's left foot and let it rest on the cushion again, not bothering with bandages. He started unwrapping Idisio's right foot.

"This time is different, Azni. I've offended the whole of Sessin, and Pieas is after me."

"You don't know that," she said.

He paused in his ministrations and looked over his shoulder at her. "Pieas Sessin fights if he farts and someone has the gall to smile. He's killed over a wrong word before, when that word involved his sister. And I threw the girl out into the street half-dressed and named her a whore to all within hearing."

"And if you'd known she was Pieas's sister, would that have held you back?" Azni asked.

Scratha held still for a moment, looking at her, then turned back to unwrapping Idisio's foot. "No. I was too angry."

"Done is done," the old woman said. "You'll deal with what comes. Even Pieas Sessin isn't fool enough to breach my walls in hunt of you, Cafad. He'll wait for you to leave—if he even knows you've come this way."

"I covered my tracks from the road, but he'll know soon enough I haven't gone to the Stone Islands," Scratha said.

"If he has the wit to stop and ask the right questions," Azni said, "which I doubt; and if he's angry, that's even less likely to happen. If he's mad enough to hunt a full desert lord in the first place, he'll go west to the harbor, which gives you days to clear my home. Stop worrying so."

Scratha wiped Idisio's foot with the damp cloth. The pressure in Idisio's bladder built steadily. "My lo . . . Master," Idisio said, catching himself again at the last second, and hesitated, not sure how to put the matter while a woman of obvious status stood in the room.

The eunuch hadn't covered how to say *I have to take a piss* in front of a noblewoman.

"Almost done," Scratha said without looking up. "Let's talk on something else, Azni." He set Idisio's foot down and sat back.

"Fine," the old woman said. "Go get the boy a chamber pot before he floods my floor. I don't want him walking yet."

Idisio felt a deep heat climb into his face as Scratha stood and left the room without comment.

"I've raised children without benefit of servants," the old woman said, smiling. "I'm not so easily embarrassed as all that."

She did have the kindness, when Scratha returned, to leave the room while Idisio relieved himself.

"Master," Idisio said after the chamber pot had been decently lidded again and pushed to one side, "who *is* she?" He decided that using the term 'my lord' might trip him up in the future; better to start using the 'proper' public term now and avoid, as much as possible, using actual names aloud. That seemed safe enough.

Scratha sighed and settled to the floor, leaning back against the wall with his long legs stretched before him. "She *used* to be Lady Azaniari Aerthraim," he said. "She left her family and married Lord Regav Darden."

Idisio's jaw loosened. The streets of Bright Bay called those two families dangerous. Darden had a reputation for ruthlessness and the Aerthraim raised caution from mystery. And they were supposedly as amicable with one another as fire and oil.

"After Lord Regav died," Scratha said, smiling slightly at Idisio's stunned expression, "Azni decided that she'd had enough of living in the deep desert and moved here. I've stayed with her often in recent years. She's one of the few people I trust." His expression darkened. "I've always been careful to keep that secret, to avoid drawing danger down on her."

"I can take care of myself," the lady in question said as she came back into the room. "Really, Cafad, after all I've taught you, don't you know any better than that?"

Idisio's master bent his head and said nothing.

"You need to rest, Cafad," Azni said. "Go get some sleep. I'll bore your boy here back to his own rest, and teach him a few things he'll need to know if he's to play at taking care of you." She smiled at Idisio. "He hasn't slept at all," she added in a loud whisper. "Worried over you, no doubt."

Raising his head, Scratha rolled his eyes and heaved himself to his feet. "I had a lot to talk to you about, Azni," he said. "Don't make it sound something it wasn't. This boy doesn't need any help with his ego."

"Of course," she said, tone bland, eyes bright with mischief.

He shook his head and snorted. "We leave in the morning," he said, and left the room.

Azni smiled as she watched the tall man walk away, then turned to Idisio with a brisk motion. "Now, tell me about yourself. Everything. I know Cafad didn't even bother asking your name; typical of him. I tore him raw over that. Even servants deserve respect, especially if they have to put up with someone like Cafad."

"That's all right, *s'a*," Idisio said, feeling clumsy and awkward. Ancient as she seemed, she still had a graceful and cool demeanor that he'd never been faced with before. "I mean, I'm used to not accounting for much."

He wished he hadn't said it as soon as the words were out; her gaze sharpened instantly, like a blacktail hawk about to drop on a mouse.

"Cafad said he caught you trying to steal from him," she said. "You're a street-thief, then?"

Idisio nodded, feeling the color rising to his face again. He couldn't stand to meet her stare any longer. "I never knew my parents. Some beggar-thieves raised me, but they never pretended to be related. They were always clear they'd found me as an abandoned infant."

He bit his lip at the prickling pain of that—and at the recurring vision of a pair of wild grey eyes staring into his. Why had that been so vivid an image? And why did he feel it was important? He shrugged and turned his attention to talking.

"The street thieves waved me around, when I was a baby, to get sympathy and coin from the nobles; when I grew too old for that I took up thieving myself. I've been living the streets my whole life." He grimaced, wondering why he was babbling so much to a near-stranger, then knew: to avoid thinking about those haunted grey eyes.

She said nothing for a while. He could feel that intent stare burning into him. At last she said, "You've been used for more than sympathy."

"I grew up on the streets, whaddya think?" he started to say, intending it as a hard-edged warning to back off; found his voice choking off into unexpected hoarseness and then silence halfway through. He shut his eyes, tears prickling against his eyelids; biting his tongue hard held them back.

"Yeah," he husked after a moment.

"Idisio," Azni said, "I'm not prying, and I'm not offering pity. Life is what it is, ugly and bitter and sweet and fine all together. I've been through my own rough times, and so has Cafad. But we probably had more support than you ever dreamed of knowing. You surviving this long means you have more strength, in some ways, than many people. Keep that in mind, if Cafad ever tries to intimidate you. And remember this, too: he's not as hard-hearted as he tries to act."

She drew a breath, lightened her tone, and began to talk of less serious things. Idisio, relieved, let himself be drawn back out into conversation and even shared some of the funnier stories from his life on the streets.

They talked for the remainder of the day, until a fire had to be set in the stove and bowls of stew ladled out of the large pot. They talked by candlelight as they ate, as she cleaned up, and by the time Idisio dropped back to sleep on his pallet, his head spun from the things he'd learned. Politics and family ties, blood oaths and noble secrets and gossip, and, woven in here and there, casual comments on the best way to mend clothes, cook food, and ride a horse.

A few words from her had explained more about that than hours of his master's cursing and admonitions. He also had a better idea of what it had meant for Scratha to change his name and take to the road, with his true name in official disgrace and his true person in the king's service. If he'd simply gone traveling as Lord Cafad Scratha, with his desert holding empty and unprotected, desert law would have given rights to any who chose to occupy it for a year's time. He could have come home to find himself homeless. But by placing his land in the king's hands and his true name in temporary public disgrace, the king himself had to keep the holding open for Scratha, whether this journey took months or years.

As even a temporary holder of a desert fortress, whatever the legal fiction involved, the king had just acquired certain rights and the other desert families certain obligations. The traditional independence of the desert families from the actual kingdom had just developed a small but significant political vulnerability.

"He's always been rash," Azni sighed. "Rash and quicktempered and hard to reason with. He regrets afterwards, but never remembers long enough for next time. Your worst task, Idisio, will be keeping his temper under hand and him out of trouble. I don't think he really has any notion what he's done, choosing to travel as nothing more than a court researcher. He has no idea what it's like, not being treated as a noble. He thinks he does. He really, truly, doesn't."

She shook her head slowly. They went on to other topics, and finally she declared herself too tired to talk further. She left the room with a gracious goodnight and a lit candle by his pallet; he blew it out and settled back on his cushions soon after.

Idisio stared into the darkness of a room gone quiet but for late-night insect noise and tried to think it all through. He didn't get far before the darkness crawled inside him and swallowed him into sleep.

His feet didn't hurt. The throbbing, aching pain of the previous two days was completely gone. His muscles still protested the unaccustomed exercise of riding, but his feet, unswollen and unblistered, slid back into the hard black boots without complaint.

Azni gave Idisio a jar of salve. "For next time Cafad works you too hard," she said with a smile, and pressed another onto Idisio's master with an admonition not to waste them. Scratha treated the small earthenware jar with a respect that told Idisio it was a precious gift; as if his miraculously healed feet weren't evidence enough of that.

His horse remained placid and obedient now. It snorted and shied occasionally when a sand-grouse or tizzy-lizard darted out from underfoot. Idisio, more comfortable with riding every mile that passed, held his seat and patted the side of the beast's neck until it calmed again. He noticed that his master's horse hadn't even made that slight twitch of reaction, plodding along uninterested in bird or lizard.

"He's a good rider," Azni had told Idisio the previous night. "Better than perhaps he even realizes. He's got a gift with animals. But he's impatient with anyone who doesn't grasp a skill as quickly as he does. If it comes natural to him, then it should be easy for all; if it's hard for him, then it doesn't need doing by anyone."

Scratha turned abruptly in the saddle and stared at him. "Where do I begin?"

"Pardon?" Idisio blinked, startled.

Scratha waved impatiently for Idisio to move forward beside him.

"Where do I start?" he repeated once the two horses were abreast.

"I don't understand," Idisio said, completely bewildered. His master's dark eyes bored into him as if expecting a better answer.

"With this stupid history!" Scratha said. "What do I write about? What do I even call it? When do I start? It's all nonsense." He stared ahead, brooding and dark.

Idisio drew a breath slowly, holding back a grin. "You could start with Lady Azni."

"No," Scratha said immediately. "She's not to be mentioned at all. I want her left alone."

"Then start with the first village we come to."

Scratha pulled his horse to a halt and sat still. "But what do I *say*?"

"I don't know, my . . . Master," Idisio said. "I can't even read."

Scratha stared at him for a long moment, then said, "I'll have to fix that. I'll need you to be able to read soon."

Idisio nodded, speechless. He'd always wanted to learn to read, but it was a hard skill to pick up in the streets, where reading meant time away from making money for survival. He'd always been told most lords preferred their servants illiterate.

"I'd like that," he said.

"We'll start tonight," Scratha said. "And you have the right idea. We'll start with the first village. There's one just outside Bright Bay, isn't there? By the marshes?"

"Ye-e-ess," Idisio said reluctantly, "but—"

"Then we start there." Scratha shook the reins, turned the horse's head more south than east, and nudged into a trot.

Chapter Four

White sand, blown over the wide paving stones of the King's Road by the ever-present sea breeze, scraped under the horses' hooves. Alyea treasured the sound. The road and the alabaster sands of the coast both petered out at roughly the same time; once that grating *shiss* stopped, she would be in alien territory, completely dependent on the handful of advisors and guardsmen who had been sent with her. The advisors rode horses of a bloodline second only to the News-Riders' mounts; the guards walked behind.

"You need to strike a delicate balance between appearing lazy and appearing hasty," the bony old man riding beside her said. "Both can get you killed; both *will* lose you respect. Four days to reach Water's End. No more hurrying than that, no less easy a pace than that. Three way-stops and we'll be in Water's End midday on the fourth."

Lord Eredion Sessin had said something similar about respect, during their meeting with the king two nights ago.

"The desert holds its own time," he'd told her. "You're good at the northern courtesies, but those won't do you any good in the south. We're a slow folk, but far from stupid; in the time northerns rattle off five wrong answers to a question, we've thought through twenty and only say the right response. Hurrying won't gain you any respect, so learn to slow down." Shortly afterward, he'd been called away and hadn't been able to speak with her again before she left. Now she depended on Chac for the information she'd expected to get from Lord Sessin.

Chac had always been something of an enigma. He'd been close to

Oruen, helping plot the overthrow of the former king, but beyond that she knew little about him; he lived just outside the Seventeen Gates, had no family, held no status she could determine, and refused all formal recognition or invitations from anyone with noble blood. But Oruen had seen fit to send Chac, along with Micru, to accompany her south, so apparently part of the old man's mysterious past included knowledge of the southlands.

She looked sideways, studying his leathery, sun-wrinkled face for a moment, then said, "When were you last in the desert, Chac? The true desert."

"Years," he said, his gaze on the distant arc of the Crescent Mountains to the southwest. "Many, many years. I used to go once a year on a desert walk to clear the sludge of the city out of my veins."

"And to look for the wife that ran away," Micru said from Alyea's other side.

Chac's thin lips drew back from his teeth. He stared straight ahead, his hands crushing the thick leather reins, and said nothing. Alyea repressed a sigh; why Oruen had sent two men who so fiercely hated each other she couldn't understand, but the animosity had been made clear before they even passed through the southern gates of Bright Bay.

"Why did you stop going on desert walks, Chac?" she said, shooting Micru a sharp, repressive glare.

For a moment, she thought Chac might refuse to answer, too aggravated by Micru's repeated barbs to talk any longer, but at last he said, "Ninnic. That stupid Travelers' Law made it impossible. I couldn't afford the taxes; they were doubled on the south gates."

"And the guards paid more attention to who went in and out," Micru noted, not turning his gaze from the near-sleepy examination of the terrain ahead. Chac seemed unoffended by that comment, so either it had missed its mark or it actually hadn't been intended as an insult.

Alyea shook her head. "Gods preserve us from those days ever coming again," she muttered, not aware she'd spoken aloud until Chac answered.

"Asking the gods to save us from that madness," the old man said, "ignores the fact that the gods permitted it to happen in the first place."

"The gods do as the gods do," Micru said. "Anger at the gods is foolish and a waste of time. *You* ought to know that by now, Chacerly."

Chac stiffened, a dangerous light in his eyes.

Alyea said sharply, "Stop it, both of you! We're barely clear of Bright Bay. If you're going to act like squabbling children the whole way, I'll turn around right now and ask Oruen to pick new advisors for me."

They both turned to look at her, visibly astonished. Micru's dark eyes narrowed slightly, while Chac's almost disappeared in the wrinkles of his squint; she wondered if she'd gone too far. Sworn to protect her or not, angering one of the Hidden was stupid, and she suspected Chac could get thoroughly nasty as well.

After exchanging a brief, calculating glare in which hostilities were wordlessly suspended but not forgotten, both men turned their attention stiffly forward and fell silent. Alyea let out a long breath and wished, uselessly, that horses could grow wings and fly them all direct to Scratha Fortress.

Alyea stood on the edge of a steep drop and stared at the vast spread of the Goldensea, far below and to the west. The sun had melted into a bronze-gold puddle on the water. Small dots were moving towards the coast: probably fishing boats bringing in the day's catch. The air, darkening towards dusk, felt clear and sharp in her nose.

The erratically climbing path had already taken them higher above sea level than she'd ever been before. Sand colors had gradually shifted to white, then grey, then changed entirely to pale brown rock; the stench of a busy coastal city gave way to the sweet, thick, and earthy tones of scrub-sage and clay dust. The transformations created an entirely new landscape, one she needed to stand still and adjust to. When Chacerly went to direct the lodging arrangements in the way-stop behind her, she took the opportunity to move to a nearby overlook spot.

From the coastal lowlands of Bright Bay, the Horn climbed sharply to a near-mountain height. Jagged cliffs rose on one side of the trail; a steep drop lay on the other—and which side was the cliff might shift with no apparent transition.

Court sages liked to argue over whether the Horn was a natural place or an aberration created by the gods. It rose too high, too sharply, and the weather patterns were all wrong, said one side, while the other argued it was proof that nature was far more complex than mankind's limited mind could understand.

Alyea closed her eyes and breathed deeply, then looked out at the ocean. That water had always been close enough to dip her toes into, with less than an hour's walk; now it was close to a day's walk, if a path so short could be found across the broken ground of the Horn.

Soon it would be farther yet, and after that, gone from sight. The land past the Horn widened into another vast continent, and her path lay straight down the center. Scratha Fortress sat deep in the sands of the true desert, a ten-day ride from the east coast, easily three times that to the west coast. To the south would be only more sand, and beyond that, the forbidden Haunted Lands and southern jungles.

She shivered. The breeze swirling up to her felt cold, misty, and unpleasant compared to the warm evening sea breezes common in Bright Bay this time of year. She turned away and headed for the inn.

Way-stops in the Horn were the only places for merchants and travelers to pause overnight. At this one, indoor rooms and stables proper were reserved for important people; commoners pitched their bedrolls and sheltered their mounts in low-walled enclosures covered by heavy, waterproof canvas tents. In deference to her noble blood, Alyea had a room indoors. Chac had told her to keep her status as king's representative quiet for the moment, out of concern that someone might try to challenge her holding of Scratha Fortress before she took actual possession of the land.

She couldn't see that happening, but had to defer to Chac's judgment. Not for the first time, she wished she'd had a chance to talk with Eredion Sessin about protocols and courtesies; he'd seemed much easier to talk to than the sour old man. Certainly *friendlier.* Chac had barely said two words since her morning rebuke.

Chacerly waited for her by the door of the inn house.

"Hurry," he said as she approached. "The evening meal's almost ready. Go clean up."

She was tired from the long day, sore from the miles on horseback, and wanted nothing more than to sit in quiet to brood. "Can't I eat in my room?"

"No," he said. "Get moving." He followed her into the inn, caught up to her shoulder where the narrow passage widened just enough, and said in a low voice, "One thing I'll tell you again is that you *ought* to have brought maidservants."

"I don't like servants," she said. "All they ever did was spy and tattle, and the ones that didn't were hurt for it. I'd rather take care of myself."

He grunted. "It looks bad. One woman with all these men. Not even women in the guards. I don't like it."

"I'll be fine," she said, pushing the door to her room open, and shut it in his face before he could argue further.

It didn't take her long to strip out of the dusty leggings and tunic, sponge off road grime, and slip into a dress. Managing without servants had given her a certain impatience for lingering over simple tasks like dressing.

She turned, examining herself in the long mirror. The fabric hugged her narrow shoulders and arms just enough to show line, not bone; the squared scoop of the neck showed her collarbones but nothing lower. A thick band of gold and silver thread brocade wound around the waist, and the skirt hung long and fully pleated. Thin red and gold shoes, little more than slippers heavily worked with a brocade that matched the waist pattern, and a long, thin gold chain with a single hematite marble finished the outfit. Her hair she left loose and brushed out carefully until it lay in a silky cape over her shoulders and back.

Satisfied both by her appearance and how quickly she'd managed it, although her mother would have been horrified at her "unseemly haste", she gave the mirror one last warm smile, practicing the expression, then turned to the door.

Chac, waiting outside, looked her over critically as she stepped out of the room. After a moment, he nodded and produced a thin beaded bracelet.

"Right hand," he said, and fastened the string of beads around her wrist. "Don't take it off."

It seemed simple enough; small, round pieces of some dark green gemstone interspersed with squared off, unevenly sized pieces of thick white shell, threaded on a thin golden wire.

"What does it mean?"

"It means you're wearing a bracelet," he said, his expression closed and hard. "It means you're not a servant. Now mind you don't toss and flutter like you're the prettiest in the room. You'll get yourself a name you won't like later on."

"I don't," she started, indignant.

"I've *seen* you do it," he cut her off. "Quiet. Modest. Eyes down. And use your ears and eyes before your mouth."

"It's only a way-stop," she protested.

"No such thing as *only,*" he said. "Not anywhere south of Bright Bay. *Everything* is important, here, and everyone could be. Pay attention."

"All right," Alyea said, feeling thoroughly rebuked. Trying to move in a properly humble manner, she followed the old man down the inn passage. "What should I be looking *for*?"

He waited until they'd left the narrow corridor and emerged into the open air before speaking again. As they walked across the rough ground towards the dining hall, she regretted her choice of thin slippers. Even the raked-out sandy path, lit now with pole lanterns to either side, held numerous pebbles and sharp rocks. She stepped with care and tried to divide her attention between Chacerly's quick, low voice and the path ahead.

"Deiq of Stass is here," the old man said. "He's a big man, big and dark."

"Thanks for the warning," Alyea said, her heart sinking.

"You know him?"

"I don't think we've been introduced, but I've seen him in court now and again. He always made me uneasy."

"With good reason. Stay away from him." Chac seemed about to say more, then shook his head, his lips pressed tight. "Just . . . just stay away from him," he finished at last. "And don't make him angry."

"Gladly," Alyea said fervently. Deiq's dark stare always seemed to be sizing up everyone around him for their value to his own personal amusement; she had no interest in speaking with him or drawing his attention in any way.

"He's the only one of real status I've seen—not rank, he's no noble, but he has influence." The old man grimaced and changed the subject. "Remember that you have to earn respect. Your family blood means much less here than it did in Bright Bay. Stay quiet until you're spoken to."

"And if nobody speaks to me?"

"Then you enjoy a meal in silence for once in your life. It won't kill you."

Alyea snorted, annoyed at Chac's brusque reply, but they entered the dining hall without a single suitable retort coming to her mind.

The dining hall was a long, low building with five bench-seat tables. The center table, set with silver salt-cellars and a thickly embroidered, linen table-covering, was obviously for the most important guests; the outer tables, by similar indications, sat successively less worthy folk. Guards and servants were placed at the outermost tables, which had only bare wood and small, rough wooden bowls of coarse salt. Chac steered her to the center table, close to the door; after a quick, assessing glance up the mostly empty table, he said, "Sit at the end here, my lady. I'll take a table over."

She settled obediently on the wide, wooden bench just as a deep, brassy note from a hidden gong filled the air: once, twice, a third time. People began to stream into the room and sort themselves out into seats; Alyea noted several subtle clashes over the seats at the center and flanking tables by newcomers. There were few enough people and more than enough seats, however, so the disputes faded away with little more than an evil glare here and there.

Alyea recognized a few faces, high-blood merchants and low-end nobles who had swirled through Bright Bay her whole life. One or two, catching sight of her, smiled and nodded brief greeting; she returned the amiable gesture in kind.

Deiq of Stass sat high at the other end of her table, watching the room with lazy interest. Alyea managed to lean over and adjust her slipper just before his searching gaze reached her area of the table, and took her time about sitting back up. A quick glance reassured her that his attention had fixed on a plump woman at the next table over; she let out a thin sigh of relief.

She risked looking around the room herself, trying to keep her gaze casual. Micru, still in rough but clean trail clothes, had chosen a spot among the servants, laughing and joking as if he were nothing more than a low-born himself. Chacerly, at the next table, already seemed deep in conversation with the people around him, merchants by the look of them.

Wide wooden doors opened at the far end of the hall. Alyea had assumed they led outside, but a rich, savory smell filled the air as servants marched in carrying huge platters of food.

The richest dishes were brought to the center table, the simplest to the sides; roast pheasant and puff-bread on silver platters for nobles, roast chicken and black bread on wooden slabs for lesser men. The servers placed the food on plates for the more powerful, left the platters on the outer tables for the servant-classes to argue over.

Servants placed delicately-arranged helpings of white beans and feathery greens, thin slices of roast pheasant and puff-bread, small globes of creamed rice balls, and long strips of steamed black mushrooms on the silver plates. Alyea applied herself to her food silently, keeping a pleasant expression on her face. After the long day of riding, she wanted thick food, not this fluffy stuff. Hopefully Chac could get her some dark bread and cheese from the kitchens later.

"Beautiful, aren't they?" a thin voice to her left said.

Alyea turned her head, relieved that she wouldn't have to sit silent all through dinner, and smiled at the woman sitting a bit more than arm's length away. "It's all lovely."

"The mushrooms, I mean," the woman said. She was short and well-fed, with greying brown hair framing a contentedly round face. "I've never seen them quite so large."

Black mushrooms from the Horn were often the size of a dinner plate and, although a delicacy, weren't all that uncommon in Bright Bay. Alyea took a closer look at the woman, noted the northern roundness to her face, the simple cut of her dress, and the lack of jewelry, and tried not to wince.

"Everything's so much larger here," the woman went on. "It's lovely. I imagine you grow your gardens all year round, here, don't you? I wish I could. You can keep basil going all year, I imagine—am I right?" Her smile was open and innocent as she waited for an answer.

Alyea stared, taken aback. Did this woman think nobles *gardened*? "I . . . I wouldn't know."

The woman seemed to take in Alyea's dress for the first time.

"Oh, dear," she said, her round face flushing. She glanced around the room, seeming uncertain and flustered. "I'm sorry. Have I sat at the wrong table?"

"No," Alyea said after a moment, ashamed of her initial, snobbish reaction. Everyone could be important, Chac had warned her; Alyea decided, a bit impishly, that those words should apply to an ignorant northern as well as anyone else in the room. Let him rebuke her for over-friendliness; she'd throw his own words back in his face.

"Are you sure? I could . . . move. . . ." The woman glanced over her shoulder, visibly reluctant to leave the good food in front of her for the lesser meals on the further tables.

"Absolutely," Alyea assured her, flashing the warm, practiced smile. "You're fine. There's plenty of room here, no reason to move, and you've already got food on your plate. Please, stay and talk to me. I'm Alyea, of Bright Bay. You're from the northlands?"

"Well . . . yes," the woman admitted, relaxing. "I'm Halla of Felarr."

"What brings you all the way through the Forest and into the Horn, *s'a* Halla?" Alyea asked, interested now. Most northerns, and especially women, *didn't* travel this far, and definitely not alone, as Halla seemed to be.

The woman picked at her food uncertainly for a moment before answering.

"My son," she said finally. "He wanted to travel to Bright Bay. I couldn't stop him, and my husband's dead five years. Rebon went off with a merchanting caravan, hired on as a clerk; he's a good boy, a smart boy." She swallowed hard. "He never came back."

"How long has he been gone?" Alyea asked.

"Three years," Halla said. She stared at her plate, took a listless bite. "The merchant he worked for is dead two years back, killed in a riot in Bright Bay. I don't know where my son is. I've spent the last four months in Bright Bay, trying to find a trace of him; the only word I gathered, finally, is that he might have been seen going into the desert with a group of southerners, as a slave."

Alyea nodded, unsurprised, and said nothing.

Halla shook her head and poked at the food on her plate.

"Everything is so strange here," she said after a moment. "I don't know what to do. I ought to turn back now, to get home on what money I have left." She laughed, a sharp humorless bark. "Not that I'll have much to return to. All my savings are in this venture, and I have no man to help bring in more."

Alyea ate quietly for a time, considering, then said, "I'm headed south, and I could use a maid, *s'a*, if you've the interest in a job."

The round face brightened. "That would be perfect, *s'a*," Halla said. "I've been a merchant's wife for most of my life, but I've done my share of serving the wealthy. Would you take me on?"

"I will," Alyea said.

"I'm so grateful—"

The northern woman's voice stilled as a male tenor interrupted softly, "My lady?"

Alyea turned to look up at the man standing behind her. He wore the colors of the way-stop, grey and black, and the slash embroidered on his sleeves marked him as a dining-hall servant. A bracelet on his right wrist ran through a gamut of grey hues, in three rows of precisely-matched beads.

"Yes, *s'e*?"

He bowed briefly. "*S'e* Deiq asks the favor of your presence closer to his hand."

Startled, she glanced up the table. The big man's brooding dark gaze had fixed directly on her; not the best of manners but a clear sign that he'd take refusal of the offer poorly.

Don't make him angry, Chac had said.

Alyea stifled an annoyed sigh.

"We'll discuss this more after dinner," she told the woman. "Wait for me outside when the tables clear, or speak to Chacerly; he's the oldest man at that table—see?" Reassured by Halla's quick, bobbing nod, Alyea stood, schooled her expression to neutrality, and walked towards the head of the table.

As she moved, conversations ebbed; heads turned to watch her. Then, politely, the noise resumed. She sat across from Deiq, inclined her head in greeting, and waited. A fresh plate was placed in front of her and swiftly filled, along with a clean cup of water and a small goblet of white wine.

"I believe I've seen you before, Lady," Deiq said once the servants withdrew. "In Bright Bay."

"I grew up there," she said.

His eyes narrowed. She smiled and turned her attention to her food.

"What brings you to the Horn?" he asked.

"Scratha."

A thin line of broad teeth showed briefly in a slight smile. "Busy man."

She gave him the full weight of a direct, emotionless stare for a few seconds, and went back to eating, leaving the prompt unanswered.

He chuckled. "You're more than Scratha's worth. Come with me instead."

"I've business with Scratha," she said without looking up.

"You're not the first," he said. "Nissa of Sessin went through here wailing over him not long ago."

She stayed quiet, trying to keep her chewing slower than the sound of her pulse hammering in her ears. Close up, Deiq was *disturbing* in a way she couldn't quite place. And he seemed to be the only person at this table not wearing a beaded bracelet; she resisted the urge to study him for other jewelry, not wanting to give him the wrong impression.

"Mm," he said after a brief silence. It sounded thoughtful, and she glanced up to see him looking at her with narrowed eyes. A wider smile than before curved his mouth. The moment showed her that he wore no earrings or necklaces. "I remember where I've seen you before. You were always wandering about behind that skinny nothing."

"Who is now king," she said without taking offense. Oruen *had* been a gangly, unremarkable man until Chacerly's tutoring had straightened his stance and paced his movements.

"What's the king's woman doing headed down the Horn?"

"Do you call every woman you befriend *yours*?" she countered.

"What are you doing headed down the Horn?" he said with no visible annoyance or contrition. His gaze rested on her thin bracelet of green and white; his lips shifted as though resisting a smile.

Alyea shrugged. "King's business," she said, and cursed herself silently for answering that way; she'd intended to say "my business."

"King's business," he repeated, and grinned. It wasn't a particularly friendly expression. "Must be important or he wouldn't have sent such a good *friend*." When she didn't rise to that bait, he nodded as if satisfied and said, "You know, you really are far too smart for Scratha. Or for Oruen. You're wasted on them. I'm headed south in the morning, out to the east road. I'd be honored for you to travel with me, Lady. I think I'd like to get to know you better."

She felt a pressure behind her eyes, a velvet not-quite headache.

"I take the King's Road," she said, wishing she knew a more tactful way to refuse.

"That's a longer way," he said, "and a harder one. You'll get seasick from all the hills you'll travel over. The coast road is smoother, and beautiful. And from the lovely port of Stass I can arrange a ship to take you to Agyaer, no charge, and so much less riding."

"The King's Road is a shorter way," she said, not looking at him, "and a neutral road."

"Ah," he said, as if she'd said a great deal in few words. They finished their food in silence.

The dinner dishes were being cleared away and replaced with bowls of clean sand before he spoke again. Scooping up a handful of sand and rubbing it briskly between his palms, letting the grains drizzle onto the floor at his feet, he said, "Do you know what neutrality means, lady?"

She shook her head as she cleaned her own hands, tucking away the thought that he also displayed no rings on his large hands. Did the lack of decoration mean no status of note—or too much to mention? She'd have to ask Chac, and hope for a straight answer.

"Neutrality means," Deiq said, "being a whore to every man while letting him think he's the only one." He stood and smiled down at her. "It's a wonderful dance. I look forward to sharing it with you."

Before she could form a reply, he turned and walked away towards the entrance of the dining hall. After a moment, when her breath unlocked itself from its hard stop beneath her ribs, she used it to swear: quietly, but at considerable length.

Chapter Five

The village of Kybeach sprawled, small and smelly, along the edge of marshland. Idisio had heard stories about this village from fellow thieves who'd wandered down the Coast Road, but somehow their descriptions of the low-tide funk hadn't quite matched the sheer intensity of the real thing.

Accommodations, he remembered being warned, were low quality at best and rat-havens at worst; nobody of station stopped here long. And nobody shifty ought to, because Kybeach held a reputation as the most singularly narrow-minded, hostile village in existence. Although Idisio tried to explain that to Scratha, the man seemed deaf to reason.

"It'll need chronicled, then," Scratha snapped when pressed. "Best the king knows what's on his doorstep, don't you think?"

Idisio shrugged and dropped the argument, hoping the man's attitude would change when they reached Kybeach; but if anything, the swamp stink seemed to tighten Scratha's resolve.

The only possible word for the stables was *foul*. Scratha, checking at the door, snorted in abrupt fury, looped the reins over a nearby post, and ordered the startled stable-boy to bring him a muck-rake and shovel. Idisio, pressed into unwilling service, tied a cloth over his nose to block the worst of the smell and began to dig out the accumulated filth.

The stable-lad peered at them dubiously and made no move to help. "Merchant Lashnar won' like you handlin' his mare," he muttered. "She's pregnant. She's sensitive, you know. He won' like it."

"Then tell him to come move her outside," Scratha snapped without turning.

"Yeah, tell him we're busy doing *your* job for no damn pay," Idisio muttered, earning a black glare from the boy, who slouched away with ostentatious indifference.

Not long after that, a determined stride carried in, not a merchant, but a young woman with ash-blonde hair, bright blue eyes, and an undeniable bounce in certain areas of chest and hip. Idisio, aware of his sweaty, filthy appearance, grimaced ruefully: probably the only pretty girl in Kybeach and she'd never look at him twice after this.

"What are you two doing?" she demanded, planting hands on hips and scowling at them. "Baylor's in a fuss over you pushing him aside and complaining over filth that isn't. . . ."

Her voice trailed off as she caught sight of the piles of stable sweepings near the outer door. Her eyes widened in disbelief.

"You're never been in these stables, have you, *s'a*?" Scratha said, straightening. He studied her with a coolly detached appraisal.

"Not for a while . . . I've been busy helping at the inn. . . ." She edged forward and peered into the noisome darkness of the stable. "Good gods. It's disgusting! What has he been *doing*?"

"Rough guess, nothing," Idisio said. She swung a sharp glare at him.

"There's one horse in a half-decent stall," Scratha said, leaning on his rake. "That'd be the merchant's mare, I take it? Needs moved. Tell him to come do it."

Her chin came up, annoyance replaced with determination.

"I'll do it," she said. "I'm his daughter. You two draw back a bit if you would, please; she's always more skittish than usual this close to birthing. She ought to have peace and quiet, not be moved around and aggravated . . . oh, my father's going to be *so* angry. . . ."

She marched past them, muttering under her breath. After she'd led the gravid mare out of sight, Scratha resumed working without any comment, but his movements held a renewed ferocity. By the end of the day the stables were clean, the horses noticeably happier, and Idisio markedly more sour. Scratha, for his part, had a satisfied, if still dour, expression on his face as they sponged off with the freshly refilled, much cleaner water of the horse trough.

The stable-boy, who hadn't offered so much as a finger's worth of help all day, crept back into sight, glaring with a deep resentment.

"You gon' get me fired," he accused.

"If the mare had foaled in that filth, you'd have lost them both," Scratha said, lip curling. "Would the merchant have cared for *that*, Baylor?"

The boy blanched, as if Scratha knowing his name were a piece of witchcraft, and slouched to the stable doors. After a brief look inside, he turned a smoldering glare at them, his resentment no less.

"Outsiders," he said. "Think you're better'n everyone else."

Scratha shook his head with a snort and offered no other reply.

"Supper, Idisio," he said, directing one last brooding glare after the stable-boy, and steered Idisio out of the stable.

Even with windows thrown wide and lanterns lit, the tavern remained a dark and smoky place, little more than a wide room with a scattering of scarred tables. A serving girl, the attractive lines of her broad face and generous curves soured by a thoroughly sullen expression, advanced as Scratha and Idisio settled at a corner table.

"What can I get you?" she demanded. "We got chicken pie, roast gerho, biscuits, an' pot-greens; long-ale, mead, and red wine." She recited the list with an air of one put out by the effort it required to speak.

"That would be fine," Scratha said serenely.

She stared at him. "What, alla that?"

"Yes," he said, as if surprised. "There are two of us. I'll have wine with supper, please." He turned an inquiring look on Idisio.

"Wine," Idisio said absently, trying to think how to explain to the man what he'd just done.

The girl snorted and swished away indignantly, and Scratha frowned after her. "Did I say something wrong?"

Hoping that it hadn't been a rhetorical question, Idisio took the opening and said, "I'd guess a pie's usually split between four people, with maybe a lump of boiled greens thrown in to be generous. For us to order so much is. . . ." he searched for the right word and finally concluded, "wasteful."

"Wasteful!" Scratha sat brooding again for a time.

When the girl came back and thumped two heavy wooden mugs of red wine onto the table, he gave her an intent, searching look. Mistaking his interest, she returned a much kinder look than she'd offered before, swaying her hip to one side and breathing deeply.

"Your food'll be out soon," she said in a voice grown suddenly soft. "You're staying at the inn tonight?"

"Yes," Scratha said, his eyes narrowing, "but I have no need for company, thank you."

She pouted, her earlier sourness returning instantly, and left them in a huff.

"Wasteful," Scratha said in a low voice, frowning down at the mug and turning it slowly in his wide hands. "Is that how you see it, Idisio?"

Idisio hesitated, cautious in his answer.

"I can understand it," he said at last.

"How can a quarter-pie and a handful of greens be expected to feed a man after a full day's work?" Scratha demanded. "It's nonsense! It's a child's portion." He turned one hand over and frowned at a developing blister.

"I've survived on less," Idisio answered, hoping that wouldn't remind Scratha of his street-thief origins. It seemed safer to keep that memory in the deep background of the man's mind.

"As have I," Scratha said, "but that doesn't make it a generous portion to serve to a traveler."

Idisio shook his head. "These aren't portions like at that palace dinner, Master," he said. "Most people don't eat several small courses. They make do with one, so it's a lot bigger. Look—here it comes."

Gerau stared in disbelief as two servers, each with heavily laden platters, advanced on their table. "*That* much difference?" he muttered.

"Yeah," Idisio said, holding back a grin. "That much difference."

The servers plunked down the platters and withdrew, leaving the heat of their sullen glares behind with the food.

One platter held an entire large pie. Around it had been arranged six biscuits, a wide bowl heaped with pot-greens, and a small bowl of coarse salt. On the other lay the largest roasted haunch of marsh lizard Idisio had ever seen. The entire creature must have easily weighed over twenty pounds when living.

"Gerho," Idisio muttered, staring at it. "Wasn't this Ninnic's favorite food?"

"Yes," Scratha said absently, looking over the food. "I see now that I should have ordered less. I'll remember that."

He reached out and tore a chunk of meat free, wiped grease away with a piece of biscuit, and bit in contentedly. Idisio shuddered and reached for the pie instead.

Some time later, when their appetites were slowing, Idisio said, "The man to the side, over there, has been watching us since the food arrived."

"I know," Scratha said, unalarmed.

Idisio shrugged and returned his attention to the food.

A few moments later, the man rose from his table and approached them openly. He was a tall, thin man with bony hands and a long face. Bright blue eyes under an untidy mop of blond hair and a tan to his skin that came from sun, not heritage, marked him as northern-bred at least in part.

"Greetings, *s'es*," he said, bowing courteously. "May I join you?"

"Certainly," Scratha said amiably, motioning to a chair. He seemed completely at ease, very unlike the nearly hostile, reserved silence he'd displayed at the king's table.

The man sat down, relaxed and smiling, and cast a glance at the almost empty platter of gerho. "Do you like the meal?" He caught the server's eye and waved peremptorily, then rubbed his hands together briskly at her puzzled scowl.

"I do," Scratha said. "Very filling, and tender meat. The cooks did a fine job with it."

The serving girl dropped two thick pieces of cloth on the table and retreated without a word.

"You're fond of gerho, then?"

"I am. Are you the breeder?" Scratha picked up one of the cloths, tossed the other to Idisio, and began wiping his hands free of grease.

The man appeared delighted by Scratha's perception. "A man of rare wit, you are, *s'e*," he said. "Yes indeed. Asti Lashnar, humble gerho merchant, at your service. I understand you rescued my prize mare from dreadful conditions earlier. I'm in your debt."

"No, you're not," Scratha said, and changed the subject before the man could protest. "Are all your gerho so big?"

"Oh, yes," the merchant said. "I've a pen at the edge of the marsh. Perhaps you'd like to come see them? I've some over five feet long."

"Not tonight, thank you," Scratha said. "Very impressive, that size."

The man swelled with pride. "They have to be large. I have built a thriving business of these creatures, supplying them direct to the king's table, no less. The common gerho is simply too small to sustain profitable dealing. I've bred them for years, *s'e*, over ten years, and this latest litter is the finest yet."

"I believe I've seen you in Bright Bay," Scratha said.

"Indeed, indeed!" the man said. "I've spent quite a bit of time there. I've no doubt you've seen me. In and out of the king's court, I was, for years. But business . . . is not what it was."

"King Oruen dislikes gerho?"

"Bitterly," the man agreed, appearing despondent. "I've tried to gain audience with him, had my own cook prepare the best dishes possible; no good. And what the king won't eat, the nobles won't touch; I'm on the edge of ruin, with over two dozen of the beasts left to eat me out of all profit gathered over the years."

Idisio, catching the glitter in his master's eye, knew Scratha was tiring of his attempt at gracious mannerisms. The merchant, unaware of his danger, rattled on.

"I'm looking for a partner, my lord, a man of wit and distinction, refined taste and honesty, who could help me find a new market. Are you perhaps headed up the road to Isata?"

"Yes," Scratha said, "but I'm no lord and I'm not interested in hauling along a load of gerho."

"Oh, no need, no need," the merchant said quickly, half-laughing. "Perhaps I should have said, rather than partner, that I seek a sponsor, such as I had at court for many years."

"Neither will I give you coin to finance your venture," Scratha said bluntly.

The merchant licked his lips and tried again. "Of course not. Coin isn't the sort of thing a nobleman uses for arrangements, and you're a noble by your bearing, refuse the title as you will. I can offer . . . inducements, to sweeten your temper towards an alliance with—"

"What are you offering?" Scratha cut in.

"Something of far more warmth than coin," the merchant said. "An alliance of great benefit to both of us. My daughter's of age, a fine girl, untouched in any way; you saw her earlier. Perhaps she might suit your interest."

Scratha stared at the man for a long moment, expressionless. The merchant returned a nervous smile, his confidence visibly crumbling around the edges.

"Are you offering me your daughter's hand or sending her for my bed?" Scratha said at last. He sounded mildly curious, but his dark, desert-hawk stare never lightened.

"She's a good girl," the merchant started, rallying into indignation.

"Then you're offering her hand," Scratha interrupted. "You throw your daughter at every noble that comes through, or am I the first?"

"I resent your implication!" the merchant said, flushed now. "My daughter is pure and untouched!"

"Regardless," Scratha said. "I'm not noble, and not interested."

The man's face crumpled a little. "But the potential benefits, my lord," he said, rallying quickly. "Refusing this alliance, why, it, it would be as if Saint-King Wezel had turned away the philosophers searching for the fountain of gold in the center of the Holy Marshes—"

"The world would be a great deal better off if that had happened," Scratha interrupted. "I'll do without the salt of the *Ugly* Marshes gladly if it would erase the damage the Northern Church has done over the years."

The merchant's blue eyes narrowed sharply.

"I see I mistook your nature," he said stiffly, and rose. "I apologize for troubling you, *s'e*."

Scratha inclined his head in farewell as the merchant marched from the tavern. "Whoremongering fool," he said, not lowering his voice. Heads turned in startled, frowning response.

"Master," Idisio said, his own voice low and urgent, "*Please* don't talk like that."

Scratha turned an annoyed stare on his servant. "What, are you suddenly bashful of strong language?"

Idisio drew a breath, spoke with care.

"You're not traveling as a nobleman," he said, keeping an eye on the people who were staring at them now. He had a feeling Scratha was used to relatively fair fights, not bar brawls; if any of the men at nearby tables were good friends with Lashnar, things could get ugly fast. "You don't have protection against attacks."

"You worry too much," Scratha said. "We're still within stone's throw of the outer edges of Bright Bay. And I can handle any attacks."

The moment of tension in the tavern passed, and drinkers returned to their ales without more than a disgusted head-shake. Idisio relaxed a little and turned most of his attention to the conversation with his master.

"Winning a bar brawl easily would draw questions about who you are," Idisio pointed out. "A King's Researcher wouldn't be a weapons-master, would he?"

"Mmph." Scratha frowned, considering. "You may be right. Again." He paused, then added thoughtfully, "I think you may actually turn out useful after all."

Idisio resisted the impulse to roll his eyes.

"I'll keep your caution in mind," Scratha said. He finished scrubbing grease from his hands and dropped the thick cloth napkin on the table. What had been left on the platters would feed another three men of average means to bursting, but Scratha clearly had no care for that.

Wasteful, yes, but more than that, a dangerous advertisement of wealth. If Idisio had seen a man like Scratha walk into a low tavern in Bright Bay and order such a meal, his finger-knives would have been busy seconds later, and the man's lodging stripped of all wealth within the hour.

At the thought, his stomach turned sour. "I ask your leave," he said hurriedly. "I need to go find an outhouse."

"You don't need permission to piss," Scratha grumbled, flicking his fingers at the door. "Go, go already. Good gods. . . ."

The rest of the man's grousing faded from hearing as Idisio almost bolted from the tavern. It took only a few moments to be at the door to the nearby inn. Brushing past a burly, sour-faced youth just emerging, he headed for the room they'd booked earlier in the day. Hearing a low whistle as he rounded the corner, he lunged forward at top speed and caught a girl against the wall as she darted from their room. A woven basket clattered to the ground as she batted at him.

"I was cleaning," she said indignantly. "Get your hands off me!"

"Cleaning us out, like," he said, recognizing her immediately as the merchant's daughter. Up close, the soft curves he'd admired earlier pressed against him; he tried to shift his grip and stance to avoid embarrassing himself. He told himself to think of her as nothing more than another street-thief, not one to trust in any way; that helped cool his blood.

"Are you accusing me of theft?" she demanded.

"Takes one to know one, they say," he said, baring his teeth in a humorless grin. "Come on, girl, hand it back and I'll say nothing. I'll even throw in a silver round for your trouble."

"I have nothing of yours!" she flared.

"And what were you doing in the room, then? It needs no cleaning; we only just arrived."

"I don't have to answer to you," she snapped, and began to push at him to release her.

"Then I'll take it to the village elder," he said. "Or I could mention it to your father, Asti Lashnar the gerho merchant."

Her bright blue eyes widened.

"Please don't," she said, sounding worried. "I swear to you, I have nothing of yours. I was passing by, to clean another room, and saw the door open. I went in to check that everything was all right, and was just coming out. I saw no signs of theft."

She looked more frightened than the situation called for, especially given the spirited determination she'd shown earlier. Judging it to be an act, Idisio shook his head and said, amiably, "Sure. I'll go with that story, once you give me what you took, and see that you get a reward as well."

"*No*," she said, vexed. "Are you dense? I'm telling you truth."

With no sound to warn of his approach, Scratha's voice made them both jump. "Is this what you had to rush away from table for, Idisio?" He sounded amused. "Surely you could have found a different place. A corner of the stable, perhaps?"

The girl's face flooded with bright and mortified color. Idisio hastily released the girl and stepped back. "It's not like that—"

"Really," Scratha said, and moved past into the room. "Your business, then. Just don't wake me, please." He closed the door behind him.

Idisio and the blonde girl stared at each other for a moment in horrified silence; then the absurd humor of the situation prompted him into a reluctant grin.

"He won't say anything," Idisio assured her.

"Best not," the girl said firmly. "There's nothing to say. And I *don't* have anything of yours. Good night!" She scooped the basket up, ostentatiously lifted the lid to show Idisio that it was empty, and hurried away.

He let her go, not seeing any other option than wrestling her to the ground and searching her; the thought of being that close to her again brought another rush of blood to his face. No, best to let that be. He'd check to see how much was missing when Scratha was safely asleep and none the wiser; and if it was a large sum, he'd track the girl down and get it back. A small sum his master would likely never miss, and if the girl's father ran under as bad a string of ill-fortune as he'd claimed, the girl could use it better than Scratha.

Idisio waited a few moments, steadying his heartbeat, before stepping into the room. Scratha had already sprawled, breathing in deeply peaceful sleep, on what passed for a bed here: little more than an ankle-high wooden support topped with a straw pallet, rough linen covering thrown over and a thin blanket for chill nights. He'd left the table-lantern lit.

Idisio paused just inside the doorway, pulled the door shut behind him, and examined the room carefully in the flickering light. He could see signs that their bags had been disturbed, but whether his master had gone through them before stretching to sleep or a thief had been at them he couldn't tell.

He moved forward, knelt by the untidy pile of bags, and rummaged gingerly through the contents. Although he could have sworn the bag of coin had been tucked further down in the pack, a judicious look in the bag showed the right volume of coin inside. If anything had been taken, it had only been one or two, not more than that; he had a sharp eye for weight and volume.

So the girl had been telling the truth. What had she been doing in their room, then, and why had she come darting out so quickly at the whistle? Idisio closed up the packs, deciding it wasn't his concern, as long as his master's money and belongings were intact.

Glancing around the room once more, he shook his head at the careless way Scratha had tossed his clothes over a chair, leaving his money pouch on top without a worry in the world. He'd have to convince Scratha to let him carry the money.

Idisio grinned. A common pick-thief of the streets of Bright Bay, asking a noble to put a pouch full of gold and silver in his care? Scratha would be mad to think of it, and even more foolish to refuse. The way the man spent his coin, he'd lose every silver bit before they crossed the Great Forest.

Idisio tucked Scratha's money pouch into the bags at the foot of the bed, set his boots to one side, laid out the thin blanket on the floor beside them, and curled himself protectively around the bags.

A noise woke him some time later, a scuffle and a muted cry that had him on his feet and to the window immediately. Pushing the shutters wide, he saw, in the pale light of a beginning moon, a shadow hurrying among deeper shadows. It rounded a corner, and the night was still again. Nobody else stirred; possibly nobody else had heard. If Idisio hadn't been in the lightest of dozes, mistrustful in a strange place, he likely wouldn't have heard it, either.

He hesitated, staring out into the night, listening for a few more moments. None of his business, he told himself. If something dodgy was happening out there, he was best in the room with his master, not out running into the middle of it.

But nobody else seemed to be investigating, and it had sounded like a female voice crying out. His mind on the blonde girl, Idisio couldn't resist the urge to make sure that whatever the problem, she hadn't been involved. Baylor seemed the type to take out his dull-witted resentment on anyone weaker, and she'd brought the news of his neglect to her father; a few ales to fan the flames, and she'd be a prime target.

Idisio slipped from the room and padded, barefoot, towards the outside door. The worn wood of the floor felt warm and silky underfoot, crisscrossed by rough scars left by dragging heavy objects along the hallway over the years. Nobody stood at the front desk, nobody seemed to be watching for late-night arrivals, and the door was unbarred. Idisio eased it open and edged through, letting it close again silently.

The noise had come from the west, the direction their window faced. He hurried towards the edge of the marsh, taking care to keep to the shadows, ears and eyes alert for any other movement nearby.

The houses thinned out well before the ground grew damp. The leading edge of the wetland lay yards from the closest home, which Idisio noted sourly had windows only on the eastward side. To the south, dimly visible, hulked a wide, low-walled enclosure, half in swamp, half on dry ground, with walls that slanted inwards at their tops. Idisio guessed it to be the gerho pen, and hoped the trail didn't lead there.

Swamp-frogs and crickets chirred, chittered, and squeaked as he advanced slowly, studying the open ground. Tracking had never been his strength, but in the pale moonlight he saw a flurry of prints in the soft ground, to and from the village proper, leading into the swamp. He guessed that two, maybe three people had come and gone this way. One of the prints was light and small, possibly a child's or a woman's foot. Another had broad toes and a heavy tread, and the third looked long and narrow, leaving little more depth to its print than the smallest had. All had been barefoot; not surprising on a warm night, especially if stealth was required.

Lovers sneaking off to spend time together? Idisio couldn't conceive of any romance enduring the stench that hung over the black mud. He hesitated again. It *really* wasn't any of his business. But if it had been nothing more than that, judging by the silence, he'd find nothing, and be reassured, whereas if he went back now, he knew he'd never get to sleep.

Curiosity had gotten his nose skinned before, but now as always, he couldn't resist finding out more. Two lovers, maybe, but there were three sets of prints made recently, which made a lover's meeting unlikely. If it had been a struggle, there might have been a rape, two on one; that thought sent his blood boiling and his feet moving forward again recklessly.

Following the tracks, he found, to his surprise, that although the ground did soften considerably, the oozing mud and water stayed to either side, not in front. The path rose and firmed further, until the tracks vanished in an area filled with springy marsh-grass. Idisio wasn't skilled enough, by dim moonlight, to make sense out of broken leaves or stems. He stood in the knee-high grass helplessly, looking around.

He saw the slightest shadow of an opening to one side, where the taller reeds all around had been pushed aside hard enough or often enough to acquire a permanent lean. It was the only possible path he could see, and he moved towards it cautiously, suddenly mindful of marsh snakes and pinching beetles. He silently called himself a fool for setting bare feet here at night.

But someone else had, and recently; he could only hope that they had scared away anything dangerous in the nearby area. And something urged him on, more than curiosity: something verging on the disturbing intuition he'd followed all his life.

The ground past the bent reeds continued firm underfoot and within a few steps opened up into a kind of rough clearing wide enough that several steps would cross it. Surrounded by tall cattail reeds and fluffberry bushes, clumps of towering silver grass, and even a wrinkled, tangled blackthorn tree, it was a cozy enough spot for privacy if one could ignore the stink.

A crumpled form lay in the middle of the cleared area, and the paleness of blonde hair stood out even in the dim light from a thin moon. Sucking in a hard breath, he scrambled to her side and dropped to his knees, reaching out to touch her gingerly.

"*S'a*?" he said, hoping for breath, for movement, for tears. She lay too still. Touching her throat, something felt wrong; moving his hand up slowly, he found her head twisted at an awkward angle, warm blood still oozing from a vicious cut on her lower left jaw.

When his fingers encountered that wetness, he jerked back, breathing hard, and hurriedly wiped his hand on nearby grass. Nausea heaved through his stomach. He knew death when he saw it.

Moments later, he was on his feet and sprinting back through the marsh, wanting to put as much distance between him and the body as possible. At the edge of the marsh, he paused, undecided—should he rush to rouse the town or get himself to safety? By the time the girl was even missed it might be late tomorrow, and he could be miles down the road with Scratha. Idisio knew, from stories more traveled thieves had told, that Kybeach always looked first to outsiders for crimes. Deciding at last that crying for help would be too risky, he started back to the inn, determined to press his master into leaving at first light if at all possible.

"What's that?" a voice called out, and a hand-lantern slotted open, light falling on Idisio, fixing him where he stood. "Who's this?"

Idisio stood, frozen in sudden panic, staring at the wavering light as the man approached. "Good eve, *s'e*," he said idiotically.

The bobbing light revealed an old man, wrinkled by sun and salt and poverty. He peered at Idisio suspiciously. "Who're you, boy, and what do you wandering around the marsh at midnight?"

"I couldn't sleep," Idisio said. "I like to walk when I can't sleep."

The man grunted, sharp dark eyes sweeping Idisio from head to foot. "You like walking in the marshes at night? Dangerous thing to do. Quicksand not far out there, and we've had problems with marsh asps of late."

Idisio glanced down at his feet; they were muddy enough, even though he'd been on largely dry ground, to make the observation undeniable.

"I didn't go far," he said, feeling a light sweat break out across his whole body.

"Quicksand *shifts*, boy," the man said severely. "At times it's right at the edge of the village, you know."

Idisio doubted that, from what little he knew of marshland, but wasn't about to stand out here and argue with an old man bent on impressing him.

"I won't do it again, *s'e*," he said. "I didn't realize it was that dangerous."

His position had become even more tenuous, now that someone had seen him out here at night. It would be only his word against the village that he had nothing to do with the girl's death. He considered confessing to what he'd found; but the old man's suspicious gaze didn't give him confidence that his story would be in any way believed. Of all the people to confide in, this would likely be the worst: an old curmudgeon who wandered the village at night, peering and prying to see what wrong he could catch people in.

He let out a long breath of relief when the man, with only the barest courtesy, turned away and shambled off in another direction. Abandoning stealth, Idisio sprinted for the safety of the inn—

And landed face-down not far from the door he'd been aiming for, his hands catching the weight just before his nose slammed into the ground. His sore wrist screamed a sharp reminder of two days ago. It took Idisio a moment to realize he'd been tripped. The understanding was helped by a large form that bulked over him, shouting: "Here's a thief who's been roaming the town while we sleep!"

"No," Idisio panted, rolling painfully to a sitting position, "no, I just—"

"You outsiders, you're all alike," the person standing over him said. Idisio guessed his attacker older than himself, but somewhat less than a full-grown man. Imposingly built, broad-shouldered and dark, he wasn't someone Idisio would care to wrestle. Another moment gave recognition: he'd brushed by the boy hours before, on his way into the inn to check their belongings.

A faint aroma came from the large boy, but Idisio was too distracted to put name to smell.

"A thief! A thief!" the large boy shouted again. "Wake up, wake up!"

"No," Idisio said desperately, and started to get up. A solid poke from a meaty hand put him quickly back on the ground again. The boy's breath in his face clarified the mysterious smell: wine. Probably quite a lot of it, by the slight sway in his stance.

In a rush of footsteps, people emerged sleepily into the road.

"What's this, what's this?" voices said in ragged chorus, like a flock of seagulls crying after scraps, and light pooled around them from lanterns, candles, and torches. "What's going on here?"

"I found him sneaking around," the big youth said, swelling proudly. "I don't see why any honest man has business sneaking around at night."

"Why were *you* out, then?" Idisio retorted, and earned a black glare for the words.

"I have work to do," the youth sneered. "I'm watching merchant Lashnar's mare now."

"True," said a voice. Asti Lashnar stepped forward, his blond hair tumbled in sleepy disarray around his face. "Is she all right, Karic? Were you shouting something about her?"

"No, the mare's fine," the boy assured him quickly. "I stepped out for some fresh air, and saw this one sneaking about. When I saw him sprinting back here like a demon snapped at his heels I knew he'd done something wicked and I had to stop him."

No way out of it now. As soon as they realized the girl's absence, they'd lay it all at his hand, and Scratha might or might not believe any protests at that point.

"I heard a noise," Idisio said, "and I went out to find what caused it."

The old man from the edge of the village arrived in time to hear that, hobbling with surprising speed, his eyes gleaming at the promise of mischief ahead.

"You told me you couldn't sleep," he croaked maliciously. "Story changes now, do it? Funny that nobody else hear this noise, hah?"

"He's lying again," the older boy said positively. "Master Lashnar, is your daughter safe within the inn? I don't see her here."

The gerho merchant, as if startled, looked around. "That's odd. She was supposed to be working the front desk of the inn, for night arrivals. She should have been first out when you shouted. Perhaps she's out checking on the gerhoi." He sounded dubious.

"I bet he lured her out," the dark-haired boy said. "I saw him staring at her, earlier in the day. And he's been in the marsh—look at his feet!"

"I found him just having come out of the marsh," the old man croaked, excited now. "He admitted wandering about out there!"

"No," Idisio said, desperately trying to regain the chance to speak. "No, I went to find out about the noise—"

"Likely story," the gerho merchant bellowed, enraged now. "What did you do with my daughter?"

"Excuse me," Scratha said, moving people firmly out of his way as he advanced through the crowd. Unlike the others around him, he was fully dressed, even to the boots, giving him an undeniable air of authority. The babble of voices fell silent and people moved out of his way.

"Idisio? What's going on?"

"He's lured my daughter into the swamp and done something foul with her!" the gerho merchant cried, lunging forward to grab at Idisio's shirt. With a swift movement, Scratha held the man back.

"Let the boy speak, please," Scratha said, forcefully enough to quiet even the furious merchant. "Idisio?"

"I heard a noise, and I went looking for what caused the noise, and I found her," Idisio said, all in a rush. "It's the blonde girl, the merchant's daughter, I don't know her name, she's in the swamp, she's dead, someone's killed her and *it wasn't me!*"

By the time the arguing had died out and the relevant people—most of the village, it seemed—had gotten dressed and ready to trek across damp muddy ground, the sky had greyed towards dawn. The gerho merchant had wanted to rush straight out to see for himself what had happened, dragging Idisio by the ear if need be, but more sensible people held him back.

"It's too dark yet," said some, "we'll be sure to step on marsh asps and stinger beetles. Wait until there are more of us, with more light."

"*He* made it out and back, a stranger to the marshes yet," the merchant replied sourly. Only Scratha's flat refusal to allow Idisio to move from his side turned the issue. Lashnar stormed away to dress and didn't return for some time.

Scratha and Idisio went back into the taproom of the inn, followed by a suspicious crowd that seemed intent on keeping them in plain sight. Scratha said little as they sat and waited; Idisio said nothing. Nobody spoke to them.

Asti Lashnar's face had a tinge as grey as the sky, and his breath shared the same wine-stink that Karic's had borne, as they finally trooped across the open ground, following Idisio's directions.

"See," Idisio said as the ground began to soften underfoot, "see, the tracks. . . ." He stopped, staring in dismay.

The soft ground had been thoroughly trampled by someone or something; the tracks had been completely overridden.

"Convenient," Scratha said in Idisio's ear. Idisio nodded glumly.

"So much for your proof," the merchant snorted, looking at the muddy chaos, then gestured imperiously to Idisio. "Show me my daughter, boy."

Scratha laid a hand on Idisio's shoulder and propelled him forward. Idisio stopped at the edge of the swamp, searching doubtfully in the muddy ground for the path he'd used before.

"Having second thoughts, boy?" the old watchman sneered, pushing close. "Feeling that rope around your neck?"

"Watchman," Scratha said, "another word and my hands will be around *your* neck. Be still."

"Here," Idisio said hastily, stepping forward and prodding at the ground with a toe. "Yes. Here." He glanced at the gerho merchant. "It's a narrow path; I don't think two aside can walk it. Follow me, please, *s'e*, and step where I step only."

"The whole village need not attend," Scratha added. "*S'e* Lashnar is the only one involved out of your village, and I will go as the boy is my servant. The rest of you, stay here."

Something in his voice drowned, stillborn, any protests.

As they picked their way through the swamp, the back of Idisio's neck kept prickling. Visions of the enraged gerho merchant's hands wrapping around his neck kept distracting him. He wouldn't dare, Idisio kept telling himself. Even so, he took great care to stand well out of Lashnar's reach when they reached the small clearing.

Lashnar moved forward like a man in a dream, kneeling beside his daughter, and stared for some time without touching the body. Scratha moved forward as well, just as slowly; but his attention stayed fixed on the ground, and he walked all the way around the edge of the clearing before turning his attention to the girl.

"Don't touch that," he said sharply, as the merchant reached forward towards something on the body that Idisio couldn't see.

The merchant looked up, all belligerence gone, a sick and dreadfully pale look to his face. "Why not?"

"Let me look first," Scratha said. He urged the merchant to his feet and nudged him aside before squatting to examine the body himself.

The grey light of the sky now flushed towards true dawn, and the chirping of the crickets gave way to the wake-up calls of swamp birds. Rat flies, bite-bugs, and tiny flying roahas stirred their translucent wings and flitted about. Idisio, standing still, numb and exhausted, felt as if he had stepped into a timeless moment of unreality. The merchant stood with a blank look on his face, hands hanging limp at his sides, staring at his daughter's body.

Finally breaking his motionless examination, Scratha stretched out a slow hand and removed a dagger from the girl's stomach. After wiping the blade clean on the dew-damp ground beside him, he stood and turned a bleak look on the two watching him.

"Her neck might be broken, from the punch that laid her to the ground," he said, "but what probably killed her was this."

He held up the dagger. Even in the dim light, Idisio could see the ebony handle and slim blade of one of his lord's throwing knives.

Chapter Six

"You told me not to make him angry," Alyea said reasonably.

"You did worse," Chac said, his jaw hardening further. "You intrigued him. Now he'll tag our heels to find out what we're up to."

Alyea sighed and resisted the impulse to look over her shoulder. That morning, Deiq of Stass had sauntered up with a broad grin to announce he would be traveling with them. He'd bowed with perfect grace, smiling amiably in the face of Chac's glower, and had taken himself to the back of Alyea's group. So far, he'd stayed there, showing no interest in speaking with anyone.

"At least I have a maid now," she said, hoping to divert Chac's annoyance. They'd given Halla one of the pack mules and redistributed the load, ignoring the woman's protests that she'd be fine walking. "Aren't you happy about that?"

"I *was*," he said, "until I found out you'd more or less invited *him* along as well."

"What makes him so dangerous that you're frothing over him being at our tail?" she demanded.

He slanted a hard frown at her. "Sometimes a bit of silk would go better than salt, you know," he said.

"Just answer the question."

He grunted and shook his head, then said, "Deiq of Stass is a little bit of everything: merchant, socialite, explorer. He's been to every port, east and west, even Terhe and Sand."

"Terhe?" Alyea said, impressed. "That's a dangerous voyage."

The old man stared straight ahead, his face grim again. "Deiq uses his wealth to buy land. That's not such an easy thing, past the Horn. You have to get agreement from every village master and desert lord within a hundred land miles of the edges of the land you've chosen. That's expensive, and damned difficult."

"How much land has he bought?" she asked.

"One estimate I heard," the old man said, "is that overall it works out to a little over twice the size of Bright Bay."

Alyea had stood on the highest tower of the palace and surveyed the vast, sprawling city beneath her; twice that size was a staggering amount of land for one man to own.

"What does he *do* with the land?" she said. "How was he ever allowed to own so much?"

"He turns it into farms," Chac said. "If you've eaten fresh fruit or vegetables over the last few years, it's likely they've come from Deiq's land. How he was allowed—he's a persuasive man, and held out a benefit that everyone could appreciate: money. And a few other things, I think."

She wasn't about to let him leave it there. "Like what?"

"Possibly drugs; there are rumors he has connections to Darden and F'Heing. But I think he uses physical charms to enthrall people into giving him what he wants. He's seduced at least two village masters into granting him land rights that I'm sure of, and he's not picky; one was male."

Alyea raised a skeptical eyebrow. "I don't believe a man can play that game."

Chac shook his head. "Women aren't the only ones who know the art. He's quiet about it, but I'm fairly sure he's bedded his way through noble ranks from Bright Bay to Terhe. If he were a woman I'd call him a whore."

"Sounds like he'd give the northern s'iopes a heart attack," Alyea said, a sour taste in her mouth, then remembered the comment the big man had made at dinner the night before. "He names himself a whore; says that's what neutrality means."

"Does he," Chac said, unsurprised. "He's as neutral as it gets, then. Here's something for you to think on: the wife of Sessin's new Head of Family, Lord Antouin Sessin, just happens to be Pieas's mother. Her eye wanders when her husband's out of sight, and there's rumor she was pregnant before marrying Antouin. I have to think Lord Sessin knows about his lady's indiscretions; it seems no secret. But for some reason there's no open notice made of it. Deiq's been a visitor there for years, and there's some quiet speculation as to who Pieas's father really is—but it's risking your life to say that openly."

Alyea felt her stomach roll unpleasantly. "Gods."

"Indeed," the old man said. "You've caught the eye of a desert asp, Alyea. If Pieas is Deiq's son—well. You could find yourself strung up as a witch, called out as a whore, or sold off as a slave. The king's authority is thin, down here, and by the time he even heard of your troubles it would be far too late."

Alyea glanced back nervously, looking for Micru. He was still walking with the guards.

"We'll protect you," Chac said, following her gaze, "best we can, but we can't ward you from yourself, Alyea. If you ever find yourself alone with Deiq of Stass, you can be sure it's not from lack of attention on our part."

Alyea swallowed hard, her face flaming. "I'm not that much a fool, Chac."

"You've been acting it," he said. "I'm glad you're starting to see sense finally. Find a way to lose Deiq's interest. *Fast*."

The setting sun gilded the buildings as the traveling party entered the second way-stop between Bright Bay and Water's End. This one was larger, and the public space sprawled along a relatively flat stretch of land with a stable, an inn, a separate tavern, and a few small shops. All the long, low buildings were built of a chunky, dull red-grey brick that could only have come from brickroot fields.

The tiny, wide-leafed brickroot plant had a tenacious root system that dug through the harshest clay soil, binding it so tightly that one could literally slice chunks from such ground, remove the surface part of the plant, set the hard dirt in the hot sun to cure, and a week later, use them for bricks. Constituting a major—and profitable—Horn industry, any flat surface was generally farmed to support the stubby little plant. Alyea had heard that there were villages whose overall elevation had dropped several feet over the years, from the constant brickroot farming.

This way-stop seemed no exception. They passed several wide, carefully fenced-off areas filled with brickroot plants. The buildings stood notably higher than the brickroot fields; some had ramps or stairs leading up to their front doors. The ground around those buildings looked as if it had been carved away over the years for brick. It gave the community a ragged, poverty-stricken appearance that the worst parts of Bright Bay would have been hard pressed to beat.

The stench of a garbage pit greeted them as they rode past the first outbuildings. By the time they reached the inn, Alyea's mood had gone as sour as the air. She wasn't cheered by the discovery that she'd be sharing a room, not only with Halla, but with strangers as well; far less selective than the first rest stop, this one mixed nobles and commoners in its small rooms without hesitation. Alyea's room held four narrow, low beds, which were little more than straw-stuffed sacks on brick bases.

Halla had insisted on taking care of Alyea's horse as well as her own, and Alyea put up little argument over the matter, too tired to even think clearly. She dropped both packs on an empty bed and looked around, meeting the gaze of a thin young woman perched on the edge of another bed.

Remembering Chacerly's admonition that anyone here could be important, she pushed aside her foul mood and offered pleasant greetings to the young woman, who wore northern clothes and a petulant frown.

To her surprise, the girl responded, in a distinctly northern accent, "Oh, good gods, I'm glad *someone's* talking to me at last! I'd always thought southerners were polite, but nobody's said a *word* to me in days. Sorry, I'm chattering. No offense intended."

"None taken," Alyea said cautiously, studying the young girl. Probably not above fifteen; and her northern accent absolutely didn't fit a face and body that a desert lord's by-blow would have been proud of.

"I'm Gria," the girl said with a wide smile; then, as if guessing Alyea's thoughts: "From Isata. Cousin to the Marq; second, third, I'm not entirely sure. My mother could probably tell you to the last drop of Isatain blood, but I'm lousy with bloodlines."

Alyea found herself smiling at young Lady Gria's brash cheer. "Alyea of Bright Bay. Cousin at some remove to one of the royal bloodlines. Second, third, maybe eighth; I can never remember. What brings you to the Horn, if it isn't too rude to ask?"

"Not at all," Gria said. "I'm getting married. Or at least, that's what my mother hopes. There's a desert lord looking for a wife to his son and contacts into a northern family of rank, and my mother loves the idea of the influence and bragging rights she'd gain through that, so we set out to be part of the grand auction. I've been harangued every step of the way so far on the proper way to throw myself at the feet of a desert lord. Tell me, is it anything like groveling before a s'iope?"

"Nothing at all like that," Alyea said, frowning.

"I was afraid of that," Gria said with a mock sigh. "Well, maybe it won't be a complete disaster. Then again, maybe I should pray that it is. I don't know that I'm ready for marriage just yet."

"Don't you get a choice in the matter? I thought Isata was fairly liberal."

"Oh, it is," Gria said. "But my mother isn't. She's devoted to the Northern Church, follows their every whim. My father was more reasonable, but he died a few years back, and it's just not worth the strain to fight her on most things. At least marrying will get me away from her."

Alyea glanced at the last bed, which showed no signs of even having been sat on, although two carry-bags sat neatly beside it.

"She's off praying," Gria said. "She prays for an hour before every meal, and an hour after the meal, and every other time she can get on her knees. I refuse to do that, which drives her wild, but that *is* a battle I'm willing to fight. My knees just won't take it." She drew a breath. "I was forbidden to leave the room without her, but I think she'd make an exception if I had a cousin to the royal family at my side. We don't need to mention the word 'distant,' do we?" She grinned hopefully, dark eyes wide.

Alyea laughed. "They'll be ringing the gong for dinner soon," she said. "Let's go get some decent seats."

"Not even a proper shrine to the Four. It's a disgrace, after all the s'iopes have done for the southlands. I actually had to kneel on bare dirt, can you believe it? Dirt! Like some heathen."

Alyea tried not to roll her eyes. Sela, a small, bony woman with wide-set, prominent eyes and high cheekbones prone to flush with emotion, had descended upon them moments after the gong. She'd sputtered furiously at Gria for leaving the room until Alyea was introduced, then spent a few moments almost fawning before dropping into a seat and a diatribe at roughly the same time.

Her voice had been steadily rising. Heads turned, frowns appeared.

"My lady," Alyea said, very aware that she didn't want her face connected with this kind of talk, "it's not wise to speak like that here. Please, keep your voice down, at the very least; better not to speak of religion at all."

"I'm on kingdom soil," the woman declared, "and protected by kingdom law."

"Kingdom law needs kingdom guards to enforce," Alyea said brutally. "You see any here? I don't. Please, let's speak of something else."

The woman looked around for a moment, seeming rather startled.

"They wouldn't *dare*," she said, more quietly.

"My lady," Alyea said, "trust me. You're a long way from kingdom law right now, whatever the boundary maps may say. And moving further every day." She paused, then decided to risk voicing the question. "If you disapprove of the southlands so much, why accept an offer of marriage to a southerner?"

"Oh, he follows the Four," she said. "He's a good man, an honest man, I was told."

"Who told you *that*?" Alyea said. The notion of any desert lord following the gods of the Northern Church was beyond absurd. "And what is this desert lord's name?"

"Why, *machago* Ierie told us," she said. "He's a matchmaker. He said Gria was the most promising match he'd found, and begged leave to escort her to the lord right away. . . ." Her voice trailed off at the expression on Alyea's face. "What's the matter with that?"

"Is Ierie traveling with you?" Alyea asked, trying to keep her tone level.

"Yes, of course," the woman said. "He's over there, with the guards; he's the one with the heavy pox mark on his left cheek."

Alyea lifted her gaze to the man indicated and realized he'd been watching them. They stared at each other for a long moment; then the man's lip curled into a sneering smile. He looked away, leaning over to whisper something in the ear of the man seated to his left. There were five guards seated around Ierie, all dark, flat-faced deep southerners, muscled and scarred.

A chill shivered down Alyea's back as Ierie straightened and stared at her again, speculation in his gaze now. She hesitated, weighing the risk, then decided Chac and Micru could protect her from any reprisals Ierie might aim her way.

"My lady Sela," she said quietly, "I don't know much of the old language, but I know that word. *Machago* does not mean matchmaker, it means slave-master. Those guards are not there to protect you. They are there to keep you and your daughter from running away. Did you sign anything?"

The woman stared at her in blank horror. "I . . . what . . . well, yes, but . . . that's absurd! It was only a contract that he would escort us, that we wouldn't choose someone else as a guide."

"Did your daughter sign anything? What language was it written in?"

"The same contract," the woman said, drawing herself up and looking offended. "Of course it was in the desert lord's native tongue, but our s'iopes assured me it was a clear and legitimate document and I could sign it with no worries. Machago Ierie was their guest while in Isata. He's a good man; he gave generous donations to our church while he stayed with us."

Alyea resisted the impulse to drop her head in her hands and growl in frustration. Generous donations? More likely bribes. But she knew better than to say that aloud.

"My lady," she said carefully, "desert lords do not send servants to the northlands to find pretty young ladies of desirable family for their sons. Every desert lord I have ever known—" Which consisted, at this point, of Eredion Sessin, but Sela didn't need to know that. "—would have to be threatened with imminent death to even consider the notion, and would likely choose death. You are not taking your daughter to a potential betrothal; you are taking her to be sold. And quite likely you will be beside her."

"That's impossible," the woman said, the flush along her cheekbones a bright crimson now.

Her daughter's face had, in contrast, been growing steadily whiter.

"Oh, dear gods," Gria said, hardly more than a breath.

"Don't you listen to her! I don't know what game you're trying to play, young lady," the older woman snapped, "but I'll tell you this: I'll trust my s'iopes' word over yours. They are the favored of the gods; they cannot lie."

"My lady," a familiar voice drawled behind them. "Do me the honor of sitting with me? They're about to start serving the food." Deiq smiled down at her, darkly handsome and completely implacable.

Alyea let a breath hiss through her teeth and considered the merits of refusing him flat out; but open hostility wouldn't help, and she was glad of the chance to get away from this stupid northern woman and her doomed daughter. She rose from her seat, nodded goodbye to the flustered women, and followed him to the head of the table.

Deiq didn't press her with conversation until after the food had been served and she had eaten several bites. Instead, he watched her thoughtfully, his dark gaze unreadable.

"It's unusual," he said at last, "for a slave merchant to allow his purchases to sit at a noble table."

Alyea paused and set the food back on her plate, feeling suddenly ill. "They don't know yet. The mother thinks she's on her way to a marriage auction for a southern desert lord."

"You tried to tell them." It wasn't a question.

She nodded and glanced down the table at the women being discussed. The mother was eating rapidly, still looking indignant; the girl stared at her food, picking at it slowly. "The mother doesn't believe me. The girl does."

"Interfering with a machago can be dangerous," Deiq said. "There's a reason he hasn't told them yet. There's a reason they're allowed to think they're still free nobles. I wonder what it could be?" His gaze went to the side table where the slave-merchant and his guards sat.

"Easier to transport willing victims," she said.

His dark gaze returned to her face. "Very true. Once again, I'm impressed, Lady Alyea. You are a rare one."

She almost groaned. Acting stupid might have lost his interest. Too late now.

He smiled. "Your advisors don't want you to have anything to do with me, yes?"

She bit her lip and resisted the impulse to cast a beseeching glance at Chac. He couldn't help her. "Yes."

"Ah." He smiled and turned his attention to his food for a while. At last he said, "This northern woman. Who is she?"

"Lady Sela and her daughter Gria. Cousins, I think, to Isata's Marq at some remove."

"I know that line. Yes." He smiled as if at some private joke. "I understand what's going on now. How interesting."

He went on eating placidly, and Alyea picked at her food and fought against asking the obvious question. Deiq just as obviously *wanted* her to ask, to need something from him. She knew the game, and wasn't playing. The northern woman was nothing but another damn fool who trusted her stupid Church too much; a shame, and sad, but it wasn't the first time this had ever happened, and wouldn't be the last. Alyea had a job to do and it didn't involve rescuing stupid northerns. Chac would be beyond furious if she even tried, especially with Deiq's eye on her.

Best to keep silent.

Deiq seemed to accept the quiet. He said nothing more the rest of the meal. As the dishes were cleared from the table, he cast her an amused glance and said, "Thank you for this conversation, my lady. It was most enjoyable." He scrubbed the cleaning sand briskly between his hands, rose, and strolled away.

"I tried, Chac, I swear," she said the next morning, as the old man glowered at her.

"He's still at our tail," the old man said. "You must not have tried very hard."

Alyea ground her teeth and resisted a strong urge to justify and defend herself—time to start taking some control before she turned into a puppet. She searched for a suitable rebuke, a sharp enough comment to set the old man in his place, and came up empty.

They rode in silence for a while. Alyea's annoyance slowly evaporated in the warming air. The mist that had greeted them in the morning burned away reluctantly, leaving the faintest of hazes behind for a while; then that vanished, and the dew that clung to the increasingly shrubby plants around them disappeared as well.

The ground still sloped noticeably upward. Ragged rock faces rose and fell around them like madly tossed crates. The path itself was relatively smooth, heavily traveled and worn underfoot, but narrowed in many places to allow no more than the width of a cart to pass. At one such spot, Alyea happened to be looking up at a long needle scrub pine that seemed to be growing out of a tall cliff to one side—and saw movement where there should have been stillness.

"Chac," she said, trying not to sound panicked.

"Don't look," he said, not moving his eyes from the path before them. "It's offensive."

She took her eyes from the thin man in grey-patterned clothes who seemed to be hanging, unsupported, against the side of the rock face above them. He blended into the lichen and scrub-covered rock perfectly; if he hadn't moved just as Alyea looked up, she never would have spotted him.

"Who is he?"

"They," Chac said, in a quiet, correcting tone, "are the *teyanain*. Singular, *teyanin*. The watchers of the Horn. They guarantee the neutrality of the path we're on."

Alyea swallowed, feeling a chill run along her arms. "I thought *teyanin* meant some sort of desert demon," she said. "My nurse used to threaten me that the teyanain would come get me if I told a lie."

Her childhood imagination had painted an image of monsters twenty feet tall that breathed flames and carried barbed whips in both hands. Now that she thought about it, that seemed a rather similar image to the one the northern s'iopes called up when talking about their gods.

Chac nodded, still looking straight ahead. "Teyanin could be loosely translated as 'desert dread.' They were the arbitrators and enforcers of the desert; the keepers of the old laws. When the tribes split, the majority of the teyanain went south. As the kingdom developed, the remaining teyanain found a place for themselves in the Horn. They don't have the authority in the kingdom that they did in the desert, but they hold absolute rule along this road. That's why this road is safe—and why it's dangerous. As long as you hold your peace, you're safe, but start any kind of squabble or fight here and you'll be cut down from above without remorse or question."

Alyea resisted the urge to look up again. "How many are there?"

"Nobody knows," Chac said. "Best guess, two or three thousand. It's never been a large tribe, and they're particular about who marries into it, and who has access to their villages." He paused, glanced sideways at her. "Took you long enough to notice them. I thought you'd pick up on them yesterday."

She stared at him, openmouthed; he shrugged and looked back at the road ahead.

"We passed four yesterday, and the one you finally noticed was the second today," he said. "And for every one you see, there's likely four or five more, hidden better. They don't mind being seen, every so often, just as a reminder that they're there, but don't make the mistake of staring."

She reflexively started to look up; stopped herself just in time and stared hard at her horse's ears until the urge passed.

"Gods," she said at last, badly shaken.

Chac grunted and said nothing. They rode for a time in silence. Alyea noticed that the group was unusually subdued, and when she looked over her shoulder, her men all had their eyes straight ahead, their shoulders stiff and tense. Only Micru seemed completely at ease, but still showed a reluctance to survey the area as he normally did.

"They know," she said, looking back to Chac.

"Of course they do," the old man said a bit tartly. "Every one of the men with you has been through the Horn, along every road there is, more than once. Did you think you'd be given fools?"

"What happens when someone who doesn't know comes through here?" Alyea asked. "Like those northerns?" She'd told Chac about them the night before, after dinner; as expected, he'd dismissed them as fools and told her to leave them to their doom.

"They make allowances," he said. "But they've seen the men here before, and they have good memories. They won't be making allowances for any of us except you; and given that you're surrounded by men who do know better, that leeway will be very short."

"Why haven't I been told any of this before?" she demanded, suddenly angry. "I grew up in the king's court and never heard *anything* of what I've learned the last few days!"

"The politics you grew up with have to do with the northlands," Chac said. "Not the desert. Most northerns prefer to forget anything exists past Bright Bay, and the desert lords like being left alone, so they encourage that."

Alyea shook her head, brooding.

"How am I going to do this?" she said at last. "I thought I knew something about the desert lords. Now I feel like a child waddling into a bonfire."

"About time you figured that out," Chac said dryly. "That's exactly what you are."

Her earlier resentment and anger returned. "And you're to keep me from burning myself?" she snapped. "You'd do better at that if you talked more about what I'm walking into, don't you think?"

"Thought you'd never ask," he said.

"Ask?"

"First thing you need to learn," he told her, unaffected by her anger. "You don't assume anyone's going to help you, here. You ask, and you acknowledge that even the asking puts a debt on you, whether or not you get the help you're after."

She glared at him. He kept his gaze to the front, serene, even smiling a little.

"You're being paid by the king to help me," she said.

"But you're the one directly benefitting from it," he replied. "There's your first lesson in desert logic. What the king is paying for is my guiding you to the Scratha fortress, and a willingness to help you learn. You acquire your own debt every time you ask for advice or help."

"Lunacy," she said.

"If you don't learn that lesson," he said, "the rest are useless, and so are you."

She turned a fierce glare to the front, staring at outcrops of rock and unoffending scrubby brush, chewing her tongue against the curses crowding her throat. *Breathe in. Breathe out.* The lessons of aqeyva nudged at her mind. *Breathe. Focus on the breath. Let everything go, just for a moment, and focus. Focus. Breathe.*

After a while, she let out a long, slow, controlled sigh and nodded. "I would be deeply in your debt, *s'e* Chacerly of Bright Bay," she said very quietly, very steadily, "if you would be so kind as to instruct me as you think best."

"Well spoken, if rather broad," he said. "Better to define the terms more closely, or you'll find yourself serving as a pleasure-girl in a noble's brothel."

Breathe. Focus. Breathe. She must not lose her temper, must not haul off and knock the old bastard off his horse. Her mind stayed blank. Everything she came up with sounded worse than her first attempt.

"I don't think I know how to ask," she said finally.

Chac let out a sigh. "*Now* I think we can get somewhere."

Chapter Seven

Scratha waited until he and Idisio were in their room with the door shut before allowing his anger to surface. Idisio dodged out of the way as his master's hand shot out.

"I didn't," he said quickly, putting some space between them. "I swear, Master, I didn't kill her."

Scratha advanced, angling to trap Idisio in a corner. Judging that avoiding him again would only make matters worse, Idisio let himself be steered back against the wall. He allowed the man to get in one heavy blow, then sagged to the ground with an arm raised defensively. It seemed to ease Scratha's temper; he stepped back and stared down at Idisio.

"You stole my knives," Scratha said. "Where's the other one?"

"I didn't!" Idisio protested, peering over the top of his arm. His cheek throbbed; he'd have a bruise before long. At least Scratha hadn't been wearing any rings.

"I saw you rooting through my pack," Scratha said. He crossed his arms; his black glare tied knots in Idisio's stomach. "You thought I was asleep."

As the man spoke, Idisio poked a tongue around in his mouth, checking for loosened teeth; they all seemed solid.

"I was checking to make sure nothing had been stolen," he said. "I saw that girl coming out of the room and thought she might have taken something."

Scratha stared at him for a moment, then shook his head. "Either that's the worst lie I've ever heard, or it's truth. And I know you lie better than that. Get up and tell me what happened."

Idisio climbed to his feet, watching his master carefully; there were still lines between Scratha's eyebrows, but the anger seemed to have passed. Idisio settled on the edge of a chair and said, "I was afraid someone was thieving through our room while we were eating. So I went to check, and caught that blonde girl as she rushed out of our room; she said she didn't steal anything, and you came in while we were arguing it."

Scratha's eyebrows rose into a deeply skeptical expression.

"I know how it looked," Idisio said. "But I couldn't get her to admit she'd taken anything, so I let her go and checked the packs to see if anything was missing. I thought you had your knives with you; I didn't realize you'd left them in the pack."

He went on to detail his later search for the noise that had woken him, and the hurried, interrupted flight. He made sure to phrase his intent as a return to his master's side for advice, and although Scratha gave him a dark, frowning look at that, he let the lie rest without question.

His master picked up the knife from the side table, stared at it a moment, then started to sit on the bed. Idisio heard a faint hissing rattle, and opened his mouth to shout a warning; Scratha spun around and stabbed the knife into the mattress, then leapt backwards, almost crashing into Idisio. Idisio hastily scrambled out of the way, only to find Scratha's hand clamped on his shoulder.

"Hold still," Scratha ordered. "Not a muscle. Not a sound."

Idisio, heart thudding in his chest, did his best to still his trembling hands.

After what seemed an eternity of silence, Scratha let out a long breath, released Idisio's shoulder, and moved towards the bed again. He stood staring down at the spot where his knife stuck out of the mattress, let out another great sigh, and said, "You didn't ask if this girl left anything *behind*, by chance?"

Idisio edged forward, staring wide-eyed at the scarlet and black stripe twitching limply across the bed. "Marsh asp. You're lucky it didn't bite you."

"It did," Scratha said. For the first time, Idisio noticed his master held his left hand cradled in his right.

The words crashed into Idisio like a hurricane wave. "You . . . oh, gods, I'll go get the—"

"Stay here."

Halfway to the door, Idisio turned in place, feeling rather wild-eyed. "What? You need the healer, I have to go, that thing's deadly—"

"I don't need some village bumpkin of a healer," Scratha said through his teeth. "Get that thing off the bed."

It took all Idisio's courage to approach the still-writhing snake, yank the knife free, and use the tip of the blade to knock the thing onto the floor well away from them. As it fell, the head and body parted ways, landing several inches apart; Idisio shuddered and shut his eyes. He prayed silently that Scratha wouldn't ask him to take the snake out of the room. He didn't think he could stand that.

Scratha stumbled to the bed and sat down, pulling his legs into a desert-style fold. His face beaded with sweat and began to lose color rapidly.

"I have to get you help," Idisio almost whined in desperation.

"Sit back down," Scratha said, "and shut *up* for a moment."

Idisio sank into the one chair and pulled his own feet up, suddenly terrified that more snakes would creep out from the floorboards and attack his bare feet. Realizing he still held the knife, he started to set it aside on the table, but Scratha shook his head.

"Keep it to hand in case of more vermin," he said. "If that snake was left here on purpose, there's likely more than one slithering about."

Idisio tucked his feet more tightly against himself and stared around the room, his heart hammering ever louder in his ears. "Why would someone do that?" he gabbled.

"Don't know. Damn stupid way to try to kill someone." Scratha breathed deeply and shut his eyes. "Probably just coincidence. But stay here," he mumbled. "*Stay here.*"

"I will, Master," Idisio promised, his hands clenched tight around his knees. The man was about to die, and then what? Idisio would be alone with a village certain of his guilt. He shivered and shut his own eyes, not wanting to watch the final spasms as the poison worked through his master's system.

Scratha's breathing disintegrated into a series of hoarse pants. He moaned, coughed violently several times, then, incredibly, spoke.

"Idisio. I'm not going to die. Stop looking so idiotic."

His voice sounded blurred with pain but strong; Idisio opened his eyes and stared in unconcealed astonishment. Scratha still sat upright, sweat thick on his face, his hands trembling, but his eyes fierce and clear as ever.

"It takes more than a swamp asp," Scratha said, pausing for breath between each word, "to kill a desert lord. Are there more snakes in the room?"

Idisio tore his fascinated stare from his master's face and scanned the room hastily. "I don't see any."

"Good enough. Now think: that girl. . . ." Scratha stopped, breathed unevenly for a while with his eyes shut, then went on. "Ground was trampled. Why?"

"Someone was afraid their footprints would be easy to match to a face," Idisio said, sitting up straight. "There were three sets. One likely hers, small and thin and light; another large and splay-toed, deep in the mud from a heavy person, and a third long and thin, a skinny man, I'd say, not much heavier than the girl."

"The deep one," Scratha said. "Not that many large folk here."

"Still too many for easy pointing."

Scratha nodded. His breath came more easily now, and some color had returned to his face.

"Washcloth," he said, pointing to the stand. Idisio scrambled to hand him one of the worn cloths and watched as Scratha wiped the sweat from his face with an unsteady hand.

"Master. . . ." Idisio said tentatively.

"I'll be fine, Idisio," Scratha said. "Let's go talk to the village master."

The village master turned out to be a short, stocky man with grey hair clipped short against his skull and wide, blue eyes. His gaze moved to the developing bruise on Idisio's cheek, held Idisio's eyes for a long, questioning moment, then scanned upward to the tall nobleman.

"Can I help you, *s'e*?" he said without warmth.

"I believe my servant had nothing to do with the girl found dead in the swamp," Scratha said bluntly. "We will stay until the person responsible is found." He seemed to have recovered almost completely during the walk to the village master's house, but Idisio noticed that he leaned heavily on any supporting surface available.

"You've not been accused of Kera's death, *s'e*."

"I know that," Scratha said, and shifted casually to lean against the doorframe, arms crossed. The long sleeves of his shirt, while undoubtedly hot, served to hide his swollen arm. "But how many here believe us both innocent?"

Silence. The man's blue eyes watched the tall nobleman warily.

"You don't even believe it," Scratha said.

"You've obviously got a temper, *s'e*," the village master said, face expressionless.

Scratha opened his mouth, face darkening, then slid a glance sideways to Idisio and sighed.

"True enough," he said. "But it's a far cry from that to sticking a knife in a girl's stomach."

"Nobody in this village would have killed Kera," the master said. "There was no reason."

"We had no reason, either," Scratha retorted, his dark eyebrows scrunching again. "Would you be so kind as to listen to our account before making up your mind?"

Thin lips pursed for a moment; then the man nodded once.

Scratha rapidly summarized his own and Idisio's movements since arriving in town.

"I'll swear to the truth of those words on my blood," he finished.

Idisio almost groaned aloud. That phrase was *only* ever used by southern nobles.

The village master's expression changed instantly from skeptical to shocked. He backed up a step, staring at the tall man.

"I beg your pardon, my lord," he stammered. "I meant no offense . . . please . . . the blood oath isn't necessary. You don't need to stay until this is all sorted out."

Scratha closed his eyes briefly, his lips tightening.

"No offense taken," he said at last, looking at the man again. He swayed a little, caught himself against the doorframe. "And I will stay, because I want to clear my name and that of my servant."

"Your name is without stain," the man said hastily, looking ever more confused and afraid. "We would not dare accuse—"

"Let's skip all that. I'm *s'e* Gerau Sa'adenit, nothing more or less." He glared until the man gave a shaky, wide-eyed nod of agreement. "One of the prints my servant saw was made by a heavy man, barefoot, with wide-set toes. Who here matches that description?"

The old man lowered his gaze to the floor, frowning as he thought for a time, then said, "We have perhaps ten large men in the village. Four of them might have been foolish enough to walk into the marshes at night barefoot. Two of those are married, and one of them has been ill for the past three days with fever."

He paused. "But none of them ever had words with Kera, or even a hard glance at her that I heard of. Asti Lashnar is very protective of his daughter's honor. He'd planned on finding her a good marriage in Bright Bay his next trip."

Scratha snorted and opened his mouth. Afraid of what might emerge, Idisio cut in first, ignoring his master's sharp glare: "Men, you said. Are you counting boys?"

"Boys," the village master said slowly, drawing the word out. "No, I can't think of any."

"How about the one tripped me up and roused the village?" Idisio said.

"Oh, Karic?" the old man said, eyebrows rising in apparent surprise. "Well, yes, but . . . well, yes. But he was tending merchant Lashnar's mare all of last night, and he's gone to deliver news to the next village on."

"He was working with another boy, wasn't he?" Idisio said. "Baylor?"

"Yee-ess," the man said, his frown deepening. "But—"

"Let's go talk to Baylor," Scratha suggested.

Face wrinkled in clear reluctance, the village master finally nodded and said, as he shut the door behind him, "He'll be at the stables."

"What, Lashnar's trusting him with the mare again?"

"There's nobody else, with Karic out of town," the village master said. His lips thinned as though he'd regretted saying that much, and he stalked towards the stables without looking back.

"No," Baylor said positively, this thin face hard and hostile as he looked at Scratha and Idisio. "He was here, with me, all night. Lashnar tol' him to stay an' make sure everything was good, as he don't trust *me* with his mare no more." The boy's expression suggested a fair amount of money had been involved in the lost job.

"Thank you, Baylor," the village master said in a tone of poorly hidden relief, and started to turn away. Scratha didn't move from his spot on a hay bale. Neither did Idisio.

"All night?" Idisio asked. "Not even left to go empty his bladder?"

"All night," the stable boy repeated, glaring at Idisio.

"How about you?" Idisio said. "Did you wander out for a bit?"

"No!" the boy said, indignant now. "What are you, deaf? I said we was both here all night!"

"I smelled wine on Karic's breath, when he knocked me down," Idisio said. "How can you drink and not have to piss?"

"We don't drink around the horses," Baylor said, but his eyes flickered to the village master as he spoke. A child could have caught the lie.

"Then where did he go to drink?"

"He didn't! I didn't! Look, I've work to do. I can't stand here—"

"You're not done yet," Scratha said as the boy started to turn away.

"Let him be!" the village master said. "He's answered your questions."

"He lied," Idisio said with absolute certainty. "Kera's the one ran to her father and lost him the position of caring for Lashnar's mare. A few drinks and he'd be angry enough to take it out on her."

Baylor's ears were turning pink. "I'd never hurt Kera!"

"Your prints led into the swamp," Idisio said. He pointed to the ground near the boy's feet. "And your feet are still muddy. What were you doing out there?"

"I wasn't—" Baylor scuffed his feet, a panicky look on his face; he stopped abruptly and stared at them, eyes rimmed with sudden dampness.

"Do you think Karic will back you, if you're accused of murder?" Idisio said before anyone else could speak. "Do you think he'll step forward to save you?"

"That's *enough*," the village master said, but Baylor crumbled.

"I didn't hurt Kera," he said, tears spilling down his cheeks now. "I didn't. I swear it. I don't know who did. She ran into the swamp after dinner, crying, and I followed her to see what was wrong. She wouldn't tell me, and I was supposed to meet Karic at the stables, so I had to go back."

Idisio shook his head and wished he dared interrupt to call the boy a liar; but Scratha's mood still hung too chancy, and collecting another bruise for insolence seemed too likely.

Unheeding, Baylor went on, "Karic was at the stables, and he was in a bad mood, and after a while he said he had to take care of something, and he left. And next thing I heard from him, he was shouting to rouse the village about a thief." The stable boy looked at them with wide, imploring eyes, and sniffled, wiping his sleeve across his nose.

"How did you know where to find her?" Idisio asked. He'd seen the best cons in Bright Bay collapse in wholly fake tears before; Baylor wasn't impressing him.

The tips of Baylor's ears reddened again. "There's a place she goes sometimes." He looked away and swallowed hard. "Went, I mean. I like wandering around in the swamp, it don't scare me. She asked, a while back, if I knew a place where you could be alone. I had a place I went, sometimes, not far out, but real private, and when she asked I showed it to her. I thought, well, maybe. . . ."

"You thought she wanted you to be alone with her," Scratha said.

The boy nodded miserably and wiped at his nose again. "But she didn't. She said *thank you* and never mentioned it again, but I saw her go into the swamp sometimes at night, and. . . ." He faltered again, and looked at the ground.

"And you followed her," Idisio said, wondering if he might be wrong after all. Desert lords were supposed to be able to *smell* a lie, but Scratha seemed to be accepting the story. Perhaps living on the streets had made Idisio too cynical. "You wanted to know what she was doing."

The boy shrugged, not meeting their eyes. He kept his gaze on the ground and shuffled uncomfortably in place.

The village master looked steadily more horrified as the tale went on.

"Baylor," he said, voice hardly more than a whisper, "was she . . . meeting someone out there?"

Baylor swallowed hard and nodded.

"Was it. . . ." The village master faltered, then fell silent.

"Who was it?" Scratha said, much more sharply.

The stable boy looked utterly miserable as he wiped at his nose again, glancing around as if searching for an escape.

"Karic," he said at last.

The village master let out a faint moan. "I *told* him. . . ." he said. "*Damn* the boy. Lashnar's going to kill him."

"He's a right, if Karic killed the girl," Scratha said without sympathy, and turned away from the trembling boy before him. "He won't be back."

The old man bristled but, under Scratha's dark stare, said nothing.

Idisio almost hissed in frustration. He *knew* Baylor was still lying, but Scratha and the village master seemed to be accepting the story without reservation.

"Why would Karic kill her?" the village master said, rallying. "If they were lovers, why would he kill her? I'd sooner believe her father killed her for dallying outside his plans."

Scratha shot the village master a curious look, a mixture of puzzlement and contempt. "He'd kill his own *daughter* for taking a lover?"

The village master blinked, flustered. "Well, wait, no, that's not what I—"

"Did she have any friends that she might have talked to?" Idisio interrupted, afraid of where this would lead. Scratha frowned at him but let it pass without further reaction.

"Her father didn't let her have any friends," the village master said with poorly concealed relief at the change in subject. "But she worked at the inn; maybe the innkeeper knows something of who she talked to."

"She was friends with one of my serving-girls, Seshya," said the innkeeper. He shook his head, his chins quivering. "I don't know what I'm going to do without Kera. She was the quickest hand at changing the linens and cleaning a room, and the only honest one I could find to mind the till."

"Don't let Lashnar know she talked to that woman," the village master said dryly.

"You think I'm a fool?" the innkeeper said. "She wasn't allowed to talk to any girls, stand up to any of the dances, join any sewing circles, smile at any boys. Villagers weren't good enough for her father; he wanted a marriage to some noble lord of Bright Bay. He didn't want anything to sully her reputation. Seshya was the only one that would risk Lashnar's anger and spend time talking to the poor girl."

"A whore with a heart of gold," the village master said with a sigh. "That's an old story."

"And usually a false one," Scratha said tartly. "Let's go talk to this woman."

The serving-girl's expression was as sulky as it had been the night before, intensified by a certain disordered appearance from having just woken up. Her clothing had been loosely fastened and not too thoroughly at that; as she swayed sleepily against the doorframe to her small room, flashes of round, soft skin showed through.

"Whaddya want?" she said. "Pardon, Master, but I'm only just asleep."

"Busy night?" Scratha said. She narrowed her eyes at him over the village master's shoulder and sneered.

"We're here about Kera," the village master said sharply, bringing her attention back to him.

"What about her?" the girl said, mouth still twisted unpleasantly. "She isn't here."

"She's dead," Scratha said. "Murdered."

The haughty look faded into pale shock. "I had nothing to do with it."

"You've been talking to Kera behind Lashnar's back," the village master said, ignoring her protest. "What did she tell you about Karic?"

The girl hesitated, then shook her head. "Nothing."

"Seshya," the village master said, voice flat.

"All right," the tavern girl said. "He was after her. He wanted her, and she couldn't figure how to tell him to get lost."

"Try again," Scratha said, voice hard. "Truth this time."

Idisio stared at Scratha in astonishment; the girl *had* been telling the truth. How could he not hear the honesty in Seshya's voice? The man certainly wasn't showing any signs of the famed desert lord nose for veracity.

"That *is* truth," the barmaid flared, straightening. "You think she was a whore, just because she talked to me? She didn't like him. He kept following her, trapping her in odd places when her father wasn't around, trying to get a kiss and a feel. She came by here crying about it more than once, asking how to fend him off without having her father involved."

"Why wouldn't she go to her father?" Scratha asked.

She made a scornful, impatient noise, and leaned against the doorframe again. "Karic would just say she threw herself at him and he turned her away."

"Lashnar would believe Karic over his own daughter?"

"You've met the man; what do you think?" She shook her head. "Karic knows how to play Lashnar. Kera's a *woman*. Under Lashnar's damn Church beliefs—oh, don't wince, Master, you've cursed the s'iopes yourself—Kera wouldn't have had a chance."

The village master avoided their eyes. "Too many cups," he muttered defensively. "Nothing more."

Scratha shook his head, seeming mildly amused for a moment, and said, "The merchant is grieving honestly enough."

"For the loss of his chances to marry into status and save his precious business," Seshya sneered. "That's all."

"So she wasn't a whore," Idisio said. "Was she a thief?"

"No," Seshya said, looking surprised. "Never that. She'd badger me about returning an accurate count of a drunk customer's change." She blushed and avoided their eyes.

"Is Karic a thief?" Idisio asked, frowning.

Seshya shrugged. "He's too clumsy to pick pockets, but he's more than happy to pick up something left unattended. Why are you asking about Karic?"

"He was supposed to be watching Lashnar's mare last night," the village master said. "He slipped away in a bad mood after midnight, and Kera was killed sometime after that."

Seshya didn't hesitate. "He was here. He needed someone to . . . talk to." She shrugged at their combined looks of disbelief. "Baylor's better with animals than Karic is, but Karic's better at keeping to Lashnar's good side, so they team up to get jobs out of the man. Then Baylor does the work and Karic does as he pleases. Sometimes he comes to talk to me, when I don't have anything better to do." She smirked.

If she was lying, she was better at it than Baylor. Not at all unlikely, but still. . . .

"If he's better with animals, how could he let the stables get in such a state?" Scratha demanded, scowling.

Seshya shrugged. "I don't know. I've never been particularly *close* to Baylor." She smirked again.

"When did Karic leave you?" Idisio cut in before Scratha or the village master could deliver the retorts visibly forming in their mouths.

"Just before dawn."

"So he couldn't have—*Damn*." Idisio spun on his heel and ran for the stables.

Idisio sank onto a partially breached bale of hay and stared at the empty stall, cursing quietly under his breath, until Scratha, the village master, and Seshya hurried into the stables a few moments later.

"Gone," Idisio said, pointing to where his horse had been. "Long gone. Probably ran as soon as we rounded the corner."

"Karic took her out to the swamp," Scratha said, staring at the empty stall, "willing or unwilling, depending who you believe; fought with her, because I don't believe Baylor could have delivered that punch. Left her unconscious on the ground, and then Baylor came looking and was so upset over what he saw as her choosing Karic that he killed her—with one of *my* daggers? No. None of that makes sense. We're missing something." He glowered, brooding and shaking his head.

A labored grunting caught everyone's attention, and Scratha moved to look into another stall.

"Lashnar's mare is foaling," he said. "Looks like she's in trouble. Do you have anyone else skilled with horses in the village?"

"Some," the village master said, "but not a one would touch this mare. Lashnar's got an evil temper when things go wrong, and he's already strung tight. I won't even ask. Karic and Baylor were the only ones that man trusted with his precious horses."

Scratha stared at the village master with an expression that made the man back up a step. "You'd let this mare die for the sake of a man's temper?"

"Lashnar's misfortunes are sent by the gods," the village master said. "Who are we to argue that or prevent his just punishment?"

Seshya snorted and rolled her eyes; the village master shot her a stern glare and added, "I may not like the s'iopes, but there's truth in the holy word they preach."

"It's not a punishment," Scratha said sharply, "it's a mare struggling with labor. Lashnar's misfortunes are his own; do you really think the gods would inflict trouble on a dumb beast to punish a man?"

The village master shook his head without answering and walked out of the stables, face set.

Scratha made a hissing noise, as if restraining himself from a vile curse. "Get out. Not you," he added as Idisio started to stand. "You stay here. I'll need help."

Seshya left without protest. Scratha blew out a hard breath as he studied the struggling mare.

"If we ride now," he said, "we could catch the boy, I think." He sighed, cursed again almost absently, and went into the stall. "We'll catch up with him on the road, sooner or later," he added over his shoulder.

"At least the mare will foal in a clean stall," Idisio said.

His master shot him a sour look and said nothing.

"I still don't understand *why*," Idisio said, hours later. "What could have made Baylor kill her—if he did, and not Karic? Why did he steal those knives? Did he plant that snake in our room? Did she? Why? How was Karic involved? Is he coming back?" He threw his arms wide in a gesture of frustration. "I could go on forever!"

Scratha, face almost grey and lined with exhaustion, dipped a cloth in the trough and slowly scrubbed the blood and mucus from his hands.

"Some things never get solved," he said finally. "We're clear of the charge, and that's all I care about. If we come across the boys on the road, I'll have some hard questions for them to answer, but we've no real authority unless we can get them in front of a village judge." He dropped the cloth on the ground and stretched, putting his hands into the small of his back and arching backwards with a grunt before straightening again. "At least we saved the foal and mare."

"It doesn't seem fair," Idisio said. "Not knowing why, I mean."

His master's mouth twitched into a faint smile. "Fair? From a street-thief who tricked his way into my service after trying to steal my purse?"

Idisio shrugged, too tired to be embarrassed by the barb. "That was survival. I hate not knowing the answers when I have questions."

Scratha's smile faded. He looked to the south, brooding, and said under his breath, "So do I."

Chapter Eight

The following night, Deiq again called Alyea to sit by him but offered little conversation until their plates were being cleared away. Then he said, lazily, "You'll be in Water's End tomorrow, Lady Alyea."

She nodded, wary at his ostentatiously casual manner.

"Where will you go from there, I wonder?" he murmured, gaze fixed on her face, a faint smile on his own lips.

Hopefully away from you, she thought but didn't say; he seemed to read the words in her carefully expressionless gaze and laughed.

"I'm hurt, my lady," he said. "I get the feeling you'll be relieved to be out of my presence."

She dropped her gaze to the table, unable to think of a reply that might turn that too-bright, intent gaze away.

"Come," Deiq said abruptly, standing. "Walk with me."

She rose at the urging of his hand on her wrist; while he didn't grip tightly enough to hurt, the contact felt as unbreakable as a steel cuff.

"*S'e,*" she said, "I'm afraid I need to retire for the evening." She cast a rapid glance towards the side table where Chac sat. He rose and moved towards them.

Deiq turned his gaze to the old man and smiled. His grip didn't loosen. "Your advisor is welcome to trail along behind us. I want to show you something, and mean you no harm."

"Let go of my wrist, then, *s'e,*" Alyea said in a quiet, level tone.

Deiq looked at his hand on her arm as if surprised, and let go.

"Forgive me, my lady," he said as Chac reached them. "I forget the strength of my grip at times."

Alyea stepped back a pace.

"My apologies for alarming you, Chacerly," Deiq said to the old man before Chac could speak. "I only wished to take the lady for a walk to see the moon rise over the Kingsea. It's a spectacular sight in the Horn. Would you come with us? I think the lady has heard some of the unfounded, evil tales about me. Your presence would ease her fears."

His gaze, bright and predatory, stayed on the old man's face as if studying each line for a weakness.

Chac looked at Alyea, questioning; she nodded, seeing no politic alternative to going for the walk.

"I think it more proper," the old man said at last, "for Lady Alyea's maid to attend her. I will send the woman to you, my lady. *S'e*." He gave a short, stiff bow and turned away.

"Ah, he's so devoted to proper courtesies," Deiq said, and laid gentle fingertips against Alyea's shoulder. "Let's move outside to wait for your servant, shall we?"

He used a light touch rather than an iron grip, but it carried the same sense of undeniable force. She allowed him to urge her from the room and took a seat on a wide bench just outside the dining hall. The tall man gracefully stepped aside, standing more than an arm's length away. In the flickering torchlight, his smile seemed a mocking thing of shadow and smoke, and he stayed silent until Halla appeared. The woman looked severely flustered, her face pale and her greeting too bright.

"*S'a* Halla," Deiq said, sounding grave and concerned. His smile disappeared. "You seem distraught. Is something the matter?"

"Not at all," Halla said too quickly.

Deiq moved closer to the nervous woman, until she had to tilt her head to stare up at him. "Was the meal unsatisfactory?"

"No," Halla said, "no, it was very good." She backed away a step, dropping her gaze.

"You're not pleased to see me?" Deiq said, not moving. "You were quite friendly the last couple of days, *s'a*. Is something different?"

Oh, gods, Alyea thought, *please tell me she hasn't gone to bed with him, please, oh gods, what a disaster that would be. . . .*

"I've offered you proper courtesy," Halla said, her back stiffening and her jaw firming. "Don't you make it sound as if I've done more!"

Deiq stared at her for a moment, then laughed, the tension along his shoulders relaxing.

"My apologies. I didn't mean to make any such implication. I seem to be growing careless tonight. The wine must have been more potent than I expected."

That would have held more weight, Alyea reflected sourly, if she'd seen him call for anything but water at dinner. But Halla, ignorant of the lie, seemed warily relieved.

Deiq turned and held out a hand to Alyea. "My lady. Shall we walk?"

She rose without accepting the offered help, motioning Halla to walk behind her, and followed as Deiq strode across the cleared courtyard. He started along a narrow path at the far end.

"Where are we going, *s'e* Deiq?" Alyea asked.

"There is an excellent and very quiet spot not far from here," he said over his shoulder, "with a lovely view."

Alyea glanced back over her shoulder, reassuring herself that Halla followed close; she didn't like the sound of this at all. Deiq had made it plain, in his advance on Halla, that he could easily master the plump woman if he chose, whatever her bravery at the last moment.

"Don't worry so much," Deiq said, stopping and turning to look Alyea squarely in the face. "Your maidservant is not the only one watching us at the moment. Your safety and honor is beyond any question, my lady." He grinned and started off again.

Alyea took a deep breath and followed, her heart hammering.

"My lady," Halla whispered from behind, "do you think we ought to go back?"

"But why should we?" Deiq said without turning his head. "A simple walk to see a beautiful sight; where's the harm?"

He stopped and faced them again, his dark eyes glittering as he stared at the northern woman. "From the way you're acting, *s'a,* one might think you'd heard some of the false and wicked stories about me that have also frightened Lady Alyea. One might wonder about the words Lady Alyea's advisor has been putting against my name."

Alyea motioned Halla to silence and moved to block the northern woman from that intense stare. Deiq's gaze shifted to her face, and a smile spread across his features.

"You protect your servants," he said. "That's a generous way, and one little seen in Bright Bay of late."

She returned glare for stare, and he finally shrugged and turned around again. His pace increased; the two women scrambled to keep up.

The narrow path opened abruptly to a wide bare space. The ground softened underfoot: not quite sand, nor the clay of the lower Horn. A line of trees and scrub lay behind them, their branches looming, feathery shapes in the darkness. Overhead, thousands of stars lit the infinity of sky. Ahead of them, perhaps sixty paces, the ground dropped abruptly into a series of harsh chasms and gullies that seemed to descend forever, a rocky slope that rolled down and down and down. The rising moon, even at just past half full, dropped stark shadows to bring that rocky turmoil into sharp relief. Far below and farther east, water glinted, a shifting of light patterns at the edge of a larger, steadier net of lights: a port city.

Alyea stood silent, staring out at the vast sight.

"That's the Kingsea," Deiq said in her ear. He'd moved to stand beside her. "And the port of Stass."

"Incredible," Alyea said with complete honesty. "I've never seen anything like this."

"Few are brave enough to leave the King's Road to see sights like this," Deiq said.

She glanced sideways at that, suspecting malice; but his face, in the moonlight, held amusement. He was teasing her.

"Did you know," he said, his gaze returning to the view, "that the word *king* actually comes from a very old southern dialect, from before the Split?"

"Yes. I know. *Kaen*, meaning leader."

"Ah, your tutors gave you heretic knowledge?" He grinned at her.

"No, my nurse—" She stopped short. "Never mind."

He studied her with sharp understanding. "And one day your nurse, who told you heretic stories, went away and never came back," he said softly. "I'm sorry."

She shut her eyes against sudden tears and bit her tongue to keep from answering.

After a moment, Deiq let out a small sigh. "I know a number of spots like this along the road I'll be taking tomorrow," he said, his tone resuming its dry detachment. "There's a side trail that leads from here to Port Stass; not a safe road for horses and guards and advisors. Chacerly has never taken it. He knows better than to try. He won't follow you down that trail, if you come with me."

Reasonably steady now, she opened her eyes and studied his dimly lit profile. His gaze rested on the port city far below, and his expression seemed merely thoughtful.

"I'll offer my company again," he went on. "Please, come travel with me. I'll get you to Scratha safely. Your advisors aren't men to trust."

His voice flowed over her, smooth and warm and undeniably appealing. She wondered if Chac could simply be jealous of a younger, more attractive man. Perhaps she could travel with Deiq and meet Chac at Scratha Fortress . . . it might be a good idea to make the trip shorter . . . she shook her head sharply.

"No, thank you," she said, more harshly than she'd intended.

He didn't seem offended.

"Consider it overnight, Lady Alyea," he said, and Alyea shut her eyes again. His voice *dragged* at her, insidiously compelling. She had a disturbing feeling that if he pressed her right now, she'd agree.

"I don't need to," she snapped, taking refuge in anger. "I'm staying with the advisors the king's given me."

"Rather than a man you've only just met," he said with a faint sigh. "I understand. But most of your fear comes from Chacerly." He looked at her, his gaze shadowed. "He gives me far worse of a name than I deserve, I'm afraid. And isn't giving you a good enough one."

She avoided his stare and watched the moonlight reflecting in slow, dancing patterns from the waves far below.

"The men you ride with," he said, dropping his voice to a near-whisper, "aren't the ones to trust. They serve you in name, but they watch you with the care of men with two masters. I'll help you, if you ask."

"At what price?" Alyea said, forcing herself to sound cold.

Deiq smiled. "I don't play the games *s'e* Chacerly does," he said. "I'll help you because I want to. Because you're far too good to waste yourself on the games of a man who needed help to take the throne from a mad, weak ruler in an unstable kingdom."

"I doubt you do anything for free, or without advantage to yourself," Alyea said sharply.

His voice swayed in a soothing cadence that raised her heartbeat and scrambled her thoughts. "The advantage I seek is your respect. Nothing more complicated than that."

She stared at him, unsure how to answer that.

He straightened, his voice becoming more distant and formal, but a faint smile slanted the corners of his mouth into a sardonic expression. "Are you ready to be escorted back to the way-stop?"

"Yes," she said, forcing speech through a suddenly dry throat.

Halla's face, as they turned to leave, almost matched the white of the moon.

Chac's good humor returned after Deiq left their party, and he rode beside her, pointing out native plants and animals and relating endless stories about them. The legends and folklore should have been fascinating, but Alyea couldn't keep her attention on the old man's words.

Halla rode as far back as she could, away from Alyea, and her expression had been troubled and distant all morning. With a faint gesture of apology to Chac, Alyea took the opportunity of a narrow spot in the trail to drop back in line, fetching up beside her maidservant.

Halla shot her a frightened, almost resentful glance.

"My lady," she said, and put her gaze firmly forward.

"Halla," Alyea said, "what's the matter?"

The northern woman's shoulders shifted in a faint shrug. "I didn't know what I was getting into, hiring on with you. I don't like being threatened. I confess myself glad to be nearing Water's End and the finish of my hire."

"Threatened?"

"Chacerly made it clear that Deiq wasn't to touch you. He said he was holding me personally responsible, and the way he said it I've heard before. It was a threat, nothing less. And you can't tell me that Deiq's muscling into my face wasn't intimidation. I don't like it. I may not have as much status as you, but I've my own dignity to think of."

Alyea rode for a bit in silence, thinking over what the woman had said, before responding.

"What do you think of Deiq now?" she asked finally.

"I don't like him, and it's clear your advisor doesn't like him," Halla said, "but he's a powerful man in his own right, and that voice! He could melt butter with it. Left my knees weak. I don't know how you stood against it."

Alyea snorted. "Not easily."

"Unmarried women are nothing but trouble and strife around single men," Halla said unexpectedly. "You ought to have a husband or guardian on this journey with you, to keep the unwed men at a proper distance."

The irony failed to amuse Alyea: Chac had demanded she have lady servants, while Halla wanted a man for protection.

"Halla," she said patiently, "no man is going to take me without my consent." She left out the word *again*. "I've trained with fist and knife for that very reason."

"You'd strike a man?" Halla's eyes went round and shocked.

"If he tried to rape me, I'd kill him," Alyea said. "Halla, I grew up in Bright Bay under Ninnic. I learned to protect myself."

The words sounded like posturing to her ears, and she wished she hadn't spoken so confidently. But Halla didn't know about Pieas, or about Ethu. *Gods, don't think about that right now!* A familiar tight prickling filled her throat.

"King Ninnic was a godly man," Halla said stiffly.

Alyea's temper flared sharply. "Ninnic was a raving lunatic with a taste for torturing anything he could get his hands on," she snapped. "Your home isn't that far from the main route; you must have heard about it."

"Those stories are lies," Halla said with the arrogance of misplaced certainty. "Deceit spread by the southerners to destroy our faith."

Alyea made an impatient gesture. "I *lived* through it. Halla, I've seen men gutted and left to die in pools of their own blood because your *godly* Ninnic wanted to see how long a man could last with his intestines all over the floor. I've seen men and women who did nothing worse than protest such treatment of their families skinned alive on the same principle."

Halla's face scrunched. She made a vague fluttering motion with one hand, as if wanting Alyea to be quiet. The other hand clutched the reins tightly, knuckles white.

Alyea didn't stop. "Three of my maidservants were seized for Ninnic's amusement. He would choose and discard women like toys, throwing them to his guards after he tired of them. Most of the time they didn't survive past the guards' handling, but if they did they were kept as court prostitutes for the lower nobles. I've seen your precious s'iopes flay men to death for trying to protect their women from that. These women were taken regardless of whether they were married or widowed or even past puberty. One of my maids was twelve."

"That's *enough!*"

"It's not nearly enough," Alyea snapped. "That's barely the beginning of what I've seen. Don't you ever lecture me or anyone who lived through that on Church morality!"

She fell silent, breathing hard. She'd done her best to forget the past; the rant had been a mistake. She'd have screaming nightmares tonight.

Halla said nothing. She had a hand over her heart and a glazed look on her pale face.

"One of the first things King Oruen did when he took the throne," Alyea said more quietly, "was to order that entire hall razed to the ground and rebuilt on the other side of the palace. He said too much evil had gone into that hall for him to ever sit in it again. The ground was salted, burned, and surrounded by a fence that's always locked. It's going to stay that way forever. He doesn't want anyone to forget."

Halla's eyes glittered with held tears, and her gaze stayed determinedly ahead of them.

"The priests wouldn't do that," she said, in an attempt at her former stiffness; then, unwillingly: "Did you really see that?"

"I really did," Alyea said, and tried to gentle her tone. "I don't know what the priests north of the Great Forest have been doing, Halla, but down here the Church isn't a good name to carry on your banner. You walk around with a fistful of northern prejudices showing and you're likely, at best, to get killed."

"At best?" Halla said, her face and shoulders stiffening again.

Alyea felt a surge of pity for her; but reality was what reality was. It would do the woman no favors to let her go with her illusions intact.

"There are worse things," Alyea said, "than a quick death."

Chapter Nine

Mindful of Idisio's still-healing feet but wanting to spare their remaining horse as much strain as possible, Scratha insisted on their periodically switching off between walking and riding. Idisio made no complaint, although after a while the effort of heaving his tired body back up into the saddle almost seemed not worth the trouble. When the horse began to visibly droop and plod, Idisio and Scratha both started walking—and Idisio realized he'd been wrong. It had definitely been worth the trouble.

Fortunately, they reached the next village less than two miles later, although the sun hung low behind them and their shadows stretched long in front by the time they arrived.

Obein obviously had more pride than the marsh town of Kybeach displayed; the rough stones of the village streets were free of drifting sand, and the entry road had been recently swept with a rake-like brush. They'd seen two more News-Riders headed east and three more carts taking northern goods west, the last less than an hour ago, but the only tracks visible were their own.

"There's such a thing as too clean," Scratha said sourly. His temper had been markedly poor since the snake bite.

Idisio grinned. "I'll bet the stables are better here."

Scratha glowered at him.

"And if the stables are clean," Idisio went on, "the boy in charge will have more wit than Baylor seemed to. And that'll mean he has an eye for details, won't it? So he'd have noticed something odd, like a boy from a poor village riding by on a rich man's horse."

"You don't need wit to spot that," Scratha said.

"But you do need quick wits to do something about it," Idisio said, and watched his master's face lighten in comprehension.

"You may be—"

"Useful. Yes, I know," Idisio sighed.

Scratha checked, turning a startled stare on him. "Have I said that so often?"

Idisio glanced at Scratha's narrow face, assessing, and risked an honest answer. "Yes. You have."

Scratha grunted, pursing his lips thoughtfully, and said nothing as they entered the stable yard. A girl, muddy, disheveled, and sweaty, emerged in response to their repeated calls, curry brush held in one hand and a fierce frown on her face. She glared around as if looking for someone, muttered a curse under her breath, and finally turned a less unpleasant expression towards them.

"Good evening, *s'es*," she said. She considered Scratha's horse for a moment, her expression thoughtful; for some reason, Idisio didn't think she was judging quality.

Idisio glanced down the long row of stalls. The purple of a News-Rider horse tabard had been draped over the door to one stall; the red and yellow flag of a high-ranking bard hung at the edge of another. Most of the stalls had a flag of some sort by the door, marking them as occupied, but two were still empty, by the look of it.

The girl followed Idisio's gaze and wiped sweat-darkened hair from her forehead. "There's a lad should be around here to help you, but I don't see him. If you could wait a moment? I'll just finish up with this mare and be right out to settle your horse."

She glanced around again, as if thinking about shouting for the absent stable hand, then shook her head and returned her attention to the two travelers before her.

"I can take care of my horse," Scratha said, offering her a charming smile, "if you'll point me to a stall. No need to worry after your lad."

She nodded, appearing relieved. "Silver half-round for the night, *s'e*," she said. "Either of those open stalls at the end will do."

Scratha's eyebrows rose, and Idisio sputtered indignation.

"The other stalls are less," the girl said with a shrug. "Box stalls are more expensive, and all we have left. You get a bag of good Arason horse-feed for the price, so it's not all that bad a deal, *s'es*. Take it or tie your horse to the hitch by the tavern." She went back into the stall from which she'd emerged without a backward look.

Scratha smiled. "We'll pay it," he said quietly as Idisio opened his mouth to protest. "Let be. Why don't you spend some time talking to her while I get this beast settled in?" He patted the horse's neck fondly. "Find out what she saw yesterday."

Idisio blew out a resigned breath as his master led the horse away.

The girl had left the top half of the stall door open. He moved over to it and looked inside. She was brushing down a trim, red-brown mare, singing softly. The mare's long, dark-rimmed ears flickered this way and that, and she snorted and jerked when Idisio appeared.

"Easy," the girl said, and glanced over her shoulder. "She's skittish. Stand still and don't speak loud. What do you want?" Her voice remained pleasantly soothing, as if talking to the horse.

Idisio tried to keep his voice quiet, which was the best way to convey a lie anyway. "My master thinks I've a ham hand with a horse. He told me to stay out of his way. I figured, watching you I could pick something up, maybe."

Her gaze turned considering and sharp. He had a feeling she didn't believe him, but she said only, "Huh," and went back to brushing.

Idisio watched her in silence for a while. Even muddy and with straggles of hair sticking to her face, she still had a fine, narrow face and curves in places that he tried not to stare at. He aimed his gaze at her hands, focusing on her movements; but as the girl leaned and stretched, other parts of her kept intruding into his peripheral vision and distracting his best intentions. He was glad of the waist-height stall door between them.

When she straightened to cast an assessing glance over her work, he cleared his throat and said, "You do this all day?"

"I'm the best at it," she said. She patted the mare's neck and turned to ease out of the stall.

Idisio stepped aside hastily and glanced down the row again. Looking at her, close up, was even worse than staring from several feet away.

"You know," she said, staring at him, "there's a great bruise to the side of your face. Run into a door?"

Idisio's grin faded.

"Something like that," he muttered.

"Huh," she said after another hard stare at him, and turned away. After securely bolting the bottom half of the stall door, she moved to the next stall, which had a small black flag beside it. Both halves of this door were closed. "You'd probably like to see this fellow." She unbolted the top half of the door and swung it open.

A familiar, fine-boned nose poked out inquiringly.

The girl watched him narrowly. "This one yours, too?"

"Yes," Idisio said, rubbing the silky nose. "How did . . .?"

"Well, if you want him back, you owe me for two horses," she said.

Idisio stared at her. "Two?"

"I gave Baylor and Karic each a horse in return for this one," she said. "They were lucky to get that much; I won both those horses two days ago from some stupid northern who thought he could beat me at five-card."

Idisio's jaw sagged. "Both of them? When did they leave?"

"Early this morning," she said. "And yes, both of them. Baylor came riding into town yesterday, face white as Horn salt, and went to find

Karic. The two of them came to find me a while after that, asking for horses; the only thing they had to trade was this one. I thought it a fair deal."

"Baylor stole this horse from us," Idisio said. Something bothered him about the girl's story, but flustered as he was by her nearness, he couldn't focus enough to tell what was wrong. She smelled of sweat and horse and an odd, subtle spice. He wished the stall door still stood between them. He prayed she didn't look down.

The girl shrugged. "That's not my problem. You want him back, you pay me his worth."

Idisio looked down the row and saw Scratha stepping out of the box stall. "How much do you want?"

"Five gold rounds," the girl said. "Less than this one's worth, I'd say, but that's what the northern valued his two horses at, so I'll settle for that."

Idisio began to protest; Scratha's hand on his shoulder stopped him. His master considered girl and horse.

"Five?" he said at last.

"You have good hearing, *s'e*," the girl said.

Scratha nodded. "Desert blood," he said absently, and held out half a silver coin. "Here's for the other. I'll think on it and let you know. Come, Idisio, let's get some rooms and dinner."

Ignoring the surprise and displeasure on the girl's face, Idisio hurried after his master.

"They both ran," he said. "Why both?"

"There's more going on here than a girl being murdered," Scratha said, frowning. "Talk to her again after dinner. And don't believe everything she says. She gave you that information without any prompting; I never trust people who do that."

"She seemed honest. I can read people pretty well."

Scratha shot him an amused glance. "I think your judgment may get a bit skewed when it comes to attractive young ladies."

"Was she? I didn't even notice how she looked."

Scratha arched an eyebrow and observed, "You're better at lying when your heart's in it."

The inn, like the rest of the town, proved considerably cleaner than Kybeach's dingy offering. Wide, low-silled windows with shutters flung wide let the last rays of sunlight into western-facing rooms and brought the first glimmer of dawn into the eastern ones. Low beds of colorful southern flowers and herbs edged every side of the building, and the occasional gust of wind kicked up a cloud of aroma that reminded Idisio of his walk through the King's Gate gardens.

This wouldn't be a cheap inn. The owner, or perhaps the whole village, obviously knew it had a good position here, just where travelers out of Bright Bay wanted to rest a bit, and travelers from the north wanted to tidy up before arriving at the king's city. If Kybeach ever cleaned itself up, it could suck business away from this town, being closer; but nothing could ever take care of that marshland stench at low tide.

The sign brought an odd expression to Scratha's face. Idisio struggled to decipher the lettering on the sign while his master stood staring at the door, and finally worked out that it read "Cida's Haven." Scratha shrugged in response to Idisio's puzzled stare and led the way inside.

A plump woman at the desk greeted them cheerfully, wide, dark eyes surveying them critically while her mouth grinned.

"Good eve to you, travelers," she said. "Two rooms?"

"One," Scratha said.

"We've one east and one west left," she said. "Busy road lately, it's been, since the change in kings. They're both the same price, five silver for the night and another silver for room service." She winked.

Idisio felt his face crimson.

"Just the room," Scratha said. "East, please."

She gave them another appraising glance, her eyes lingering on Idisio's bruised face, and nodded. "Sunrise room it is. Five silver bits, please . . . thank you." She slid a key across the counter. "Down the right hallway, fourth door on the right. You'll need to be out by noon."

Scratha started to turn away, then swung back abruptly. "Are you called Cida?"

The woman's expression became opaque, like a window on a misty day. "That's the name of the inn."

"But is it yours?" Scratha asked.

"The inn was here before I was born, *s'e*," she said. "*My* name is Alre."

Scratha smiled and turned away again, seeming satisfied.

"Good eve, *s'a*," he said over his shoulder as they left the main room.

"What was that about?" Idisio asked when they were out of the woman's hearing range.

"Nothing important," Scratha said, still smiling.

"You lie better when your heart's in it."

"So does everyone."

The tavern attached to the inn boasted well-dressed, quiet, and refined patrons who had no objection to paying outrageous prices for the food and wine. And no fear of northern priests, apparently: a dice game rattled in one corner, a card game shuffled at another table, and aesa smoke twisted and faded in the breeze coming through several wide windows. The smell of cloves, ginger, and other exotic spices from past the Horn drifted in the room, and the dishes carried past on large silver platters steamed richly with their own unfamiliar aromas.

No corner tables were open, which obviously would have been Scratha's first pick; finally the man settled for a table against the wall, near the dice game. A serving girl arrived at their table seconds after they sat down. Her clothing hovered just on the edge of propriety and drew attention to places Idisio didn't think he should stare at. He dropped his gaze to the table.

"Southern white wine," Scratha said to the serving girl.

"And for you?" she asked, shifting a little as she looked at Idisio. The move put her round hip entirely too close; she smelled of sweetened ginger. Idisio shut his eyes.

"Get him the same," Scratha said. "And a platter of whatever that dark-haired girl just brought by, enough for both of us."

"Yes, *s'e*," the girl said.

Idisio kept his eyes shut until Scratha said, voice matter-of-fact, "She's gone. You're safe."

Idisio risked a glance; the girl had left. Scratha seemed thoughtful rather than amused.

"My eyes are tired, that's all," Idisio said, knowing it sounded lame.

Scratha left it alone. "Have you ever heard of aqeyva?"

Idisio blinked. "Ack what?"

"I didn't think so," Scratha said. "It's an old discipline; not many people still know it."

"Fighting?" Idisio said.

"Not entirely. It's a discipline, and I can see you need that badly."

"What makes you say—"

"Pretty girls," Scratha said succinctly, his mouth twitching in clear amusement. Idisio bit his lip and looked away, deeply embarrassed. "I'll start teaching you tonight, after you talk to the girl at the stables."

"I don't even know her name," Idisio protested, suddenly not wanting to talk to or even look at another female form tonight. "Or where to find her."

"Go back to the stables," Scratha said. "She likely sleeps there."

Idisio sighed. "Yes, Master."

Further conversation ended with the arrival of their meal: two enormous, glazed earthenware bowls each containing a generous portion of meat, tender, dark, and rich with spices; a pile of noodles; long strips of steamed root vegetables; snap peas still in the shell; and black beans in a tart sauce.

Scratha had only finished half of his meal when Idisio scraped the last of the meat juices from his bowl and let out a satisfied belch. Scratha raised an amused eyebrow; Idisio shrugged, sat back and said, briefly,

"Stables." He received an equally short nod in response, stood, and left the room.

Stars glittered high and distant overhead; the half moon still lurked low in the sky. Just enough light from torch and moon filtered over the gravel path to let him make his way to the stable without fear of stumbling. Idisio paced his step to a casual amble. He didn't want to look like he was rushing to see the girl again, or hurrying to the stable for whatever reason. Moving fast drew attention.

A sudden cold fear rose in his gut; would this girl, too, be murdered when he arrived? He put the thought aside, scolding himself for being foolish, and forced his quickened step to slow again.

He found her sitting on a bench set against the wall to one side of the stable doors, staring at the stars with an expression of weary contentment. She watched him come up the path without comment, and moved over to make room for him to sit beside her.

He hesitated, then sat, feeling awkward and stupid again.

"I didn't get your name," he said. "I'm Idisio."

"Riss," she said, and leaned back against the side of the stable, drawing her feet up to rest on the edge of the bench. The move put her face behind him; he scooted back, balancing his own heels on the edge.

She smiled, her gaze on the stars above, and said without looking at him, "Did you decide if you want your horse back yet?"

"My master hasn't decided," Idisio said.

Riss turned her head to stare at him. Torch-cast shadow dappled her face. Nearby, a long, leafy branch swayed in the light breeze, shifting dark lines erratically across her pale hair. "You didn't come here just to get my name. What do you want?"

Idisio knew when he could dance around a topic and when a straight answer was the only way to go. "Karic and Baylor."

"Karic's the Kybeach runner," she said. The darkness made her expression hard to read. "Anytime there's news, he brings it, stays for a day or two, and goes back."

Idisio waited, and after a few moments she added, "Baylor was runner for a couple of weeks when Karic was sick."

The boy stared at his feet, frowning. "Why did they both run from us in Kybeach?"

"You think I know?" the girl said with a shrug.

"Yes," Idisio said. "You care about the horses too much to just give over without a good reason."

He didn't look up, but he could feel the girl studying him critically.

"You're smarter than you look," she said.

"Thanks."

She ignored the heavy edge in his voice. "You're welcome. What do I get for telling you?"

Idisio had an offer ready. "A gold round."

"No, thanks."

He looked at her, astonished. Nobody turned down money. Especially not that much money. "Two rounds?" he said, tentative, hoping Scratha wouldn't be angry at the amount.

"I don't want money," she said. "I want you to take me with you when you leave."

He stared at her, speechless.

"I'm not offering to pay my way with my body," she said sharply, "so you can just stop looking at me like that."

"No!" Idisio said, feeling color rush to his face instantly. "That's not what I—"

"I'm tired of being here, that's all," she said, cutting him off. "I'm tired of being a woman in a small village, where everything's going to be the same for the rest of my life. I'm tired of seeing people ride in, talking about wonderful places far away, and then leave for more adventures while I sit here mucking out stalls and currying horses."

He shook his head against the torrent of words, at a loss for a response.

"If you won't take me," she said with fierce intensity, "I won't say another word." She rose and stormed into the barn.

Idisio stared up at the stars, shaking his head wordlessly for some time, mouth opening and closing like a landed fish.

Eventually he sighed and followed her into the barn.

"No," Scratha said. "*No.* Absolutely not."

"I gave my word," Idisio said.

"Your word means nothing in this."

Idisio shrugged. "As you like. I'll tell her she's not going after all." He started to turn.

"Wait," Scratha said.

Idisio looked back, keeping his gaze guileless and inquiring.

"That was too easy." Scratha studied him for a moment, his dark face drawing into a fierce, intimidating scowl. "She did tell you something, and you're not going to tell me, are you?"

"I made a promise," Idisio said. "If she doesn't go, she didn't tell me anything."

"Mmph." After a long moment, his master nodded. "All right. What did the girl say?"

Idisio relaxed a little. "Karic's the town runner for Kybeach. A couple times, he couldn't make it, and Baylor came instead. The town runner before Karic was a man named Gessen; he ran the news for fifteen years before disappearing one day. Riss said it was odd, that Gessen disappeared just when he did, but she wouldn't tell me why. That's part of what she's going to finish telling us once we're on the road."

Scratha sighed and pressed the bridge of his nose with his fingertips.

"Worthless," he said. "Is there anything else that might be of value?"

"She wouldn't say anything else," Idisio said. "Not until we're on the road and she's sure of us, she said."

Scratha barked humorless laughter. "Sure of *us*? What of our safety around her?"

"She's not. . . ." Idisio started, then fell silent.

"Anyone that manipulative isn't one I'll sleep easy around," Scratha said. "Keep your eyes off her chest and on her eyes, Idisio. I'm starting to get used to having a servant now; I don't want to lose you."

Idisio nodded glumly.

"For my part," Scratha said, "while you were out, I managed some information-gathering myself." He looked smug now. "Somewhat more valuable than your own."

"From the innkeeper?" Idisio said.

Scratha's gaze sharpened again. "How did you know?"

"You were practically drooling over her." Idisio flinched as the words came out of his mouth, unable to believe he'd been so cheeky; but Scratha shook his head, unoffended.

"There's a free room she holds aside for runners," he said, "but Karic and Baylor always stayed at a house near the edge of town, a place with a bad reputation. She'd like to see the people there run out of town, but they've got too much influence with the new village elder; another man she doesn't think highly of. She says he stepped up to lead a little over a year ago. The last elder died childless, so the village gathered to choose a new one. This new man surprised everyone; nobody seems to admit choosing him, but he landed the post."

"She likes gossip, or did you tickle her toes for that much?" Idisio said.

Scratha smiled, looking like a well-fed cat.

"Neither," he said. "We're related."

Idisio stared, mouth hanging open. "*What?*"

"In the Great Hall of Scratha Fortress," Scratha said, "hangs a huge tapestry tracing our ancestry to before the Split. Every desert Family has one. I've spent a fair amount of time looking at it over the last few years; for one thing, I had to add in the death dates." He cleared his throat and looked away for a moment, expression bleak. "One name I wasn't sure of: a girl who ran away from an arranged betrothal. I heard the story many times, and the tapestry had no death date for her. I always wondered, and I always hoped, but I was too afraid to go looking and find out."

"Cida," Idisio guessed.

Scratha nodded. "Cida," he said. "The innkeeper's *s'e-natan*—her father's mother. Cida apparently ran away with a stableboy she'd fallen in love with; that was never mentioned in the story I heard, but I'd guess that's because it was too shameful to admit. She walked out on an important political betrothal, after all." He smiled. "Cida had four children, two boys and two girls, and each of those had children. Alre—which is an old family name, by the way—is the only one who stayed in the area. The rest have scattered throughout the kingdom; doing very well, from what she says, and none have the least idea that they're related to Scratha. She's the only one who knows the full story; she chose not to pass it on to any of her children."

Idisio shook his head, impressed. "Lucky you came this way after all, then," he ventured.

But Scratha's gaze had turned distant; he frowned, seeming not to hear Idisio's comment. "It should have been passed down," he murmured, as if to himself. "I have some searching to do."

"Why?"

"Because my family is matrilineal," Scratha said, focusing on Idisio again. "If there's a straight female line remaining, I want them back in the fortress where they belong. From what she says, the female line is north of the Forest, probably in Isata."

"What if they—or she—isn't interested in going south?"

Scratha shook his head. "I won't have the fortress empty any longer than I have to," he said. "It's a tremendous relief to know that my line hasn't ended with me after all. Although I'm sure my *s'a-netan* would have been horrified to hear of the Scratha line being mixed with northern blood, I'll take it with gratitude."

Idisio decided not to press the question of reluctant relatives. Something in his master's expression warned that it was time to shift the subject. "So what's the innkeeper's relation to you?"

"*S'a-nashan-kai*. I think you'd call it mother's-side cousin, twice removed; but that's a cold, short way to say it," Scratha said, visibly relaxing. "I don't care much for your northern tongue sometimes. *S'a-nashan-kai* covers that it's not a straight matrilineal relationship, and there's status involved . . . it would take too long to explain." He sat down on the edge of the bed and kicked off his boots. "We leave at first light. Tell your girl to be ready."

"She's not my—" Idisio started.

"Don't be so literal. Go."

Idisio stomped out, feeling thoroughly aggrieved and not quite sure why.

The back of his neck was wet. His shoulders were wet. His hair was wet. His feet were soaked. And seeing his master riding in comfort, whistling to himself quietly, only worsened Idisio's temper.

It was, of course, his own fault. He'd let himself fall prey to Riss's intent, thoughtful stare, and wound up offering to let her ride. Moments later he'd been trudging sullenly beside the horse, because somehow riding with her behind him, or before him, seemed like too much invitation to embarrassment.

He *should* have followed their example and taken his hooded cloak out of his saddlebags as soon as the clouds started to gather overhead, but he'd been lost in brooding until the first splash on his nose woke him to the impending deluge. After a frantic scrabble in the bags, he'd got the cloak on just a few moments too late. He wasn't cold, not at this time of year; the air was muggy and the rain warm. But he *hated* being wet, and hated being laughed at more. He couldn't prove they were laughing at him, but he could *feel* it.

So now he slogged, increasingly angry, along a muddy road with a steady grey curtain of torrential rain coming down around them. They found nowhere to stop, no shelter to be had, and even if he'd been riding double with Riss their pace would have been held to the same slow plod because of the mud and the poor visibility.

Even the News-Riders that passed by barely managed more than walking speed. The Riders and their mounts, covered in froth and spattered mud, looked even more miserable than Idisio.

"I should have stayed in Bright Bay," Idisio muttered. "I always had somewhere dry to sit out the afternoon storms."

"You're welcome to go back," his master said without turning, his voice sharp.

Idisio's heart skipped a beat, accelerated briefly, then slowly stuttered back to normal. How had the man heard him? He hadn't spoken loudly, and the pouring rain should have masked the words.

"Sorry, Master," he said.

Riss slanted a questioning stare at him. So she hadn't heard his words; that was some reassurance. He shrugged in response and went back to staring at the ground.

Not long after that, Scratha said, "Village ahead."

Idisio looked up. The rain had finally thinned, and buildings could be seen through the grey haze, sturdy ghost-shapes that grew more solid the closer they came.

"Must be Sandsplit village," Riss said, annoyingly cheerful.

"*Sandsplit?*" Idisio said before he could stop himself. "What kind of stupid name is that for a village?"

Riss shrugged. "It's a coastal town, and it sits at the crossroads of the Forest Road, the Sandlaen Port Road, and the Ugly Swamp Road; name makes sense to me."

Her reasonable tone only annoyed him more.

"Stupid," he said, wanting a reaction from her, a good fight, anything to take his mind off how his feet squished and his hair plastered flat against his neck.

She ignored him. Scratha ignored him. They passed the first fences, wattle-woven constructions within which pigs as sullen as Idisio huddled under cover. On the other side of the road, a chachad bird screamed challenge as they passed, its bright red throat puffing out alarmingly; it ruffled equally red feathers into a wide-winged show of ferocity and stalked along the fence line on long black legs. Idisio caught glimpses of three-toed, wickedly taloned feet before the mud covered them on the next stride.

Idisio stuck out his tongue at the huge bird.

"Brave from over here, aren't you?" Riss said from above him. "Why don't you go within the chachad's reach and do that? Who's being stupid now?"

He glared up at her. "Get off my horse."

"All right," she said, pulled the horse to a halt and slid off, landing lightly in the mud. She proffered the reins to Idisio, a smile on her face that missed pleasant by just a hair.

Scratha dismounted as well, turning a dark stare on Idisio that cooled his temper immediately. "*Your* horse?"

Idisio swallowed.

"Sorry, Master," he muttered again.

Scratha pinned him with that glare for another moment before shaking his head and turning away. Wordlessly gesturing for Idisio and Riss to follow, he led his horse towards a long, low-roofed building nearby. Wide double doors and a horseshoe nailed to the left of the door marked it as a stable.

The wide doors slid open as they approached, and two grooms came out, both women. They gave the wet, tired horses critical, assessing looks, accepted the coin Scratha handed them, and led the beasts away with a minimum of conversation.

Saddlebags in hand, the travelers slogged through the steamy damp to the next building, which had been painted a cheerful blue and had a bed painted on the door. A carefully lettered wooden sign hung over the door.

"Traveler's Rest," Scratha sighed. "How creative. Let's get inside before it starts raining again."

The door opened into a wide, dim room lit by a handful of table-lanterns and what grey light came through the flawed glass blocks of the few windows. There were a scattering of tables and chairs, all sturdy, all heavily worn and scarred by years of use. A few people looked up as the travelers passed, examined them with vague indifference, then returned to their low-voiced conversations.

The desk at the far end of the room seemed to serve as both bar and inn desk; Scratha headed for it without hesitation.

"One room, three people," he said to the innkeeper, a thin man with small, dark eyes, grey streaks in his dark hair, and heavy pox-scars on his face.

The innkeeper looked them over with more interest than the people at the tables had shown. His gaze fixed on Scratha longest.

"One room for three?" he repeated. "What name do you give, *s'e*?"

"Gerau Sa'adenit."

"Gerau Sa'adenit?" the innkeeper said, his small dark eyes narrowing. "Hold a moment. News-Rider left something for you this morning." He reached under the counter. "Two silver rounds for the three," he added, putting something wrapped in dark, waterproofed fabric in front of them. "One bed in the room. All we have left." He ostentatiously avoided looking at Riss as he spoke.

Frowning, Scratha took the packet and slid it into his saddle bag. He shot Idisio a quick, questioning look; Idisio nodded.

Scratha handed the innkeeper the silver and said, "Do you serve food here, *s'e*?"

"Wine only," the innkeeper said, "and that only in rainy season. Rain wine, I call it. It's wind wine up north."

"Mulled wine?" Scratha said.

The innkeeper nodded. "Pot on the fire now, if you'd like some. Silver bit each cup, and a finer drink you won't find short of Stecatr. You can eat next building over, at the Grey Salt Tavern, or you can try the Raven's Wing a bit further down; it's cheaper but not as good food."

"You're from the north?" Scratha said, handing over another silver round. "Keep it."

"For that, you can drink the pot dry, if you like," the man said with a smile that showed gapped and crooked teeth. "Yes, I used to live in Stecatr. Fine city, fine people, but my bones got to aching so much in the cold winters, I decided to move south. I was told profits were soaring down here, with all the new traveling going on; and so far that's held true."

"How long ago was that?" Scratha said.

"Oh, not long," the man said. "Four months or so. Met a man wanting to move northwards; he bought my Stecatr inn, I bought his, easy trade. We're both happy. Odd thing, he didn't seem the type to run an inn; but that's not my never-mind. He paid a goodly price for my place, and let me pay far too little for his. Eh, his foolishness. But you'll be wanting to get to your rooms and dry off now; I'll get another pot of rain wine going, to make sure you'll have plenty when you come back out. Third room on the right, down that hallway. I'll send a girl with some towels." The man grinned at them, bobbed his head, and hurried to a table whose occupants were signaling for more wine.

Scratha smiled. "Well," he said quietly as he ushered them from the main room, "there's at least one uncomplicated man left in this world. Nice to know."

"Don't you mean honest?" Riss asked. "That's the saying, one honest man left in this world."

Scratha shook his head, still smiling, and didn't answer.

The Grey Salt Tavern was the sort of place Idisio would once have considered prime pocket-picking ground. Even now his hands twitched a bit from habit, and he found his eye drifting to thick purses and wallets carelessly attached to broad waistlines.

Scratha's hand clamped casually, if a near-bruising hold could be called casual, on Idisio's shoulder a moment later: no mistaking the message. Idisio ducked his head and focused on the floor. The grip shifted to a light touch, but Idisio's mood had already gone sour.

He'd felt so much better after a hot mug of rain wine, a thorough rubdown with damp cloth and dry towel, a change of clothes, and a hasty finger-rake through his hair to tidy it up a bit. He'd felt, for just a few precious moments, like his old, cocky, sure self. But Scratha's stern pinch brought him back to the moment, reminding him that all the skills he'd been so proud of mastering, as a street-thief, were worse than useless now.

They settled at a table, Idisio still keeping his gaze firmly on nearby things and doing his best to avoid any appearance of casing the other customers. He didn't need another look, anyway; he knew everything he needed to know. *Would* have needed to know, he corrected himself hastily. He wasn't a thief any more. That had been survival, not something he loved or needed to do.

But at least he'd been a *good* thief. Now he'd become a moderately adept servant to a banished desert lord pretending to be an ordinary person. The morning and evening lessons Scratha had set him on reading and writing were hard, and frustrating, and made him feel stupid; and though the aqeyva lessons hadn't started yet, he had a feeling they'd be even worse.

He didn't like feeling stupid. He didn't like being laughed at. His master could get along with Riss as a servant, couldn't he? And a couple of those gold rounds would take Idisio a long way, and likely wouldn't be missed for a while. Idisio could. . . .

. . . could sneak away with a few coins and fewer skills and wind up working the streets of another city, a northern city, one that Scratha would eventually pass through. Returning to Bright Bay was out of the question. He'd be laughed out of town, at best; at worst, picked up by the King's Guards and taken into the royal presence to explain his return without Scratha. He likely wouldn't survive long in any case, and he'd never be happy working as a pick-thief in any city, not after seeing the glory that came to hand when one had noble status or real money to spend.

And it seemed likely Scratha would take Idisio's desertion as personal insult, or proof of deep lies all along, and hunt him down to put that remaining ebony-handled blade in his back.

He glared at his hands and didn't look up when the server came to take their order.

"Idisio," Scratha said, snapping his fingers impatiently, then, to the server, "Oh, hells, give him some more mulled wine. It might sweeten his temper. All round, yes. Thank you. And a meal, whatever's hot and fast." The server went away again. "Idisio. Look at me or I'll knock you across the damn room."

Idisio raised his head. "Yeah?" The look in Scratha's eye made self-preservation kick in, and he modified it to, "Yes, Master?"

His master's mood had darkened since their arrival as well. While Idisio sponged off road grime, Scratha sat in a comfortable armchair and read the folded sheets of parchment the News-Rider had left for him, all covered with tightly scrawled writing. Scratha started frowning almost at once, and by the time he'd finished reading, his expression could have melted sand into glass.

He still looked in no mood to tolerate disrespect from a scruffy street-thief turned lackluster servant. His tone remained distinctly sharp as he said, "It's time to ask Riss to fulfill her promise, as we've carried her this far. I thought you might like to hear it, as you seem to like getting answers to your questions."

"Yeah," Idisio said, straightening with real interest now, and offered an apology that was close enough to truth: "Sorry. Rain always makes me grumpy."

"Mmph," Scratha said, and turned his stare to Riss without more comment.

She stared back as fiercely and said, "You don't hit him again. Ever. Not even a threat."

Idisio stared, his jaw loosening at that unexpected demand, and Scratha looked as taken aback himself. Silence hung, uncomfortable and taut, for a few breaths as Scratha stared at Riss; then he transferred his gaze, more thoughtful now, to Idisio.

"All right," he said at last, in an oddly muted tone. "I won't. Now *talk*."

She shifted uncomfortably, all aggression fading. "Well. . . ."

Scratha put a hand over his eyes and sighed noisily.

"I should have known," he murmured.

"You don't actually know anything?" Idisio demanded, appalled. "You *lied* to me?"

"Oh, shut up!" she flared. "Like you would have done different." She dropped her head on her arms and began to cry.

Scratha regarded the girl without surprise or sympathy. "At least you didn't try to hand off another pack of lies," he said. "Tell us what you do know about Karic and Baylor. The truth, this time. Not the horse trading nonsense."

She straightened, sniffling, and squinted at him dubiously. "How'd you know? I thought you bought it."

"*I* was watching your eyes, not your chest," Scratha said tartly.

She colored a deep and honest red; Idisio felt his own face flare to match.

"Why was it so important for you to get out of Obein?" Scratha asked. "What are you running from?"

She twisted her hands together on the table, the crimson of her face washing away to a stark pale nervousness.

"It's all together," she said, barely audible, and stared at her hands as she went on, "Karic . . . always . . . well, he was nice, at first. He came by every time he was in town . . . and said I was pretty . . . and . . . I mean, normally I wouldn't fall for that, but he was so. . . ." She made a vague gesture with one hand, not looking up, then immediately clenched them together again.

"He seduced you," Scratha said, sounding more impatient than sympathetic. "So?"

She flinched a bit at his tone and snuck a hasty glance at his face. "Well, he always brought a bottle of wine with him. And it seemed odd, somehow, but I could never figure why, exactly, except that he seemed more fond of ale than wine." She shrugged, her lips thinning. "I thought wine was more romantic, anyway, so I didn't give it much thought at first. Then I started wondering where he was getting the wine; it was in a strange blue bottle, like I've never seen made along the coast or sold in our tavern. I asked him about it. He said it was a southern wine and specially made, that he only brought me the best."

Scratha's face became grim. The server brought three mugs of hot wine, but nobody touched them as Riss went on, still staring at the table. She seemed relieved to be spilling the story.

"One night, not long ago, he said he'd meet me, in the stables, where we always. . . ." She swallowed convulsively, her hands clenching more tightly for a moment. "He ran late, and I went to find him. I was worried. I knew the people he spent time with weren't . . . nice people. I thought they might have hurt him, because he said that he was getting out of their company. He said he had a bigger contract to hand, and that he'd be rich soon, and not need to run news and messages across little coastal towns. And I thought, maybe, they'd gotten angry at him for leaving . . . I don't know. I just got scared, and went to find him."

The chatter of the tavern and plates of food being set in front of them filled the silence while she visibly tried to find words for what had happened next. Idisio cast a hungry eye at the platter but knew better than to touch it just yet; he'd eat it cold, most likely, but better that than annoy Scratha by interrupting the girl's story.

"I hadn't realized. . . ." she said at last, almost whispering again. "I'd thought he just didn't understand . . . what kind of friends he'd chosen. I was *stupid*."

"What did you see?"

She looked up, then away, then down at her hands again, as if wishing for a way out of saying it aloud. "I didn't dare go in, not alone, not in the evening like that, but I looked in an open window. And he was just picking up one of the blue bottles, and setting down coin for it. I heard him talking. Heard him saying . . . that he needed to start buying two bottles soon, because I was building a tolerance. . . ." She dropped her head in her hands and fell silent.

"Had to be dasta in the wine," Scratha said with immense distaste, and grimaced. "Damnit. Was he dealing, or just buying?"

"Dealing, I think," she said in a muffled voice. "A lot of things made sense after I saw that, questions I'd never really thought about because I was too eager to keep his favor . . . I thought he loved me."

"So what happened then?"

"I ran back to the stables, and rousted the other stable lad from his sleep, and told him I was feeling ill and to plead apologies to Karic when he came by, and I ran off and hid and cried half the night. And in the morning, he'd left. I didn't see him again until this last time." She straightened, her eyes damp but her voice steady. "Of course he came by to see me, and had that damn bottle, and I told him I knew what he'd been doing, and that I didn't want him near me again. And he said that I was an idiot for turning him away, and that I'd misunderstood a coarse joke. I didn't believe him, I told him to go away and stay away, and he laughed. He said I'd be crawling back to him soon enough, and he left. But then Baylor came in on that stolen horse, and I couldn't help it, I had to find out what was going on, so I followed them . . . they went around the corner of the stables to talk, and I crept close and listened. . . ."

She paused, her lips thinning, a hard light in her eyes.

"I'm not cut out for stealth," she said simply. "They caught me."

Scratha pursed his lips and said nothing. Idisio, horrified, didn't know what to say. They all sat staring at each other for a long moment of dreadful silence.

"They dragged me back into the stables with a hand over my mouth and a knife at my throat to keep me quiet," she said in an eerily even tone. "The stable lad was gone, it was my turn on duty that night. I usually am; I like being awake at night . . . Anyway. Karic brought out a little bottle, about this tall—" She held thumb and forefinger apart to illustrate. "—and made me drink it all. And said nobody would believe me and that if I even tried telling people what happened, his friends at the edge of town would get me. And that I was to lie to you, and tell you they ran north, through the Great Forest. But I know they're going south, to Sandlaen Port, and I know they have a contact here in Sandsplit named Yuer."

Scratha started at that name; his face seemed to darken instantly.

"Yuer!" he said. "Gods help us all, *he's* involved in this? And he lives *here*? I thought . . . hells. Go on."

She shrugged, looking down at her hands again, her back straight and stiff. "I don't remember much after that. I woke up the next morning out in the main aisle of the stable, with several people, locals and travelers, staring at me; I wasn't . . . dressed, and I reeked of wine and . . . well." Her mouth tightened. "You know. And Karic was right, nobody believed me. They said I'd been acting the whore with Karic for months, and everyone knew I was nothing but a useless slut, and even my own parents turned me out for shaming them. The stable master only kept me on and let me sleep in the stables because I'm so good with the horses, but the way he looked at me—he'd have cornered me himself soon enough. And after that would come the village. I couldn't . . . I couldn't stand that. I'm stupid, but I'm *not* a whore."

"And what did you hear Karic and Baylor talking about before they caught you listening?" Scratha asked, his frown unwavering.

She ducked her head. "That they'd killed a girl, back in Kybeach." Her voice broke. "And they'd tried to put the blame on an outsider, and it wasn't working, and so they had to run. That's when they caught me—I gasped when I heard them talking about murdering the girl, and they heard me."

Scratha tilted his head to one side, frowning at her. "Mmph. And that was two nights ago now?"

She nodded mutely. He studied her for a moment more, then shook his head.

"Eat," he said abruptly, turning his attention to his own plate. "I need to think about this, and it's best done on a full stomach."

The steam had long ago faded from the platters, but even cold the food tasted good. Idisio shoveled it down enthusiastically, feeling a bit guilty that her horrible story hadn't dimmed his appetite in the least. Scratha ate with equal speed and gusto, while Riss picked over her plate listlessly, her determined show of strength fading at last.

After the plates had been cleared away, Scratha sat back and said, without preamble, "Look at the mugs. Now close your eyes and tell me what they look like. Riss, you first."

Riss cleared her throat uncertainly. "It's . . . it's grey. It's made of metal. It's got a design on the side. Something with animals. A fox and some birds, I think."

"Idisio?"

"Silver alloy," Idisio said promptly. "Stands about as high as my hand is long, about as wide around as my palm. Handle embossed with birds in flight, body boss of three birds being stalked by a fox. I don't know what's on the side away from me, but I'd guess it's probably the three birds in flight and the fox missing on the pounce. There's a dent on the near side rim. That's all I remember."

Nobody spoke for a few moments.

"Open your eyes," Scratha said finally.

Riss had developed a glazed look. "How in the s'iopes' seven hells did you remember all that?"

Scratha grinned. Idisio had never seen him look so pleased.

"Very good, Idisio," he said.

Idisio relaxed, feeling a sudden glow. "Thanks."

"Riss," Scratha said, "you'll learn. Don't worry. It's impressive that you remembered as much as you did. You'll both take to aqeyva lessons just fine."

"Ack what?" Riss said, and looked confused when Idisio and Scratha started laughing.

Scratha pushed to his feet, dropping a generous amount of coin on the table. "Let's go. I want to talk to Yuer before we turn in for the night. I've some questions for him, and I want both of you along as witnesses."

With those alarming words, he ushered them out of the tavern.

Chapter Ten

The bulk of Water's End sheltered in a natural bowl. Cliffs rose to all sides, some over a hundred feet high, and the path sloped steep and narrow down a hand-carved pass in the ancient rock. Sentries dressed in eye-catching white perched high along the cliffs: steady on impossibly thin ledges, supported by sturdy rope and leather harnesses. Long metal braces lined the tops of the cliffs; by the look of it, the sentries could slide sideways several feet in either direction.

To Alyea, the engineering of those braces seemed as much a marvel as Oruen's solarium. How could they secure perfect metal rods into solid rock? Incredible. But this wasn't the time to ask about that.

"Are those teyanain?" Alyea asked Chac after a single swift, furtive glance upwards.

"No," the old man said. "Their authority stops at the ridge we just crossed. Water's End has its own guards. Every desert family tithes to support Water's End; some of them send their young men and women to train here as guards for a time. It's something of a coming-of-age ritual, serving time here as a guard." He glanced up and sighed.

"Did you serve here?" Alyea asked, prompted by the wistfulness in the old man's expression.

"Yes," Chac said, and pulled his horse to a halt. "Lead your horse down by hand."

Alyea glanced back as she swung off her horse. Micru had already dismounted and stood ready, hand on bridle. "Do the guards get upset if you ride down?"

"No," Chac said. "Trail's too tricky to ride."

"What about caravans?"

"Different trail," Chac said. "There's three north trails. One two-way trail for caravans; you have to pay to use that one, and it's a hefty fee. One free trail for walking out, one free trail for walking in."

The rocky, sandy ground underfoot proved slippery and treacherous. Alyea placed her feet with care and tried to avoid having her horse step on her toes. That quickly turned out to be a lost cause as they slipped and scrambled their way down the narrow trail.

"Why . . . isn't . . . the trail . . . wider? Smoother?" Alyea panted halfway down. Sweat trickled down her face, funneling into her thin shirt; she'd look a proper mess when they reached bottom.

"Why should it be?" Chac said over his shoulder. He moved like a cat over the uneven ground, guiding his horse easily, and didn't seem the least bit out of breath. "Deep southerners don't want much to do with the northlands. This serves as a natural barrier to kings that get a mad notion of taking over the desert Families' lands. If anything gets past the teyanain, they won't make it past this."

The idea of an invading army trying to make it down this slope brought a sour smile to Alyea's lips.

"What about the other trails?" she said, jerking her foot away just as a heavy hoof slammed down. Hard boots weren't helping; her feet felt bruised and she suspected at least one toe might be broken already. "Or ports?"

"The other trails both have their own tight spots, and you have to have a recognized guide to make it through," Chac said. "The ports wouldn't be friendly to invasion attempts, either." He fell silent, his attention on navigating a tricky turn.

They were nearly at the bottom of the trail. Water's End spread out before them, a patchwork of stone buildings, some two and three stories; tents, at the edges, and even, incredibly, lush patches of garden greenery. Alyea had been expecting something much cruder, from Chac's comment at the first way-stop.

"I thought you said Water's End wasn't much," she said as they descended onto relatively level, wide ground again.

"Never said that," the old man said. "Just said it was a larger version of the way-stops, and it is. Prettier, too." He drew a deep breath and surveyed the area as the guards finished the descent and gathered behind them.

Alyea looked as well, and forgot her sweat, her disheveled appearance, the dirt and dust on her clothes, her aching feet.

The scent of desert rose and whitemusk flowers, feather-herbs and bitter onion, fresh baked bread and citrus fruits all clashed in her nose. With a shift of the faint breeze, those aromas faded into the dust, dirt, and sweat of a busy camp in hot weather. The smell of metal lent a tangy accent to the air, and nearly everyone seemed to be wearing a sword or dagger.

People wearing brightly patterned, lightweight fabrics filled the winding streets. Most wore their hair either intricately and tightly braided against their skulls or completely shaven. The predominant skin tone ranged from dark brown to black, a shade she'd rarely seen in Bright Bay; as Chac had said, the deep southerners wanted little to do with anything north of the Horn. Here and there she saw the bronze or burnt-almond skin tone and hawk-like face of an old, noble bloodline; crowds parted before those visages. The people moving out of the way didn't even seem to glance up first, as if they felt the presence before seeing it.

A cacophony of laughter, shouting and arguing filled the streets, punctuated by the erratic screams of caged desert birds. Now and again an asp-jacau howled or whined; there were more of those creatures here than Alyea had ever seen in one place, all neatly groomed and obediently trotting behind their masters. Some wore gold, silver, or gem-studded collars; a few had swirling patterns bleached or dyed into their fur.

Alyea blinked wind-flung dust from her eyes and looked at Chac, feeling overwhelmed and helpless. He stared at her, his expression thoughtful; when she met his gaze he nodded as if coming to a decision.

"This way," he said.

The group wound through a seemingly erratic path, past tents, buildings, and gardens, finally halting again in the courtyard of what must surely be the largest building in Water's End. It stood three stories high, block upon huge limestone block set and firmly cemented together. The wide windows on the upper stories were flanked by heavy, metal shutters, currently open and fastened securely back to the sides of the building.

A nearby stable building, large enough to house fifty horses in comfort, boasted a fenced enclosure with thick grass and three thick-trunked oaks with huge, abundant foliage. Several horses dozed in the shade created by those giant leaves, their tails twitching idly.

Small statues of rearing horses, dancing children with jugs in hand, and howling asp-jacaus dotted the central area. Water poured from each statue into a stone trough, which ran for several feet before turning into an underground pipe.

"Incredible," she breathed.

"Aerthraim engineering," Chac said, sounding smug. "Wait until you see inside."

Grooms trotted towards them, smiling cheerfully; one rattled off a question: "*Ka-s'eias, ahaki t'ass ekita? Pahaki t'ess?*"

"I'm sorry," Alyea said, "I don't. . . . "

"*T'ass, s'eias, essata; keyassa natoya su-s'a Peysimun,*" Chac said. "Let them take your horse, Alyea."

Feeling suddenly lost, Alyea let the nearest groom lead her horse away. "What did they say?"

"They asked if we were staying at the enclave or just stabling the horses for a while," Chac said. "I told them we were staying, and gave him your family name so they can bring the baggage to our rooms."

"What's *ka-s'eias*?" Alyea said. "I haven't heard it that way before. *S'eias* is a mixed group of people; what does the *ka* make it?"

"It's unique to the deep southlands," Chac said. "Means they're not sure of our exact status, but know we're not commoners and want to offer proper respect. 'Honored' is probably the closest translation. Now that they know you're a northern noble, you'll find everyone calling you *su-s'a*: northern lady."

"What are they going to call you?" Alyea asked, with a touch of mischief.

Chac's expression went remote. "Chacerly."

"What, no term of respect?" Alyea teased, and immediately regretted it. Chac didn't even look at her. His expression changed from remote to stony.

"No," he said curtly, and started towards the enclave building.

Alyea hesitated before following him. She couldn't imagine what the old man could have done to lose even the most basic term of courtesy before his name, especially in the deep south where respect counted for everything. Deiq's words came back to her: *the men you ride with aren't the ones to trust . . . they watch you with the care of men that serve two masters.*

For the first time, Alyea wondered if she and Oruen were the ones Chacerly served.

Chac reached the door to the enclave and went inside without even looking behind to see if she followed. She put her suspicious thoughts aside for the moment and hurried to catch up.

Considerably nicer than the last way-stop, this room held a single bed and a lower cot for a servant to sleep on. Halla looked around the room, seeming uncertain, and sat on the cot with a lost expression.

"What's the matter?" Alyea asked, dropping her pack on her own bed and sitting next to it.

"I don't know where to go," Halla said. "I've been asking and asking after my son along the trail, and nobody knows anything."

Alyea thought about Chac's lessons on southern custom, sighed, and said, "Halla, I have to explain something to you."

She sketched out the obligation concept as clearly as she could. The northern woman looked steadily more baffled.

"I have to pay for someone to tell me where my son is?" she demanded at last.

"Well, not with coin, and no--" She forestalled the woman's gathering indignation. "Nothing to do with sex. You don't have to sell yourself. But you have to have something to give in order to get any information about your son."

"So the people I asked could have been lying?" Halla looked perplexed. "Why would anyone lie to a mother looking for her son?"

"It's nothing personal," Alyea said. "That's just the custom here. I'm having to learn it myself; Bright Bay isn't like that."

Halla sat brooding, frown gathering deeper, and finally said, "No offense, my lady, but your southern world is madness."

"Just different from your customs," Alyea said. "That's all."

"No," Halla said, shaking her head. "Any place where people could lie to a mother seeking her son is completely mad."

"They may not have lied," Alyea said. "They honestly might not have known. Don't think the worst until you have to."

"I have nothing to offer," the northern woman said.

She looked so miserable Alyea couldn't help crossing to sit beside her. She put a hand on Halla's shoulder. "Chac told me there's an old saying: sooner or later, everything comes through Water's End. We'll find word of your son here. I'm sure of it. And don't forget, you have some status by being my servant. Don't be afraid to use my name; it might tip the balance."

"But won't that put you in debt?" Halla asked dubiously.

"Maybe," Alyea said lightly, "but I'm sure I can afford it. Go on, go ask around." She gave the woman a few small coins. "Buy me one of those wonderful red silk tunics I've seen people wearing around here."

Not that she wanted the tunic, but the errand would give Halla a reason to be out on the streets talking to vendors; the northern woman's nod held instant understanding. "It may take me some time," Halla said, testing, and Alyea nodded.

"Take as much time as you like," she said, smiling.

"Thank you, my lady," Halla said with deep sincerity, and hurried out the door without a backwards glance.

Still smiling, Alyea crossed to the window and watched: the northern woman emerged into the street and headed for the market with eyes modestly lowered and a stride that held nothing but purpose. People moved out of her way, as they did for the desert lords, without really looking; then seemed oddly perplexed, glancing back over their shoulders at the northern woman.

Behind her, Chac coughed, alerting her to his presence; she half-turned and motioned for him to join her at the window.

"It's a busier place than I expected," she said when he stood beside her.

"It's the heart of the southlands," he said, frowning down at the street. He seemed less than pleased about something. "Where's your maid?"

"I sent her on an errand."

"Alone? Are you mad?" He stared at her.

She shook her head, remembering how people had moved out of Halla's path. "She'll be fine, Chac."

"This isn't Bright Bay, damn it," he said, unaccountably upset, and went to the door. She heard him speaking with one of the guards in a low voice; he returned to her side a few moments later, his frown eased only slightly. "They'll find her. Don't *ever* send her out without an escort to protect her. Don't try walking alone, yourself, not here. It's not safe. You don't have the status for it just yet. Gods know I've been trying, but it's not taking hold."

She turned her head to look at him. "What do you mean, you've been trying? What have you been doing?"

"While you've been chatting along the way with Deiq," he said tartly, "I've been trying to arrange alliances to keep you safe on the road and get us to Scratha Fortress. So has Micru. It's not been going well at all. We haven't received a single invitation to visit any Family yet. That's bad, Alyea, that's very bad. Past Water's End, your only source of water and food is the fortresses. You don't just show up at the gates and bang on the door to say hello. You need an invitation. And we don't have one. Not one."

"Why didn't you tell me this?" she demanded. "I could have—"

"You don't know *how,*" he cut her off. "If Deiq hadn't taken an interest in you, I would have introduced you round each dinner and maybe had better luck; but all they saw was you sitting with *him*, and they wanted no part of that. He's not trusted much, south to north, commoner or noble."

"You could have said," she complained.

"I *did* tell you to get rid of him," Chac reminded her impatiently.

She grimaced, wondering if Deiq had understood the impact his attentions would have; if it had been calculated. *I can get you to Scratha Fortress safely,* he'd said, and promised help if she asked for it.

"Damn it," she said aloud.

"Yes." Chac seemed about to say something else, but then his attention drew sharply to the street again; she leaned, looking to see what had caught his eye.

Gria and her mother stumbled by below, wrists weighed down with heavy chains and cuffs. The guards in the party walked very close to the women, and Alyea could make out a dark bruise on the older woman's face. Sela seemed to be halfway between shock and apoplectic rage; her daughter's expression alternated between blank and frightened. The machago Ierie, cheerful and smug, sauntered down the street in front of the small procession.

Alyea felt her chest tighten at the sight. "It isn't fair. It isn't right. They believed him; that's their only crime."

"I doubt it," Chac said. "Do you really think a machago would make the long trip just for one pair of northern women? They upset someone powerful enough to pay a slave-trader to come all the way past the Horn and steal them away to a place they'd never escape."

Alyea stared down at the street, hardly seeing the crowds now. The slave trader's party had passed out of sight now, around a corner.

"Deiq knew," she said under her breath.

"What?" Chac's attention sharpened on her. He scowled.

"He said he knew what was going on with them," Alyea said. "But he didn't tell me. I didn't ask," she added to the fierce glare the old man directed at her.

"Good," Chac said. "At least you did *that* right." He rubbed his temples. "I have to go make some arrangements. I'll be back soon. Stay here; for the love of the gods, *don't* go out there until I've secured *something* for an alliance." He walked out without looking back.

She sighed and went back to staring out the window.

Not long afterwards, a firm knock rattled the thin door behind her. She crossed the room and opened the door with her expressionless public face firmly in place, and held to it with all her might a moment later as machago Ierie grinned at her unpleasantly.

"Lady Alyea," he said. "A present for you."

Behind him, the two northern women glared at Alyea as if they held her responsible for the situation. Four guards loomed behind, their attention completely on the slaves, ready to grab them if they tried to bolt.

The bruise on Sela's face, at close range, looked very dark, and very large.

"A *present?*" she said sharply.

"From *nu-s'e* Deiq," the man said. "He has purchased these women and wishes me to give them into your care."

"When did this happen?" she demanded.

"My lady," Ierie said, unruffled, "the hallway is not the best place to hold this discussion."

"You certainly aren't entering my room!" she said before thinking.

He shrugged. "Do you accept this gift or not, Lady Alyea?"

It had been sensible, before, to stay out of the troubles of the northern women. It would be beyond madness, now, to refuse the gift; another kind of madness to accept. She'd made herself an easy target for whatever game Deiq had set up. He'd guessed her sympathy for the northern women, and now she owed him a debt beyond paying, whatever phrasing the machago used to hide it.

If this was a gift, she was an asp-jacau.

"Yes," she said at last.

Smirking, Ierie produced a leather document case and handed it to her. "Your paperwork, my lady. You are now wholly responsible for these *mac'egas;* the mark on their bands is registered with the Water's End *hayrar* under your name. If they attempt to leave Water's End, by any road, while not in your presence, they will be stopped and returned to you."

Alyea felt her stomach curdling from the intensity of Sela's stare.

Ierie stepped aside and motioned for the two women to advance. Alyea opened the door wider and moved out of the way as the northerns, prompted by an ungentle shove from the guards behind them, stumbled into her room.

"The cuffs," Ierie said, "do not come off. They will be slaves, south to north, for the rest of their lives. I recommend you do not try to take them back into the northlands, but that is your choice entirely. Good day, my lady."

He turned and sauntered away, his guards following.

"Gods," Alyea said under her breath, and closed the door. She stood staring at the plain, scarred wood for a few breaths, gathering strength and sorting her thoughts, before turning to look at her new slaves.

"You tried to warn us," Gria said miserably.

"How convenient," her mother snapped. "And now you *own* us, do you? Let me tell you, I don't accept it! I want this cuff off and I intend to bring charges in front of King Oruen!" She brandished her arm at Alyea, as if intending to use the heavy metal cuff as a weapon.

"He said they don't come off," Gria said.

"Nonsense. That was just to scare us. We'll be free of this mistake soon." She fixed Alyea with a stern glare. "Won't we, *my lady*?"

Alyea drew a deep breath and sank into a chair. "No," she said. "I'm afraid not."

Chacerly examined the proffered hand soberly. He shook his head after a moment of tapping and poking at the band, and looked up at Alyea. He'd been furious on finding the two northern women in Alyea's room, but that anger seemed to have vanished now, replaced with a deep concern.

"I haven't seen this in years. I thought it was a lost art."

"Art?" Sela said bitterly.

Chac sat back on his heels and looked up at her, then stood.

"It is an art," he said. "What it's used for may not be. Look—see that silver twisting through the metal?" He pointed to a fine network of shining lines woven through the duller metal of the slave cuff. "That's called *ugren*. It's a rare alloy. There's nothing I know of that cuts or melts it, once it's hardened and set. And as it's contacting your skin, it's likely bonded to that as well. Attempting to remove the cuffs could rip your flesh right down to the bone beneath."

Sela stared, her face bone-white. Gria moaned softly, looking ill.

"It's not a common slave cuff," Chac said harshly. "Whoever hired

Ierie to come get you wanted to be damn sure you'd never be considered free again, north to south."

Alyea put a hand over her mouth.

"Oh, it gets worse," Chac said, turning a fierce glare on Alyea. "Far as I know, only ones who know how to put on an ugren cuff without killing the slave are the teyanain. And when *they* get involved, *everything* goes to all the hells. On top of it all, you said *Deiq* bought these women, and presented them to you as a gift?" He shook his head, lips tight. "What a damn mess. Did you ask him to get involved?"

"*No*," Alyea said as strongly as she could without shouting. "Not even a hint."

Chac studied the northern women for a moment, seeming to consider something, then looked back at Alyea. His expression had acquired a chilly, frightening detachment. "You have two options," he said. "The first one is to find out who they were going to be sold to originally, and send them on to him as a gift."

Alyea shook her head. "I won't do that. "

"Then you have to kill them," he said.

She stared at him, shocked. Sela whimpered. Gria shivered, huddling closer to her mother.

"They're dangerous by their very presence," he said. "You're under a debt while they're in your service. You're involving yourself in political games you know nothing about if you keep them alive, and it could destroy you. What you're doing is more important than two northern women. Let me--"

"If you lay one hand on them, Chacerly," Alyea said with measured chill, "I will see you stripped and sent into the deep sands to die."

They matched glares for a long, silent moment.

"It's safer to be rid of them," he said. "You don't know what you're doing."

"I don't believe in killing innocents to save myself some trouble," she said. "And they're legally mine. Not yours. I make the decision on this."

"You're letting emotion drive you," Chacerly said. "Not reality."

"I said *no*."

His lip curled for a moment, then he shrugged and said, "As you will, my lady. I'd advise asking them some very hard questions, if you're still listening to anything I have to say."

"You're my advisor, Chac," Alyea said, trying to lighten her tone. "I always listen. I just make my own decisions about your advice."

"Talk to them, then," he said. "Find out what's going on before it catches up to you. I'd offer to help but I doubt you'd care for my methods."

He turned and left the room without another word, shooting the northerns one final dark, misgiving glance as he passed. Alyea sighed and let herself fold into a chair. Before anyone could speak, Halla burst into the room, beaming. Her smile faded as she took in the two women sitting on Alyea's bed.

"What—" she started, a frown beginning to form.

"I'll explain later," Alyea said, and made a peremptory gesture for the northerns to be silent. "What is it?"

Halla studied the women for another moment, her forehead furrowed in concern. "Perhaps this isn't a good time?"

"It's as good a time as any other," Alyea said. "Out with it."

"Well, it's like this," Halla said uncertainly. "I . . . I think I've had word of my son."

"That's good," Alyea said, unable to summon up more energy for enthusiasm. "What did you hear?"

"I was . . . I went to the washing square . . . and spoke to the other women there. And men! They have men doing the washing here, my lady."

Alyea's smile felt more genuine now. "And someone there told you about your son?"

"Well, I said I was looking," Halla said. She seemed to have forgotten the two sullen northern women. "I told my story, and explained how I was working for you while I searched for my son. One of the women said she'd seen a northern boy locally, one with a light slave cuff on; she said that means he was working off a small debt or something minor, and would be free to go once that was up. She didn't know his name, but gave me a description and an address."

"Go find out, then," Alyea said. "What are you waiting for?"

Halla hesitated again, twisting her hands together nervously. "Well, my lady, I'm fairly sure it's my son; the description fits, right down to the mole on his cheek. It's just . . . the man he's working for . . . she said it was Deiq."

Alyea shut her eyes and muttered, "Why am I not surprised?"

She stood and crossed the room to the small desk. As she'd expected, she found writing supplies inside; she pulled them out and swiftly wrote a brief note, blotted it, and rolled it up. At a loss for a seal, she spotted several lengths of ribbon in the drawer and used one to tie the parchment roll securely. The other three women watched her with varying degrees of silent bewilderment.

Alyea handed Halla the note and said, "Take this to the local judge, the *hayrar*. It's an affidavit that Peysimun Family will be personally liable for whatever debt or service your son has incurred, and to release him into your care immediately. Make them write you a note transferring the liability and take it to the place your son is staying. I'm sure he'll know who to present the release to."

Halla held the note as if it were the most precious thing she'd ever seen.

"Thank you, my lady," she whispered, her eyes filling with tears.

"Go on," Alyea said, and the woman almost ran from the room.

"Does this Deiq make a practice of holding slaves?" Sela demanded before the door had fully shut behind Halla. "I thought it illegal!"

"In the kingdom, it is; but we're all far from home, Sela. And before you launch another tirade, keep in mind that I *did* try to warn you!"

"And what could we have done?" Sela cried. "Run, and be captured? Or run, and find out you were lying, and disgrace ourselves beyond hope? What else was there to do?"

Alyea sighed. "Why would anyone want to enslave you in the first place?"

"How should I know?" Sela snapped.

"It cost someone a lot of time and money to bring both of you down here and put those cuffs on your arms. Why are you so important?"

"You'd know more about southern reasoning than I would," Sela said nastily.

Alyea rubbed her temples, trying to ease the beginnings of a monstrous headache, and murmured to herself, "I can see this is going to be a long night."

Chapter Eleven

The building that rose before them measured no larger than any other in the village, and hardly seemed as opulent as the palace in Bright Bay. It did, however, have carefully trimmed hedges, neatly shaped rosebushes, a paved courtyard, a small stable to one side, and two armed guards at the plain wooden door.

The guards watched them approach without a flicker of emotion crossing their broad faces. Idisio felt a chill crawling along his spine as he came closer. He'd seen eyes like that before—in men who killed for coin.

Scratha seemed undisturbed by the cold stare of the guards. He strode up to them as arrogant and assured as he'd ever been in the King's Palace and stopped just out of their reach.

"We're here to see Yuer," he announced.

"Yeah, we figured that," one of the guards said, surveying the three visitors with a dark squint. "Either that or you want to sell the girl, and she don't look whipped enough for that."

"Yuer," Scratha repeated coldly.

"Yeah, go on in. He said you'd be here tonight."

Scratha checked mid-stride and turned a hard stare on the guard. "Excuse me?"

"You're expected," the guard clarified, and jerked a thumb at the door. "Go on in already. Unless you've changed your mind about the girl?" He leered at Riss. She shrank back.

"No," Scratha said, and pushed the door open. He strode in without looking back. Idisio and Riss almost tripped over each other crowding in behind him.

The small room beyond held little more than a comfortably smoldering fireplace and four low, wide chairs set around a short-legged round table. Idisio rocked to a stop and stared in unabashed fascination at the man in the chair facing them.

There was a lot to stare at: skin like a bleached hide pulled too tight over prominent bones and a face filled with a mass of drooping wrinkles, as if all the spare skin had somehow migrated there. Wispy, dark hair scraggled along a pale scalp. The man smoothed his long-fingered, almost skeletal hands repeatedly over a thick, dark red lap-blanket, although Idisio found the room uncomfortably warm.

Bright dark eyes stared back at Idisio, and the man's thin mouth twisted into a wide grin.

"Please, come sit," the man said in an astonishingly clear bass. The sound of that rich tone coming from the frail, wrinkled form made Idisio's jaw drop again. "Hot tea?" He leaned forward and lifted the ceramic teapot, tilting it to fill three small cups with a rich, steaming amber liquid. The scent of cloves and cinnamon filled the room.

Scratha didn't move. "You expected us."

"Of course. And I must say it's lovely to see you again, my *lord*." He arranged each of the small cups a little distance apart from each other, choosing each spot with careful precision, then looked up at them. "Oh, do sit down. I get a twist in my neck so easily these days."

"I thought you'd gone further north," Scratha said.

"Oh, it's far too cold up north," the man said. "Speaking of which, the tea is getting cold." He blinked at them with a lizard-bright sparkle in his eyes. "Won't you sit and have tea with me?"

Scratha drew in a long breath, let it out through his teeth, and slowly sat in a chair, motioning Idisio and Riss to follow suit. Idisio sat down gingerly and reached for a small cup of tea without really thinking about it. He passed one to Riss and the last to Scratha, uncomfortably aware that the wrinkled man seemed to be watching him attentively.

"Idisio, Riss," Scratha said, "this is Yuer."

"Ah," Yuer said, reprovingly. "You didn't introduce me properly, my lord. It should have been *ferahd* Yuer, son of Lord Regav Darden and *dista* Atha; you'd say *bastard son of a whore,* I think, in the northern tongue."

Scratha's face tightened. "I saw no need to introduce that."

"I'm not ashamed of it," Yuer said. "I can hardly claim to control my birth, can I? And my mother was a favorite of Lord Regav's until his unfortunate meeting with that Aerthraim bitch."

Scratha's face settled into a dark frown. "Yuer, don't bait me."

"Still fond of dear old Azni, are you? Well, spare me a moment of fun," Yuer said. "I have so little of it these days."

Scratha shook his head and didn't answer.

"And you think you have no time for my foolishness," Yuer said.

"Well." He sipped at his tea, his gaze shifting among them. "Perhaps you don't, at that. But time is an odd thing, isn't it? I recall you saying once that if you never spoke to me again in this lifetime it would be too soon."

"You've said the same of me," Scratha said. "And I've said many things over the years, some of which should have been left silent."

Yuer made a faint coughing noise, almost but not quite a sniggering laugh. "Now you admit mistakes? Could these children have made such a difference? Could you have possibly have grown . . . *attached* to them?" His eyes glittered. A chill ran down Idisio's back at the tensions rising in the air.

"Stop it," Scratha said, his stare as flat and dangerous as a snake's. "That's enough, Yuer. This is today. If all you're going to do is rake through the past, I'll leave, and then I'll send my report to Lord Oruen. He'll take great joy in hanging you one piece at a time from each of the Gates."

In the silence, the sound of rain came pattering gently against the window shutters. Idisio stifled an impulse to bolt from the room.

"Ah," Yuer said at last, his voice soft. "You do have a compelling argument there. I am fond of my skin remaining intact, such as it is." He poured himself more tea and sipped thoughtfully for a few moments.

Idisio glanced at Riss. She slouched back in her chair, both hands curled round the small cup, looking deeply unhappy.

"Politics are never simple," Yuer said at last. "And they reach into the past further than any of us have been alive, and will echo into the future far beyond our children's lives."

"Politics or profit?" Scratha said.

Yuer smiled briefly. "Politics is all about profit on some level, whether that be coin or other gain; successful profit involves understanding politics. You worry over a few pounds of dasta and esthit and redweed moving south to north, untaxed, illegal. In your mind, it is all wreaking horrible havoc in all lives involved. But it's such a small, small piece of the overall politics that it's hardly worth noticing . . . unless, of course, current politics move attention to that tiny piece." He sighed.

"Dasta is illegal in the northlands," Scratha said. "The Church bans it, and Lord Oruen has backed that ban."

Yuer grinned and shook his head. "A knife is not evil. The hand that holds it can use it to cut bread or cut throats. Look to the hand, not the knife."

"I'm looking for the ones who seek out assassins to sell their knives to."

"Why?" Yuer asked, still smiling. "You're no King's Guard or secret enforcer. Why would you worry over the nonsense of the northlands?"

"I want to know how it gets through the Horn," Scratha said. "If Darden has corrupted the teyanain, that's valid desert business."

"Corrupted?" Yuer's smile broadened. "The teyanain are incorruptible."

"Then how can they let your carriers move through the Horn?" Scratha said, leaning forward and putting his cup on the table with a hard click. "There's a two-hundred-year-old agreement on that!"

"Agreements change," Yuer said. "Initin the Red was a wise man, a good leader, but he couldn't predict that when he died, his chosen successor would refuse the throne and turn control of the kingdom to a minor branch of the royal family."

"What?" Scratha sat up straight, scowling. "You don't believe that old nonsense, Yuer. It's never been anything but a madman's rumor."

"Madness for madness," Yuer said mildly. He poured himself another cup, shook the pot gently, and set it back down. "I'll have a servant make more."

"I want you to explain how you can give any credence to that mad story."

"Because I know the name of his chosen successor," Yuer said. "And because the families of Mezarak, Ninnic, and the other mad kings had never shown any evidence of instability before taking the throne. Their madness came from a curse laid on the line for forsaking the proper order of things."

"Who?" Scratha demanded.

"You won't believe me." Yuer smiled. "You'll call me a liar and a fool."

A faint noise brought Idisio's attention to Riss. She'd begun drowsing in her chair, empty teacup held loosely in her hand. The rain must have put her to sleep; Idisio had to fight the urge to let his own eyelids slide closed.

"Say it and let me judge," Scratha said.

"Ienna Aerthraim," Yuer said. "Mother to Asoana Aerthraim, who gave birth to Osenna Aerthraim, who gave birth to Aziarna Aerthraim, who gave birth to your darling Azaniari Aerthraim. They run a matrilineal heritage, like Scratha does."

Idisio found himself blinking rapidly. The list of names had been so similar in sound—a standard complaint by northerns about the desert Families—that he'd completely lost track. But it *sounded* as though Lady Azni, who had been so kind to him and given him that miraculous salve, should have been in line for the throne in Bright Bay.

What a different world he would have grown up in if that had come true!

Scratha shook his head slowly. "How did you come to find that out?"

"The teyanain keep records of everything," Yuer said. "They have books going back to before the Split. Every king had a teyanin attend his court as a record-keeper since the beginning of the kingdom; that is, up until Ienna refused her calling. After that the kings refused to allow a teyanin the post of record-keeper, and as a result the royal line bears a curse."

Riss snored softly. Yuer glanced at her and smiled.

"That's not possible," Scratha said. "I would have—"

"No," Yuer said. "You wouldn't have known. Even your beloved Azaniari probably doesn't know. Ienna wanted no part of a throne; she wouldn't have told her descendants. The Aerthraim have never accepted a public office that would bring them notice. Ienna passed the throne to one of her lovers."

"I don't believe any Aerthraim would dishonor her family that way," Scratha said, and stood, expression grim. "If all you have to go on are slanderous falsehoods, I'm through listening."

"I did say you'd call me a liar," Yuer noted, looking amused. "But I've been through the records of every desert fortress that would let me in, and a few that didn't know of my presence, before I was *encouraged* to leave the southlands. On my way through the Horn I gained access to the books of the teyanain. There's no argument with the facts!"

"How did you get into the books of the teyanain?" Scratha demanded.

"I rendered them an indispensable service," Yuer said, and his grin turned unpleasant. "You don't need that story. I think this is more important right now."

"Go on," Scratha growled, settling back into his chair.

Yuer glanced at Riss, then at Idisio. A faint frown passed across his wrinkled face, barely noticeable. "First, more tea."

A gesture brought a quiet servant into the room with a second teapot, almost identical to the first, and four fresh cups. After tea had been poured and the tiny cups taken in hand, Yuer said, "Those books I studied . . . each of them from a different point of view, each of them with a tiny piece of the overall truth. I doubt too many people have seen as many of them as I have, to see such a complete picture."

"You flatter yourself," Scratha said, frowning over his tea. "You're no wise scholar, Yuer."

"Not when you last knew me," Yuer shot back, "but people do change, don't they? I think I could name a few myself, and I know you can." His gaze moved, rather speculatively, to Idisio for a moment.

Scratha snorted and shook his head, but sipped his tea and made no other argument. "Go on with the story."

"It's interesting," Yuer said, leaning forward a little, his eyes narrowing, "that this boy is still awake. I'd expected *you* to be awake, not him."

The room suddenly seemed very quiet, and very warm. The soft rain outside faded to an occasional *plink*. Idisio stared at his tea in horrified understanding.

"You tried to drug us?" he squeaked, and bit his lip at the cracked, whiny sound of the words.

"It's always been one of Yuer's favorite games," Scratha said dryly. He took another sip of tea, his dark stare fixed on the wrinkled old man. "I'm surprised, myself, that you're still awake."

Idisio stared at his master, appalled and feeling rather betrayed. "You *knew?*"

"I expected it," Scratha said, not looking away from Yuer. "The question is why he'd risk it."

Yuer smiled. "I knew I'd at least slow down your servants," he said. "With them asleep, you'd be less likely to run before Pieas gets here."

Scratha sat up straighter. His scowl made Idisio cringe into his chair reflexively, even though he knew he wasn't the target.

"Pieas!" Scratha said; the name came out as a dire curse.

Yuer smirked. "Yes. I received a bird-messenger this morning that he was on your trail and to hold you against his coming."

Scratha snorted. "You think I would have *run* from that little *ta-karne*? He's been all but disowned by his own family, he's on the run in disgrace, and he's got a blood-right call on his head. I certainly wouldn't hesitate to kill him, in or out of your home, Yuer."

Moving with exaggerated care, he pulled several sheets of parchment from his pouch and tossed them on the table.

"Read it!" he said. "A message from the king's own hand, telling about Pieas's disgrace."

Yuer grabbed the folded papers. His dark eyes scanned the close-set lines of writing rapidly: page after page, four in all. He read through them again, more slowly, then looked up at Scratha.

"Pages are missing," he said.

"The others held no relevance to you."

Yuer looked down at the pages, shaking his head slowly as he settled back in his chair.

"Disgraced," he mused, rattling the parchment. "That changes . . . quite a bit."

"I won't hold the mistake against you," Scratha said, baring his teeth in a thin, humorless smile. "We all make mistakes, after all. Even you."

"Apparently so," Yuer murmured, his gaze distant. "It seems I have some talking to do with Pieas when he arrives—which ought to be soon."

"Even disgraced," Scratha said, "he's still the child of a powerful desert family. I'd advise against killing him yourself. There's enough other people after him for that."

"Oh, I'm not too concerned over killing him," Yuer said, and his expression sent a shiver down Idisio's back. "I've other methods for expressing how upset I am with him. And other reasons besides this incident."

A faint rattling sound, like feet scraping against gravel, came clearly from outside. One of the guards opened the door and looked in, his broad face furrowed in a frown.

"Man running," he said briefly. "Got by us, think he was listening. Follow?"

Yuer sat up, his face flushing with instant rage. "He was *eavesdrop-*

ping? On *me?* He *dared?* Yes, gods damn you, bring him to me!"

The door clacked shut as the guard sprinted away. Scratha and Idisio both leapt to their feet and headed for the door. Idisio checked just shy of the threshold, turning a worried glance back to Riss, who still drowsed peacefully in the chair. Yuer flapped a thin hand at him impatiently, the gesture serving as reassurance and imperious command all at once; Idisio nodded and bolted after Scratha.

Just as they reached the main village road, the light haze of mist condensed into a heavy, thundering downpour. Idisio's foot hit a mud slick; he went down hard and spat mud along with curses while rolling clumsily upright. A hard hand caught in his armpit and yanked him the rest of the way to his feet.

"Let the guards get themselves soaking wet searching like fools," Scratha said in Idisio's ear. "Stables, Idisio. He'll have to get back to his horse to run anywhere in this weather."

Idisio slogged after Scratha as fast as he could; whatever had been in that tea seemed to be affecting him at last. His legs seemed filled with sand and his body worked sluggishly; he fell behind despite his best efforts, and Scratha disappeared into the downpour ahead.

Unable to move another step, Idisio stopped, panting. Not far ahead, a woman screamed; the sound jolted him back into motion. A handful of steps later, a thudding sound barely gave him time to fling himself out of the way as a large black horse thundered by, rider crouched low on its back.

"Looks like he got away," Idisio muttered, picking himself up off the ground for the second time, and trudged, in no hurry at all now, towards the stables.

Scratha stood in the center aisle of the stable, his expression bleak as the weather and three deep scratches threading blood trails down one cheek. He glared at a woman who crouched, weeping, at his feet.

"Get up already," Scratha snapped.

She raised a shaking arm over her head and cowered, as if expecting to be struck. Idisio, unable to help himself, moved forward and crouched beside her. He could feel Scratha's hard glare on the back of his neck.

A splotch of damp mud slid off his head as he leaned forward; it splatted on the floor right next to the girl. She flinched further into herself and whimpered.

"*S'a*?" he said tentatively.

Her thin, bruised face tilted up towards him, revealing wide, wild eyes and a desperate stare.

"Don't let him hurt me," she whimpered. "Don't let him—"

"He won't hurt you, *s'a*," Idisio said. The pattern of bruises and cuts on her face and arms warned him against trying to touch her right now. Overhead, Scratha breathed heavily. His looming, intimidating presence filled the air with an almost palpable anger.

Idisio risked saying, "Master Scratha, could you . . . back up a step, please? Maybe a few steps?"

Scratha growled but moved back two long steps. "He threw her at me. The little *ta-karne threw* her at me." He touched the ripped stripes on his cheek gingerly. "*Damn* you," he added.

"He hit me," the woman whimpered, quivering. "Don't let him hit me again."

"She clawed my face," Scratha said unsympathetically, glowering.

"He won't hit you again," Idisio reassured the woman. "I promise. I won't let him."

"Then she'd best not claw at me again," Scratha retorted. "Get up, get *up*, woman! What in the hells are you doing here? Who are you? Why did Pieas leave you behind?"

"Wian. I'm Wian. I'm Lady Alyea's . . . I was. . . ." The woman shuddered and shook, crying again, and refused to say anything else.

"I think she's best off resting to calm down," Idisio said, looking up at Scratha. "And having a healer look at these cuts. Some of them look infected."

"Hells," Scratha said. "All right. Let's get her back to Yuer's."

The woman looked up sharply, her face turning a stark white. A moment later, her eyes rolled back in her head and she slumped in a thoroughly unfeigned faint to the dirty stable floor.

Scratha blew out a hard breath, then crouched and gathered the limp form into his arms. He stood with as little effort as if he'd picked up a sack of feathers. Which might not, Idisio admitted to himself, be far off; the rips in Wian's dress showed a gaunt form barely above starvation.

"Maybe we shouldn't take her back there," Idisio objected. "She seemed upset when you said Yuer's name."

"All the more reason," Scratha said. "Time to find out what in the hells is going on here."

That plan proved fruitless. Seeing the limp girl in Scratha's arms, Yuer summoned servants to take her away and dismissed his guests with unmistakable finality. Idisio shook Riss awake; muzzy and confused, she followed them tamely out the door and back to the inn. By the time Idisio finished cleaning himself up and changed into dry clothes, Riss had recovered enough to know she'd missed something important. Idisio filled her in while Scratha went to bathe.

"He *what?*" she said several times, each one more incredulous and furious than the last. As Idisio finished the account and Riss drew breath for an obvious tirade, Scratha returned.

"He *drugged* me!" Riss began, just as the desert lord stepped back into the room. "I'm going to—"

"You'll do nothing," Scratha cut in. He shut the door behind him and regarded her soberly. "You weren't harmed. Let it go, Riss."

"How could you have left that girl with him?" she demanded, turning her anger on Scratha. "How could you trust him like that?"

"Yuer always goes with his highest profit," Scratha said. "From his reaction, he wants the girl alive. He'll get her back on her feet sooner than any of the village healers could. He *was* a promising ketarch student, at one time. He knows a lot about medicines."

"And drugs," Riss said bitterly, unappeased.

Scratha shrugged. "I never said he's a nice person, Riss, or trustworthy. But the welfare of a strange girl Pieas dragged along, probably for his amusement on the road, isn't my concern. At this point, even finding Pieas isn't all that interesting to me. He's useless. He *ran*. Whether he went north or south, he's finished. He'll never be anyone important now. Nobody would touch him as an ally, after such a show of cowardice. And he's offended Yuer, which is as good as a death sentence in itself. No. Let him go. I've other business to attend to, more important issues to consider."

"Like what?" Riss demanded, still scowling. "You can't just leave her behind!"

"Of course I can," Scratha said sharply. "If *you* want to stay with her, feel free. I'm sure she'd appreciate a friendly escort back to Bright Bay. Or take some coin and be on your way alone. The same applies to you, Idisio," he added. "I won't need a servant much longer. I'm going back south."

They stared at Scratha in shared disbelief.

"But . . . you were told . . . you promised," Idisio stammered idiotically.

"Back *south*?" Riss said, suspicion and anxiety mingling in her expression.

"I humored the king with this nonsense assignment," Scratha said. "I wanted to see what he'd do, given the chance at a desert holding; now I know." His expression darkened. "He explained in his letter what's been happening, and I can't believe he's fool enough to think I'd stand for it. He's making a hash of everything. I'm going home, and taking my lands back, and he can squeal all he wants from Bright Bay. There's nothing for me past the Horn anymore."

Riss put a hand over her mouth, eyes wide. "Chance at a desert *holding*?" she said, the words almost inaudible behind her palm. "The *king*?"

"But the king," Idisio protested.

"Has no true authority over me," Scratha said. "Desert business comes first."

"You're a *desert lord*?" Riss breathed, her face starkly pale. She twisted her hands together. "I beg pardon, my lord—"

"For what? You're done nothing wrong, Riss."

"I've argued . . . been disrespectful. . . ."

"You thought me nothing more than some idiot noble on a fool's errand," Scratha said brusquely. "Let be. I'm not angry." He pulled the money pouch from his bags and tossed it on the table. "Split what's left and go your own ways. I don't need servants in the southlands."

Idisio didn't hesitate. "No. I want to stay with you."

Scratha frowned at the refusal, then cocked an eyebrow at the latter statement as though surprised. "Why?"

"Oh, Master, just the other day, you said you couldn't do without me," Idisio said, deliberately calling to mind his initial ploy in front of the king. Scratha's mouth twitched; clearly he recognized the reference.

"Mmph," he said. "I said I'm getting used to having you around. Fine. I'll take you, if you insist. But Riss—"

"I stay too," Riss said, rather unexpectedly, and wouldn't look at either of them. "I can't very well go home again. And traveling alone isn't a good idea for a woman, whatever money you give me. I'd rather stay with . . . in good company." She colored a little. "My lord. If you permit."

Scratha cast a shrewd glance at Idisio and smiled. "Very well. Get some rest, then. It's a long ride to Sandlaen Port, and I want to leave early."

Chapter Twelve

"I told you," Sela said, "I don't know!"

Alyea sighed. Brief though her aqeyva training had been, she'd learned to read people fairly well; and one of these two, if not both, knew something they weren't admitting. She'd tried every way she knew to charm the women into trusting her, but even Gria now regarded her with open hostility.

She stood and crossed to the door, leaning out to speak to the guard. "Send for Micru," she said, then withdrew into the room again.

"So you're going to torture us?" Sela said, her expression bitter and her voice shrill with tension. "See the kindness of the southern lady, Gria?"

"Why do you think that?" Alyea asked.

"I've seen that look before," Sela said, tossing her head. "I know your kind, my *lady*. Start out kind and turn to whips when you don't get what you want." She spat on the floor.

"*Gods*, you're an idiot," Alyea said, and turned her back on the woman.

A light tap sounded at the door; Micru slipped into the room, his flat, dark stare taking in the entire room in one professionally quick sweep. "My lady?"

"Do you know who these women are, Micru?" she asked.

He surveyed them for a long, silent moment, considering. "I know *what* they are."

Sela stared at Micru as if beginning to feel fear for the first time.

"Slaves," she said, in an attempt at scorn. "That's obvious enough."

"*Ugren* slaves," Micru said, and settled into a chair. He studied the women, one knuckle resting against his mouth. "Northerners. Quasi-nobles. And fools, beyond a doubt."

They stared at him warily.

"Fools," Micru said, his tone eerily, almost hypnotically, flat. "Fools who thought they could buy their way into a place beyond money."

"I wasn't interested in going south!" Gria shrilled suddenly. "She *made* me! She's the one after money!"

Sela moved, snake-fast, and slapped her daughter hard.

"Be quiet!" she snarled.

Micru smiled. He crossed to the door; opening it, he told the guards, "Remove the older one. Stay with her in another room."

"No!" Sela shrieked, bracing herself in front of her daughter. Alyea forced herself not to react as two guards wrestled the woman out of the room.

Micru shut the door again.

"Now that your mother isn't here," he said as he settled back into his chair, "tell us what you know, girl. It may save both your lives."

His tone held an offering of hope, not a threat, as though he truly sympathized with the girl and wanted to help her. Astonished, Alyea watched Gria crumble.

"She's not my mother," the girl said. Her gaze stayed fixed on a point somewhere past Alyea's left knee. "Don't hurt her. I'm the one they want."

The words threw all the possibilities Alyea had considered into chaos. She opened her mouth to speak, caught Micru's sharp gesture, and stayed silent.

"I've always known I was a foundling," Gria said, still in that lifeless voice. "It never made any difference. She always treated me as her own. She couldn't have any of her own, and her husband never produced any bastards, so I was the best. . . ." She stopped, shut her eyes, and swallowed hard.

"Best chance at an heir?" Micru said.

Gria nodded. "My children will be treated as full blood of my adopted father's line," she said. "Would have been." She raised her left hand, looked at the cuff, let it fall back into her lap.

"Did Sela's husband ever try fathering children on you directly?" Micru said with implacable, emotionless logic.

Gria shook her head, her expression still blank. "When that . . . that man came, it seemed so good, so wonderful, that we might gain that status . . . and the s'iopes said it was an honest offer. She's always trusted the priests. And she . . . talked me into it. Into going south. I didn't want to go, I had someone . . . but they didn't approve." Gria opened her eyes, brimming with tears now. "Mama Sela insisted on coming. She knew I'd run away . . . and they promised she'd be sent back with my first male child. The s'iopes said it was in writing, in the contract, that it was legally enforceable and honest . . . they said it was truth sworn to under all four gods." She wiped at her eyes, staring at Alyea appealingly now, ignoring the man in front of her.

"A southern slave trader would hold no bond under a Northern Church oath," Micru said. "Past the Horn, those oaths and those papers don't carry the weight of a grain of sand in the deep desert."

"We found out," Gria said bitterly, and wiped at her streaming eyes again.

"Why are you the one they want?" Micru said.

"I don't *know*," she said. "I really don't. I just know I'm the one they wanted. I heard Ierie talking with his guards, once, when they thought I was asleep, about killing Mama Sela. They decided I'd be more pliable if she was around."

Micru hummed to himself softly, his expression troubled. "When and where were you cuffed?" he said at last.

"Just outside Water's End. Some men appeared. I never saw them before. They were frightening." She shut her eyes. "They drugged us both, but I didn't fall asleep. I don't know why. I wish I had."

"Frightening," Micru said patiently. "Why?"

"They looked . . . cruel. Uncivilized. Some had bright blue tattoos."

Micru sat up straight, his eyes intent now. "Was it here?" He pointed just below his right collarbone.

Gria opened her eyes to look and nodded.

"Did it look like a swirled star?"

She nodded again, mutely, and Micru stood up. "Keep her close, Alyea," he said. "Keep her very close. And keep a dagger closer. Stay here. I'll send more guards."

"Wait," Alyea said as Micru turned for the door. "What's going on? What does the swirled star mark mean?"

"Chacerly's made a mistake. A very, very big mistake. Don't trust him any longer."

"What—"

The door swung shut behind him, cutting off more questions. Moments later, three guards pushed through, their expressions grim, and took up stations around the room.

"What in the hells is going on?" she demanded. They looked at her briefly and didn't answer.

Alyea stood and walked towards the door; the nearest guard put out a hand in warning, shaking his head. She sat back down, furious and trying to decide who to pin it on: Micru, for abandoning her without answers, or Chac, for apparently creating the situation. She had just about settled on being angry at herself for ever getting into this spot when the door opened again and Chac strode in.

He nodded to the guards and crossed to the bed. Alyea rose; he ignored her, looking down at Gria instead for a long, thoughtful moment.

"I was right," he said finally, "you should have killed them both. Too late now."

Alyea pushed between him and the girl.

"You tell me what's going on!" she said, all the frustrated restlessness of the last several hours flaring into sudden aggression.

He stared at her. For just a moment, his face lit with a rage worthy of a desert lord; then it dissolved into stoniness again.

"We're leaving," he said. "It's not safe here for you now."

"Why not?"

"I don't have time for your stupid questions," Chac said. He stepped back and signaled to the guards. "If she doesn't follow me, knock her out and carry her. Bring the other girl as well."

The old man strode to the door. Two of the guards moved towards Alyea without hesitation; the third, frowning, said, "Wait . . . this isn't what Micru said—"

Chac turned and flung out a hand, almost too fast to follow; something small and dark whipped through the air and buried itself in the doubtful man's neck. The guard sagged, clawing at his throat, eyes wide and astonished. Before Alyea could do more than open her own mouth in surprise, the remaining guards moved in front of her, blocking her view. She heard gagging noises from behind them, like a man desperately trying to breathe; then a sour smell in her nose took her into darkness.

Alyea awoke hot and muzzy, with sweat pooled under her back and legs; she groaned and rolled to her side. Wiping an arm across her face to clear sweat-blurred vision, she propped herself up with her other elbow and looked around.

She lay in a wide, low-ceilinged carriage, on a low bed with thick cushions. A bench seat nearby held a neatly folded pile of clothes. Latticed windows took up most of the walls on three sides; the fourth had a simple latched door.

A tiny, thin, hot breeze wandered through the lattices. Sounds came from outside; people talking, people walking around. The smell drifting through the air set her stomach rumbling, although she couldn't place the aroma.

She ached all over, stiff and sore as if she'd been bedridden for days, but she wasn't tied or, as far as she could tell, hurt. But she *was* incredibly hungry. Alyea sat up slowly, looked down at herself, and added *naked* to that list.

"There's a jug with some water by the bed," a voice said from outside the carriage. "And a cloth, to wipe off the sweat before you get dressed. Clothes on the bench."

Alyea turned her head, staring through the lattices, feeling suddenly trapped and exposed.

"Don't worry, northern," the voice went on. "Nobody can see you, and nobody cares anyway. Hurry up."

Alyea took a deep breath and reached for the jug.

Cleaning off the worst of the sweat gave her a sense of preparing to face whatever waited outside. The clothes turned out to be a deep-southern style she'd rarely seen in Bright Bay, and one she'd never thought to wear herself: a long silk robe, brightly colored and almost transparently thin, with a wide, braided-silk belt. The front dropped into a deep V; bending over would display everything.

She tried to remember how the women of Water's End had managed to move in these robes without being immodest, but her attention hadn't been on that at the time. She suspected she would quickly disgrace herself in this outfit.

"C'mon already, northern," the voice said.

Alyea shrugged the robe around her shoulders and fastened the inside ties and outer belt. She didn't see any shoes or slippers; after a moment of looking around helplessly, she went to the door. Half-expecting it to be locked despite the urging to come out, she rattled at the latch tentatively and jerked back when someone tugged it open from outside.

"C'mon already," the voice repeated. "Food's ready."

She stepped forward cautiously, looking around, and saw a short man with dark skin watching her with amusement. His long shirt, cut from a rougher cloth than her robe and a sharp white color, draped like scarecrow clothes against his spare frame; his leggings almost matched the clear blue sky overhead. His bare feet showed noticeable calluses.

"I don't bite," he said.

Sand gritted against her feet as she came through the doorway. It shifted and sank underfoot as she walked a few steps away from the carriage. Questions ran through her mind: *Where am I? Who are you? What's going on?*

She stayed silent and studied her surroundings. The carriage had no wheels, only long poles to either side; she understood why when, looking to one side, she saw four muscular men sitting under a rough shelter of hide and wood, eating what looked like stew from small wooden bowls. Two more men were busy dousing the small cookfire and disassembling the charred cooking spit.

Sand lay in all directions; great, rolling swells of it, with only a faint haze of mountains to the west to break the monotony. No sign of Chacerly, Micru, Halla, Gria, or Sela. More questions, more worry; she set her teeth lightly in the tip of her tongue to keep from asking. If any of the rules Chac had taught her applied, she would be in debt for the answer;

and right now, she couldn't afford that. Being alive and unhurt might be a debt all in itself, for all she knew.

"Come," the man said from behind her. "Eat."

She resisted the pull of her stomach and turned to look at him. His amusement deepened into an actual grin; she let her stare grow into a glare.

It didn't seem to bother him.

"Eat," he said again, and made shooing motions with his hands, directing her towards the tent.

Alyea drew a deep breath and walked towards the stew pot. Three small wooden bowls and carved spoons sat on a small tray, and a large ladle hung from the side of the stew pot. She scooped out a bowl of stew, trying, as she moved, to watch the men nearby; they showed no interest in her. They ate silently, staring straight ahead, faces dull and slack.

"Over here," the small man called. She followed him around the side of the carriage. A thick, coarsely woven mat had been spread on the sand; another, larger one slanted overhead to shade the area.

Alyea settled down on the mat as gracefully as she could and began to eat. A few mouthfuls into the stew, the mild spice taste flared suddenly into an eye-watering heat. Alyea had laughed when northerners choked on food she considered almost bland; now it was her turn to gasp and cough, and her guide's turn to laugh.

But: "Don't bite into the cactus peppers," her unidentified guide said without any hint of laughter, glancing down at her as she sputtered. He unhooked a leather bag from his belt and passed it to her. She stared at it uncertainly.

"Hah, northern, like this." He took it back, upended it over his mouth, and squeezed; a cloudy liquid squirted into his mouth.

She tried it, managing to get most of the liquid into her mouth, and swallowed through almost pure reflex. The fire of the cactus pepper faded, replaced by a vile sourness; she coughed and almost gagged at the lingering taste.

"What was *that*?" she said when she could speak again.

"*Perroc-s'etta,*" the man said. "Cactus milk. Fermented."

Alyea drew a careful, deep breath, and set the bowl aside. "I'm done, thanks."

"Finish eating," the man said, unsmiling now. "You need it. Just don't bite any of these. . . ." He leaned down, dipped forefinger and thumb into her bowl, and pulled out a long, white strip Alyea had thought to be some sort of potato. "Cactus pepper." He dropped the pepper in his mouth and chewed with a contented expression.

Alyea shuddered, considered refusing to eat, and decided this man would probably pour it down her throat if he had to; he had that look to him—friendly, to a point, and business after that. If that had been the expression on her own face while questioning Gria and Sela, small surprise the women hadn't trusted her.

Alyea certainly didn't trust this man: not with questions, not with answers should he ask any himself. She ate the soup quietly and set the bowl on the ground when she finished.

He picked it up and walked away. She stared out at the heat-bleached landscape before her and, on impulse, went back to her aqeyva lessons. *Let thought fade,* Ethu had taught her. *Let the questions go; fear and anger and worry all become irrelevant.* She'd never been very good at it before, but somehow, in the utter, heat-hazed stillness of the desert, it seemed simple. Soon only her breathing registered, rasping in and out of her throat. Even the sweat trickling down her face faded from notice.

At last she took a deep breath and opened her eyes. The small man squatted in front of her, an arm's length away, an odd expression on his face as he watched her.

Calm, centered, and alert now, she picked up on details she'd missed earlier: the pattern at the edge of his shirt, the calluses on his fingers—and on the edges of his hands. Micru, and some of the other Hidden, had hands like those. A dark tattoo looped around and around his left forearm in a flowing, twined line. She'd seen that mark in an old book, one Chac had saved from the Purge and given to Oruen. This man followed one of the old gods: probably Comos, the god of neutrality.

She met his dark stare without flinching. "*Nu-s'e,*" she said. "I am *su-s'a* Alyea."

He nodded slowly. "*Ka,*" he said. "I'm honored by the gift of your name. I am Juric, *taska*. Courier, carrier, guide, and watcher."

"*Ka,*" she said. "Thank you for the food and drink."

He smiled a little and stood, stepping onto the sand without apparent discomfort. Alyea glanced at the thick callus on his feet and stayed put, then looked up at the sky to check the sun. The endless blue sky had shifted into blazing streaks of orange and violet; she'd been in aqeyva trance for hours. No wonder he'd been looking at her like that. She'd never stayed in trance that long before; nobody she knew ever had.

He smiled at the expression on her face. "The desert tends to take time from you," he said. "Why are you here?"

It had the feel of a formal question, almost a riddle game. She considered, watching the tiny shifts in his face as he returned her gaze; she thought about the tattoo on his forearm and what it implied, and finally said, "Am I here?"

"I am here," Juric said. "You are here. Why?"

She drew a deep breath, let it out very slowly, and gambled. "Ask the wind."

A moment of silence hung, while he stared at her; then he smiled again, but it held a dangerous edge this time. "You do not follow Comos."

"I've never been called, no."

"Alyea," he said, abruptly dropping out of the formal tones, "*do* you know why you're here?"

She stopped herself before she could say: *because I'm an idiot*, and swallowed.

"No," she said. "I don't. I'm ignorant."

"Ignorant," he said, "not stupid."

She stared at him. Had he heard her unspoken words?

He smiled. "I also trained in aqeyva, Alyea. For much longer than you have."

Alyea tried to smooth her expression to the blandness Juric had shown a few moments ago.

"Not bad," he said, grinning. "Keep practicing."

She set her teeth in her tongue to stop the questions she dearly wanted to ask.

He nodded, as if pleased at her continuing silence, and motioned her up and off the mat. She found, to her surprise, that the sand felt warm, but hardly as scorching as she'd expected. Juric lifted the two mats, then rolled them up into one thick bundle with quick, professional movements; his gaze swept the sky and surrounding sands, darting back to his work now and again.

The rolled mats held in one hand, he gestured to the carriage.

"Get in," he said.

She obeyed without protest, noting in passing that the men had broken down their tent, bundled the poles and fabric into a neat cylinder, and kicked sand over the remnants of the small fire, obscuring it completely. Under the steady evening breeze beginning to flow across the sand, all traces of their passing would be gone within hours.

She shivered, feeling vulnerable and frightened again, and sat on the low bed. After a few moments, Juric followed her in, shut the door behind him, and after tucking the rolled mats under the bench seat, settled on the bench almost across from her. The small space suddenly seemed much smaller, and his dark stare less friendly.

Juric rapped his knuckles on the wall by his head, and the carriage lurched as the men lifted it. The carriage swayed; a low chanting came from outside, cadence time in a foreign tongue. They moved forward, carried on the shoulders of six strong men.

"Machago," she said in a low voice, glaring at Juric. "You're a slave-master."

He shook his head. "*Taska*. Courier. Carrier. Errand-boy. I'm not their master."

"They're slaves."

"Of course," he said. "But not bound slaves. They're working off crimes and debts. Once they work off their due, they'll be free with no stigma."

"Crimes," she repeated, careful to keep it flat and non-questioning.

He smiled, showing even, white teeth. "We don't have time for the formal games, right now; you'll incur no debt by asking open questions. Except," he added, holding up a hand as if she'd jumped to speak, although she'd made no move. "I tell you when you can ask questions, and you have to answer my questions honestly."

She considered, looking for traps, and finally nodded. "Accepted."

"Ask," he said. "Two questions."

She drew breath, chose carefully from the myriad of worries, and said, "Where is Gria?"

His eyebrows rose, as if he'd expected a different question. "Your ugren slave? With the *hask*."

She debated asking what *hask* meant, but she suspected he meant Chacerly, and she had a more important question in mind.

"Why is Gria so important?" she said instead.

His smile faded. He studied her for a few breaths, that odd look on his face again, and finally said, "The *hask* underestimated you badly. You're better off with me. I ask you in return: what do you know of desert Family bloodlines?"

"Everyone's related," she said before she could stop herself, and bit her tongue.

His amused look returned.

"True," he admitted. "Another question: have you heard of the blood trial?"

"I've heard the words," she said, "but I don't know what they mean."

"To become a full desert lord, men must go through the blood trials," Juric said. "Each man's trials are different, but all must be tested by Callen followers of Comos, of Ishrai, and of Datda, the old gods of the desert. All three Callen must be unanimous in their agreement that the supplicant is worthy to become a desert lord. Not all who apply are accepted to go through the trials, and not all who are accepted survive."

She waited. He nodded, approving, and went on:

"Different families have different rules on who is allowed to become a desert lord. Sessin will only allow their full-blooded children to attempt the blood trials. Scratha has always been less . . . particular, but perhaps that is because their matrilineal reckoning ensures the blood will stay in their family in the end."

He bent and slid open a thin drawer from under the bed. Lifting out a thick tan shawl, he handed it to her and closed the drawer. She draped the wrap around her, only now aware that the temperature had begun to drop rapidly. The sand-colored shawl felt thick and warm; she hugged it tight and said, "Thank you."

"The Callen take whatever applicants come to them," he said, ignoring her gratitude. "Once in a while, a supplicant comes who has not been sent by a Family. This is exceptionally rare, but it has happened before. Cafad Scratha was one such exceptional person; his entire Family was slaughtered while he was out on a desert vigil. Nobody remained to back his application, and the other Families, for whatever reason, would not put their names behind his. He opted to take the trials without a sponsoring Family. It was the only way he could become Lord of Scratha Family and remain in possession of his lands."

His voice came from a gathering shadow as the light faded. Alyea shivered again, tucking the shawl closer around her body. She thought about asking if they could light a candle or hand-lantern, but the dark didn't seem to bother Juric, and the carriers apparently could see well enough.

"Understand, Scratha Family has always been highly respected as scholars and diplomats," Juric's voice went on. "They studied old writings and were always able to smooth over political difficulties. A gathering was considered lacking if a Scratha lord did not attend. They brought families to a peace-table that had glared at each other over drawn daggers for hundreds of years. Their highest achievement was something nobody believed possible: the arranged marriage of Cida Scratha to Lord Evkit of the teyanain."

"The what!" she said before she could stop herself. "I never heard of that!" *And why would I?* she thought, annoyed with herself. *I didn't even know the teyanain existed before traveling south. I'm starting to act as though I grew up here; how ridiculous!*

"It never happened," Juric said. She couldn't tell in the darkness whether he sounded sad or amused. Too much depended on the speaker's face.

It occurred to her that he couldn't see her, either. That relaxed her nerves considerably.

"Cida was willful and stubborn," Juric said. "She ran off with a commoner the night after the announcement of her engagement to Lord Evkit. She destroyed literally years of negotiations and agreements. Her desertion was a mortal insult to Lord Evkit."

Alyea sat very still, staring at the faint silhouette of Juric's head.

"The teyanain are very bad people to insult," Juric said. "Scratha Family found themselves no longer welcome at any of the other Family gatherings. Their allies fell away, leaving Scratha Family open and vulnerable. Scratha guards deserted with no warning. Their food animals fell ill with strange diseases; their wells clogged unexpectedly. One by one, the lords of Scratha abandoned them or died; one changed his allegiance to Darden Family. Another, according to rumor, went south, possibly hoping to find help from the Forbidden Jungles. He was never seen again."

"They just ran away?" Alyea said, incredulous.

"Desert lords, like all people, have their personalities and quirks and fears," Juric said. "And it's a rare human that won't at least consider jumping from a rapidly sinking ship, especially when there's a sound and ready vessel at hand to step onto."

"But if they hadn't left. . . ."

"If this, if that," Juric said. "I'm telling you what happened. I'm not saying the lords of Scratha acted very admirably during that time. Do you want to hear the rest?"

"Yes," Alyea said, putting aside her anger with an effort. "Please, go on."

"One after another, the desert lords of Scratha left or died," Juric said. "The wells dried up. The people began to starve. And nobody would send aid. Not a single family. Not even the Aerthraim. It was said the line of Scratha was cursed."

The carriage rocked and swayed, the hoarse breathing and soft chanting of the men carrying it the only sound.

"And then," Juric said, "Cafad Scratha went out on his first walkabout, as part of his training to become a desert lord. He returned to find every single member of his family dead and the floors covered in their blood."

"I'm surprised he survived this long," she said, then covered her mouth, appalled at her heartless comment.

Juric didn't seem to mind.

"Scratha is matrilineal," he reminded her. "Cafad is male. In the long term, he's meaningless. He'll never have the authority a woman could gain, no matter how many children he has. He's gone through the blood trials, and he's Lord of Scratha, but it's a house without walls. Nobody's ever challenged his status: why bother? Desert Family guilt gave him everything he has. Of course, nobody's ever found Cida Scratha, either; she's been presumed dead for years."

Breath caught in her throat as the implications connected in her head.

"Oh, gods," she said, horrified. "Gria's the heir to *Scratha*?"

"Your slave is a foundling," Juric said, "raised by a northern lordling. She would need a full Scratha lord to speak for her bloodline before that notion could even be hinted at publicly."

"A foundling the teyanain wanted badly enough to put an ugren cuff on," she said.

"Questioning the ways of the teyanain," Juric said, "is a shortcut to a cursed life."

She let out a long breath and thought about it. "I've been blundering about like a horse in a glass shop," she said.

"True."

Alyea shook her head, wishing she could read his face, but it remained invisible in the darkness. "Chac should have told me all this," she said. "Long since, I should have known what you just told me. I would have handled things differently. Why didn't he tell me?"

Juric made no reply. She heard him shift, and scraping sounds; a moment later, a small lantern flared. He quickly hooded it to allow only a faint leakage of light, then hung it on a long-shafted hook. Alyea watched it sway for a moment, almost hypnotized by the motion, then tore her gaze away and looked back at Juric.

"To be a desert lord, you have to go through the blood trials," Juric said. "Quiet. Don't speak. Listen to me. Only the blood trials will give you the authority you need in this situation. The king's word isn't good enough here, and your advisors knew that.

"The *hask* arranged for you to go through the trials, but it's a farce. He doesn't think you can do it. He intends you to fail. I believe you can succeed."

He waited, his shadowed stare fixed intently on her face.

Alyea stared back, frozen, unable to believe what he had just said. She had to take *three* potentially fatal trials just to serve as king's proxy at Scratha Fortress? Madness.

Another piece turned over and connected: a full desert lord had to verify Gria's bloodline. None of the other Families, from the sound of it, would offer such a concession, and Scratha had been banished to the Stone Islands; calling him back could take months.

Furthermore, Juric's words implied that if Alyea survived the blood trials, she'd be granted more authority on the basis of her gender than Cafad had ever held. The logic of that escaped her, but this wasn't the time to argue southern customs.

Alyea could name Gria heir to Scratha and annul her slavery. *If* she survived the blood trials.

"How long do I have to decide?" she said, barely above a whisper.

"The *hask* bid me bring you to him for your first trial," he said. "But I am a Callen of Comos, follower of the winds. I answer to myself alone, and my trial is always the first to be given. At your request, I can begin your trials. But once begun, you must continue; you cannot change your mind halfway through."

She shut her eyes, feeling ill. Events had spun too far from anything she'd expected. Every time she thought she understood, something else knocked her off balance. Juric had said he thought she could do it; did that mean he favored her, or was that a simple assessment without bias either way?

"I'll do it," she said at last. "With you to start the trials. Let's get this over with."

He lifted a hand and rapped sharply on the side of the carriage. "Then we begin now."

Chapter Thirteen

Idisio discovered two things over the next several days. The first, and most obvious, was that he hated sea travel. He hated the constant motion, he hated the enclosed spaces, he hated the fact that he couldn't leave if he wanted to. He hated that if something happened and the monstrous thing sank, he'd be dead because he'd never learned to swim.

He didn't get seasick, but he couldn't sleep and his appetite vanished. He couldn't decide what felt worse: sitting in the tiny cabin they'd been given and staring at swaying walls or sitting out on deck watching the swaying waves. Shortly after they boarded, Scratha handed him a thin sheaf of blank parchment, a pen and inkwell, and a bound book of children's stories to practice his still-uncertain skills; but the idea of trying to concentrate on writing exercises soon held little appeal.

He couldn't even vary the monotony by visiting the horses. They'd been left in Sandsplit Village as a "gift" for Yuer. Idisio suspected more politics he didn't understand had been involved in that gesture.

The second thing he realized was that he missed Riss's company. She'd been very quiet since that first night at the inn. She could be found out on deck in all sorts of weather, just walking or standing by the rail, staring out at the waves Idisio hated so much. She hadn't given Idisio more than a distracted wave and a half-hearted smile since they boarded.

And Scratha didn't seem inclined to talk either. He spent most of his time brooding: standing at the rail himself, staring south and west. His replies to comments or questions remained curt and mostly uninformative; Idisio gave up trying within a day of leaving Sandlaen port.

The sailors, on the other hand, talked. In fact, Idisio sometimes thought they never shut up. One in particular, a brawny man with developing streaks of grey in his bright red hair and a thick coating of freckles everywhere else, seemed to always be singing, talking, or laughing. Sea-songs, old ribald desert tunes, northern hymns, slave work-songs: the man seemed to know every tune ever penned in the kingdom. The second day out, he sang a verse that made Idisio sit up and stare, unable to believe the man's gall:

There was a king, a lovely king
Who loved a lady fair
He didn't hold her to himself
But let her spread her wares.

He grinned at Idisio's shocked stare, and went on to the second verse:

And in the town they said of him
The rot had caught his brain
The lady fair, that spread her wares,
Should not be seen again.

"A little off-key, I think," the man said, and ambled over to where Idisio sat openmouthed. "At least, by your face."

"I can't believe you're singing that," Idisio said.

"What, 'The Lay of Dusty Rose'? You've never heard it before?"

"I've heard *of* it," Idisio said carefully. "But it's banned, with an execution order on anyone who sings it."

"Oh, if I only sang *allowed* songs," the man said, "I'd have nothing fun to sing about." He turned away and went back to his work, lifting his voice in another verse, one Idisio hadn't heard before:

The lady she stayed by her king
(And by all the town as well!)
And when the time came for her end
They rang the great king's bell.

The king he went quite mad with grief
And screamed out like the crows
For ten days full he mourned his whore
Whose name was Dusty Rose.

"Gods," Idisio said under his breath. He understood now why the singers he'd heard had never made it past the second verse before being firmly evicted from the area.

The next four verses became increasingly explicit as they told the story of the sorrowing king's decision to take his lady's name for his own, and his death, shortly after that, from the "rot" that had killed the original Dusty Rose.

Upon finishing, the sailor turned and bowed in all directions. The others roundly ignored him, although one or two grinned.

"Ah, talent is never appreciated," he said, coming to stand beside Idisio. "Red."

"Sorry?" Idisio said, startled.

"Red," the man repeated. "My nickname. Red. Kinda hard to forget." He raked a hand through his hair.

"Oh," Idisio said. "I'm. . . ." Not for the first time, he wished he had a nickname like that. The only tag he'd carried on the streets had been "Lifty": not a name to introduce oneself to honest people by. "Idisio," he finished.

"It's true, y'know," the man said unexpectedly.

"Sorry?"

"The song. Dressed up a bit, but true at the core. That's why it's banned."

Idisio had grown up hearing the gossip and back-door history of Bright Bay, but *that* notion had never crossed his ears before. "Really?"

"Really," Red said with a straight, earnest face, then laughed again. "Don't take it all so serious, Idisio. You worry yourself into an early grave that way."

He clapped Idisio on the shoulder and sauntered away, whistling. Within a few steps, he'd broken into another song:

There is a lake, a ghosty lake
Far to the north it lies
And they say should a woman draw near
She gets a big surprise. . . .

The words faded, drowned out by the creaks and pops of a ship under full sail.

"He's mad," a voice said from behind Idisio.

Turning, Idisio saw another sailor looking at him from a few feet away.

"Don't pay him no mind. The more attention he gets, the worse he is. You're just a new audience for his nonsense."

"I figured," Idisio said, feeling vaguely disappointed for some reason. "But. . . ."

"What?"

"Well . . . is it true? That song?"

The sailor sighed. "That's the bitch of it. He's at his craziest when he's telling truth."

Red turned out to be the best part of what became too long a voyage. Scratha stayed moody. Riss continued to ignore him. The other sailors, talkative as chatterbirds with each other, gave Idisio only the briefest of noncommittal nods as they went by. Only Red displayed openly friendly behavior. Idisio couldn't decide whether to take the man seriously or not, but he was always entertaining. When the sailor worked on deck, Idisio usually tried to find a spot nearby.

Red only repeated the song about the "ghosty lake" once. It told of a lake to the north of the Great Forest, populated by strange creatures that seduced innocent women and stole any children that came from the union:

And the king he heard of this
By his pious advisor's word
"Evil" they named the lake
But truer to so name the priest's heart. . . .

It wasn't a funny song; it didn't have a regular rhythm or rhyme, and it cut closer to the bone than the one about Dusty Rose. The song painted the king as overshadowed by his Northern Church advisors, and a helpless plaything of their malice; Idisio, suspecting the song referred to either Ninnic or Mezarak, had his doubts on that view.

Red didn't bow for applause afterwards, and Idisio decided against asking for the truth of that song; he didn't want the answer. He stopped following Red around, afraid of hearing more songs like that. He chose instead to spend his time on deck standing at one of the rails, staring out at the passing view.

To the east, the Kingsea seemed to stretch in an endless sheet of frothed blue and green; to the west rose the Horn. Red sometimes paused beside Idisio, dropping a casual remark or two before moving on again.

"That bump up there," he said once, pointing over the starboard rail, "that's a fair-size way-stop. I been through there. Strange people; they've been digging the dirt out from around their houses so long, most of 'em look like they're up on little pillars."

"Why would they do that?" Idisio asked, mystified.

"To build more houses," Red told him, and wandered away again.

Idisio squinted up at the distant ridge Red had pointed to, thought about it, and decided the man had been pulling his leg. Nobody could be that foolish.

But in a rare moment of conversation with Scratha, his master confirmed the sailor's story.

"Brickroot grows thickest up there," Scratha explained. "It's a profitable business and the main Horn industry. Most buildings in the outer desert areas are made of some form of brickroot blocks. I know the waystop he mentioned; they've carved their existing soil down to the underlying rock in places. Stupid, really; there's no replacing the dirt they're selling. They'll have to look for another means of income soon."

Something about that thought prompted Scratha into another brooding fit, and Idisio slunk away without his absence being noticed.

Another time, Idisio stood watching a ship passing to port, some distance away, when Red stopped beside him. The sailor squinted and said, "Merchanter. Look, Idisio: see that flag? Pay attention to those colors. That's out of Stass; one of merchant Deiq's ships, carrying sweets and fruit. Man makes a living on it. You ever try *suka*?"

"Once or twice," Idisio said. His mouth watered at the recollection.

"What did you have? A stick or a chew?"

"A stick," Idisio said. The soft candies had been more expensive, and so harder to steal; he'd never tried, more concerned with survival than sweets.

Red rummaged in a worn belt pouch and handed Idisio a small, soft candy wrapped in brightly colored paper. "Here. Try one of these."

It tasted even better than Idisio remembered. The soft taffy clung to his teeth, giving him a moment's worry that he'd be scraping it off with a splinter, and then abruptly dissolved into nothing more than a lingering sweetness and a marvelous memory. He rolled his eyes and sighed blissfully. Red grinned and nodded.

"Thank you," Idisio said fervently when the last scrap of taffy had melted away. "That was wonderful."

"Wish I had more for you," Red said, "but I got to save a few for my boy."

"You have a son?" Idisio said, and tried to think of the usual thing to say next. "Um, how old is he?"

"I'm not sure," Red said. He turned to stare south with an expression not unlike Scratha's brooding look. "I just found out about him. Maybe ten, maybe fifteen by now. I don't know. I lost track of the years, somewhere along the way."

"Um," Idisio said, at a loss again.

"Don't even know for sure he's mine," Red said, still staring into the distance. "But he's got red hair, and that's not so common in the southlands. Well." He shook himself, gave Idisio a distracted smile, and moved away.

They passed by the port of Stass that night. Idisio was disappointed when Scratha told him, the next morning, that he had slept through it; he'd been hoping to stretch his legs on land. Scratha had insisted that they all stay below during the stop in Bright Bay, to avoid being seen–a sensible precaution, and Idisio hadn't argued. But he'd been looking forward to seeing Stass Port, and said as much aloud.

"You didn't need to wake up," Scratha said. "I paid the captain extra to provision heavily in Bright Bay so we wouldn't lose time stopping there. We're headed for Agyaer."

Idisio still didn't understand his master's driving urgency, unless it was to get off this wobbling monstrosity called a ship. But Scratha still wasn't talking; every hour they traveled further south, the more he drew into his proud, isolated lordly shell. Idisio, seeing the flickering of madness in the man's eyes almost constantly now, prudently withdrew and avoided him as much as possible.

Riss took to staying in her cabin, coming up less and less frequently for air. Even Red became curt on occasion, although he always apologized immediately and profusely, and went out of his way to make Idisio laugh again. The other sailors went on ignoring everything, doing their work, gathering in clusters to rest, and dispersing to work again.

Idisio busied himself with reading, writing, and practicing aqeyva meditations. The meditation provided the most relief; he found it possible, even easy, to slip into a trance for hours. Any long stretch of time when he wasn't aware of the ceaseless swaying around him was perfect as far as he was concerned, and soon he spent more time in trance than out of it.

Even so, the voyage stretched out too long and too lonely. Idisio let out a long breath of deep relief at the cry of "Agyaer!"

The port city sprawled along the coast for miles before the docks came into view. An imposing slope of rock dwarfed the city, which spread mostly across the broken and erratic skirts of that wall. Caravans, mules and people could be seen trudging up a wide stair cut into the cliff. Looking at that steep path, Idisio had a bad feeling that they'd be climbing it themselves soon.

Closer to the ship, tiny coast-hopper boats rowed busily back and forth along the shoreline, laden with everything from huge baskets of fruit to bolts of fine cloth. The sounds of singing and laughter drifted across the water, punctuated with drum beats, rhythmic and arrhythmic all at once. Idisio stood at the starboard rail, entranced.

"Welcome to Agyaer," Red said, leaning on the rail beside him. His eyes were bright, his expression expectant as a child about to open a gift. "See that, over there? That blue roof? That's where Yhaine lives. I'd almost forgotten about her. Years ago and more than one bottle, as the saying goes. I'll be seeing her soon enough, and my son." He shook his head, eyes fixed on the distant, barely visible roof until it was lost to sight.

"How did you find out?" Idisio ventured, not sure what to say. "About your son, I mean?"

"Ran into an old friend of mine, one I hadn't seen in years," Red said, craning as if in one last attempt to see the roof. "I've been working Stone Island and Kismo ships out in the Goldensea; more profit to be had, more exciting. But excitement gets old, and so have I. This side of the Horn has nice, easy work, long as you stay on coast runners like this one. I wouldn't go on one that tacks out over the open water of the Kingsea, not me. What was your question?" He looked back to Idisio, his bright blue eyes puzzled. "I'm sorry. I've been losing track of things lately. Can't seem to stop thinking about Yhaine."

"You answered it," Idisio said, trying to smile.

"Oh, good." Red smiled vaguely, then his expression sharpened. "Idisio—would you . . . d'you think you could go with me?"

"Ah. . . ." Idisio blinked, taken aback. "Go where?"

"To see Yhaine," Red said as if it should have been obvious. "I don't know, I just . . . I haven't seen her in so long." He turned and looked back at the passing town, brooding again. "You don't have to come to the door with me, just . . . just walk me there. I'm afraid I won't make it all the way to her door if I go alone."

"What do you think will happen to you on the way?" Idisio said, utterly confused. What good could a scrawny boy do against something that could overpower a large man like Red?

"I'm afraid I'll bolt," Red said starkly, his hands tight on the rail and his gaze straight ahead. "I'm scared, Idisio. You'll remind me of what I'm going for. Just you being there will remind me."

Idisio opened his mouth, shut it again, and swallowed. He wasn't sure if he'd just been handed a compliment or called a child.

"I don't know if I can," he said. "My master's in a hurry for some reason."

"I'll have a word with him," Red said with sudden determination, and turned on his heel, almost sprinting away before Idisio could say a word to hold him back.

"Oh, *no*," Idisio said, and ran after him.

The desert lord's stare seemed to bore into the sailor; Red endured the examination with stubborn determination.

"You're telling the truth," Scratha said finally. It wasn't a question.

"Yes, my lord," Red said, voice shaky. "I wouldn't dare lie to a desert lord, my lord."

"Don't let him get hurt," Scratha said.

"No, my lord. I won't, my lord."

Scratha glanced to Idisio. "Do you want to go with him?"

Idisio opened his mouth, not sure how to reply, and was astonished by the strong "Yes, my lord!" that emerged.

Scratha stared at Idisio for a long, narrow-eyed moment, then nodded. "I have arrangements to make anyway. It'll take time, and we'll have to lodge here tonight. I'll be taking two rooms at the Silver Sands Inn; come back there when you're done."

He even gave Idisio a half-round of gold to spend as he liked.

"Wages," Scratha said in response to Idisio's incredulous stare, "and rather overdue."

Idisio barely had time to stammer thanks before Red grabbed him by the arm and hustled him off the boat.

"Good man, your master," Red said. He seemed hardly aware of what he was saying. "Lord, I mean. Desert lord. Sorry about that."

He switched abruptly into an explanation of how the houses they passed had been built, then rattled on feverishly for several blocks, seizing topics apparently at random. At last, he fell silent, released Idisio's arm and slowed to a more casual walk. His eyes looked a bit wild and his breath came in unsteady gulps; after a few more steps he stopped.

"I can't do it, Idisio. I can't. It's been too long. He's got to be at least ten by now. Older. Maybe even fifteen. I've never been good with time. Gods, I can't do this. They won't thank me for interfering now. I'm mad to be thinking of doing this."

He turned on his heel as if to retreat; Idisio grabbed him by the arm and said, without thinking, "Red, I'd love my father to come find me!"

Red froze, staring down at Idisio. "You never knew your father?"

"No," Idisio said. "I grew up on the streets of Bright Bay as an orphan." He looked away from Red's horrified gaze, feeling intensely embarrassed at the admission. He hadn't intended to say it; hadn't even known he felt that way. He'd meant to say something encouraging to bolster the man's resolve, not expose an old hurt he'd thought long ago healed over.

"Oh, gods, Idisio, I'm sorry," Red said. "I had no idea. I wouldn't have asked . . . you must think me completely heartless."

"No," Idisio said, trying to smile. "I think you're great. Just don't run away. That's why you brought me, right? To keep you from running away?"

Red stared at him for another moment, then nodded sharply and turned back around. "Let's go," he said, and strode forward.

Chapter Fourteen

The slaves settled in a silent circle, their attention fixed on the ground in front of them. Juric guided Alyea to the opposite side of the carrier, away from their view. He spread the mat on the ground and motioned her to stand on it.

"Take off your clothes, and sit," he said, stepping back several paces. He sank to the ground himself, sat cross-legged, and stared at her with a challenging gaze clear even under the faint light from stars and waning moon.

She drew a shivering breath, uncertain. Would she fail the trial if she refused? Or would obeying be a failure? Was the test to see if she blindly obeyed a strong voice or used her wits to choose her own path? Would Juric kill her the moment she failed? She had a feeling she'd never see the death blow coming.

So much rested on her sketchy memories of what the deep south believed; she wished she'd spent more time reading with Oruen about that. It had never interested her very much. What had that old book said? Comos represented neutrality. The god of the winds, the god of balance, everyone stood transparent before him . . . and transparent could be translated, loosely, as 'naked.'

She stripped off the loose robe and sat, fervently hoping she'd remembered it right. A light breeze feathered against her skin, chilling her instantly; she shivered and hoped even more strongly this wouldn't take long.

"You called on Comos earlier without knowledge," Juric said. "I forgive the ignorance. You did not know me as Callen. Never call on a god blindly. They will answer, and mortals often regret their reply; and the followers of a god can be less gracious yet."

She bowed her head, not sure what to say.

"If you had to choose between your two ugren slaves," Juric said, "which would you give life, and which sentence to die?"

Alyea knew this game. She'd heard Chac drill Oruen with questions like this, day after day.

She slowed her breathing and focused, centering herself to speak from the calmest, most objective place possible. That had been Chac's first lesson: politics demand that you decide from the mind, not the heart, and that mind must be perfectly still. But did Juric look for the same answer Chac would have wanted?

"Gria to live," she said at last.

"Why?"

"The death of Sela would cause lesser ripples," Alyea said, choosing her words with care.

"How do you know?"

Another question Chac had made Oruen answer countless times.

"I only know what I see," she said. "What I see tells me Gria has more power to change the world around her than Sela."

"Is that a reason for Gria to live, or to die?"

Alyea hesitated. Chac had never asked that question.

"To live," she said at last.

"Because she has power? You would kill those without power, then?"

Although Juric's voice remained completely emotionless, Alyea had a bad feeling in the pit of her stomach now. He'd maneuvered her into a trap, and she didn't know the way out.

"That isn't what I meant," she said at last.

"When you follow the words of another instead of your own wisdom," Juric said, "you often speak other than you mean. Try again, Alyea, without the crutch of the *hask*'s teachings this time. I will give you a second chance, which others would not. Which of your slaves would you sentence to die, if *you* had to choose?"

What she said next surprised her. Words bubbled up as if freed from a long-sealed vault: "I would ask them to choose. It's their lives, not mine; why should I decide their fate?"

A long silence hung between them.

"Always use your own wisdom," Juric said at last. "If you die from it, at least you die with honesty in your mouth. If I asked you to mark for death one of the slaves that carried us here, what would be your answer?"

"It would depend on the reason for the death."

"Why?"

"If it was a madman's whim, with no just cause, I would refuse," she said. "I would protect the slaves as best I could. If the reason was good, I would ask first for the slaves to choose, and pick only if I had to, and as blindly as I could."

"You lived under a madman who took your slaves from you. Is this how you acted then?"

She licked suddenly dry lips and sat very still. How had he known that? A chill ran down her spine. "No. I was afraid."

"Is fear a reason to allow another to die that you may live?"

Tears dripped from her chin onto her bare chest; the moisture slid slowly around the curve of her breasts, leaving a damp trail that chilled her further.

"No," she said. "It's not a good reason."

"Reason," Juric said, "is not good. It is not bad. It is what it is. Fear is a reason, anger is a reason, love is a reason. Good or bad does not attach. That is the way of Comos, to see the truth of what is. Aqeyva comes from Comos, and it is a powerful tool. Masters of aqeyva can hear the wind, which circles the world and knows everything that has ever happened and will ever be. With that understanding, it is impossible to judge right or wrong, good or bad."

Alyea listened, frowning at the dimly lit figure in front of her. "Even Ninnic? Even Mezarak and Pieas?"

"What you see as a monster," Juric said, "is the least part of a man. The slaves that carry you are named *comisti*; they have been convicted of crimes ranging from theft to rape. They appealed to Comos, and were granted the following terms: they are sworn to silence. They will not look at nor speak to anyone but their master. They will be worked hard and relentlessly for all the days of their sentence. At the end of their service, some comisti find themselves called to the service of a god; others go on about their lives. But whatever their choice, their debt is paid, their crimes forgotten as if they never happened. The only sign they bear of their service is a small, easily hidden brand. That is the justice of Comos."

"And if they repeat the crime, or commit another?" Alyea asked.

"If a comisti appeals a second time to Comos, they receive the same terms as before, with one difference: this time, when their service is up, they will be granted an honorable death. There will be no dishonor to their family or bloodline."

Juric held up a hand to stop Alyea as she began to speak again. "Enough questions. I have another for you; if the choice was between the two of us, that one must die, what would your answer be?"

The words remained as emotionless as before, but the hair rose on the back of her neck. She thought back over everything that had been said. Her breathing steadied and slowed as she considered, and she found herself slipping into a light trance. She allowed it, deciding it couldn't hurt to have more clarity of mind. As her pulse settled, she found herself on a mental high ledge of sorts, looking down at the question from a distance.

Did she deserve to live? What had she done that made her life of value?

Her faults, her mistakes, from childhood on, paraded in stately logic before her. She'd failed, not once, but many times; she hadn't protected her servants, hadn't listened to the people around her, hadn't lived her values at all. She'd believed herself special, all her life, better than a commoner because of her blood; later, she'd thought herself better than the court because she'd been seduced by a man who later became king.

Not easy to look at, even from a distance. She could feel tears rolling down her face and dripping onto her chest again, steady as her pulse. Many of the thoughts that appeared she'd never consciously been aware of before; but she could see now that her life had been filled with selfish, fear-driven motives.

She turned her attention to what she *had* done well, and another series of past decisions unrolled in front of her. She'd tried, to the best of her abilities and knowledge, to do right; and how could sacrificing her life help anyone? Ignorance and arrogance had influenced her life, but not ruled it; bright spots offset the painful memories. She'd found the courage to dismiss all her servants rather than risk losing any more to royal mishandling. She'd stepped in front of Chacerly to save a pair of obscure northern women. She'd had many discussions with Oruen, before and after he took the throne, about the standard beliefs about women and what she wished could change. Some of the changes he'd started had come from their long talks.

She'd done poorly, and she'd done well.

And Juric likely felt the same way about his life. Did he have more or less worth than she did? Should he die for her to live? Should she die so that he could live? The breeze stirred her hair, drew her attention away from her thoughts, pulled her into feeling every shift and whisper against her skin.

She opened her eyes, the answer clear in her mind at last, and found Juric watching her, his head cocked slightly to one side.

"I do not have the wisdom to choose between our lives," she said steadily, "and would ask the wind to decide."

He stood, motioning her to rise; she obeyed, stood unafraid and naked in front of him, waiting for his decision.

"The test of Comos is the test of the self," Juric said. "It is a test of the ego, to see if you can set your own wants aside for the larger good. You cannot be a desert lord if you put your own fears before the good of those you rule and protect. You cannot be a leader if you listen only to yourself. You must recognize when you are too close to make a decision, and allow another to step in. The desert is harsh, and life is not fair; a cowardly or arrogant leader would cause many deaths. That is why a full desert lord must have the approval of Comos."

He paused. She trusted her instincts and stayed quiet.

"You pass the test," he said at last. "You may bear the mark of Comos.

Come here." As she approached, he drew a small glass box from a pouch at his waist. "Turn. Hold still."

He smeared a cold paste on her mid-back, in a precise pattern no larger than the palm of her hand. A breath later, the cold turned to fire, and she screamed without intending to, dropping to her knees. His hands locked around her wrists, and she realized she'd been trying to claw at her back to get the stuff off.

"Quiet," he said in her ear.

She gasped and forced herself to a muted whimpering, and finally to silence, but couldn't stop the tears or the trembling. Dimly, she sensed that Juric had released her hands; she bent forward, crouched like an animal on the ground, and tried to breathe through the scorching agony. Her breath came out in uncontrollable hoarse gasps.

Seconds or minutes or hours later, she felt pressure and a coolness as Juric smeared another, thicker paste over the first. The fire cooled, as if doused by ice water, and abruptly the trembling shifted to shivering. Her muscles began to loosen from their pain-locked tension; then the stars went out and darkness graciously took away sensation.

Alyea woke to darkness and the feel of a thick dressing on her mid-back. She'd been laid on her stomach. She lay quietly for a while, examining her memories; she must have fainted from the exhaustion of enduring that much pain. She'd seen people do that before, and they generally woke stiff and cramped, almost unable to move.

She stayed still, blinking, letting the sway of the carriage soothe her frayed nerves. She could feel Juric nearby, hear his breathing. If he had the aqeyva training he claimed, he knew she'd woken, but he said nothing. Letting her think, maybe, or waiting to see what she would do now, or possibly in trance himself. From the even serenity of his breathing, she guessed the last to be most likely.

Finally she risked movement. A finger first, twitching experimentally, then the hand, bending the elbow, and finally shifting the whole arm slowly to one side. No pain, no stiffness. She moved the other one similarly, took a chance and propped herself up on her elbows; nothing twinged. The dressing shifted with her, with no feeling of cracking or sliding off.

"Wait," Juric said then, and partially unhooded the lantern again. He put a gentle hand on her shoulder. "Pain?"

"No."

"Lay flat again, and hold still."

She couldn't help tensing as she settled back down, expecting him to rip the dressing off her back along with a layer of skin.

His hands patted the dressing lightly here and there, as if testing. He made a clucking, satisfied-sounding noise, worked his fingers under the edges, and slowly rolled the mass up. It didn't hurt; rather, it felt as if a layer of wet cloth had just been removed.

"Done," he said.

Propping herself up, she saw a bundle of fabric in his hands: mottled with an evil, greenish yellow ooze and interspersed with flecks of thick white, like rotted milk.

"The fire of Comos," Juric said, holding it up, "removes many evil things from your body. Your first purification is complete." He dropped the mess into a leather bag, peeled off thick black gloves, and dropped them into the bag too. Tying the bag tightly shut, he pushed it to one side and sat back. "Hungry?"

Even after seeing that revolting mess, her stomach growled at the word. She sat up the rest of the way, shifting into a cross-legged posture without conscious thought. He smiled and handed her a spoon and a bowl of the same stew she'd eaten the day before.

"I removed the cactus peppers," he said. "Eat safely."

She ate the cold stew, watching him steadily as she chewed. He sat quietly, eyes closed, indifferent to her intent regard.

"Where to now?" she said when she finished, and held out the bowl. He took it without opening his eyes and set it on the bench beside him.

"The trial of Ishrai," he said. "We'll be there by morning. Sleep."

"Will Chac be there?"

"No. He waits at the trial of Datda."

"Where are my slaves, and my servant Halla?"

"I already told you that," he said. "They are all with the *hask*, and safe."

"Chac wanted to kill Sela and Gria," Alyea said, unable to resist pushing a bit more. "If they're with him, how can they be safe?"

Juric opened his eyes and smiled at her.

"They are safe," he repeated, then doused the lantern. She heard him sliding the panels near him open, and a chill breeze filtered in through the latticed windows.

"He will not harm them. Sleep."

She twisted her lips in a silent snarl, then sighed. He clearly had no intention of telling her anything else; but his advice made sense. She didn't have anything else to do, and her head still felt thick with exhaustion. As she stretched back out, he draped a thick blanket over her. It occurred to her then that she still didn't have any clothes on. For some reason, that didn't bother her at all.

Dawn had just begun to streak pale colors across the dark sky when they came to a halt. Unable to sleep, Alyea had finally taken refuge in an aqeyva trance. The shift in movement shook her out of the meditation; she opened her eyes and looked at Juric.

He leaned forward and laid her robe across the foot of the bed, then stood.

"Dress and come out when you're ready, *ka-s'a* Alyea," he said. He offered her a deep bow, an odd maneuver in such a cramped space, before leaving.

She took a deep breath, reaching for the calm from the aqeyva trance, but it had shattered beyond recovery. Her whole body seemed filled with a buzzing tension: not quite anxiety, not quite expectancy. She'd passed one test; would she pass another, and one more after that?

She pushed the blankets aside and slipped the robe over her head. Juric had called her *ka-s'a*: *honored lady*. It meant progress: she'd earned status in his eyes at least. She held to that thought as she stepped out of the carriage.

Juric and the comisti were nowhere in sight. A chunky spire of worn rock towered before her, easily two hundred feet high and almost that wide. Two tunnel openings were visible from where Alyea stood; one seemed hardly large enough for a child to crawl through, while the other stood wider and taller than a large man's reach.

A woman stood in the wider tunnel mouth, watching Alyea. She looked to be shorter than Alyea, unless distance deceived, and considerably rounder. She wore a robe of either deep green or black; hard to say in the still-dim light. When she saw Alyea looking at her, she lifted a hand in an unmistakable beckoning motion.

Alyea stopped an arm's length from the plump woman. Up close, the robe color proved a deep, rich green. Probably past childbearing age, the woman had dark hair marked with the distinctive iron grey streaks of an aging deep southerner, and her angular face held a network of thin lines. She studied Alyea with dark, lively eyes; after a moment, her sober expression split into a wide smile.

"Welcome to the Qisani," she said in a thicker, more musical accent than Alyea had ever heard before. "Please follow to me." She started walking away as Alyea puzzled out what had been said.

Alyea hurried after the woman, catching up in a few swift strides.

"No need to run. I do not move so fast. You could take nap and still catch up." The woman laughed, the sound bouncing rich and full from the curved stone walls around them.

Alyea slowed her pace and looked around as they walked. Just past the entrance, the tunnel took a sharp turn to the right and narrowed briefly. Sturdy doors leaned loose against the wall before the turn. They looked just the right size to wedge into the tunnel as a barrier; Alyea remembered tales of skin-shredding sandstorms in the deep desert and shivered.

The walls around them held few tool marks, as if mostly blasted through by years of sandstorms. Alyea glanced back over her shoulder, wondering how often the storms came.

Lamps were set every few feet. Alyea paused briefly to examine one: it seemed a simple oil lamp, a rough, lumpy glass globe set in a sturdy iron bracket; but bright green liquid showed inside, and the flame burned whiter than any she had ever seen.

She put her question about that aside with all the others; one day, she promised herself, she'd sit down with a native and twist his arm as hard as she could until she had everything answered.

Ahead, the passage opened into a wide room. Alyea followed her guide into the room and stared, mouth open in unabashed shock. A deep pool of water filled most of the room. Trays of plants floated at the edges, supported by some sort of inflated bags. Alyea recognized some of the herbs, but most of the plants were foreign to her. More than one bore brightly colored flowers. Wide stone benches lined the walls of the room, some with thick, colorful cushions on them. The room felt warm and humid, and seemed empty of other people.

Light without a source filled the room; looking up, Alyea noticed several slanted openings in the ceiling and the gleam of mirrors high above. That had to be Sessin's craft; she'd heard of such things in tales of what the palace had once been. The s'iopes had long ago made sure to smash all such "demon-spawned" things in Bright Bay beyond recovery.

Some people had said, very quietly, that "demon-spawned" meant anything Wezel or his priests did not understand.

Alyea took another long look at the room, marveling, before focusing her attention on the woman.

"This is the *ishell*," the woman said, looking around with a satisfied air. "Do you need to empty your bladder?"

"Yes," Alyea said.

The woman pointed to the opposite side of the room and politely turned her back. Alyea moved around the edge of the pool and found a chamber pot that seemed to have been carved from solid rock. She lifted the heavy lid carefully, holding her breath against the expected stench; but the pot looked as clean as if it had never been used. A large pile of clean moss, beside the pot, had an obvious purpose. When she finished, she set the lid back on the pot and walked back to join the woman.

"Refresh yourself," the woman said, indicating the pool of water.

Alyea hesitated. This didn't seem like a common bathing room, somehow; it felt like a place for sacred ceremonies, with chanting, drumming and prayer. Dunking her whole body in seemed disrespectful. She settled for kneeling at the edge and dipping her hands in, with a silent moment of gratitude for the presence of so much water in such a dry place. She wiped her damp hands over her face and stood, turning to face her guide again.

The woman nodded, seeming pleased. "You are cautious. That's good. Water is to honor. Even the water you passed will be used for curing lizard skins. Nothing is wasted here."

She seemed to expect a reply, but Alyea couldn't think of one.

"Come," the woman said after waiting a few moments, and turned to leave the room. Alyea followed her, increasingly confused; had she failed the test already?

Her guide turned down a side passage that Alyea hadn't noticed before, probably because it slanted sharply back towards the entrance. This passage also led steeply down; rough ridges had been carved in the floor to improve footing. The lamps they passed sat in deep alcoves and gave off a more muted light than the ones by the main entrance.

No other passages seemed to branch from this tunnel, but Alyea stayed too busy watching her balance and footing to look around. At last the slope leveled out, and the tunnel widened into a cavern: man-made this time, with smoothed-over chisel marks all over the walls.

A large, curved table took up half of the room, with matching benches arranged on either side. Four women in plain white linen robes sat on the benches, eating what looked like stew from small bowls. A large black pot, identical to the one Juric's slaves had used, sat to one side, supported on a thick metal tripod over a small fire pit. Only faintly glimmering coals remained beneath, but steam still rose from inside the pot.

"Sit," the plump woman said. "I will get you food."

Alyea thought about refusing; she'd had enough of the spicy stew already. But it seemed rude, and she might need the nourishment, so she nodded and sat down near the other four women. She picked a spot carefully, not too close to be intrusive, not so far away as to seem unsociable; they looked up at her, offered bright, friendly smiles, and went back to eating without a word.

"They are under vow of silence," the plump woman said, returning with a bowl and wooden spoon. She set them on the table in front of Alyea and moved to sit across from her, exchanging nods and smiles with the others.

"Why?" Alyea asked, hoping it wasn't a rude question, and prodded at the stew with her spoon. She couldn't see any cactus peppers, and the stew looked and smelled different than Juric's had; she risked a bite.

It tasted creamy rather than sharp, the vegetables soft and the broth thick. Not long ago she would have thought it bland; now she thanked the gods it didn't have cactus pepper in it.

"They have taken shelter with Ishrai for crimes," the woman said readily. "They do not speak until they fill term of service."

Alyea shifted uncomfortably. It seemed tactless to speak about the women as if they weren't there, but none of them seemed the least bit offended.

"It is all right," the woman said, catching her discomfort. "They would say to you themselves, but they are not allowed. Ask me, ask anything."

"Juric told me about the comisti," Alyea said. "I assume this is fairly similar."

"In many ways, yes," the woman said. "These women are called *ish-raidain,* and they serve the Qisani until released."

Alyea sorted through questions carefully. Whether this conversation served as a test or just a friendly chat, she didn't think she'd be granted unlimited time for questions. Each one had to count.

"What is the Qisani?" she said at last.

"This," the woman said with a broad sweep of one thick arm. "This marvelous, wonderful place. Aerthraim dug out many rooms for us, Sessin gave us glass lamps and oils, F'Heing and Darden have given herbs and plants. All Families, even lesser ones, donated something. All Families support, tithe every year, keep us sustained. This rock has always been sacred place. Conclave gave it to Callen of Ishrai as haven, long time ago, many years ago."

After Juric's silence, this woman almost overwhelmed Alyea's tight nerves.

The woman sat smiling at her contentedly, completely at ease, and said, "I am sorry I do not introduce myself or ask your name. I know to you northerns that is rude. We do not use names here. Only *ishai-s'a* is allowed to use names. She will be here soon."

Alyea took that to mean the woman in front of her wasn't the Callen who would be testing her. Her tension eased sharply, and she turned her attention to the remaining stew with far more appetite.

"It is good to see someone enjoying stew so much," the woman said. "We have it almost every day, and so it becomes dull."

"I'll take anything without cactus peppers in it right now," Alyea said.

"Oh. . . ." The woman looked dismayed, then puzzled. "But it does have cactus peppers."

Alyea stopped eating immediately and poked with the spoon through her bowl again, searching. "I don't see any."

"We chop up fine," the woman said. "Oh, I understand. Your comii-taska is from Shakai region. They cut cactus peppers in strips, and leave inner membrane on. That is where heat lives."

Alyea nodded, relieved. "Thank you. I was in tears when I bit into one of those strips, but he just dropped one in his mouth and ate it like it was nothing."

"Shakain do not think a meal is good unless they burn their mouths," the woman said. "And they actually *like* perocce water." She shuddered. "Tastes very bad. Most people do not drink it unless they have to."

"He had something he called *perroc-s'etta,*" she said. "Is that. . . ."

Stifled giggles stopped her question. The women around the table stared at her, smothering their amusement behind their hands. The youngest of them turned bright red. The guide rattled off something in the desert tongue to the women, and they dropped their hands and turned their attention back to their food, looking rebuked.

"Do not say that in public," the guide said, returning her attention to Alyea. "Is crude, is rude word. Let me think how it would translate for you." She thought for a moment, then said, "*Perroc* is cactus; *s'etta* is male . . . fluid. Do you understand?"

Her stomach lurched. "Yes," she said, swallowing hard. "Unfortunately, I do."

The guide looked surprised for a moment, then shook her head violently. "No, no," she said, looking frustrated. "It is only from a cactus, but the Shakain name translates that way. There is not anything mixed in." She made a face, as if disgusted at the thought.

Alyea breathed a sigh of relief. "Why do they call it that?"

"The Shakain are very male," her guide said. "They celebrate men, do you understand? Everything men. Very unusual for a Shakain to take the path of Comos. Comos is not male, is not female. Callen of Comos must to be . . . neutral. Not sex. Not. . . ."

She grimaced and made a motion with one hand like scissors opening and closing. "Do you see?"

Alyea stared at the woman, horror-struck. "They have to be *castrated*?"

"Yes, yes, that is the word," the woman said, cheerful again.

"Women too?"

"No, no," the woman said, waving her hands. "Women understand balance better than men. But they have to be past the time of blood to go out in the world. Younger women stay with their, with their. . . ." She grimaced, shaking her head. "I cannot translate it."

"With their teacher and community," a new voice said from behind them.

"Yes," the woman said, and bowed her head. "My thanks, *ishai-s'a*."

"And mine to you. *S'a* Alyea, if you would come with me?"

Alyea stood, studying the woman who had just entered the room.

The *ishai-s'a* stood easily a foot taller than Alyea. A thick braid of dark hair, pulled forward over her left shoulder, reached to her stomach. Her face had the angularity of an old desert line, but Alyea couldn't place which one. In contrast to the guide, this woman looked as if she didn't have any extra fat on her body, other than in the generous curves that her thin robe did absolutely nothing to conceal.

Alyea remembered a Bright Bay saying: *A woman to make a eunuch cry.* This woman, without making a single seductive movement, fit that description perfectly. Alyea wondered if that was why she stayed hidden away in the middle of nowhere: surrounded, presumably, only by women.

The tall woman waited patiently, smiling; Alyea realized she'd been staring. "My apologies, *ishai-s'a*," she murmured hastily, dropping her gaze. She could feel a flush starting to climb across her face.

She heard a series of choked noises from behind her that could have been laughter.

"No, *s'a* Alyea," the tall woman said, "you have not earned the right to call me that yet." Her dark stare moved past Alyea to the table beyond. The sounds from the other women stopped short.

"Gods," Alyea said under her breath. She felt fumbling and hopeless, afraid to even speak now. "I'm sorry."

"You only repeated what you heard, and that was a word you should not have heard yet," the tall woman said, still staring past Alyea at the now-quiet women. "You will learn. Come with me."

She led Alyea back to the ishell and motioned her to sit on one of the benches. Eyeing the stone surface, Alyea chose one with a cushion. The woman drew a curtain across the doorway; it looked like hundreds of rough glass beads, strung on individual lines, and settled in place with a gentle chinkling noise, swaying slowly for some time.

The tall woman moved to sit beside Alyea, turning herself sideways, and sat cross-legged; Alyea copied the movement, careful to keep space between so their knees didn't touch. The woman's presence was close to overwhelming; not sexual, exactly, but *powerful*. Alyea felt as if she sat within reach of a blazing fire that produced all the impact of heat without burning her flesh.

"You may call me *ka-s'a-ishrait*. That translates to 'honored Callen woman of Ishrai,'" the woman said. "If that is too long, simply '*ishrait*' will serve." She smiled. "The other term means 'sister under Ishrai.' It should not have been said in your presence; you do not bear our mark. If you pass your blood trial, you may use that term; not before."

"I'm sorry," Alyea said again.

The ishrait shook her head. "Apologize once. If your words are not accepted the first time, they will never be accepted. It is a weakness to apologize many times."

Alyea nodded.

The woman studied her for a moment, seeming to deliberate, then said, "You are a problem, *s'a* Alyea. Do you understand that? No. I can see you don't." She sighed. "The blood trials are not a short process. The trial for Comos alone can take weeks to months; you went through it in less than two days. The trial of Ishrai should take a full year and should come last. You will be given less than a week. You are being given very short trials, and out of proper order."

Alyea picked a question carefully. "Why have the trials been shortened for me?"

"Politics," the ishrait said. "You are, as I understand it, in a unique position: King's Emissary, proxy holder to Scratha lands, and sent with a *hask* and a *sheth-hinn* as advisor and protector. You own two ugren slaves, one of whom may upset a very delicate balance in the southlands. You're under the protection of a *thass*, but the teyanain are hunting you in defiance of that protection."

"Pardon, ishrait," Alyea said, "I don't know most of those terms. I can't fully understand what you're saying."

"*Sheth-hinn* is an assassin," the ishrait said.

That had to be Micru. "What about—"

"*Thass*," the woman said, cutting her off, "is a person with great status, beyond even noble rank. It is not your king," she added, seeing the expression on Alyea's face. "Your king has little status in the southlands. I have been asked not to tell you the name of your thass just yet."

Alyea reflexively began sorting through names that might suit. Chac? But Juric had spoken of him with utter contempt. Or had it been Chac Juric referred to, after all? What if one of her guards was actually the mysterious *hask*?

The ishrait smiled, as though sensing Alyea's confusion, then went on, "When your thass asked to bring you here to be tested, it alarmed me deeply. The involvement of the teyanain only makes matters worse. You put us all in danger, *s'a* Alyea. This is not a good place for you to be." She glanced at the pool with a frown and seemed to hold herself back from saying more.

Alyea shook her head slowly, then stopped, afraid the ishrait would see it as rejection. A question finally came clear, and Alyea worded it with care: "Will shorter tests be open to political challenges?"

The ishrait sighed. "No," she said. "That's part of my concern, *s'a*. The reason the tests take so long is that they involve instruction to prepare the supplicant for the trial. You are having the trials without any preparation. You cannot imagine how dangerous that is, especially for the trial of Ishrai. I am astounded that Juric granted you the mark of Comos. I know Juric; he would not have granted you more than one mistake. Most supplicants are given three, even after months of preparation, but Juric is a very hard man."

Alyea felt a sharp chill run down her spine. "He told me that by giving me a second chance he was giving more than most Callen," she said.

"Were those his exact words?"

Alyea thought back. "'I will give you a second chance, which others would not.'"

"Callen are allowed to lie during the blood trials," the ishrait said. "But he must like you. He only twisted his words. It would have been kinder for him to say 'I will only grant you one mistake, where most give three; be warned.' But that is not Juric's way, especially with a woman. He has served Comos for many years, and he does try to be fair, but he was raised Shakain and has not totally lost that bias."

"Or his love for cactus peppers?"

The ishrait's smile returned. "Every time I see him, we hold a contest to see who can eat the most cactus pepper before reaching for tea. I am not Shakain, but I come from a village near the Haunted Lands, and their spices are far bolder than in Shakai. Juric was not always a Callen, and neither was I; we traveled together for many years, and he still comes by whenever he can. It is very likely he volunteered to test you so that he could come see me."

"I thought. . . ." Alyea started, then bit her tongue.

The woman seemed to understand. "Eunuch? Of course," she said. "But that does not stop a friendship, does it?"

"I'm sorry, ishrait," Alyea said. "That was rude."

"It's a common reaction from northerns," the ishrait said. "We believe the choice to give up that part of life is a powerful decision. Anyone strong enough to do that, for whatever reason, should be respected and honored, not mocked as a weakling as northerns do."

Alyea thought of the fat, sour old eunuchs she'd seen in the courts all her life, and the spare, vibrant energy of Juric, and had to agree a vast difference lay between the two.

The ishrait drew a deep breath and let it out slowly, closing her eyes while she exhaled. "*S'a* Alyea, Juric no doubt told you that once you begin the blood trials, you cannot stop. That was truth. I should not tell you this, because the decision should come from the soul, not the mind, but there are two exceptions he would not have mentioned. One, you may break from the trials by swearing service to one of the three gods as a Callen. Callen renounce *all* claims in the world; family, status, bloodline, political power . . . slaves . . . lovers. We are removed from all debts and dishonors, and nobody can lay hand on us for past actions. Once we go into the world again, of course, we are held accountable for actions from that point on; but anything prior to the oath is gone as if it never happened. Not even the teyanain would dare breach that beginning neutrality."

Acana paused, watching Alyea's face closely, then went on, "The other option is to volunteer to participate in another supplicant's blood trial. That is considered a holy service and frees the volunteer from all previous commitments and challenges, wiping your past clean just like the first option. But the decision to accept a volunteer rests with the Callen administering the trial, and you may only volunteer once in your entire life; so if the Callen rejects your offered service you cannot try elsewhere. I do not recommend you take that option. But it is your life, and your choice. I cannot advise you further on the matter."

The ishrait dropped her gaze to her linked hands, a faint crease across her forehead, and waited for a reply.

Alyea considered, looking at the issue from as many angles as she could think of. Distilled to bluntness, what the woman had said was: *You're racing against death. I don't think you're going to win. Here's a way out.*

Juric's words came back to her: *The test of Comos is a test to see if you can set your own welfare aside for the larger good.* What would happen to Halla,

Sela, and Gria if she abandoned her responsibility to them because she feared for her own life? What about the trust placed in her by the king? What would happen to Scratha Fortress and lands, if the representative sent to hold them walked away from that position?

"I thank you, ishrait," Alyea said finally, "but I won't do that. I won't turn away from the people that are looking to me to carry this through. I won't turn away from myself. If I die through the trials or through the teyanain, at least I'll die with honor."

The ishrait looked up again, a broad smile appearing. "Now I do believe you passed Juric's test without flinching," she said. "I will allow you to take the blood trial of Ishrai."

Alyea hadn't expected that; but looking back over what Juric had said, and untangling his words, she understood. *Not all supplicants are accepted.* But he hadn't told her, directly, that each and every Callen had to accept her individually.

She shut her eyes and swallowed hard, realizing what a fine edge she'd been walking; then wondered how many lies the woman had just told her.

Callen are allowed to lie during the blood trials.

She'd have to watch the ishrait very carefully.

"Come," the ishrait said, swinging her legs off the bench and standing. "I will prepare you for the trial."

Chapter Fifteen

The house with the blue roof had a matching blue door, and the small yard around it looked neat and tidily kept. Several large pots of herbs and vegetables stood in the sunniest parts of the yard. For some reason, Red frowned when he saw that, and checked his step.

"The rose bush is gone," he said under his breath, looking around.

The door opened just then, and a tall, heavy-set woman came out, carrying a small bowl and a knife.

"Good day," she said amiably, then squinted at Red. "Do I know you, *s'e*?"

Afraid the man was about to bolt, Idisio elbowed him lightly in the side. It seemed to break Red out of his paralysis.

"Ah . . . I'm looking for Yhaine," he said hoarsely.

The woman's stillness warned Idisio of trouble before she spoke.

"I'm sorry, *s'e*," she said. "Yhaine died years ago."

"And . . . and her son?" Red said in a near-whisper. "The boy?"

The woman came a few steps closer, studying him. "I remember you now. You're that sailor she was fond of for a time. I'm her older sister Filhane."

Red nodded. His expression held a heartbreaking mix of dread and hope. "The boy, *s'a*?"

"Why do you ask?" the woman said, cocking her head to one side, a hard light in her eyes now. "You think you're the father? Bit late in the day to come knocking, isn't it?"

Red began to shift his weight back, as if readying himself to retreat.

Idisio kicked his ankle and said loudly, "He only just found out, *s'a*. Have some mercy, would you?"

The sailor looked lost and bewildered at the unexpected support. Filhane transferred her hard-eyed stare to Idisio, who glared back with every ounce of street-thief gall he could muster.

"He only just found out," Idisio repeated, more softly. "Look at his face, *s'a*, if you doubt his sincerity."

Filhane took a long look at Red, then sighed. "I'm sorry," she said. "Listen to me then, sailor: you may have bedded my sister, but I doubt you knew her. Let go of the romantic memory I can see in your eyes. She wasn't like that at all."

Red frowned and opened his mouth to speak; Filhane held up a hand and went on. "She was sweet, when she wanted something. And mean as a roused micru when she was denied. She actually did like you; that's why I remember you. But I'll bet you never saw her mean streak, or the *esthit* she used."

"That must have been after. . . ." Red began.

"No," Filhane said. "She started using *esthit* when she was ten. I couldn't stop her. Nobody could. Our father beat her time after time after time and couldn't make her stop. I begged and pleaded and screamed at her. Nothing worked. I'll guarantee that every time you saw her, she was lost on dream-dust."

Red began to look angry now, sullen, as if he wanted to argue. Filhane didn't give him a chance.

"Here's something else for you, to take the shine off that romantic memory of yours: you weren't the only man she was bedding back then," she went on remorselessly. "Don't look like that. Did you hold faithful to her, when you were in another port?"

Red opened his mouth, shut it again, then looked at the ground, a deep flush beginning to crawl up his neck.

"I didn't think so," Filhane said. "Believe me, sailor, as much as you don't want to hear this, I wish I didn't have to say it more. But my sister was a whore, and addicted to esthit, and no amount of wishing will make it different."

Red took a deep breath and rubbed the back of his neck with one large hand. "Thank you, *s'a*. That's a good hard lesson you've handed me. I'll leave you in peace."

"Wait," Idisio said, grabbing the man's arm hard, just below the elbow, as Red began to turn away. "The boy. What about her son?"

"He's likely not even mine," Red said bleakly. "I was a fool to think that."

"Now that I don't know," Filhane said. "What made you think he was yours in the first place?"

Idisio tightened his grip; after a moment, Red said, thickly, "The man who told me of the boy said the child had red hair."

"Red hair?" The woman's eyebrows rose. "He's seen the child, then. I never did. Yhaine was out of the house and living with another man by the time her pregnancy was showing. There was enough bad feeling between us by then that we never saw the child; it took me months to get word of her death. I always thought the child must have died stillborn, as there was no word of it to be found."

Red stood very still. Idisio, glancing up at the sailor, saw a mad glitter surfacing in the blue eyes.

"He's seen the child," Red repeated softly under his breath. Idisio doubted the man had heard much past that point. "Living with another man."

"If the child has red hair," Filhane said, "it may well be yours, after all. There aren't many redheaded sailors come through this port, and you're the only one I can remember my sister taking up with during that time. I'd track down that man she was living with, to find out what happened."

"I'll do that," Red said. "Do you know his name?"

Filhane frowned, thinking for a moment. "Something like Ikle or Itckl."

"Iticali?" Red said.

"Yes, that was the name," Filhane said. "You know him?"

"That," Red said through his teeth, "is the old *friend* who told me about the boy." His hands clenched into fists.

Filhane retreated a cautious step. "I don't know much else," she said. "I think Iticali was in the service of some desert lord at the time. Perhaps he placed the child with his lord's family."

"Which lord?" Red said.

"I don't know, sailor," Filhane said. "I have no more answers for you, but I do have work to do. Please, take your righteous anger elsewhere; I've no time or help for it. I gave up on being angry about my sister years ago."

Red turned without a word and walked out of the small yard; and this time, Idisio made no move to stop him.

"Boy," Filhane called as he turned to follow the sailor.

Idisio paused, casting an inquiring look over his shoulder.

"If you do find the child . . . send me word?"

Idisio nodded, not trusting his voice, and ran to catch up with the fast-moving sailor.

"Not our problem," Cafad Scratha said, some hours later. "Absolutely not. Don't even think about it this time, Idisio. We've enough problems as it is. Don't add a randy northern sailor to the pile."

"But—" Idisio started.

"*No*," Scratha said. "He'll have to find his own answers."

"You're a desert lord, though," Idisio said, persistent against Scratha's gathering scowl. "You could get answers he couldn't."

"I swore I wouldn't hit you again," Scratha said through his teeth. "Don't make me break that promise. Let it go, Idisio. You don't know what you're asking."

"Then *tell* me," Idisio said. "How am I any good to you if you have to protect me from my ignorance?"

They matched glares; then Scratha sighed.

"I should have left you in the streets," he said, without any real force. "Asking for anything, whether it be favors, goods, or information, carries a price in the southlands. I don't want to be indebted to someone for the sake of a foolish northern sailor."

Idisio breathed a quiet sigh of relief. The strangeness had left his lord for the moment, the dark track of his thoughts diverted to something less important. And this language he understood; the street thieves of Bright Bay operated in much the same way.

"I'll pay it," he said.

Scratha stared at him. "You can't. You have nothing to pay with, Idisio. It's a generous offer, but it's not possible."

"I can," Idisio said, sure of himself now. "What kind of things would another lord ask for?"

"It could be anything," Scratha said. "And it's not the lords that you need to worry about; it's the hirelings and mercenaries. Some of them are . . . not kind. Idisio, no. Let this northern find his own answers."

"What's the worst thing they could ask for?" Idisio pressed. "What's the worst you've ever heard of being asked in exchange for this kind of information? It's pretty trivial, isn't it, asking after a lost child?"

Scratha drew a deep breath and shut his eyes. "You don't want to know."

"I do."

"You *don't*," Scratha said without opening his eyes. "It's foul."

Idisio waited, not speaking, until his lord finally looked at him, then said, in as emotionless a voice as he could, "I've probably done it already, whatever it is. That's part of growing up in the streets."

Scratha stared at him, looking horrified.

"The people that raised me didn't give free handouts," Idisio said. "They wanted a profit out of their effort. That's how it is. That's why I jumped at the chance to go with you." He paused, drew a deep breath, and forced his tone to become flat and hard. "If you don't help Red, I'll go asking myself."

"*No*," Scratha said, and it was an order, carrying an unspoken threat that Idisio would be lucky to escape with bruises if he disobeyed.

Idisio swallowed hard and threw his last die, praying his hunch about Scratha's one vulnerability turned out to be right.

"I used to dream, at night, that my father would come find me," he said. His voice wouldn't obey him; it wavered and stuck. At least he wasn't crying. "I used to think one day, everything would be all right, it would all turn out to be a bad dream or a mistake. Someone would rescue me. But nobody ever did, my lord; I pulled myself out on your tail, and you were kind enough to let me. Not everyone is that lucky."

Scratha started to speak, stopped, swallowed hard, and said, "There's nothing saying he's on the streets, Idisio."

"There's nothing saying he's not," Idisio shot back.

"*Sessii ta-karne, i shha!*" Scratha spat, suddenly furious; the moment passed quickly, and he rubbed his temples as if to ease a headache. "Fine. I'll ask around. If you *swear* to keep your own mouth shut."

"I promise," Idisio said readily. "What did all that mean, just now?"

"If you ever learn the old language," Scratha said, his expression still sour, "you're welcome to punch me for what I just called you. Now go away." He tossed Idisio a gold round. "Take Riss out for a good meal, and buy yourselves some proper desert clothes. I don't have time to see to it now. If you run out of money, tell them to send me the bill. And go find Red; tell him to come see me."

"Yes, my lord, thank you, my lord," Idisio said, and bolted before the man could change his mind.

He went after Red first, reasoning that the search would be quicker without a girl tagging along. It didn't take long for Idisio to be glad of that decision. Several of the streets and taverns he passed through in his search made him nervous, and a female face would have caused a riot in at least one of them.

He finally found the sailor, sitting alone in a dark and musty-smelling wine shop, staring at an almost-full glass of wine. Judging by the bartender's expression, the sailor had been sitting without drinking for some time.

"Idisio," Red said, looking up with a distracted frown. "What are you doing here?"

"Looking for you," Idisio said. "My lord wants to see you."

"What for?"

"I talked him into helping you look for your son," Idisio said, and watched the dour expression lighten into incredulity.

"Why would he do something like that? Why would you?" Red stood, leaning forward onto the table as if in need of the support. "You walked me there, like I asked; you don't owe me anything else."

Idisio shrugged. "Better hurry, before he changes his mind."

"Gods," the man said, and threw a silver coin on the table. "Where do

I find him?"

"Silver Sands Inn," Idisio said. "Wait, I'm headed back there too—"

But the sailor had already slammed through the door and was almost running down the street. Idisio sighed, offered the sullen barkeep a shrug, and followed.

Not in a hurry now, he found himself paying more attention to the people he passed, especially the younger ones. Ten to fifteen, Red had said; no older than Idisio, and with bright red hair. Something about that tugged at his memory, disturbing him. He'd known a boy with bright red hair once, in Bright Bay; could it have been . . . ? But that was ridiculous, of course. He put it out of his mind.

Once or twice his step slowed too much, and he found himself the target of coarse invitation by nearby whores, male and female alike. He'd never liked those offers, and with old memories churning fresh in his mind, liked them even less. He shook his head each time and hurried past without speaking.

He made it back to the inn without seeing a single naturally red-topped head, male, female, adult, or child. There were even more people in this town with dyed hair than there had been in Bright Bay, but the colors here tended towards blue and yellow and even white, all in strips, usually set in dozens of long, tight braids. An astonishing number of people, young and old, were shaven completely bald. Many wore thin, hood-like head coverings that wrapped around the face, leaving only the eyes visible.

As Idisio entered the inn, he belatedly thought about what he'd just done: challenged a desert lord and offered himself as payment for whatever debt was incurred. Jumped in on the side of a near stranger, a *randy northerner* as Scratha had named him.

He'd lost his mind. What had he been *thinking*?

Traveling away from the city had softened his survival wits. He'd had it too easy, too safe, for too long; he'd jumped straight into madness without even looking first.

With barely a glance at Idisio, the innkeeper told him the room numbers, sounding thoroughly distracted. Idisio offered thanks with little more coherence. His troubled thoughts carried him blindly to the door of the room he would be sharing with Scratha. He could hear voices inside, and decided Red and Scratha were best left alone for the moment. Riss had the next room over; he moved to it and knocked softly on the door.

After a moment, he rapped harder, and that brought an indistinct mutter from inside. It sounded like an invitation, and Idisio, mind still fixed on the enormity of what he'd just done, pushed through the door and stepped inside.

More bare skin than Seshya had ever shown him presented itself.

"Ohdeargods," he said, and slammed back out of the room, eyes shut tight. Weak-kneed, he leaned against the opposite wall and tried to think of a way to pretend he hadn't just walked in on Riss with no clothes on.

He hadn't managed anything beyond slowing his racing heart by the time the door opened. Riss stared at him, wearing a light robe and looking bemused herself.

After a moment, she said, "Your hearing's not much good, is it? I *said* 'wait a minute.'"

Idisio shook his head dumbly, looking anywhere but at her.

"Gods, you're an idiot," Riss said after a moment, sounding impatient. "Come on in; don't stand there in the hallway. You look like you're about to faint."

"No," Idisio said, aware that his voice was emerging at a rather higher octave than usual. "That's all right, I just. . . ."

"Oh, for the love of the gods," Riss said. She grabbed his arm, yanked him into the room and closed the door behind him. "Haven't you ever seen a girl without clothes on before? It's *hot* here! I was trying to cool off. Sit down."

He shook his head, still at a complete loss for words, and sank into the chair she pointed to.

"Was there something important, or did you just barge into my room for fun?" Riss said waspishly.

"Ah," he said, intensely grateful for a question he *did* have a good answer to. "Lord Scratha wants me to take you out for a meal and to buy some clothes. Proper desert clothes, he said." He took a chance and opened his eyes again.

"Good," Riss said. "Everything I have makes me sweat. Did you find the sailor's boy?"

"No," he said, staring determinedly at the floor. "He's gone. . . ."

He felt a sudden dizziness, and a hot, dry wind whispered against his cheeks and forehead. The taste of sand rolled against his tongue. A memory rose, of the red-haired boy he'd known and his odd mannerisms; he *had* been southern. He might have been Red's son, after all. Wouldn't that be funny . . . but the thought held no real humor against the continuing overlay of wind whispering in his mind.

The moment passed. Riss knelt beside him, her face white, gripping his arm hard. "I thought you were about to faint. What happened?"

"Nothing." He blinked, trying to focus. "I just . . . I just need to go eat something. I haven't eaten today. I think. Let's get going."

She stared at him for a moment, then cautiously released his arm as if afraid he would fall over. He stood, correcting a slight wobble before she could react to it.

"Wait outside, then, so I can dress," she said, looking as if she held back much sharper words. Idisio left the room and leaned against the opposite wall again. Like before, his knees felt treacherously unready to support him, but this time it wasn't embarrassment and shock; it was fear.

It happened again while they were walking back to the inn.

Full, content, and relaxed, he began telling Riss about the visit with Filhane and about Scratha agreeing to help. He glossed over how he'd gained his lord's support, and although Riss gave him a hard look reminiscent of the one Azni had used weeks ago, she left it alone.

"So what now?" Riss said. "Is this sailor going to be traveling with us?"

"I don't know," Idisio said, startled. "I hadn't thought of that. I figured they'd ask some questions locally; the boy can't be far from here, can he?"

"If he's been taken into a desert lord's family, he could be anywhere," Riss pointed out.

"I don't think. . . ." Idisio started, and his vision blurred again.

He felt a sense of being elsewhere and other than himself. Stone walls rose around him and silence, blessed silence, and a warmth began in his chest; the faintest glimmer of hope that it was over, that he had found a safe place at last, and an *anger*. . . .

He came back to himself, on his knees, his cheek stinging as if Riss had slapped him. His throat felt raw, and the packages he'd been carrying were scattered over the ground as if he'd thrown his arms out wide and heedless.

"You *screamed*," Riss said, her face white. Her voice trembled as she went on, "I think you made one man piss himself. I almost did. *Gods*, what's going on with you?"

"I don't know," he said. People were beginning to gather around, staring. He climbed to his feet, brushed off his knees, and started picking up the dropped bundles.

"Let's get back to the inn," Riss said. "Quickly."

"You have to tell Lord Scratha," she said once they were back in the inn. They'd gone to Riss's room by unspoken agreement; the packages were piled in a corner.

"No," he said immediately, hunching into himself. Afterimages still danced through his mind at odd moments; a phantom glimpse of red hair, a tickling urge to scream and never stop.

"You have to," Riss insisted. "He'll know what to do. What are you afraid of?"

"I'm not afraid," he said, lying altogether; the lift of her eyebrows called him on it. Before they could argue further, a knock sounded and

Scratha stepped in without waiting for invitation.

"I see where you learned your manners," Riss said a bit sourly.

Scratha cast her a puzzled look, then shrugged it aside without asking. "It's getting late. We have to get up early in the morning. If you could manage without Idisio's company, we all need to get some sleep."

"Lord," Riss said, ignoring Idisio's frantic motion to stop her, "Idisio needs to talk to you."

"No," Idisio said, ducking his face away from the dark stare turning his way. "No, I'm all right."

"He's had fits twice in the last four hours," Riss said over his protest. "He's afraid to tell you for some reason."

"Thank you, Riss," Scratha said, voice completely calm. "Idisio, come."

Idisio shot Riss a poisonous glare as he left the room; she shrugged and made a shooing motion with her hands.

"Fits," Scratha said quietly a few moments later, closing the door behind them. He moved to the edge of the low bed and sat down. "Tell me."

Seeing no point in protest, Idisio gave as much detail as he could remember of each incident. When he finished talking, Scratha shut his eyes, pinched the bridge of his nose, then sighed and dropped his hand.

"Have you been practicing the aqeyva meditations?" he asked.

"Every day," Idisio said. "Hours a day."

"Hours," Scratha repeated, and shook his head. His dark eyes scrunched more tightly closed, then opened again. "I didn't think you'd practice that much on your own. I should have paid more attention."

"Did I do something wrong?" Idisio said, bewildered. "I thought I was getting really good at it. Is that wrong?"

Scratha let out a half-snort, half-laugh. "Wrong? No. But you should have had more guidance. I should have been watching you. I let my own concerns distract me. You've been in trance for *hours* a day?" He sounded as if he hoped the answer might change to *"No, I lied."*

"It passed the time," Idisio said, trying to sound indifferent. He fought an urge to cower; the very air seemed to have darkened with the desert lord's mood.

"Do you have any idea how rare that is?" Scratha said. "I've been practicing aqeyva most of my life and can't hold a full trance more than two hours."

"It's just . . . paying attention to yourself," Idisio said, fumbling for words. "It's not that hard. I don't understand, my lord. It's no different than seeing what's really in front of you, like when you had me look at that mug; I just never thought to turn it to myself before. And it would have been dangerous, losing track of everything around me like that. But it's not that hard."

Scratha shook his head again, his expression bemused. "You make it sound so simple," he said. "Only aqeyva masters can do what you've done. And these visions, and not being affected by Yuer's drugs . . . You never had anything like this before you started practicing?"

"No," Idisio said after a moment's thought. "I've always relied on hunches, but nothing, ever, as . . . as solid as these. They're almost visions."

"That's exactly what they are," Scratha said. He rubbed at his eyes. "I think you have Ghost Lake blood, Idisio. You have too much northern in your face for anything else."

"What's . . . ?" Idisio stopped, remembering Red's song. "That's the place up by Arason? Those stories are real?"

"Oh, yes. There was more truth than myth to the tales that sent witch-hunters to Arason. How you came to Bright Bay I don't understand, and we'll probably never know, but you're *ha'ra'ha,* without a doubt."

Idisio shut his eyes. He thought he might scream. "What's a *ha'ra'ha*?"

After a brief silence, Scratha said, "It's . . . well, we'll talk about it more, later. I need time to think how to explain it. I never thought I'd have to . . . well. Go to sleep. We can talk in the morning."

Idisio accepted that decision with deep relief; but after a time of staring up through the darkness, wide-eyed and wakeful, began to regret letting it pass. At last he said, tentatively, "Lord Scratha?"

The desert lord sighed. "I can't sleep either," he admitted. "All right. I don't suppose you've learned any real history, so I'll have to start a ways back for you to make sense of the answer. That's why I've needed to think, to find the shortest way to explain." He blew out a gusty breath and shifted on the low bed. "You're not fully human, Idisio."

Chapter Sixteen

After dark, the ishell felt very different from the spacious, welcoming place Alyea had seen earlier in the day. Globes of oil similar to those in the passageways had been set on the floor near the walls at measured intervals, but gave off such dim light that most of the room lay in shadow.

Women in white robes, with hoods drawn forward to hide their faces, occupied every bench: sitting cross-legged and facing each other as Alyea and the ishrait had done earlier in the day. The pool looked like a black pit now, and not at all welcoming. Alyea couldn't tell where the stone ended and the water began. She stood in the doorway to the ishell, uncertain and unreasonably terrified, and waited for someone to tell her what to do.

A hand touched her shoulder from behind. Alyea stopped a frightened squeak just before it emerged from her mouth and turned to meet the dark gaze of the ishrait. In the eerie light of the room, the woman's face seemed a thing of stark and cold angles. The power she had resonated earlier in the day had shifted into something much broader and deeper, a thing of deep roots and old knowledge.

"Disrobe," the ishrait commanded.

Alyea slipped out of the light robe; the woman reached out and took it from her.

"Stand at the edge of the pool."

Alyea felt her way across the floor, wary of stubbing her toes. Past the benches, she moved even more cautiously, testing for the edge of the water with each step. At last a slight slickness and a dip in the floor warned her she'd come close; she stopped, turning to face the ishrait.

"There is a mat a step to your left," the ishrait said. "Sit down, facing me."

Alyea obeyed. The mat felt like a smoothly-woven blanket folded on itself to create thickness. She drew her legs up and tried to tuck her feet under herself; the room had become surprisingly cold.

"The sisters of Ishrai form a community in which the opinions of all are valued," the ishrait said. "Therefore, the first part of the test is a series of questions, one from each sister of Ishrai gathered here. You must answer to their complete satisfaction to continue. You may take as long as you like to think about the questions, but you must answer fully and honestly. Do you accept these terms?"

Alyea swallowed. "Yes."

The ishrait's voice became deeper and more formal. "Sisters, before us is a supplicant for the blood trial of Ishrai. I have granted her petition. *Taishell te s'a-naila*; the blood trial begins. She is open to you now. Ask her what you wish."

A voice came from somewhere in front of her. "Supplicant, you have no name, no titles, no status in this place of Ishrai. Does that change your purpose?"

Alyea considered the question carefully. If she truly had no name, if all her titles and privileges were stripped from her, would that stop her? Would she be free to abandon Gria and Sela, and stop worrying about them and the job laid upon her by the king?

"No," she said at last. "I will continue regardless."

Another voice echoed through the chamber. "Supplicant, do you act for yourself or for others?"

Alyea began to answer, then stopped, frowning into the darkness around her. She had to pass the blood trials because she'd been charged with holding Scratha Fortress by the king; and she wanted to do that not for his sake, but for her own. He'd handed her a powerful position: hadn't her first thought been that she would outrank Pieas? She'd agreed to the position for her own purposes. Still, she felt genuine concern and thought for others had been involved in her decisions. She considered another moment, and finally said, "Both."

"Do you always think of others in your decisions?"

"No," she said. She'd expected something similar, and had an answer ready. "I have been selfish much of my life. I see that, and regret it, and wish to change that behavior."

"Define selfish."

Alyea bit her lip. "It's thinking first of yourself, to the harm of others," she said, trying to keep from sounding uncertain.

"Who have you harmed, and how?"

She stared from darkness into the steady ring of light at the edges of the room, and didn't know what to say. The silence seemed to stretch forever. "I should have listened to my elders," she said, unable to come up with anything more coherent.

The question was repeated in an eerie flat tone that echoed through the room. "Who have you harmed, and how?"

. . . how . . . how . . . hhhhwwww . . . ohh. . . .

The whispering echoes faded away to silence.

Alyea shut her eyes, feeling suddenly ill. One chance gone; only two more left, if this went by the rules the ishrait had explained earlier. A memory rose in her mind: Ethu's fixed grimace as the whips descended again and again.

"I caused the death of a good man," she whispered. Tears spilled down her cheeks. "By not being willing to stand up for my truth, I allowed a man with more courage than I to die in my place."

"Was his death truly your fault?"

She drew breath to insist it had been, but the words twisted in her mouth.

"No," she heard herself say. Her voice came out hard and rough from deep in her throat. "*No*. It was them, the priests, not me. I wish I could kill them all!"

Alyea hadn't cried back then, hadn't cried during her own punishment, or afterwards; under constant watch, she hadn't dared display weakness. By the time that danger passed, grief had been pushed into a steely anger against the priests. But now that long-standing shield dissolved; tears came, unleashed with the force of a long-delayed wave. She bent over, locking her elbows around her knees, and found herself actually howling with anger and pain.

As if a ghost were in the room, she thought she heard Ethu's voice whispering *no tears*, but she couldn't seem to stop.

Her sobs were the only sound for a long time. When her breath slowed to occasional hitches, she sat back up, drawing an arm across her face. She looked around at the silent women and thought, *Well, I've failed this one for sure.*

Another voice spoke, from her right this time. "What teaching do you follow?"

Still shaken by her emotional outburst, Alyea found words hard to assemble. "I . . . I don't have one," she said. "I was taught to follow the northern s'iopes, but that was just to keep me alive."

"Is your learning of our ways aimed only at keeping you alive?"

Alyea bit her lip. An edge to that question warned her she'd moved onto dangerous ground.

"There are people depending on me," she said carefully. "I won't survive the trials if I don't learn your lessons, and I can't help anyone if I'm dead." Prompted by a mad impulse, she added dryly: "Personally, as well, I'd rather stay alive."

She saw no visible reaction to her attempt at humor. Even a flicker of a smile would have been tremendously reassuring; the constant, emotionless drone of the questions and the surrounding silence raised a cold sweat on the back of her neck.

"You are putting your own life at risk for the sake of another's orders. If you pass all the trials and become a desert lord, what then?"

Alyea started to say: *I'll do the task he sent me here to do.* She held the words, sensing a larger question. For the first time, she thought about the possibility of succeeding, of holding Scratha Fortress as an actual desert lord. What would she do?

Return to Bright Bay? Her new status would throw her entire family into disarray. No Peysimun had ever held rank as high as desert lord. They wouldn't know what to do with her. They'd be terrified.

Desert lords never stayed in Bright Bay for long. They wandered through and left again, ignoring the people scurrying out of their way. Sometimes they came to court gatherings; sometimes they just showed up for no apparent reason and left again a few days later. She wouldn't be welcome for very long; it would make people too nervous.

Dozens of small political alliances throughout the court would be disrupted by the fact that a minor family had abruptly acquired powerful connections. And what would Oruen do with her, a potentially dangerous new force in his court? He couldn't allow her to stay in Bright Bay unless she labored under a tight leash of his own making; and she knew she wouldn't stand for that. He likely knew that too, which led to unpleasant suspicions she didn't want to think about.

Stay in the desert? Where? Once Scratha returned and took possession of his fortress again, she'd have nowhere to go. It seemed doubtful that proud lord would allow her to stay, title or no title. In fact, Scratha would likely be furious at the move to make her a desert lord and place her in charge of Scratha Fortress. He might even call her out, to end in blood the possibility of another claimant for his place.

No matter which way she looked, death seemed to be waiting, and betrayal by everyone she'd ever trusted. She'd been an *idiot* to agree to Oruen's request. Why had he put her in this position? What *did* he want from her? She shut her eyes, nauseated.

"Gods only know," she said, and meant it; she had no better answer to give the waiting silence. "I'll deal with that day when it comes."

"Is this man who sent you here worth dying for?"

Alyea thought about when she'd first met Oruen. He'd been tall and gangly, thin and awkward, nothing to look twice at physically. He'd skirted the fringes of court life, only attending when it would have been suicidal to be seen absent.

He'd haunted the beaches of Bright Bay, stopping to pick up shells like any scruffy beachcomber, examining them carefully and setting them back down. Sometimes he threw them out into the ocean, hard, as far as they would go, or skipped flat rocks against the waves.

She'd watched him from hiding, drawn by some bitter intensity in his actions, and finally one day openly positioned herself where she knew he'd pass by on his daily ramblings. She'd been twelve at the time, he almost twice that. He'd walked by with barely a nod to her; she'd scrambled to her feet and taken up a place by his side.

He hadn't objected, hadn't said anything, and they had walked in silence for over an hour. She'd met him again the next day, and the next, and slowly they'd started to talk, far away and safe from the s'iopes and the horror of daily life.

She'd been sixteen when Oruen took her to bed, the one and only time. She always said *seduced* afterwards, but the reality was much more desperate, a day of unrivaled horror leading to a mutual need for comfort, which unfolded into the inevitable.

He'd never referred to it afterward, never approached her again; and after a few fumbling attempts of her own had been rebuffed kindly but unmistakably, she'd let the friendship resume with some distance to it. When Pieas cornered her one night, she hadn't told anyone. She'd pushed aside Oruen's questions about the bruises. She'd been afraid to bridge that distance, afraid of collapsing into his arms only for him to gently, quietly push her back with the same emotionless words he'd used before.

And now he'd gained the throne, and his return for all her help and her one-time warming of his bed had been a permanent apartment in the palace and the raising of her family back into favored status. She wasn't his concubine, nor one of his advisors. He called her a friend and allowed her to quietly visit him any time she felt the need to talk, and he still claimed to respect her judgment and observations. But she'd gained nothing significant for the risks she'd taken on his behalf. Not until he chose her, out of a court of highly qualified diplomats, to step into what she now saw as the most politically dangerous situation he'd faced in the six months he had been on the throne.

Why her? The question kept coming back. Why pick an inexperienced, relatively ignorant girl, and send her with an advisor reluctant to give out crucial information? Had he intended for her to fail? If so, if not . . . was Oruen worth dying for?

She breathed in through her nose, let the air out in a hard sigh. "Once upon a time, I would have said yes without question. He's a good man. Now . . . I don't know."

"Is your purpose worth dying for?"

Opening her mouth to say *yes*, she found herself shocked at the words that came out instead: "*Nothing* is worth dying for. You can't help anyone or anything if you're dead."

Wincing, Alyea shut her eyes, waiting. What she had said went against everything she had ever been taught, ever seen lived, ever believed before. But it felt like truth: a raw, harsh truth filled with anger at endless violence and pointless sacrifice. Too many men had marched to the palace to beg, to plead, to threaten and cajole for the return of their wives and families; their reward had been a chance to entertain Ninnic before their own deaths. Too many women had thrown themselves in front of their children, trying to protect them, only to be killed and the children taken anyway.

Honorable self-sacrifice be damned to the s'iopes' hells; it never achieved anything.

The ishrait finally spoke. "Stand."

Alyea rose slowly, massaging cramps out of her legs; the cold of the stone seemed to have seeped through the blanket and into her joints. The women on the benches were turning, facing her now, their faces still shadowed beneath their deep hoods.

"The test of Comos is the test of the ego," the ishrait said, her rich voice rolling through the room. "It asks you to set aside your own fear, your own needs, for the sake of those you protect. The test of Ishrai is the test of life. It asks you to weigh the value of living. A desert lord's life is a sacred trust and must be treated with the greatest respect. A desert lord's death weakens the entire world. The desert is harsh, and life is not fair; a reckless leader would quickly be killed and leave his people unprotected. That is why a full desert lord must have the approval of Ishrai."

Alyea swallowed, daring to hope that she'd pulled it off after all.

"You have passed this part of the test of Ishrai," the woman said. "*Taishell te s'a-lalien*; sisters, the supplicant is closed to you now. You may go."

The women stood in a ragged wave, bowed deeply in Alyea's direction, and filed silently out of the room. The clicking of the bead curtain swaying back into place went on for quite some time as the ishrait moved around the room, extinguishing oil lamps until only one remained lit. She picked it up and came to stand in front of Alyea. In the tiny island of light surrounding them, the woman's face seemed drawn and worried.

"Now comes the hard part, Alyea," she said. "Sit back down, please."

The tall woman sat down on the floor in front of Alyea, seeming not to mind the cold stone; set the oil lamp between them and shut her eyes. She looked as if she were gathering strength for a supremely difficult task.

"Women do not usually become desert lords," the ishrait said. "Let me assure you it has nothing to do with gender bias. There's a very harsh reality involved. I know that Juric told you he believed you could do this; I wish I could agree. If you had the full year to study with us, I believe you might pass, but this. . . ."

She blew out air through her nose in a hard sigh of her own, seeming frustrated, and directed another worried glance at the dark pool.

"Alyea, I'll be honest. I hoped you would fail the questioning. That would have been safer for all of us."

Alyea felt the chill of the stone reaching up her spine.

"I'm committed now," she said, hearing a brittle edge in her own voice. "Stop trying to scare me out of it."

The ishrait smiled, a brief flash of pale teeth in a shadow-lined face. "All right. Let me tell you a story, then. Be silent, and listen." She leaned forward, extinguished the last lamp, and began to speak, a disembodied voice in complete darkness:

In the beginning days of the world, there was born light, and there was born dark. There was dry, and there was wet. There was warm, and there was cold. Then there came life, with death close behind. And life took many forms, but death could take only one.

One form of life developed which could think, and knew itself, and considered future and past and present as separate concepts. And that life grew, and claimed dominion over all creatures, and built a great city, and another, and another.

That life was not human.

Alyea opened her eyes and stared into the darkness, wishing she could see the ishrait's face.

Their cities did not satisfy them. They fought, and argued over small things, and lost their way, and became deeply divided, and at last parted ways. Some stayed above ground, others fled on the wind, and others dug deep to find the secrets of the world, hiding underground as they sought for knowledge. After a long time, the seekers desired to reconcile with their estranged brethren, and emerged from the deep and the still places of the world.

But the cities were gone. All traces of the ones they had left behind were gone, without a trace. No ruins; no signs of battle; nothing. Their people were simply gone, as if they had never been.

Alyea made herself swallow in a dry throat. Her eyes were starting to hurt; she realized she'd been straining them wide, staring into the darkness as if she could force herself to see the ishrait's face. She shut her eyes and rubbed her eyelids lightly with her fingertips.

The remaining seekers were few and mostly old by that time. They had not given much thought to children, while they sought their knowledge; they had been secure in their certainty that more of their kind existed to carry on the line. Now that security faltered, and they found themselves alone.

But they discovered that while they studied the deep and the still places of the world, another life had moved to fill the quiet place left by their lost brethren. This life thought, and knew itself, and considered past and present and future to be separate concepts.

This life was human.

Alyea swallowed again, blinking. She had a dozen questions by now, but knew better than to speak. The air felt dry and cold in her throat, and her skin chill-prickled.

This is the teaching of Ishrai. This is the secret lore we hold. Callen of Ishrai and the desert lords alone know this tale. You will never repeat it.

Alyea found herself nodding obediently.

The humans and the people of the world met, the ishrait said, and Alyea wondered if she were speaking at all. The breathing in front of her seemed steady and undisturbed by words. She put the thought aside as irrelevant to the moment and focused on listening.

The humans and the people of the world agreed to live together, for mutual benefit, for mutual survival. The humans gave the people of the world a name they could pronounce: ha'reye for many, ha'rethe for one. And that suited the people of the world well enough.

And they discovered that with the right circumstances, they could have children together.

Alyea opened her mouth, caught herself just in time; put a hand over her mouth to make sure she stayed silent.

A pact was made between humans and the ha'reye, for mutual benefit, for mutual survival. The people of the world promised to use the secrets they had learned to make sure the humans had water that did not drown the land, winds that did not blow everything away, and a sun that did not scorch the land. The humans. . . .

Alyea listened to the silence for a while before realizing the ishrait wanted her to complete the last sentence.

"The humans provided them with children," she said softly.

The humans gave of themselves, the ishrait agreed. *The humans gave, once every year, one of their finest young men or women. Those chosen to serve stayed with the ha'reye for one year, and gave the people of the world a single child of mixed blood, called a ha'ra'ha, and then returned to their families unharmed. Unhurt, but* different; *and they never spoke of what had happened during that year.*

Over time, this caused fear and doubt. The ones who served were affected in different ways, and sometimes frightened their communities. After a time, some places rebelled, and refused to serve when chosen, and said they would not be bound to the people of the world. They broke away, heedless of disgrace or duty. But others remained true, and wanted to study more closely with the ha'reye, and learn their secrets.

"The Split," Alyea said involuntarily, then clamped her hand back over her mouth and bit her lower lip.

The Split, the ishrait agreed evenly. *Some humans went south, to the deep jungles, to study with the ha'reye. The remaining humans broke their agreement with the people of the world, and held back their young. And the ha'reye waited a hundred years for the humans to change their ways and understand their error. But humans, not understanding, thought they had won, and moved on, and forgot.*

The ha'reye, seeing that humans had no intention of returning to their pact, came out of their deep and still places, and took the hundred young that they were due for the past hundred years. And then they left that area. The water sank deep into the ground, and the wind moved the earth from place to place to place, and the sun scorched the land. Great farms became desert, and lovely places became barren. And the humans searched for a cause, and found none; and a few among them who studied the old ways called for the ha'reye to forgive them, and found silence.

Ha'reye do not forget as quickly as a human does, and they do not forgive as easily as a human will.

Alyea felt herself nodding in time to the steady beat of the words, almost swaying in place, and shook herself sharply back to alertness.

Humans sought their kin in the jungles to the south, and found the way closed. They tried to travel the seas, to find a new land where they might survive, and found the way closed. They tried to move into the northlands, and found the way closed. And people began to die from too much sun, and too much wind, and too little water.

And then a strange thing happened.

A single human, a young man who had studied the old lore and listened to the old stories all his life, walked into the deepest places of the desert, where the children had once been given, and offered himself.

He sat in the hot sun and let it scorch him. He sat in the rains and let them soak him. He sat while the wind blew fierce and wild around him, and did not move. And he called out over and over and over for the ha'reye to hear him, to take him as an offering under the old ways, to forgive humans for breaking the pact.

The ha'reye heard and were amazed. They answered, and lifted him from the hot sands, and eased his burned flesh, and accepted him as an offering under the old ways. But they did not forgive all humans for breaking the pact, and they did not restore the southlands to their former glory.

After the allotted year of service was up, they released him to spread the word that if humans would return to the pact for as many years as they had left it broken, the east and the west and the north would be opened, but the southern jungles would stay closed forever, and should now be known as the Forbidden Jungles. Many people laughed at him, and said the desert had driven him mad; but some listened, and followed him, and kept the pact. And the pact was honored for a hundred and fifty years, and the east and the west and the north opened, but the Forbidden Jungles stayed closed. Those who had not believed went to the east and to the west and to the north, but those who believed stayed behind, and those who agreed to serve came to be called lords of the desert. They were avoided and feared more than they were respected, but kept the pact nonetheless. And those lords had families, and they chose to live in the deep places of the desert, and choose from their families who would keep the pact with the ha'reye.

It soon became clear the choices were not blind enough; even a desert lord can make mistakes when it involves the intelligence or suitability of his own offspring. So the followers of the wind-lord Comos, the water-maiden Ishrai, and the sun-lord Datda were given the responsibility of testing those who wished to honor the pact.

Over the years and through the miles, humans have once again forgotten, but never the desert lords. On the faith of the desert lords rests the survival not only of the southlands, but the world; and they never, ever forget that.

Silence filled the darkness. Sensing that the ishrait had finished her story, Alyea lifted a trembling hand to her face and discovered the dampness of tears.

"Good gods," she said at last, shakily.

"It's a long story," the ishrait said quietly, her voice echoing in the empty room, "but you need to understand it. Any questions?"

The words came out without conscious direction: "Has the king gone through the blood trials?"

"Once, that was a requirement," the ishrait said. "It fell aside with the years and the fading of memory into myth, and the chaos of recent years hasn't helped. No, the desert lords may call him 'lord' now, but it's an empty title. Oruen seems better than the recent line, but he'll never be allowed to take the trials. He knows just enough to understand that, and to have a small idea of what that means."

"And so he sent me," Alyea said, pieces beginning to fit together at last. "To become his tame desert lord."

"A desert lord serves no man," the ishrait said. "There is no such thing as a tame desert lord. Oruen's understanding is limited, and he makes a grave error with this."

"I'm beginning to see that," Alyea agreed ruefully. "Why have I been allowed to come this far?"

"Because you have the backing of a thass."

She almost said, *who?* But names weren't used here. "Why is this thass so important?"

"Think of all you have heard, Alyea," the woman said. "There is only one thing we would bow to in this situation. What is it?"

In the quiet, Alyea's pulse seemed to thud along her temples. "The ha'reye?"

"Or the *ha'ra'hain*, their mixed-blood descendants. Some few, very few, choose to make their way in the world of the humans, rather than stay in the deep places with the people of the world. Your thass is a ha'ra'ha who has chosen to stay with the humans. He is a very rare and important man among us, Alyea; and he favors you."

The room seemed warmer now, the stone under the blanket less chill; Alyea drew a deep breath and found herself breathing moist air again. She froze, not sure when the change had occurred, and unreasonably terrified by it.

"What does that mean?" she asked, unable to keep her voice steady. "That he favors me? What am I supposed to do about it?"

A heavy sigh came from the darkness in front of her.

"There is a price for everything," the ishrait said. "You cannot avoid the duty of a desert lord if you want your title to have any weight. You must give a child, and you must spend time learning your new way. But this rather peculiar situation demands your presence in the world much sooner than a year. This ha'ra'ha has proposed and been granted a remarkable exception to the one-year rule. After all the blood trials are complete, assuming you survive them all, he has offered to serve as your teacher. He will be as your lord and master until he is satisfied that you are ready to stand on your own."

The mist seemed to be condensing onto Alyea's bare skin. Not an unpleasant sensation, but still an eerie one; she resisted the urge to wipe the dampness away.

How could she hold a desert fortress and be involved in delicate political arrangements while under orders from some stranger? Impossible. Alyea shut her eyes and tried to swallow again. This wasn't what she had expected.

"What if I choose to spend the full year with . . . with the people of the world, the ha'reye, instead?" she asked.

"It's too late for that," the woman said, sounding sad. "The agreement is made and the questions are ended. My part in this is done. *Taishell,* ha'reye; she is open to you now. Gods hold you, child. Goodbye."

"Wait—"

As she spoke, she realized that the dampness on her skin wasn't condensation, but a thick layer of some unknown fluid. With a wild eddy of warm air, a surge of the same liquid flowed up her back. It slid around to the front of her body, surrounding her so quickly she barely had time to gasp in reaction before she felt herself being lifted, rolled, and pulled in one long smooth movement beneath the surface of the pool.

Chapter Seventeen

They left town as the sky began to grey; not on horses, as Idisio had assumed, but walking, with a pack mule trudging beside them. The wide path up the slope he'd seen from the ship turned out to be gigantic steps, cut wide enough for two laden mules to pass each other comfortably. While the steps were shallow, the slope tended to be steep; within a short time his calves ached. He ignored it, brooding over what Scratha had told him the night before.

The desert lord had told a long story in the cadences of a bard; Idisio had been carried away by that smooth recital. The meeting of ha'reye and human, the Agreement reached after much negotiation, the resulting children; it all whirled together in his head. He'd had little sleep and felt thoroughly gritty-eyed as he trudged up the steps, leading the mule.

Early morning quiet didn't help his drowsiness. Their mule clopped steadily up, and others clopped placidly down. Nobody seemed in a hurry to get to the top or the bottom, and nobody rode. The steady rhythm sounded almost like a lullaby. Idisio blinked hard against the urge to fall asleep on his feet; no rail protected travelers against the increasingly long drop to the jagged ground below.

Every so often, a wider space in the trail allowed people to move out of the way of those behind, and take a rest or a meal or a piss; Idisio saw all three in a short time. His thoughts had him so distracted he didn't even blink at the last, didn't find it at all odd, just gave it a blank incurious glance and kept trudging.

As the sun warmed the air, Riss began to chatter: asking Scratha questions, laughing, being foolish. Realizing that his lord was answering patiently and even gently, Idisio shook out of his brooding to listen.

"Three," Scratha said. "Three gods, three trials, three marks. I bear all three. Full lords don't show them casually; they're sacred. Even telling you how many marks, how many trials, isn't something most would do."

"We're lucky," Riss said, and it didn't sound at all sardonic.

Scratha made a neutral noise and went on: "There's a . . . a ranking system, the *thio*, in the desert. Someone with Yuer's background and birth . . . I can understand his bitterness. He always wanted to be a desert lord, but even the Aerthraim wouldn't stretch that far, and they'll accept people into their family that no other desert family would touch."

"Why did Yuer leave the southlands?" Riss said.

"He was essentially banished," the noble said. "He'd given certain young ladies of station some . . . difficulty."

"Rape?" Riss said. Her voice trembled.

"No," Scratha said. "That would have gotten him a much more severe punishment. No, Yuer had a tendency to get drunk and say excessively rude things to nobles, especially women. He became such a disgrace that his case came before a Conclave. Everyone agreed that sending him to the northlands would be best; there would be less temptation for his outbursts. He seems to have gained some self-control, at least. Control enough to undercut a two-hundred-year-old agreement between desert and kingdom," he added. "I still want to know how that happened."

They walked in silence for a while.

"Where's Red?" Idisio said suddenly.

Riss laughed. "You don't listen so well, do you? We've already been over that."

"I was thinking about something else," Idisio said.

"I told the sailor where to look and who to speak to," Scratha said, cutting Riss short as she began to say something. "I gave him the words to use and a letter giving him my support. What he finds or doesn't find is up to him now. That's as far as I could go, Idisio. He's no longer our concern."

"Thank you, my lord," he said, and meant it wholeheartedly.

Scratha nodded without replying.

"Oh, don't be mean," Riss said a few moments later and grinned at Idisio. "Your lord's not telling you that he asked the sailor to send word if he found his answers."

Idisio shot a startled glance at Scratha; the man smiled, gaze still straight ahead.

"True," he said. "I'll admit I'd like to know, myself. I feel that there's something important about the boy, and I've always gone with my hunches." He slanted a quick look at Idisio.

"So have I," Idisio said, and felt a new energy come into his step.

The journey to the top of the Wall took two full days of climbing, with no inn along the way. Halfway up they came to a plateau where exhausted travelers could collapse; aching all over, Idisio promptly did so, heedless of being stepped on or over by man or beast.

At the end of the second day of climbing, they crested the final turn of stair to level ground. The ground wasn't the pure sand Idisio had expected, but a hard, cracked mixture of pebbly dirt strewn across an uneven surface. A long building, flung wide and low across the ground and more window than wall, sat on a rare platform of solid rock. Out front stood a brightly painted sign, taller than Idisio and wider than he could stretch his arms, marked with a simple line drawing of a man climbing steep stairs. The awkward lettering read:

TOP OF THHE WAL IN ANN TAVARNN

In the distance, a rough spire of wind-scoured rock hunched against the gathering dark. Idisio stopped, staring at it; something seemed both menacing and familiar about the formation. Before he could place what bothered him about the distant rock, Scratha prodded his shoulder and Riss his back, and he stumbled on with them, tangling up his feet momentarily. The challenge of keeping his balance without catapulting into the ground distracted him as they climbed a low stair to a raised courtyard, where waist-high stone walls flanked by tall greenery blocked his view of the outside.

As they passed through the inn's wide courtyard, Idisio glanced up: feathery tops of sand-grass and desert bamboo nodded together high overhead, forming a screen against daytime sun. This late in the evening, with the sun already a low shimmer against the western horizon, chunky stone lanterns were being lit.

Nobody spoke as they walked through the striations of afternoon shade turning into evening shadow. Riss had been subdued for some time, but Idisio didn't think it came from the long climb. Something else seemed to be troubling her, but exhaustion stopped him from asking questions.

Beyond the courtyard lay a wide room with a scattering of low, desert-style tables. Red and blue sitting cushions leaned in tall piles against the walls, some still bright and new-looking, but most faded and worn. A wide, waist-high table at the far end of the room looked to be covered with plates of food.

Scratha steered them to the nearest stack of cushions. "Take one and follow me," he said, lifting a faded red pillow and turning away.

Idisio suspected he would have charged over a bed of hot rocks for a promise of sitting down at the end, and Riss probably would have been trying to knock him out of her way. Even Scratha moved more slowly than usual.

Scratha settled on his cushion, waited until they were all seated, and said, "Customs differ here. Before we move another step, there are a few things we need to settle. First of all: Idisio. You're my servant. Servant to a desert lord means you have status."

"Thio," Idisio said.

"Good. You have been listening. Yes, you have thio. If I send you on an errand, whether that be fetching water or carrying a message or bedding a woman, you do it. You don't question. And if someone gets in your way, you tell them I sent you and to argue it with me."

Idisio stared at his lord. "Bedding a woman?" he said in disbelief.

Scratha's expression held no humor. "It's been known to happen," he said. "Politics, Idisio. It's not a nice world you've put yourself into." His manner softened. "I won't ask that of you. But I've known other lords to order that, and more. Watch yourself. You're probably in more danger than I am, here. Nobody will attack me directly, but you're both vulnerable. And ignorant."

He paused. "I didn't want to bring either of you along, remember. I was willing to risk Idisio because he's quick on his feet and with his wits. But you wouldn't listen, and I could see Idisio didn't want to leave you behind."

The last comment was obviously directed at Riss. She shot Idisio a startled glance. He felt his face turning a deep crimson and tried desperately to think of something that would change his expression to a cool aloofness.

"That's another thing," Scratha went on before they could speak. "Honesty. I'll tell you this right now: by all the gods do *not* try to lie to anyone here. You don't know who's a desert lord, who's a ha'ra'ha, who's trained in aqeyva. Best to say nothing but truth, and as little of that as you can. Believe me, if I catch either of you in even a small lie here, I'll thrash you bloody myself."

Embarrassment gave way to fear: Idisio stared into his lord's dark, dark stare and had absolutely no doubt of Scratha's deadly sincerity.

"Riss is going to have to be my servant as well, for the time being," Scratha went on. "She needs the status. You're going to have to get along, Idisio. No more childish sniping and pride contests. On either side," he added, shooting an equally intense glance at Riss, who had been starting to smile.

Her smile slid away. "Yes, my lord," she said meekly.

"If you're going to accept being my servant," he said, "you have to accept that you *will* obey every single one of my commands, no matter how distasteful you may find them. Is that a problem?"

"I'm not walking back down that bloody stair," Idisio said, surprising himself. He bit his lip but met his lord's gaze steadily.

"Good," Scratha said, and looked back at Riss.

"I'll obey, my lord," Riss said.

Scratha nodded. "There's a truth for you to tell, Riss," he said. "One you've been avoiding. It's time for Idisio to know."

Riss opened her mouth, seeming about to protest.

"That's an order. Resolve it before we move on." He met her glare, steady and grim, until she retreated to studying the table again. "There's always the option of leaving," he added. "But if you go, there's only one path: back down the Wall. I won't have either of you wandering loose up here."

He sighed. "Plates are on the food table. Help yourselves. I'll pay when we're done eating." He stood in a graceful unfolding of long legs and stalked away.

In the long, awkward silence that followed, Idisio felt like scrambling to his feet and diving for the food as a distraction, but he didn't want to be the first to move. Riss seemed similarly frozen in place.

"Oh, hells," she said at last. "Idisio, look at me."

Her tone suggested a willingness to wrench his neck permanently upright if he didn't do as ordered. He met her steady stare, doing his best not to flinch or look away.

"What do you know about dasta, Idisio?"

He shook his head. "Not much. I know it's some sort of . . . I mean, I've heard it's used for, uhm, for. . . ." He fumbled to find words that weren't too embarrassing, and failed.

"It's a highly addictive aphrodisiac," Riss said bluntly. "Southern whorehouses use it to make sure their women are docile. There are boys in the trade, too."

"I know," Idisio said. A wave of dizziness and a sense of screaming rage swept over him briefly; then it passed. He blinked and focused on Riss again. She didn't seem to have noticed anything.

"Karic fed me dasta about once a week for over a year," she said. Her lips tightened. "I never realized until I overheard him talking that night. I'd never heard of dasta before." She cleared her throat and looked away. "I realized pretty fast I was addicted."

"I gathered as much," he said.

Her expression became fierce. "It's an *aphrodisiac* addiction," she said, almost snarling. "One of the things you want when the craving hits is sex, because that's always been part of the experience, and you think that can stop the hurt of not having the drug."

He stared at her, at a loss for words.

"Lord Scratha explained all that, one night when you were asleep early, and asked what I wanted to do. He said I could bed him if I needed to, or you if you'd agree; I didn't want another man to touch me just then. He said he understood and that he'd do what he could to help me without that." She spoke rapidly now, as if trying to get it over with.

Idisio's jaw loosened. He opened and shut his mouth like a landed fish several times, conflicting thoughts and emotions rushing through him.

"He said you could take me to bed? Oh, gods," he added instantly, utterly mortified, and covered his face with both hands. "I'm sorry, Riss, I didn't mean to say that. Oh, gods."

To his surprise, she laughed. Not a joyful laugh; more a weary acknowledgment of a painful truth. "Yes. And I thought about it. But I was so hurt and so angry . . . that just wasn't an option. Just explaining it all to you was more than I could handle. That's why I spent so much time in my cabin, on the ship. I still . . . I still crave. . . ." She stopped, cleared her throat. "But I can handle it now." Her stare dared him to question that statement.

"Yeah," Idisio said, numb. She'd thought about going to bed with him? He spoke to cover the awkward silence, and made it worse: "Well, that's all right."

He dropped his face back into the safe darkness of his palms for a moment, feeling like the world's biggest idiot, then made himself look up and face her.

"I meant. . . ." He fumbled for words, and quickly gave up. "Sorry."

Her grin had more real humor in it this time. "I understand," she said, and looked away, giving him a chance to recover. "Looks like Lord Scratha found some other people to talk to."

Idisio looked across the room. Scratha had settled at a table with three other men, all dressed in desert robes, dark and hawk-faced.

"Giving us time to talk it out," Idisio said.

"Really," Riss said, deadpan; he shot her a startled glance and she grinned. She stood. "Let's go get some food."

Idisio jumped at that suggestion; it gave him something to do with his hands besides twisting them nervously and something to do with his mouth other than gape. They filled their plates and applied themselves to their food in silence. Idisio was chewing over more than the food on his plate, and had nothing to say until he'd sorted it all out. Riss had an almost serene expression on her face, as if she'd said everything that needed saying and felt content to leave it at that.

"Honesty," he said at last, tentatively. She glanced at him. Idisio poked at a ball of rice until it fell apart, revealing a strange grey paste inside. "It's not easy."

He fell silent again, not sure how to present his own truth, but knowing he needed to.

"I think that's called *quba,*" Riss said quietly, pointing at the dismantled rice ball. "It's a paste made from cactus peppers." She picked one up from her own plate and popped it into her mouth.

"I've been. . . ." Idisio started, and took refuge from speech with a bite of the quba.

A moment later he began coughing, his mouth and throat on fire. Riss reached across the table, lifted his goblet, and pressed it on him. He gulped at it gratefully. The liquid tasted like a strong, warm tea; in other circumstances Idisio would have called it bland. At the moment it tasted wonderful.

"I grew up on the streets," he said once he had his breath back, and told the rest in a rush, before he could lose his courage. He used as few words as he could and left out the most humiliating parts; still, Riss looked horrified by the time he finished.

"I'm sorry, Idisio," she said. "I've been thinking you wouldn't understand what I went through."

"Not the dasta," he said. "I never had to deal with that. But the . . . what they did . . . yeah. I have some idea." He took another bite of the rice, more carefully this time, and washed it down with a sip of tea.

"That's why you were so fierce about that sailor's child," Riss said. "Wanting to save him from life on the streets, if that's where he is."

Idisio started to nod, and the dizziness came back, a distant humming in his ears and a shrill howl of fury. His vision greyed for a moment, and he had to blink hard and rub his eyes to focus again.

Riss' stare had turned sharp and thoughtful.

"I'm just tired," Idisio said, offering a tight smile. Judging from the twitch of her mouth, she didn't believe him, but she let it go. They went back to eating in silence.

Their plates were empty by the time Scratha returned to their table. He stood over them, looking down, and said, "I've arranged lodging for the night. If you're done eating, let's go."

As Idisio stood, aches and stiffness from the long climb made themselves known. He rolled his head in an attempt to loosen the muscles and dropped into a deep leg stretch when his calves started to cramp. He straightened to find them watching him with amusement.

"You looked awfully silly," Riss said. "I thought you were having some sort of seizure for a moment."

He shrugged, refusing to apologize, and followed them out of the room. Scratha steered them through a different doorway than the one through which they'd entered; it led to a long hallway with wide, arched openings on one side that let in air and sunlight. Doors were spaced along the solid wall. Scratha stopped at the third door and touched the surface with his fingers.

"Servant quarters," he said, then pointed to the next door. "My quarters. There's a connecting door if you need me. I'd advise not wandering around alone. Get some rest. We've a long way to go tomorrow, and you'll need your wits."

He walked away. Idisio stared after him dumbly, took a half-step to follow, and stopped again. Scratha opened the next door and stepped into the room without looking back. His door shut.

"Oh, for the love of the gods," Riss said. She opened their door, put a hand in the small of Idisio's back, and propelled him inside. The room smelled of sharp and bitter things Idisio had no name for, but seemed clean.

"Bitewood and pepper," Riss noted, sniffing, and looked pleased. "There won't be any bugs here."

Idisio grinned, startled at that bit of domesticity from Riss of all people.

"What?" she said, catching his expression. "Stables need to stay free of bugs too, you know."

Floor to ceiling, brightly colored silk hangings covered the walls; Idisio guessed the connecting door to Scratha's room lay behind one of the draperies, but didn't bother looking for it. Four wide, thick cushions lay on the floor, each one easily large enough to serve as a mattress for a man Scratha's size.

The other furnishings took up almost all the remaining space in the small room: a low desk with a kneeling pad, a washbasin, and a chamber pot. A wide window covered by a light curtain of woven reeds allowed the vague evening breeze to drift through the room.

Idisio sat on one of the cushions, determined to act casual and relaxed. Riss lifted one cushion on top of another, then pointed at him.

"Lie face down," she said, moving her hand to indicate the cushions.

"Huh?"

"You're stiff and sore," she said. "We both are. You first. I'll work you loose."

"Uh," he said, his calm act completely shattered.

"Come on, I won't bite. I promise. Lie down."

Idisio cast an assessing look at Riss' expression and obeyed; at least he would be *face* down.

Riss's fingers dug into his back with surprising strength.

"Working around horses," she said as she kneaded and rubbed, finding every sore spot and stiff area, "you learn about keeping them fit and moving easily. No great stretch to move that to people."

"Great," Idisio said, the words muffled by fabric, "now I'm a horse."

Riss made a whinnying sound, and they started laughing.

By the time Riss finished working his back and legs, Idisio was grinning like an idiot. He'd never expected to feel so comfortable around a girl, let alone this one, but Riss kept up a steady stream of banter, encouraging him to join in.

Riss insisted on explaining what she was doing so that he could rub her down next, but when that moment came, Idisio found himself too terrified to lift a hand. She made a disgusted noise, pushed the mats apart, then stretched out, pulling a light blanket over herself without a word.

"I'm sorry," Idisio said lamely.

After a moment, she sat up and looked at him.

"I'm not really mad," she said. "I guess I should take it as a compliment, that you're afraid to touch me in case you're overcome by lust."

Idisio gaped, shaken and wordless at her bluntness.

"It's all right," she said. "Go to sleep." She leaned over and turned down the lamp. The darkness, pressing in close and hot, silenced any more attempts to apologize; he found his bed mat and lay down without another word.

It took him a long, aching time to fall asleep.

Chapter Eighteen

In the darkness came a hard pressure that took away Alyea's breath; then, abruptly, a growing light and a floating, empty feeling. She saw nothing around her, but felt surrounded by presence—one, many, she had no way of telling. It was just *presence,* stronger even than the ishrait's had been.

In a moment of clarity Alyea understood that the ishrait had to be a ha'ra'ha herself.

The light shifted and separated, forming pools and lines of not-light. Alyea stared at the abstract patterns for some time, watching them move, join, split, and curve, feeling the open, idiot wonder of a child learning the world for the first time.

At last she realized that the shadows and planes of light hinted at the definition of an actual, physical form. Focusing more sharply, she saw the ha'rethe in front of her for one searing moment, and as the light dropped steeply back into darkness, she screamed.

The floating, dreamy feeling returned, along with a sense of sadness that brought tears streaking down her face.

You do not offer us acceptance, a voice said. *So few humans offer us acceptance, despite all we give your kind. What do you bring us, then? What is your gift to us?*

Gift? She blinked hazily, trying to remember if the ishrait had said anything about a gift.

You must give something, the voice insisted. *It is not sharing until both sides give. What is your offering?*

"What do you want?"

We have been given many gifts, and none have asked that question. The voice sounded rather startled. It fell silent for a time, as if thinking, then said, *Tell us a story that means something to you.*

"A story that means something to me?" She paused, remembering a story one of her nurses had told her long ago. "All right. I'll tell you about Krilla."

Drawing a deep breath, she began reciting, letting the cadence of the words take over her voice.

This is a story of a distant northern village, high in the Scarpane Mountains, the village of Alonir. Although it is in the path of many of the worst winter storms, somehow most of them turn aside and leave the village untouched. Old men and women of Alonir say this is because of Lord Krilla.

Krilla lived with her mother, father, and three sisters, in this village of Alonir. She was the youngest, no more than sixteen, and very slight and homely. Her older sisters were attractive but vain, and their mother desired to find them suitable, wealthy husbands. But the wealthy men lived in the foothills and plains below the Scarpane Mountains, and the family was too poor to travel so far.

The three sisters did not like to go outside. They protested that the harsh winter winds and freezing air would ruin their looks and that they would never find good husbands without their beauty. Krilla's sisters often complained about the weather and about their poverty, but Krilla loved the winter weather, loved to dance with the wind and spin with the snowflakes. She felt more comfortable outdoors in the clean, crisp air than in the stuffy little house filled with constant complaints and sighs.

But a winter came where the wind ran colder and stronger than ever before, and her mother forbade Krilla to go outside for fear of being blown away or frozen to death.

She found the confinement intolerable, and as the days passed she became more and more upset at the quarrels erupting around her. She had always spent so much of her time outdoors that she had not seen how very depressed her sisters were over the weather, and it puzzled her.

"Why do you hate going outside?" she asked. "It's so beautiful out there."

"It's too cold!" one sister cried.

"It's too windy!" cried another.

"It snows too much!" said the third.

Krilla shook her head, confused that her sisters could so hate the very things she loved.

"Well," she said bravely, "What if these things stopped?"

Her sisters laughed at her.

"Foolish girl!" they said scornfully. "Only the Lord of Winter could stop the snow and wind from coming to our village. What do any of us have that would persuade him to turn aside from this tiny place?"

"I do not know," Krilla answered stoutly. "But I am willing to search him out and ask. What harm can it do to ask?"

"Go ahead," they said. "You won't make it beyond the village borders, the weather is so terrible. We'll be waiting here. You won't go far."

"I will!" Krilla declared, and catching up her coat and mittens, went out the door while her sisters kept their mother distracted.

The weather was indeed terrible, but Krilla knew how to dance with the wind. So she slipped through the blasts of freezing air with determination and went on. The snow fell thickly, but she knew how to whirl through the strange and beautiful patterns of the snowfall. At the edge of the village, she paused, but did not look back. Instead she looked at the very highest peak of the Scarpane range, where legend said the Lord of Winter lived.

"I hope the legends are right," she said to herself. "It will be a very long walk."

The story of Krilla also ran very long, and Alyea had demanded the entire thing over and over, until she could recite it herself. She had wandered around muttering parts of it to herself; that had inevitably led to the s'iopes finding out that her nurse was telling "forbidden folk tales" and sending her away. It had taken years for Alyea to realize that "sent away" had been a polite euphemism: *beaten to death for spreading heresy* would have been more truthful.

Just one more death to lay at the feet of the Northern Church.

Alyea kept going, throwing the words into the darkness, telling of the determined little girl walking up the mountain, trudging on without much rest or food, driven by the urgency of her quest. At last Krilla reached the top:

She was very tired, but the sight of the huge cave opening drew her on, heart pounding with hope. Approaching the mouth of the cavern, she called out, "Is this the home of the Lord of Winter?"

The echoes of her voice came back to her, and she began to lose hope. Then something moved in the darkness of the cave.

"This is my *home," said a deep, gravelly voice. "The home of the Lord of Winter is on the next mountain over."*

Krilla's legs gave out from under her, and she sat down and wept, the tears freezing on her face. "I'm so tired," she cried, "and I cannot walk that far, and have nowhere to rest. May I please rest here for a while?"

"Hm!" said the voice, and "hm!" again. "Yes, come in and rest. I will give you shelter from the wind and snow."

Krilla was too tired to be wary. "Thank you very much," she said, and went into the cave.

"Why do you seek the Lord of Winter?" inquired the voice. "Move to your right a little more, there is a soft place for you to sleep on there."

Krilla followed the directions, and found a pile of soft cloth to stretch out on.

"I am going to ask him to turn aside the winter storms from our village," she replied.

"Hm!" said the voice. "Why?"

"My family is too poor to arrange good husbands for my sisters. If the storms turned aside, we could earn enough to give them a proper dowry."

"How do you feel about the weather?" asked the voice.

"I love it," Krilla said. "I love to dance with the wind and play with the snowflakes."

"But if the Lord of Winter agrees to turn the storms away from your village, you would not have those things any longer."

"I know," Krilla said sadly. "But my family is more important."

"Hm," said the voice. "Sleep, human child. You are safe here tonight."

Alyea drew a breath, paused for a moment to rest her throat, then told of Krilla waking to discover that her host was an enormous white dragon, and that she had slept curled up on one of its huge forelegs. Realizing that the dragon must be the Lord of Winter, the child fell to her knees and presented her request for the storms to be turned aside:

"What would you give for this request?" the Lord of Winter demanded, his eyes suddenly stern and cold. "What price would you pay?"

"Anything," Krilla said humbly. "I would pay any price for this boon."

"Asking me to turn aside storms is not a light request," the dragon warned. "It will carry a heavy price."

Krilla swallowed back her fear and nodded. "I will pay it."

The dragon considered her for a moment, then said, "I will tell you the price first, and let you decide whether you still wish to pay it. You will stay with me for the winter—this one, and every one that you wish to see the village spared from the storms. You will share my bed and do anything I ask of you while you are with me. Are you still willing to pay the price?"

Krilla choked back a sob. "I am."

A tear rolled down her face and struck the layer of snow on the floor, freezing instantly into a perfect tear-shaped drop of ice.

The Lord of Winter reached out and gently picked up the tiny drop. "You are braver than many warriors. Very well. I will turn the winter storms aside from the village of Alonir."

Then he transformed himself, and became as a reptilian human, and took her to his bed. Two drops of her first blood fell to the icy floor, and froze as had the tear; and the Lord of Winter put all three aside in a small box.

Alyea paused for a moment and opened her eyes. It seemed that the darkness had eased a bit; she thought she could see the faintest outlines of a massive form before her. She shut her eyes again and went on, telling of Krilla's return to her family in the spring, of their disbelief and mocking. At last, stung by the unrelenting laughter, Krilla showed her family the gems that had formed from the frozen drops of her tears and blood, which the Lord of Winter had warned her to keep hidden:

Her family looked at the gems with wonder, and just as she thought they believed her at last, one sister asked where she had found such beautiful gems, and the second sister said she must have stolen them, and the third sister reached for the box, saying these would make a grand dowry. And Krilla's parents stepped between, and took the box away, and said they would decide how the gems would be used, and that Krilla had done well.

Krilla went to bed crying, and during the night her parents looked at the gems, and spoke together in low voices, and formed a plan. When Krilla awoke the next morning, her parents told her that the rubies would serve as dowries for two of her sisters, and the diamond as dowry for the eldest, and that Krilla herself would go with the eldest of her sisters and serve as a handmaiden in a rich man's house. When she protested that she must return to the Lord of Winter come the end of fall, her parents called her mad, and demon-ridden, and shut her in her room.

Three suitable young men were found, one for each of the elder sisters, and engagements announced as summer faded into fall. At last Krilla was taken from her room and readied for the journey down the mountain. She had been told so many times during the spring and summer and fall that she was ill, that she had imagined her meeting with the Lord of Winter, that she half-believed it herself.

But the day before they were to leave, she found by chance where the box was kept, and in secret she took one ruby back. And she remembered that the Lord of Winter had said that if she commanded it aloud, the rubies would break and that would summon his aid; and she thought, "If I am deluded, if I was ill, then nothing will happen."

She took the ruby to the fireplace, set it on the stone hearth, and commanded, "Break, ruby!"

The ruby shattered, and the banked fire came alive again, and from the flames spoke the voice of the Lord of Winter.

"Little one," he said, "little human, do you call for my aid?"

Krilla became frightened, and said nothing.

"Little one," said the Lord of Winter, "little human, my Krilla, why do you call for me?"

Krilla still said nothing, and backed away from the hearth.

"Little Krilla," said the voice of the Lord of Winter one more time, and Krilla thought the voice sounded angry now. "You have called, and I have answered, and now you are silent. One more time only I will ask; why have you called me?"

Krilla ran away, and hid under her covers for the rest of the night. In the morning the fire was just a banked fire again and there was no sign of the broken ruby; not the smallest shard remained. And Krilla became truly ill, and could not be moved. She developed a strange wasting fever that stripped the weight from her so that her bones showed against the skin.

"We cannot wait," said her family, "we must go without her."

And only the sister who could not marry because her dowry ruby had been destroyed stayed with Krilla. She was the same one who had said Krilla must have stolen the gems, and she was so bitter and angry over her loss that she did little to take care of her sister. The rest of the village tried. The priests of Alonir and of all the nearby villages prayed over Krilla, and the herb-wives and leech-doctors used their wisdom, but nothing helped.

At last in desperation they called for a healer from yet another village, a man of ill repute who was said to serve the old gods of the deep south. And this healer came, and he looked at Krilla, and asked her to tell him her story.

When she was done speaking, he said, "She speaks truth. She has seen the Lord of Winter, and made a pact with him, and shared his bed; those gems are her tears and her blood, and it is your taking them that has made her ill. These gems are a part of Krilla, and only she can safely handle them."

The priests were angry, and they threw the healer from the house, and told him never to return. And Krilla continued to get worse. The priests decided the gems were evil, and Krilla possessed by a demon; and they sent a messenger hurrying to the village at the foot of the mountain, to return with the gems. Although Krilla's parents protested, they did not dare gainsay the priests, and returned to Alonir, angry at how Krilla had ruined their grand wedding plans. And when they returned, the priests seized the box and tried to smash the gems.

But the rubies would not break, and the diamond would not break, and the priests prayed and cast exorcisms and at last demanded that Krilla break the gems herself, to be free of the evil.

Krilla could not rise from her bed by that time, and had no strength to resist their demands. When she picked up the ruby and whispered, "Break," it shattered into a million pieces instantly. And one of the shards stuck in her hand, and a drop of her blood fell to the floor; and to everyone's amazement the drop of blood hardened and became another ruby, larger than a man's fist. It was too hot to touch, and seemed filled with an inner flame.

"Little one," said the voice of the Lord of Winter from within the ruby, "little human, do you call for my aid?"

Krilla tried to speak, but the priests moved too fast, and closed her mouth.

"Little human, my Krilla," said the Lord of Winter, "why do you call me?"

But Krilla was held fast, and could not speak. And two of her tears fell on the floor, and to everyone's amazement they became great shining diamonds, larger and finer than the first.

"Little Krilla, my Krilla," said the Lord of Winter one more time, and this time his voice sounded very sad. "You have called me, and I have answered, and you are silent. I ask you again: why have you called me?"

Krilla could speak at last, because the priests, distracted by the diamonds, had loosened their hold on her to reach for the shining gems; so she cried out, "Help me, my lord!"

The ruby grew and grew at those words, and became another form, a large form, one that nearly filled the free space in the room, and took the shape of a dragon.

"I am here," said the Lord of Winter, and two great golden eyes opened in the ruby shape. "What help do you wish, my little human?"

Before Krilla could speak, her mother pushed forward and said, "She wishes to be free of you and your foul bargain, monster! Begone!"

The Lord of Winter looked only at Krilla, and he said, "Is that what you want, my Krilla?"

And Krilla looked at the Lord of Winter, and he at her.

"If I break our bargain," said Krilla, "will you still hold the storms aside?"

"No," said the Lord of Winter.

"If I keep our pact," said Krilla, "how long will you hold the storms aside from my village?"

"Until the end of our pact," said the Lord of Winter.

"And how long will our pact last?" said Krilla.

"Until you die," said the Lord of Winter.

"And when will that be?" asked Krilla.

And the answer the Lord of Winter gave struck everyone silent with wonder, even the priests; and Krilla said, "I will keep the pact, my lord; and I will stay with you not only in the winter, but the spring and summer and fall as well."

Alyea remembered that she always had interrupted her nurse at that point, asking, "What did the Lord of Winter say? What did he say?"

Her nurse had shaken her head and said, "That part of the story cannot be told, child. Nobody knows." And no matter how often Alyea pestered her, the nurse gave the same answer.

"And why would you do that, my Krilla?" said the Lord of Winter.

"Because there is nothing left for me here," said Krilla. "My family and my village will turn against me, whatever I decide."

"But why would you stay with me, my Krilla, instead of making your own way and allowing your village to reap its own rewards?" said the Lord of Winter.

And the answer Krilla gave struck everyone as the wisest thing they had ever heard, and the diamond in the box shattered, and melted, and vanished forever. But the two diamonds formed of her most recent tears remained.

Alyea had started to interrupt again; her nurse had covered her mouth gently and said, "That answer cannot be told either, child. Nobody knows. Perhaps one day you will find out for yourself, and bring the rest of the tale to your children."

The Lord of Winter smiled, and took her away; and she was never again seen in that village, and nobody ever dared climb to the highest peak of the Scarpane Mountains to seek her out. But when the wild winds screamed down the mountain, the worst of them passed around and over the village of Alonir; and the village was blessed with great harvest in fall and healthy newborn animals in spring, and a calm summer every year. And the villagers prospered, and set the two remaining diamonds in a carefully guarded glass case, and never touched them for their own profit. And they banished all the s'iopes from their village, and lived in great peace for many years.

Alyea had *really* liked that part. Even now it brought a wide grin to her face to say that line, although those words had probably been what sealed her nurse's grim fate.

One day the guards cried out and summoned the village, for the two diamonds in the glass case had shattered. And nobody could understand why, or what had happened. The healer from the next village was called upon once again, and it took him many days to arrive, for he was very old by this time, and near death. And he looked at the diamond shards, and handled them with great reverence, and blessed them in a strange language. To the amazement of all, the pieces melted and disappeared completely.

They clamored for him to tell them what it meant, and the answer the healer gave was the most astounding and joyous thing they had ever heard and they rejoiced. The villagers celebrated for many days, and named Krilla the patron Lord of their village.

Alyea hadn't even tried to interrupt at that point. She knew what her nurse would say. The ending wound through a series of thoroughly blasphemous statements that she'd loved hearing and even now enjoyed repeating:

So there are those in the north who quietly pray to Lord Krilla, and roadside shrines are dedicated to her. The priests seek to tear them down, but the shrines reappear within days or weeks. The wiser priests simply hold their notice aside and say nothing, while the foolish ones grow angry, blustering, and wear themselves out on a thing that will never change. There are no shrines to Krilla in the south, for she loves only the snowy lands, and will never stray from the Scarpane Mountains. But in the north, if one prays to the Lord Krilla with an honest heart and the desire to help others, one may find help when it is least expected.

Alyea drew a deep breath and opened her eyes.

The darkness had lifted. She stood in a simple, pleasant sitting room; a man sat in an easy chair, facing her. A wide fireplace had a blaze laid in, and the warmth wrapped around her like a gentle blanket. Another comfortable chair stood a step to her right.

"Not exactly accurate," said the man in the chair, frowning, and she trembled at the expression. "Please sit. There's a throw if you're cold."

She found herself in the chair, drawing a thick blanket around her, with no clear memory of having moved.

"I admit you tell a story well, even if it was poorly chosen," the man said. "I accept the gift."

She stared at him blankly, unable to think of anything to say. His features wouldn't stay fixed in her mind; he looked thin and hard, one moment, gentle and soft the next. A desert lord, a northern noble, a comfortably padded well-off merchant; she couldn't quite pin what he looked like from moment to moment. Somehow it didn't matter.

"That was an unfortunate choice of story," he said. "Too many inaccuracies, for one thing."

Remembering the shape outlined to her vision for a heartrending moment, she licked her lips, tested her voice with a slight cough, and said, "Are you . . . dragons?"

"No," the man said, his expression flickering into something distinctly ugly. "You have no word, no concept that describes us well. We don't care for that story. As I said, an unfortunate choice of gift. But it's accepted. Not all gifts are . . . pleasant." He drew a breath, let it out, then stood and held out a hand. "Come here. Time for *my* . . . gift. I'll give you those answers you wanted so badly."

She was on her feet again, and standing close to him, before she knew she had moved. His hands wrapped gently around her upper arms. After a moment of looking at her intently, he slid one hand up to her shoulder and back down to cup her elbow lightly. The touch raised gooseflesh on her arm and a deep shivering heat throughout her body.

His voice lowered to a compelling whisper, barely audible, speaking words in a strange language. Her vision dimmed, or maybe the air hazed. She could see his eyes, dark and intense: and then that faded and she felt the heat of his body pressing close. Darkness folded around them, and heat rose and spread through her, wide and deep and wild.

There came pain, and joy, and then an infinite, eternal tenderness that at last overwhelmed her and pulled her completely into oblivion. She heard voices in the darkness, echoes of herself long ago, asking:

What did Krilla say, nurse? What did she say that was so wise?

Nobody knows, dear . . . nobody knows.

But then another voice spoke, a young, sad voice, and it said:

Because, my lord, my family and the villagers are not evil. Some are innocent, and follow wherever they are led, without thought of their own; they do not deserve to be punished for simple foolishness. And some in the village do nothing but lead where they want to go and give no thought to the well-being of those who follow, and those people will earn their own end. But you led only where I asked to go, and rescued me only when I asked. You have used no trickery, and asked only that I decide my way for myself. You have more honor than any human I have ever met, and I will follow you for that until the end of my days.

And there came a blinding, howling pain and a searing rush of ecstasy, tumbling on and around and through each other; then the darkness came back and took it all away again.

What did the healer say, nurse? What did he say? Why did the diamonds break?

Nobody knows, dear . . . nobody knows.

Another voice spoke, an old, gentle, joyous voice, and it said:

A diamond born of tears is the hardest substance in the world. The first diamond, which broke when Krilla chose to leave with the Lord of Winter, was the tear of sacrifice; she reclaimed that piece of her spirit when she chose her path with full desire rather than from duty. The last two diamonds were born from tears of pain and anger, and were broken by the most powerful emotion in the world: love. She has come to love the Lord of Winter, to surrender her heart completely, and to utterly forgive those who sought to harm her.

Alyea felt new life pushing its first, tentative feelers into the space around her. Tenderness, gratitude, and love flowed through and around, inside and outside, weaving and wrapping and holding her, then rocked her down into a deep silence again.

What did the Lord of Winter say, nurse? What did he say, that made Krilla decide to go with him?

Nobody knows, dear . . . nobody knows. Perhaps one day you'll be the one to find out, and bring us all the answers.

Another voice spoke, rich and deep and loud and quiet all at once. It said:

If you stay with me to save your village, your life will be twice as long as the oldest of your kind. If you stay with me because you wish to be by my side, your life will be four times that long. And if you grow to love me with a true and open heart, your life will be as long as mine and you will be as a Lord yourself, and your children will be Lords of the world, and their children. But never seek to deceive me, for I know your heart more clearly and more surely than you do; and I ask of you only honesty, and will return you only truth.

Tenderness and gratitude swelled one more time; then regret and sadness wove into the silent song of emotion. She felt a searing pain beyond pain, a ripping that seemed as if it would go on forever.

This time darkness came as a merciful release.

Feeling came back in slow fragments. A deep, steady pain seemed to have seeped into her very bones. She felt a light cloth covering over her, a soft padding under her; warm air moved gently against her face. She could smell desert thyme and rosemary mixed with a soothing, rich floral fragrance she couldn't identify.

She lay with her eyes closed, with no particular impulse to do anything but rest. The pain sapped her energy and strength; she wasn't sure she could move even if she wanted to. She felt a pressure across her hips, stomach, and groin, as if a thick, weighted blanket were bound tightly around her; in that area alone the pain seemed muted.

After a while, the air moved in a different pattern, and the scent of herbs and flowers mixed wi:)th the acrid tang of human skin and sweat. Almost human: the odors held a musky tinge which Alyea recognized now.

"Ishrait," Alyea said without opening her eyes.

The woman said nothing, but Alyea sensed her settling nearby, within arm's reach to the left. The quiet steadiness of her presence seemed to ease the aches spiraling through Alyea's body.

Alyea felt no pressure to speak further, and simply rested a while more, until the red-edged waves of pain subsided to a deep discomfort.

"Ishrait," she said finally, "why do I hurt?"

In a low, barely audible murmur, the woman answered: "You may call me Acana. You have earned the right to know my name and use it as you like."

"Acana," Alyea said, feeling only a weary sort of patience, "Why do I hurt? What happened?"

"What do you remember?"

Alyea sorted through fragments of memory.

"The pool," she said at last. "You had me stand in the dark, in front of the pool, and asked me a lot of questions. And then . . . I think I must have fallen asleep, and had a dream. A nightmare, maybe. I can't recall what it was about, not really."

She had a sense of almost unendurable loss at not being able to remember the dream clearly. There had been a girl, trudging up a mountain in the cold; and a great voice, speaking from an invisible source. At one point, Alyea remembered, her own hands had been cupped in front of her and filled to overflowing with crystal-clear rubies and diamonds.

And something about that linked to a deep eroticism, and a deeper pain, but she couldn't recall clearly why.

Acana sighed. "No dream and no nightmare. But it may be a mercy you can't remember much of it." Her voice sounded very sad. "You have passed the blood trial of Ishrai, and have been given the mark. Your only remaining obligation is to your ha'ra'ha, who will guide you through the following year." *If you survive.*

The last words sounded oddly blurred; Alyea had the distinct feeling she'd just overheard one of Acana's thoughts. She didn't bother dismissing that as impossible. She'd accept a bluebird reciting poetry and discussing philosophy right now, without a twitch.

She heard Acana rise, murmur something indistinct, and leave the room. Alyea kept her eyes closed, feeling nothing but an overwhelming lassitude that denied any emotion, squashed any thought or reaction or movement. Another scent, evocative of warm, cinnamon-laced sand, entered the room as Acana's faded away, and at last a distant jolt of shock reached deeply enough to prompt a response. She knew who had arrived, just by that smell; no doubt, no chance of mistake.

Random thoughts flashed through her head. Apparently, she'd completely failed at losing Deiq's interest after all. She didn't understand how he'd gotten from Stass to wherever the Qisani stood so quickly. Chac would be furious.

But none of that seemed to matter any more.

Alyea opened her eyes and managed to turn her head to the left, each tiny increment of movement feeling slow and creaky. In the dim light of the few small oil lamps, he seemed to loom high and tall, impossibly large, until she realized she lay on a low bed and the perspective was skewed.

"Greetings, my lady," Deiq said as he knelt beside her, seeming to shrink back to normal size with the movement. He cupped her face in large, warm hands and smiled, his expression so gentle and tender that it wrenched at her heart. With that smile, some of the not-dream came back to her, and she began to cry. He smoothed the tears away with his thumbs and said nothing as she wept. When her breath evened out again, the weariness returned. She shut her eyes, and Deiq, seeming to understand, said, "Sleep, my lady. I'll stay with you."

She let the darkness take her again, unable to fight the suasion of his voice this time. When she woke, the room had filled with daylight and the smell of fresh-cut oranges. Deiq's scent hovered near at hand, and she felt body heat to her left. She opened her eyes, looked at the sunlit rock overhead, and breathed in the scent of oranges and human-*other* for a while before once again turning her head to look at him.

He sat beside her pallet, knees drawn up and arms looped around them, watching her. His face held lines of exhaustion, as if he hadn't slept for days, but he smiled when she met his dark gaze.

"Hungry?" he said, lifting a plate of sliced orange wedges.

Her stomach rumbled in response to the sharp-sweet scent. She ignored it. "Chac said you were dangerous."

"He was right," Deiq said after a moment. He set the plate down slowly, his smile fading. "And I would have told you the same about him, had you met me first."

"I've known Chac for years," Alyea said. "I've never seen him do an evil thing."

"And by inference, you've seen me do evil?"

Alyea tried to recall what she actually *had* seen of Deiq. He'd stalked through the corridors of the palace with a look she'd interpreted as predatory; now, with more experience to temper her judgment, she thought perhaps it had simply been a look of assurance. Her perceptions could well have been colored by the gossip and chatter of the court and her own family.

"You were a favorite of Ninnic's," she said at last, unable to form anything more damning in response to his question.

He made a small noise of disgust. "Favorite? No. I stayed out of Bright Bay while he was on that throne, whatever rumor may say. And I certainly didn't care for him. "

She said nothing, unable to respond this time. His tone had been edged with a long-simmering frustration.

"I told you," Deiq said quietly, lifting the plate again, "I have far worse a name in the courts of Bright Bay than I deserve. Much of it is from that old man's spite, on a matter long past and unimportant."

"His wife," Alyea said, in a sudden moment of absolute clarity. "Micru said she ran away. But you took her, didn't you? That's the only thing he could possibly hate you so much over."

Deiq picked a slice of orange from the plate and bit into it, wiping drops of juice from his chin. He chewed, swallowed, then held out the other half to Alyea. Her stomach demanded that she accept. The sight of the juice dripping down his chin ripped her willpower into splinters, and she let him place the fruit in her mouth. The small piece held the richest flavor she'd ever tasted. She found herself accepting and eating chunk after chunk. Deiq wiped her chin with a small cloth now and again.

When the plate had been emptied, he set it aside and cleaned his own hands with the cloth. Then he looked back at her, a mild, contented look on his face.

"No," he said. "I did not *take* his wife. She chose to leave him, and I agreed to escort her to another place. She is still there, and still happy, and still has no desire to see him. And I have told no man or woman where she is, and I never will, and he will not forgive me for that."

"Why did she leave him?"

"She found out the truth of who he is and what he is," Deiq said. "And she lost all love for him. But right now, you don't need to worry about him, or her, or anything outside this room." His contented expression grew more serious. He reached out and tucked her hair back around the curve of her ear. "You have a lot of healing to do in a very short time."

She shut her eyes again, hearing things in his tone that he wasn't saying; and those things frightened her.

"What happened?" she asked, hearing her voice come out wobbly and nervous.

"You passed the blood trial of Ishrai," he said. "In this case, it was more . . . literally . . . a blood trial than usual."

She remembered the ripping feeling, the disconnection, and shuddered.

"There was a child, wasn't there?" she said, the words barely more than a whisper. "They took it."

Deiq sighed. "Men have it easier," he said. "They only provide seed. Women have to give more than that. That's why it takes a year; it's easier if the woman can at least carry to full term before they take the child. When. . . ." he paused, as if searching for words. "When there's as little time as you had, they have to take . . . more. To sustain the child. Do you understand?"

Alyea lay with her eyes closed for a while. A sense of panic lurked at the edges of warm, thick layers of weariness and the deep ache still permeating her body. "Am I . . . ruined? It felt like they ripped. . . ." She couldn't finish.

"No," Deiq said. He took her left hand in both of his and spoke with slow deliberation, as if concentrating on holding his voice steady. "But it will take time for you to heal. And I don't . . . I don't know if you'll be able to have more children."

"That's all right," she said in disconnected idiot calm. "That's. . . ."

Raw panic abruptly slammed through the insulating layers, and her mumbling words turned into a long, trembling shriek. She was vaguely aware of movement, and smells changing, and someone holding her down as she convulsed; and then the searing pain came back and shredded her into unconsciousness again.

"I'm sorry," were the first words she heard when she opened her eyes again. The faint flickering of a single oil lamp set nearby showed her Deiq, kneeling beside her bed. He sat hunched forward, his head pillowed on his arms, and seemed to be talking to himself.

"Gods, I'm so sorry," he murmured again.

She cleared a throat raw from screaming, and he sat up sharply, wiping hurriedly at his face.

"Don't apologize more than once," she rasped.

He smiled, a thin and painful expression, and settled back against the wall, drawing his knees up. "Hungry?"

"No," she said. "Why are you sorry?"

He looked away, then back to her as if forcing himself to meet her stare. "You're more hurt than I expected," he said. "I thought you'd be . . . I didn't think they'd be so . . . I shouldn't have sent you here. It was a mistake."

Her dazed compassion disintegrated with a surge of anger. "You sent me here? I thought Chac arranged this!"

"Yes and no. Chacerly intended to put you through the trials, but I . . . altered the arrangements a little. Lord Eredion asked for my help in guiding you; he was alarmed when the king told him who was being sent as your advisors. They might have been good in Bright Bay, but past the Horn those were the two very worst people he could have chosen. I could have avoided your going through the trials, by giving you my backing, if you'd listened to me at the way-stop, and come with me; but you're stronger than I thought you'd be, and you resisted my best efforts. I've never had anyone do that before."

"Egotistical bastard," she whispered, her anger not the least bit less.

He shook his head, sober now and unsmiling. "No. Truth. You've a much stronger will than you think, Alyea. You may even have a touch of the blood yourself."

"What hold does Eredion have on you, to make a ha'ra'ha do his work?" Alyea said.

For the first time she saw a flash of his old arrogance; he straightened a little and said, "Nothing can *make* me do another man's work. He asked, and I agreed. The reason is between us, and not your concern."

Pain abruptly surged through her again, and she shut her eyes, gasping for breath. He cursed softly and spread his large hands over her torso. One covered her stomach and the other her chest, fingers splayed around rather than across her breasts. She sucked in breath and found it easier, and the pain eased a little.

"Acana's coming," he said, his voice curiously unemotional.

Acana came into the room, carrying a large basin of steaming water and a bundle of cloths.

"Close your eyes," Deiq said. Alyea obeyed, too sick and hurt to argue. She felt the blanket being lifted away from her legs and groin, and the heavy pressure against her lower stomach easing. With that came a storm of pain that cut her off from everything but the awareness of someone howling like a wounded animal.

Realizing that someone was herself, that part of the pain came from a throat about to give way from too much screaming, helped her cut down to a steady whimpering that still flayed her throat. At last she reduced it to a heavy gasping, the best she could do.

"Breathe slowly," Deiq said in her ear, his breath tickling her hair.

"Slow and long and shallow. Trust me. Don't gasp like that. Please. Don't scream. Slow. Slow and shallow, there you go. Listen to my voice, listen to this rhythm . . . in. Easy . . . out. In . . . out . . . in. . . ."

She managed, with a fierce effort, to follow the tempo he gave her.

"Good girl. Good. Easy . . . *gods,* can't we stop that damned bleeding?"

She had the feeling she wasn't supposed to hear that last part. It had been a harsh whisper, and directed away from her; but her hearing seemed preternaturally sharp. The slightest rustle and scrape sounded as loud as a shout.

"Just keep her breathing," Acana said, equally quiet. "The *ha'rai'nin* is on her way. All we can do is keep her alive until then."

The pressure came back, a thick feeling now, as if someone leaned on her lower torso, pressing a heavy hand between her legs. The pain eased again.

"Why didn't the Jungles—"

"Shush, she can hear you. Put her to sleep, it'll be easier to hold her still that way."

Deiq cursed again, and lowered his mouth to Alyea's ear.

"Sleep," he said, a soft, compelling murmur. "Alyea, sleep; please, please sleep."

She tried to resist, to summon that will he'd called so strong, but pain took the last of her strength, and she sank away from knowing for a time. When she woke, the room seemed to echo with an eerily familiar song, with words in a language she felt she ought to know. The room had filled with light again, and a spicy taste lingered in her mouth, as if someone had rubbed cactus pepper paste on her tongue.

A hand rested on her shoulder, a warm, large one. Turning her head revealed Deiq, asleep in an ungainly sprawl against the wall. Her movement woke him; he blinked sleepily, then sat up straight, a wide grin spreading across his face.

They looked at each other without speaking for a moment. Alyea found herself reluctantly matching Deiq's smile.

Without taking his gaze from her face, he called out in that same oddly familiar language, and with an eddy of scents, Acana and a strange old woman came into the room. Old—but Alyea sensed a power in her presence that dwarfed both Acana and Deiq.

"Lady," Alyea breathed with a profound and dizzying respect bordering on awe.

Deiq's expression shifted to startlement, and Acana raised her eyebrows. Alyea didn't care. She had no interest in anything but this strange old woman whose very presence raised goose bumps over her entire body.

"All right, all right," the old woman said, smiling as she approached. "It's taken you that way, has it? All right."

There seemed something immensely soothing about her voice and manner. When the old woman sat on the edge of the low pallet and lightly touched Alyea's arm, a shock ran through her whole body. The dizzy feeling disappeared. The old woman was just an old woman: a wise one, a healer, but not . . . not a goddess, not a ha'rethe.

Alyea shut her eyes, feeling a burst of embarrassment flood her face with color.

"That's all right," the old woman said. "It happens that way sometimes. The sharing gets everything all muddled in your head." She patted Alyea's arm gently. "Close your eyes for a bit, dear, and it'll sort itself out soon enough."

Alyea found a comforting darkness behind her eyelids, a place of absolute silence and no physical feeling at all. She let herself float there; she had no reason to leave, nothing to return for. She could stay here forever.

A voice cut into the peace, breaking the silence, calling her name over and over. She knew that voice; she didn't want to know it, didn't want to remember it. That would force her to return to the day-lit room and the pain that waited. Much nicer to stay here, floating gently in infinite darkness.

"Alyea," the voice said, and it sounded more insistent now. She felt a light, stroking pressure in a spot that might, back in that room, have been her face. "Remember, Alyea, remember Oruen, and Chac, and your ugren slaves. Remember the desert, and the Horn, and Bright Bay. Remember the ocean; remember the moonlight on the waters. Alyea, remember yourself, please, Alyea. . . ."

It all started to come back to her; she couldn't shut it out. The two foolish northerns, and the nagging, unanswered questions: who or what was Chac? Had Oruen actually betrayed her, or had he simply been a fool? Where were her ugren slaves, and was Gria really the last true-blood Scratha? These and a dozen more questions tumbled rapidly through her mind, and she knew she couldn't stay in the lovely, empty space any longer.

She drew in a deep breath, let it out in a long, annoyed sigh, and opened her eyes. Deiq knelt by her side, his hands cupping her face. Even with Deiq's body blocking her view, Alyea knew from the fading scent that the ishrait had left. By the same method, she knew that the old woman still sat in a corner.

"Alyea," Deiq said in a tone of profound relief, and sat back on his heels, releasing her face.

She stared up at the ceiling and didn't answer for a while.

"Healer," she said at last, and heard her voice coming out cold and hard. "Can I move?"

"As long as you don't jump around, ride a horse, have rough sex, or get into a brawl," the old woman said dispassionately, "you can do anything you like. In another month or less, you'll have no restrictions. You'll find you heal rather more quickly from now on than you're used to."

Alyea sat up, accepted Deiq's offered support, and stood. Once she steadied, she released his arm and met the old woman's gaze.

The wrinkled face slowly creased further into a wide smile. "You're well on your way to becoming a desert lord, with a glare like that," the old woman said, and stood. "You won't be needing me any longer. *Teth-kavit*, Alyea."

Somehow Alyea understood what that meant, although she'd never heard the word before: *gods hold you, and blessings to your strength.*

"Teth-kavit," Alyea said in return, and added, "Thank you, healer."

"You're welcome, child," the woman said, and left the room.

Alyea turned her stare on Deiq. He met it steadily, all his humor gone.

"How are you involved in this?" she said at last. "The *truth* this time. All of it. "

He made a vague motion with one hand. "Lord Eredion asked me to help."

"And why did you agree?" she pressed.

He hesitated, looking torn, then said, "He's my father. Now and again, he calls that in for a favor."

She stared at him, dubious but seeing no reason to disbelieve the statement. "So now what?"

"Now," he said, "you go to your last trial." He reached out and caught her as she wobbled abruptly. "Once you're able to stand long enough to walk ten paces," he added, easing her back down onto the bed. He sat on the edge beside her and stroked her forehead lightly. "It may take another day or two for that."

Chapter Nineteen

Sunlight without heat blazed down around Idisio, and strange, impossible shadows stretched over sand bleached of all color. Idisio knew he was dreaming, but the void where sound, heat, and sensation belonged seemed more powerful than reality. Ahead of him stood the stone spire he'd stared at earlier that evening, looming far higher and closer than it had been. Without moving, he came to within a few yards, then a few steps, then found himself standing close enough to examine the wind scars etched into its dark surface.

Se'thiss, t'akarnain, something said.

He blinked—*odd, to clearly feel yourself blinking in a dream*—and looked around for the source of the soundless voice. Nobody there.

Who are you?

Idisio opened his mouth to answer, found himself mute, and blinked again.

Speak, the voice commanded, and Idisio struggled to obey. It occurred to him that the voice wasn't speaking out loud, and with that came his answer.

Idisio, he said without moving his mouth. *I'm Idisio. Who are you?*

He heard a gurgling, hissing noise, knew it for laughter. *I call you. Come to me. I have much to ask, and you have much to learn, young one. Come to me.*

A blind terror overcame Idisio, and he tried to back away. He found himself unable to move. Pebbly sand slid over his bare toes as some invisible force dragged him forward, closer and closer, until his nose hovered a breath away from being crushed into the rock.

As his face pressed into the unyielding surface, he screamed—and woke.

Riss stared at him with eyes too wide and face too pale for that to have been his first scream. Two oil lamps had been lit, and Scratha sat nearby, his dark face unusually grave.

"Tell me," he said, and Idisio, still dazed, recounted the dream as clearly as he could remember. As he talked, he began to feel foolish almost immediately, and waited for them to laugh at him.

Scratha didn't laugh. Not a flicker of a smile passed across his face, and Riss seemed no more amused than the desert lord.

"Again," Scratha said. "What did the voice say? The strange words you heard, what were they?"

"Saythis ta arkarn something," Idisio said, the word tangling hopelessly over his tongue. "Saythiss tay arknain? I don't know."

"*Se'thiss t'akarnain*," Scratha said.

"Yes!" Idisio felt a great swell of relief. "You know it? What does it mean? I thought it was nonsense, just dream words. . . ." He trailed off. Scratha's expression hadn't lightened. "What does it mean?"

"It means," Scratha said, "that I've been a fool." He stood. "Pack. We leave now."

Dawn laid a faint hint of grey on the far horizon as Scratha led them through the courtyard. People were already stirring, or perhaps only just going to sleep; some looked as if they had been drinking for some time.

"Say nothing, look at nobody," Scratha said as they walked rapidly across the flagstones. "Not even each other, Riss."

Idisio, his stare firmly on his feet, smiled a little as Riss made a faint, disgusted noise. She'd been watching him anxiously ever since he'd awoken from his nightmare, and it had started to feel like ants crawling all over his skin. He'd always hated being stared at.

The flagstones ended in a set of shallow steps; Idisio had a dim recollection of staggering clumsily up them the evening before. His attention on his feet now, he managed the descent rather better. As soon as his feet touched the uneven ground, however, he couldn't resist lifting a quick glance towards where he remembered that frightening stone pillar to be.

"*No*," Scratha said, stepping in front of him as though he'd expected Idisio to do just that. "Not yet. Trust me. Keep watching your feet, and follow me."

Idisio blinked hard and obeyed, almost nauseated with fear now. Without being able to see the sun or stars as a guide, he had no idea which way they were going. He thought they'd turned west, towards the deeper desert and incidentally towards that stone spire; but he had no intention of looking. He saw no sense in pushing Scratha into one of his extreme moods by disobeying a clear order.

Light crept steadily through the air: the beginning of dawn. Idisio's feet, slogging through steadily deeper and sandier dirt, became distinctly visible. His calves began to protest, reminding him of how far they'd walked yesterday. He bit his lip and hoped his lord would call a halt soon, one at least long enough for him to rub the soreness out of his legs.

"Stop," Scratha said at last.

Idisio knelt instantly and massaged the beginning of a cramp from one calf.

"Idisio, look at me."

Idisio dutifully stood and raised his gaze to the angular face before him. "Yes, my lord?"

"I'm going to explain about your nightmare now," Scratha said. "Do you want Riss to hear this, or should I send her out of earshot?"

Idisio didn't need to look to know that Riss fumed at the notion of being set aside like a child. "She can stay."

"Riss, do you want to stay to hear this, or would you rather step aside?" Scratha asked.

"I'll stay."

Idisio let out a long, quiet breath. For some reason he found he *did* want Riss by his side. She seemed a steadying influence, someone who would keep him from screaming if this conversation turned into a waking nightmare like the one two nights ago had.

Scratha motioned for Idisio and Riss to sit, and lowered himself onto the ground in front of them.

"I've already said you're ha'ra'ha, Idisio," he said without any preamble. "You've never noticed before because you've repressed it all your life. Riss, shut up, I'll explain later. I don't have time right now."

Idisio nodded without speaking. Riss huffed but stayed quiet.

"So the effects, now that you've learned the stillness of aqeyva, are hitting you all at once," Scratha said. "And you're not prepared. I blame myself. I should never have brought you up the Wall. When you told me about your fits I should have shipped you straight back to the northlands. But I thought if I kept you out of aqeyva trance, you'd be safe enough. I was wrong."

"Is this a reversible thing?" Riss said sharply. "Because if it isn't, and you'd have sent him back north, he'd have had to deal with this all by himself, wouldn't he? That sounds fairly stupid to me."

They both stared at her as if she'd grown an extra head; then Scratha's expression cleared.

"You're right," he said. "I didn't see it that way. Thank you, Riss."

"She may be useful after all," Idisio murmured.

Scratha grinned briefly. Idisio forced a tight smile and waited tensely for his lord to continue. The desert lord hesitated, as if deciding what to say. When he spoke, his voice sounded unusually clipped and blunt, as if he were holding to a much shorter explanation than he wanted to give.

"*Se'thiss t'akarnain* roughly translates to 'beloved child of northern relatives'. It's a bit more complex than that, but close enough. It means you've attracted a ha'rethe's attention."

"It was a nightmare," Idisio said in feeble protest. "Just a . . . a dream."

"It was a vision, and a true one," Scratha said. "There's at least one ha'rethe that still calls this area its home, and it's inviting you over for a visit."

"I don't want to go," Idisio said, his mouth dry with terror.

"You have to," Scratha said without visible pity. "Ha'reye don't take refusal very well. The last time humans told them 'no,' the entire southlands turned into desert."

Idisio bent forward, tucking his head between his knees, and breathed deeply, trying to keep control of his stomach.

"What's going to happen to me?" he managed at last.

"I don't know," Scratha admitted. "I wish I did."

The slab of wind-scoured rock loomed before Idisio, just as in the dream: but this time there was the rising heat of the desert sun on his shoulders, the sour taste of fear in his mouth, and a distinct tremor in his hands. The sweat trickling down his face came from more than heat—and a contrasting cold lurked in his stomach, as if someone had replaced his guts with chunks of ice.

He walked forward, a step, two, then three. Scratha stayed close behind him, near enough for a grab if Idisio should bolt. That hadn't been said—it didn't need to be.

But where would he run? There was nowhere to go. Idisio blinked hard and made himself take another step, and another. A hissing noise stopped him. He looked down at his feet, searching for a sand-asp or desert viper, but saw nothing moving in the sand.

"Stay still," Scratha said very quietly, then said something else in the language of the desert, too rapidly for Idisio to follow.

Another, louder hissing came, warbling now.

"Damn," Scratha said under his breath, then, a little louder, "I was hoping it would let me come with you, but it wants to talk to you alone. Idisio. . . ." He hesitated. "We'll wait as long as we can."

Idisio stared at the lines and random markings on the rock and found he had no spit to swallow with. He wanted to say *What? Wait as long as you can? How long is this going to take? Am I going to come back?* But he couldn't voice any of that without beginning to shriek halfway through, so he just nodded dumbly.

Another faint hissing arose from somewhere in front of him.

"Walk forward," Scratha said, voice emotionless.

One step. Two steps. Three steps. The sand beneath his feet seemed to dissolve into emptiness, and he fell into absolute blackness. He managed, either by intent or sheer shock, not to scream. After a time, the feeling of falling gradually ended. He stood in complete darkness, with no sensation beyond a faint chill. The air carried no scent, no moisture, and no sound.

Idisio panted a bit, catching the breath that had locked in his throat with the unexpected fall, and finally steadied himself. He didn't know if he stood on, in, under, or near anything. The disorientation nearly terrified him into the scream he'd been holding back.

Could he move? Should his eyes be open? Scratha hadn't told him anything on what to expect, what was courteous. Maybe he didn't even know.

Idisio heard a faint hissing that gurgled, almost like reptilian laughter.

His nausea faded, replaced by dizziness; he couldn't tell if he swayed in place, but his joints felt none too steady.

"All right," he said, and listened to his own voice in astonishment. "I'm here. What do you want? I'm busy, y'know."

Talk he'd have given a tough in Bright Bay while trying to face down a potential fight. His mouth, as always, worked faster than his brain. He shut his eyes in hopeless dismay at his idiocy.

The gurgle came louder this time, and clearer. It sounded almost human.

"Are you," a thin, high voice said, oddly accented but perfectly clear. "Are you indeed."

There came a long silence. Idisio felt an odd, tickling sensation inside his skull, as though something ruffled feathery fingers through his mind. Unnerved, petrified, he stood absolutely still, eyes wide in the darkness, and tried not to move.

"You're very unusual, you know," the voice said quietly. It sounded rather more sympathetic now. "Very unusual. And interesting."

The chill deepened. Idisio shivered and rubbed at his arms.

"I'm sorry, young one," the voice said. "I'm inconsiderate. You're cold."

The air warmed, and the darkness faded; a few feet away, a small table and a wide chair such as Bright Bay nobles liked to lounge on appeared. Thick dark carpet crushed softly under Idisio's bare feet.

"Please sit," the voice said. Idisio found himself in the chair, a thick blanket drawn up around him, warm and comfortable.

"Where are you?" Idisio asked, looking around. Other than a small circle of table and chair, the darkness still surrounded the lit area like a featureless, endless sea.

"I am here," the voice said in his ear, and he jumped.

A woman sat on the wide arm of his chair, smiling down at him. Idisio forgot everything and just stared at her.

She looked barely older than Idisio, with long, dark hair that rolled over smooth, bare shoulders and generous curves barely covered by thin blue fabric. Equally dark eyes in a northern-pale and rounded face studied him intently. He saw an age and a calculation in that stare that abruptly recalled him to the fact that this had to be a veneer, not the real creature.

Without moving, he tried to harden his own gaze, to hide his initial startled interest in the form it had chosen.

She laughed and stood, walking a few paces away to another chair that must have appeared when she did.

"So you're not easily impressed," she said, sinking into the chair in a way that made him glad he was sitting down. "That's the ha'rethe blood in you, young one. Any full human would have given in without another thought."

He said nothing—he'd been impressed all right. He tried to breathe normally, not wanting her to see his struggle. Riss's face came to mind, and her laughter. He found himself breathing more easily and even smiling at the woman.

"What do you want?" he asked.

"To say hello," she said. Her full lips curved into a smile. "To find out how my northern brethren are doing."

"Hello," Idisio said. "I haven't the faintest idea. Sorry. Never met them."

"I see that now," the woman said, the smile fading. "And I'm disappointed in them. No ha'rethe should ever allow one of our children to wander alone in the world."

"I'm not one of *your* children." He wasn't sure why, but he didn't want to claim any kinship to this creature, or let her lay any obligation on him.

The woman studied him thoughtfully. She seemed almost to be frowning now, but her features weren't as distinct as they had been a moment ago. "You have a great deal to learn. I should take you in myself for teaching."

"I stay with my lord," Idisio said. "I *won't* stay with you!" He put all the determination he possessed into his voice: to his surprise, she flinched.

Her form seemed to blur for a moment, then steadied. "I can't force you. And I see you're still too young to listen to wisdom. But you have obligations, young one, that should be explained to you. Whether you want to accept it or not, you carry the essence of two races in your body. You are ha'ra'ha, and that means you serve no man. Not even this desert lord of yours. He's merely useful as a teacher until you grow to your full strength. He knows this. He should have seen what you are sooner—but he's human. I've never had much respect for their intelligence."

Idisio opened his mouth but found no words to use in protest against that faintly disdainful tone.

"Obligations," the woman said, and stood. "Tell your desert lord to start with those. It's important." She stood before Idisio's chair, looking down at him, her features sharp and clear again. Idisio shut his eyes, swallowed hard, and tried to think about Riss.

The woman snorted softly, and a moment later the cold returned. Idisio shivered and reached for the blanket. It had vanished. Opening his eyes, he found himself in deep darkness again.

"Send me the desert lord," the woman's voice whispered. "Now."

Cold crashed around him, then dissolved into a searing heat across his back and shoulders. He fell forward onto his hands and knees. Sunlight dazzled his eyes. He covered his face with one hand and whimpered. Startled movement fluttered nearby; then Scratha scooped him up as if he were a sick child.

He clutched, nauseous and dizzy, at his lord's support. After a moment, when his head cleared, he managed to gasp, "She . . . it . . . wants you now."

"Not surprising," Scratha muttered, his face grim.

Idisio drew a deep breath, tried to speak, and passed out.

It had turned to full dark when he woke, and the air held a sharp chill. Someone had draped a real blanket over him. He hunched himself under its scratchy warmth more securely and blinked, rubbing his eyes. An oil lantern sat on the ground nearby, lonely warden against darkness.

"You're awake!" Riss knelt by his side an instant later, her voice high and shrill. "Gods, Idisio, gods, are you all right? What *happened* to you?"

He wanted to crawl under the covers and hide from the fear that sparkled off her like the light from a thousand splinters of glass in sunlight. He sat up instead.

"It's all right," he said, trying to be reassuring, and glanced around. "Where's Scratha?"

"He went into that *thing*," Riss said, throwing a glance at once hostile and terrified towards the great stone. They were camped within a few feet of it, and Idisio resisted an impulse to claw his way out of the blanket and run like all the demons of the s'iopes' hells were after him.

"When?"

"Right after we got you settled," Riss said. She drew a deep breath and shut her eyes. "I don't know why he hasn't come back yet," she added, her voice steadier. "I'm getting scared, Idisio."

Idisio put a hand on her shoulder, trying to calm her.

"He'll be back soon," he said, not sure he believed it himself, and wound up somehow with an armful of trembling Riss. She curled up practically in his lap, her head buried in his shoulder.

"I don't understand what's going on," she said.

"Neither do I," Idisio admitted. "But he'll be all right. Don't worry."

"And what if he doesn't come back?" Riss demanded, sitting up a bit and staring at him, her face so close to his that he thought he could feel her eyelashes flitter against his skin.

"Worry about that when it happens," Idisio said. He found himself at a loss. He hadn't expected her to fall apart on him and didn't feel strong enough right now to handle it.

"I'm back," a familiar voice said, and Scratha stepped into the thin circle of light.

Riss scrambled away and sat nearby, her face visibly reddening in the dim light. Scratha settled to the ground in a cross-legged position and rubbed at his face wearily.

"My lord," Idisio started, then stopped, biting his lower lip hard to hold the words back.

Scratha seemed to have lost several pounds from his already-thin frame; his face was tinged with grey, and his eyes held a terrifying bleakness.

"I'm fine," Scratha said, offering a thin smile.

"What did it do to you?" Idisio blurted.

With a faint flicker of a glance towards Riss, Scratha shook his head. "Stretch out and get some sleep, Riss. We'll be moving on soon. Sleep while you can."

The cadence of his speech was hypnotic. To Idisio's surprise the girl made no protest. She simply lay down a few feet away, her breathing deep and even within moments.

"We need to talk," Scratha said.

"What did it do to you, and how did you do that just now?" Idisio demanded, caught between anger and deep, trembling fear.

"Neither one matters right now," Scratha said, an edge in his voice that stopped Idisio from pressing the point. He paused, watching Idisio for a moment, then shook his head. "Why did you refuse to let the ha'rethe teach you?"

Idisio blinked. "I want to stay with you."

"I can't teach you as much as a ha'rethe can. Even a ha'ra'ha can help you more than I."

"I'm staying with you," Idisio said, clinging to the words stubbornly, not sure why.

Scratha sighed, annoyance shifting into weary resignation. Idisio had never seen his lord so open and easy to read. That, as much as anything else, frightened him badly.

"I'll give you the best I can, then," the desert lord said, "but eventually you're going to have to go to either a ha'rethe or a ha'ra'ha."

The look on his lord's face warned against disagreeing, so Idisio just nodded.

Scratha drew a deep breath and looked at the sleeping girl. "We've been granted passage," he said in seeming irrelevance.

Idisio listened to the strain in Scratha's voice and looked at the unremitting grey of the man's face. "You don't sound happy about it," he said slowly.

"Being granted passage through a ha'rethe's private underground ways is an extraordinary honor," Scratha said. "With a rather high price." He shut his eyes and winced as if at some internal pain.

"Underground?" Idisio said, his voice suddenly high and squeaky.

"The ha'reye have passages all over the world," Scratha said without looking at him. He leaned forward a bit and splayed his hands out on the ground in front of him as if for balance. "We'll be able to go right to Scratha Fortress in less time and far more safety than traveling the sands would have given us." His voice came out slower and more ragged now, as if he were reaching the end of his strength.

"With that thing right beside us at every step?" Idisio demanded. "No, thank you!"

"Idisio," Scratha said, his voice little more than a hoarse whisper now, "I need to rest. Argue with me later, please." He rolled forward and to one side, letting his weight fall on his left shoulder and from there onto his back. After blinking vaguely at the stars for a moment, his eyelids slid closed.

"But. . . ." Idisio began. Something told him beyond doubt that Scratha was truly exhausted this time, not faking it as he had in Kybeach; he gave up and glared at the stone looming over them instead. He didn't quite dare curse it, didn't quite dare get up and bolt for the relatively safe northlands, but he thought long and hard about both options before allowing himself to drift into a dark sleep.

His dreams were broken and uneasy. Glowing eyes and seductive women appeared and disappeared randomly during visions of dank stone walls—and, oddly, that small, clean, sunlit room he'd seen before.

That room still felt full of a powerful, desperate anger and fear, but somehow it didn't affect Idisio so much this time. He felt more like a bystander watching a terrible tantrum being thrown by an exceptionally strong child. With that thought came a further sense of widening perspective, and Idisio caught a flash of red hair, clipped close to a young boy's skull, before the vision dissolved into darkness again.

Finally, free of troubling visions for the moment, Idisio slept.

Scratha shook everyone awake shortly before dawn.

"Eat," he said, pushing desert bread and hard cheese into their hands. He set a water skin by Idisio and moved to stand some distance away.

As Idisio chewed the tough bread, he watched Scratha's profile in the greying light. The desert lord stared into the distance, expressionless, showing no sign of weakness or weariness, motionless as the stone looming over them. His pack lay at his feet, ready to go.

Riss said nothing as they ate, and Idisio didn't feel like talking. He felt well-rested, although he suspected he hadn't actually slept much at all. *Nervous energy,* he told himself firmly, and concentrated on eating and keeping an eye on his lord.

Finished with their meal, Riss shook out her blanket and folded it neatly back into her pack. Idisio shoved the last of the cheese into his mouth and took a hasty swig from the water skin as he stuffed his blanket untidily away. Scratha turned only when they were finished and standing beside their packs.

"Follow me," he said.

He led them around to the other side of the stone. Unlike the eastern side, this one had more smooth spots than furrowed ridges. Scratha moved to one of the widest flat areas and put his hands on the rock. He seemed to push lightly, and the rock face swung inwards, revealing a narrow passage that sloped into utter blackness.

"My lord," Idisio said involuntarily. "I can't. . . ." His protest died under the sharp glare the man gave him.

"Well, *I'm* not afraid," Riss said, and marched forward.

"Stop a few paces in," Scratha said, his voice pitched just loud enough to carry, and motioned for Idisio to move. Mouth dry, Idisio obeyed, aware that his lord would likely drag or carry him if he stalled for another moment. Scratha had that look to him right now. Putting a hand out as the light disappeared around him, he touched a thin shoulder. He couldn't help making a muffled noise and jerking back.

Riss made a faintly disgusted sound.

"I'm not a cactus, you know," she said tartly.

Scratha joined them. A moment later there came a scraping sound, and the square of dim light from the opening disappeared. The door had closed, and no light remained.

Idisio took a deep breath, then another, fighting not to whimper.

"Ha'rethe," Scratha said, and something else, words in the old desert language Idisio had never heard before.

"Don't call that thing's attention," Idisio said, but it came out in a whisper, barely vocalized, and most of it caught in his throat.

A whitish-blue, sourceless glow filled the passage, barely a small hand-lantern's worth of brightness, but Idisio's panic lifted instantly. The dim light revealed smooth, pale stone walls, a sloping floor, and a low ceiling. Scratha stood slightly stooped, one hand on the ceiling as if to remind himself not to stand straight up.

The light sparked glittering reflection from tiny, mica-like chips in the walls; Riss grinned in delighted wonder, while Idisio sighed in relief that this passage felt nothing like the dank one under Bright Bay.

"Let me take the lead," Scratha said. He kept his voice low, and as he glanced around his expression seemed tinged with awe.

Riss flattened against the wall and let the desert lord squeeze past. Scratha led them onwards and down, the gradual slope of the passage giving way to shallow, wide steps with wear marks more towards the sides than the center. Idisio thought of four-legged creatures, like the marsh lizards of Kybeach, but said nothing.

The descent went on for a long time before leveling out, but Idisio felt no pressure or panic. The light moved with them, as though some invisible creature held an unseen lantern in their midst. The walls stayed a dry, comforting desert color, and the passage felt clean, quiet, and safe.

As they walked, the ceiling rose, bit by bit, until Scratha could stand without difficulty. He paused and ran both hands over the ceiling and down each wall, then across the floor and back up. He made an odd, satisfied noise and started walking again, trailing his fingers along the wall.

"Idisio," he said over his shoulder, "put a hand to the wall on your right. Don't look at it. Keep walking."

The wall felt smooth at first, save for a few faint bumps and creases. The irregularities gradually became more distinct, more deliberate in nature, like a pattern of some sort. Idisio struggled with the urge to turn his head and look at the wall, and compromised by slanting his eyes just a bit to the right as they walked.

To his disappointment, he saw nothing visible on the wall, even as his hand insisted there were markings clear as any black-ink writing on clean new parchment. He blinked hard, trying to force his eyes to see what his fingers felt, and stumbled, crashing sideways into the wall on his left. A wave of dizziness dropped him to his knees, breathing hard. He shut his eyes, pressing his hands to the ground, waiting for it to pass.

"I told you not to look," Scratha said, sounding amused, and hoisted Idisio back to standing. "Open your eyes and look straight on, get it out of your system." He kept his hands under Idisio's armpits, supporting him, and turned him to face the wall.

Idisio stared at the smooth tan wall in front of him. He couldn't see the slightest nub or crack or crevice, even when he stepped forward and stared at the surface up close.

Scratha let him go, allowing Idisio time to explore the wall with hands and sight, and finally said, "It's all like that. Walls, floor, ceiling."

Idisio shut his eyes and ran his hands over the wall again, shaking his head.

Riss made a faint, impatient noise. "What are you talking about? There's nothing there."

Idisio could hear her feeling along the wall nearby.

"There's nothing there," she repeated. "Just a rough stone wall."

"What does it say?" Idisio asked, opening his eyes.

"I have no idea," Scratha admitted. His grin faded. "I think it's meant to be read in all directions at once. Humans can't possibly begin to interpret it."

"But how. . . ." Idisio stopped, looked up at the ceiling, down at the floor, and felt gooseflesh rippling along his arms. "This isn't a cut tunnel."

Everyone looked up and around.

"So?" Riss said.

"It's a burrow," Idisio said. "Like a snake's."

The light flickered slightly.

"Not quite," Scratha said hastily. "Don't compare them to any kind of reptile," he added in a low undertone, bending further to speak into Idisio's ear. "They get upset."

Idisio, with a sudden awareness of how far underground they were by now, and how precarious their light source, pressed his lips together.

Scratha glanced at Riss, who looked puzzled. "It's writing," he said to her, "of a sort. It's meant to be read by touch, not sight, and it's all around the walls, which means the ha'reye probably fill the tunnel when they travel through it."

"Probably?" Idisio said. "I thought you knew what—" He stopped, suddenly confused.

"We see of the ha'reye what they want us to see," Scratha said. "Some have seen what is likely the true form. I've never been granted that." He didn't sound regretful. "Let's keep going."

Chapter Twenty

Aleya and Deiq sat on a sun-warmed rock under an overhang, watching the last hour of daylight spread glorious sprays of gold, orange, peach and purple across the cloudless sky.

"You've passed the blood trials of Comos and Ishrai," Deiq said. "There's one left."

Alyea said nothing, waiting. Ever since she'd awoken some hours ago, she found herself strangely unwilling to speak unless she had to. The sound of her own voice felt odd to her ears, and her throat still hurt, as if she'd been screaming in her sleep.

Noise of any sort crackled painfully in her ears, like a burgeoning infection. Deiq spoke in a near-whisper. They'd come outside because the echoes of human movement bouncing from the rock walls made Alyea flinch.

Outside all was beautifully silent and still, save for the occasional *whiss-scritch* of desert animals venturing into the warm air.

"The sun-lord," Deiq said finally, his gaze still far away, abstracted. "Datda. Most people won't name him. It's considered bad luck, unless you're a follower. He's the god of war, of death, disease, violence, and so on."

"I'm going to have to fight?" Alyea said when it became clear Deiq had finished speaking.

"I don't know." He rubbed the knuckles of one hand with the palm of the other and shut his eyes. "It's different for everyone."

Alyea felt her forehead wrinkling into a frown. It hadn't been a lie, exactly, but she had a feeling he wasn't telling her the whole truth, either.

He looked up and caught her staring at him. A rueful grin appeared on his face. "Yes. Going through the trial of Ishrai makes you harder to fool."

"So tell me," she said.

"I can't. There are rules to the blood trials, Alyea. I can't interfere."

She made a disgusted noise.

"Sorry," he said, sounding completely unapologetic.

"What can you tell me? There has to be something!"

He considered, watching her closely. "I can tell you," he said at last, "that if you lose, I can't help you, but you won't be bonded to me any more." He cleared his throat and looked away, seeming uncomfortable.

"Because I'll be dead. No surprise there."

"Not necessarily," he said without looking at her. "I can't say more than that. I'm sorry."

His expression, in profile, was so bleak as he stared at the horizon that she left him alone. They sat in silence, watching the sun settle into a fading glow, watching as the stars began to appear high above.

By evening of the next day, Alyea's sensitivity had eased enough that she could eat dinner with the Qisani community. The room stayed mostly silent. The *ishraidain*—women serving penance under the protection of Ishrai for various crimes—kept their vow of silence, and the Callen seemed to prefer to refrain from speaking themselves. When the Callen did talk, they used low voices that even Alyea's newly sharp hearing had trouble picking up.

There seemed no particular ranking to how people arranged their positions at table. Acana sat next to Alyea, but around them ishraidain and Callen mixed together randomly.

The stew this time tasted spicier than it had previously. Alyea found she enjoyed it; the flavors of all food seemed brighter lately. She glanced up to see Acana watching her, smiling.

"In your honor," the ishrait said quietly, "I asked for the food to be made a bit more interesting. Do you like it?"

"Yes," Alyea said, keeping her voice to the same low volume. "Very much. What's in it?"

"It's the same stew we always have," Acana said, "but we added more cactus peppers. I think it's rather similar to what Juric fed you, in fact."

Alyea took another bite, comparing memory to present, and nodded. "It is. Why doesn't it bother me any more?"

"You're adjusting your sense of taste to avoid feeling pain," Acana said. Her smile widened. "I always win the pepper-eating contests with

Juric these days. He doesn't understand why."

Alyea found herself grinning in return. "I can see this is going to be useful."

"You can also tell if there's something harmful in the food," Acana said. "Poison, for example. You'll find yourself making adjustments for that too. It's very hard to kill a desert lord. Or a ha'ra'ha," she added with a respectful nod to Deiq.

He nodded without comment and went on eating. Nobody spoke again until the meal ended and ishraidain rose to clear the dishes. Then Acana motioned wordlessly for Alyea to come with her. Deiq tagged along unasked, and as the ishrait made no objection, Alyea kept her mouth shut.

They followed the ishrait into a small, unoccupied room similar to the ishell but without a pool. Several of the strange green-oil lamps burned high but produced almost no smoke; Alyea resolved to ask about them soon.

"The lamp oil comes from Aerthraim Fortress," Deiq said in a low voice. "I'll tell you about that another day."

Alyea shot him a hard stare; he shrugged, unconcerned, and settled on a bench near the doorway. Acana motioned Alyea to sit on one end of a long bench and took the other end herself.

Cross-legged, facing Acana, Alyea watched the flickering of the lamps move shadows around the room and across the ishrait's face in patterns that didn't quite match what the physical flames should be producing. Rather than making Alyea nervous, the discrepancy seemed strangely comforting.

"You have been with us ten days," Acana said at last.

Alyea blinked, startled. "That long?"

"That long," Acana said. "Unless you apply to become an ishraidain, ten days is the limit you can claim sanctuary within the Qisani. You are under the hand of a ha'ra'ha, relieving us of the responsibility of teaching you, and you are not an ishraidain. This is your last night with us. You must leave."

Alyea took a deep breath, let it out slowly as she considered. "Can you answer some questions, before I leave?"

Acana seemed to smile a bit, although it might have been a distortion of shadow. "Some things I can answer. Some I cannot."

"Who was the healer that attended me?"

"A healer. The name doesn't matter."

Alyea rephrased the question. "What was she?"

"I can't answer that."

Alyea smiled. "You just did. She's from the Forbidden Jungles, isn't she?"

In Alyea's peripheral vision, Deiq shifted as if about to speak, but settled into silence again.

"She traveled a long way," Alyea said.

"Alyea," Deiq said quietly, "she can't tell you about the healer. Please stop baiting her."

"That wasn't my intent," Alyea said. "My apologies, Acana."

She turned her head to stare at Deiq, took a breath, and *willed* him to give an unguarded answer. "How often have *you* been to the Forbidden Jungles?"

"Not often enough," he said, his voice rough with emotion, and grimaced. "*Damnit*."

The tension in the room eased abruptly as Acana laughed. "She's going to make a *very* good desert lord," she said.

"If she survives the last trial," Deiq said.

"I don't have your doubts," Acana said, and stood. "I pity the one who goes up against her. For that matter, I admit some sympathy for you, Deiq. You're going to have your hands full."

"Tell me about it," Deiq said, sounding grumpy.

Acana laughed again, bowed to both of them in turn, and left the room.

"No honorific?" Alyea said before Deiq could speak.

"I don't ask for one," he said, and stood. He crossed the room and sat on the bench, drawing his legs up to sit facing her as Acana had been moments before. "Don't do that again, Alyea. You caught me off guard with that push."

"I wanted to find out if I could do it," she said.

"You can," he said, unamused, "but don't try it with another ha'ra'ha or desert lord. It's beyond rude, and a dangerous trick to play."

"I won't," Alyea said, chastened.

Deiq nodded, his taut expression relaxing slightly. "We leave tonight. The last blood trial is going to be held at Scratha Fortress, since that's the heart of the current dispute. We should be there by morning. Walking," he added, anticipating her next question. "Juric is long gone, and the Callen of Ishrai don't use *sharaks*—that's the word for the type of carriage brought you here."

He held up a hand to stop her from speaking. "There's something else I have to say."

She raised her eyebrows and waited.

"I know Pieas raped you," he said. "I know Oruen seduced you. I know what the ha'reye did to you felt like a combination of both. Trust me that I'll do neither. My obligations are more important than that."

She felt her face heating, and couldn't speak.

"Remember what I am," he said. "I can read people. I saw how you looked at Pieas, and at Oruen, and how they looked at you—it was as if you shouted it."

"Gods," she said, covering her face with her hands.

"Make sure you know which gods you refer to," he said, "when you say that in the southlands." He stood. "Time to go."

She wore a greyish-tan garment this time, one with a long, loose cut. Deiq wore a similar outfit, and hooked a small pack over his shoulders. She had nothing to carry; even the robe from Juric had been taken away.

Silent and tall, Acana stood in the darker shadow of the entrance to the Qisani, oil lamp in hand. She bowed to them once. They returned the bow, and without speaking turned away and began walking.

The moon hovered low on the horizon, just past full. Wan light shifted the darkness into strange, flat pools and lines, eerily reminiscent of what Alyea had seen at the beginning of the blood trial of Ishrai. She tried not to think of that: a chill still ran down her spine at the memory.

The sand lay deep and loose in spots, in others hard as a thin layer over buried rock. Deiq set a steady pace, one Alyea could easily match; still, within an hour her legs ached and cramped.

"Hold on," she said, stopping, and bent to rub her calves. "I need a rest."

"No," he said, and knelt to push her hands aside. "Not like that."

She frowned down at him. "My legs hurt."

He sat back on his heels and put a finger to his forehead, just above his left eye. "Here. Don't use your hands. *Tell* your body it's going to walk without pain."

"You're mad."

He stood. "We're not stopping again. Do it my way or I'll leave you behind." He turned and started walking again.

She cursed under her breath and jogged awkwardly through the sand to catch up.

"How?" she panted when she reached his side.

"You're in control," he said without looking at her. "Your body's a tool to get you from place to place. You control the tool. You tell it what to do. You don't have to breathe hard, either, by the way. You can control that, too."

He didn't break stride as he spoke, moving forward with the same even pace he'd used before. Alyea fought to slow her breath, distracted by the increasing pain in her calves.

"Don't force it," Deiq said, still not looking at her. "Just *know* it's under your will."

"Will you *stop* so I can focus?" she snapped.

"No."

"*Damn* you!"

He made a dismissive gesture with one hand and said nothing.

"This is what you call teaching?"

"Don't waste your energy yelling at me," he said. "Use it to focus."

She snarled, feeling rather like an angry asp-jacau, then forced her attention to her breath. Step . . . breath . . . step . . . breath. It took a few minutes to catch the rhythm; abruptly, the pain vanished, and she only felt the ground rolling past her feet. Her body consisted of breath moving in and moving out; turning that breath into forward movement, and then balancing a thousand tiny adjustments in each step. Sounds, smells, sight, the slither of fabric against her skin and the taste of the air in her mouth: all senses combined into one long liquid moment. Pain arose, rerouted itself into energy to take another step. Protesting muscles simply smoothed themselves out.

Astonished at the incredible, flowing clarity, she fell. The ground sprawled up beneath her with a hard thump, shaking her breath back into erratic gasps. Aches redoubled, cramped her into a whimpering ball for a moment, then eased.

Deiq laughed and helped her stand, brushing sand from her clothes.

"Good start," he said. "Everyone falls the first time."

She stood still, blinking to clear a doubling of her vision, until things returned to normal. Her leg muscles quivered.

"What did I just do?"

"You reached center," Deiq told her.

"It felt like an aqeyva trance," she said, the words sounding thick and blurred to her own ears, "but I was taught never to try walking while in trance."

"What you call aqeyva is the closest a human can get to the discipline of the ha'reye," Deiq said. "No full human can ever reach as far into the center as you just did. You can do it because you've traded essence with a ha'rethe; you're not full human any more."

"Am I a ha'ra'ha?"

"Not even close," he said with a patience that told her every new desert lord asked that question. "Desert lords are . . . in a grey area between human and ha'ra'ha. As I said earlier, you may have some of the blood, but it's too faint to mean much. It's given you an edge with learning aqeyva meditations, and those most skilled at the aqeyva trance are considered the best candidates to be desert lords; it's part of the blood trials."

Alyea remembered the odd look on Juric's face when she'd come out of an hours-long trance.

Deiq nodded as though hearing her memory himself. "From what I'm told," he said, "you did exceptionally well. The taska said you were a natural—that you sat for much longer than any supplicant he'd ever handled before."

She couldn't think of anything to say to that.

"Let's move on," Deiq said. "We've a way to go. Move faster this time."

He turned and started walking again.

She followed, finding it easier this time to fall into the walking trance. Time slowly ceased to matter. The stars moved overhead, the moon shifted across the sky; she felt no sense of hurry, just the steady sensation of sand shifting underfoot. The sand seemed almost to be helping her move forward, propelling her faster with each step.

Emotion peeled away in layers. The vast sky overhead and the endless, moonlight-greyed sand around them reduced everything in her life to a tiny, insignificant speck. No wonder, no astonishment remained. Her movement became more an act of will than the shifting of muscle and bone. She moved through a thousand contradictions and saw the resolution to each for a fraction of a second, brief and sharp, then lost the answer again.

If she had been capable of tears she would have wept.

As dawn began to rearrange the colors of the sky, she felt a vast sense of presence ahead. Refocusing her vision with an effort, she saw a fortress, built of enormous chunks of whitestone and granite. It sprawled across the sand, not nearly as tall as she'd expected, far from gracious—nothing but an unattractive pile of disorderly rock.

Deiq put a hand on her shoulder, slowing her to a stop.

"Take a moment," he said. "You need to come all the way back to human time and space."

He stood quietly, keeping his hand on her shoulder, as she shook off the lingering half-daze. She shuddered at a sudden feeling that everything inside her had broken beyond repair. At last the fragmented sensation eased, her sight cleared, and she studied the fortress ahead with a much different eye.

It still seemed an ungainly sprawl of blocks, the design almost haphazard; it fit no pattern she'd seen before. The walls curved here, ran straight there; rose three stories high and dropped to one without symmetry. Much of the stone seemed to have been bleached and weathered by hundreds of years of desert sun and sandstorms, but Alyea saw two large, yellow-orange patches whose crisp lines indicated a more recent history.

Several tents had been pitched well away from the walls of the fortress. The morning breeze carried the thick scent of a dung-coal fire and recently cooked food: probably the ubiquitious stew with cactus peppers. People sat on blankets spread before the tents, resting and talking quietly.

Nobody seemed to have noticed Alyea and Deiq yet.

"Stay still," Deiq said, his voice low. "They won't see us until we move. We blend in. Take the time to study everything."

She saw four tents, each large enough to hold five people comfortably. The term "tent" could only be broadly applied: these sturdy, collapsible shelters sat atop the loose sand, secured more by weight inside than by stakes and string.

Alyea realized she knew at least some of the people in front of the tents: Gria. Sela. Chacerly. Micru. She wasn't sure of the others, but something about the way those four figures shifted, the shape of their heads, a gesture, a slouch, identifed them to Alyea beyond question.

She could tell there would be no joy in the reunion. Chacerly sat with a tautness that spoke of anger and fear; Gria and Sela slouched in despairing postures. Micru sat still, but something about his form reminded Alyea of his coldblooded namesake, coiled and waiting to strike; he sat far from Chac.

Another group, this one composed of small dark-skinned men, huddled in a compact group: talking, occasionally gesturing widely. They radiated anger and danger.

"Teyanain," Alyea breathed, not at all sure she had it right; but Deiq's hand tightened on her shoulder.

"Yes," he said.

"What are they doing here?"

He didn't answer. Glancing up at him, she saw by his expression that he wouldn't.

"All right," she said. "I'll figure it out for myself."

They walked forward, the sun at their backs, and for a few steps nobody noticed the movement. Finally one of the teyanain looked up and scrambled to his feet, shouting. Moments later almost the whole camp seemed to be standing, squinting into the bright light.

Gria, Sela, and Micru stayed seated. Alyea wondered what that meant: were all three prisoners? The two women certainly had that look to them, but Alyea couldn't imagine Micru sitting tamely in cuffs, somehow.

She kept her face expressionless as she and Deiq advanced on the camp, watching where people stood and where they looked—and didn't look. The teyanain weren't glancing anywhere near the seated people, and neither was Chacerly.

The wrinkles on Chac's face deepened as he strode forward. He directed a glare at Deiq.

"You have a bad habit," he snapped, "of interfering where you're not wanted."

Deiq said nothing, his own expression bland.

Chac made a dismissive, hostile gesture and turned his attention to Alyea. "Took you long enough to get here," he said. "And where's Juric? He should have had you here days ago."

"I'm sorry I'm late. I was healing," she said, keeping her voice neutral.

"Healing? From what . . . ?" He stopped, returned his glare to Deiq. "You *didn't*."

"She did," Deiq said, and smiled. "She bears the marks of both Comos and Ishrai."

The teyanain had been hanging back a few paces, listening intently. At those words, one of them pushed forward. He stood at least a head shorter than Alyea, with the dark skin and facial structure of a deep southerner, but mysterious blue tattoos wrapped across his face and arms.

"Show them," he ordered. "Show marks."

Deiq put his hands on Alyea's shoulders and turned her to stand facing away from the onlookers. She felt him draw the loose cloth of her shirt up to show her mid-back. After a moment he let it drop and carefully pulled the left side of her leggings down a handspan to expose her hip, then tugged them back up and turned her around again. He gave her the faintest hint of a smile when she glanced up at him.

Chac let out a hiss through his front teeth. "You're a *fool*."

The teyanin leader said nothing, but seemed to be studying Alyea with markedly more respect than before.

"How is possible?" the tattooed man said. "Ishrai year not past."

"I'm standing in for the ha'reye," Deiq said.

In the deathly silence following those words, Chac's weathered face seemed to lose color.

"You can't do that!" the old man snarled. "That's not allowed!"

"The ha'reye of the Qisani agreed to it," Deiq said. "That's all the authority I need."

A murmur rose among the teyanain behind Chac. Alyea heard "Qisani" repeated several times.

The teyanain's expressions shifted to distinctly impressed. Chac jerked, lowering his chin to his chest for a moment, then took a deep breath and straightened.

"Juric was told to bring you straight here, not to the Qisani," he said to Alyea. "You should not have gone through those two trials yet. Juric will be called to account for this."

"Juric is a Callen of Comos, and a friend of mine," Deiq said with lazy amusement.

Chac's glare shifted back to Deiq, and it held a murderous anger this time.

Alyea cleared her throat.

"Excuse me," she said in a tone that brought everyone's attention sharply back to her. "I'm here to take the last blood trial. Is there a Callen of Datda here that is ready and willing to test me?"

The tattooed teyanin bowed, both hands clasped together in front of him, and when he straightened he pointed to Chac.

"Callen," he said, and stepped back three measured paces.

"*Chac?*" Alyea said in disbelief. "You can't be serious!"

The old man's expression could have melted the stone of the Qisani.

"Yes," he said finally. "I'm here to test you."

Alyea suspected events had moved far from the path Chac had intended.

"We left the Qisani last evening and have been walking all night,"

Deiq said. "I'd like to request that she be given the chance to rest before beginning the trial."

Another murmur from the teyanain. The blue-tattooed one now had an expression of open astonishment. "You walk from Qisani in *one night?*" he said.

"Toi, te hoethra," Deiq said. "I swear it to be truth. She walked by my side with the wings of the desert wind."

"You have right to rest," the tattooed man said before Chac could speak. He pointed at the tents behind them. "You use my *shall*, my shelter. Go."

"*Saishe-pais*—gratitude to your honor," Deiq said, and put a hand on Alyea's shoulder. He steered her past the watching crowd and towards a shelter that had a bright blue stripe near the entrance.

"Don't look back," he murmured as they walked. "Don't look at anyone. Just get in the shelter and say nothing until we're inside."

The *shall* was wide, round, and smelled of sun-baked, unwashed human. A light mat lay on the canvas floor, grey and worn with long use; Alyea sat on it without waiting for a prompt. She looked up at Deiq.

"What *can* you tell me," she said deliberately, watching his mouth twitch as if against a smile, "about what just happened out there?"

He sat beside her, drew his knees up, and grinned.

"Very little," he said, seeming pleased about something. "Chac expected you to be here several days ago. I made arrangements otherwise. I thought you'd be better prepared for the blood trial of Datda if you'd been through the other two first."

"Chac didn't want me to pass his trial in the first place, did he?"

"I can't speak to that."

"You don't have to," Alyea said sourly. "Gods! This is a mess."

"I've seen worse," Deiq said, and stretched out. "Go to sleep."

She stared at him for a while, watching him as his breathing evened out and his eyes began to flutter in the onset of true sleep. He said nothing more, and as the day's heat began to seep into the chill air of the shelter, it seemed to steal away the energy she'd been using to stay upright.

She didn't remember lying down, but found herself stretched out limp next to Deiq. A heartbeat after that, a darkness thicker than night drew her from consciousness.

Chapter Twenty-One

As they walked, a strange, sourceless susurrus of murmurs and whispers faded in and out of Idisio's hearing: he shivered, a prickling chill racing over his whole body. The tunnel didn't feel comfortable any longer. Once the voices began, traveling the ha'rethe's underground ways had swiftly become an experience as eerie and creepy for Idisio as the tunnels beneath Bright Bay.

Scratha, too, seemed to be listening at times, but Idisio found himself afraid to ask if his master heard the voices. The desert lord's expression held a worrying sourness, and the grey strain hadn't faded from his face yet. Riss didn't seem to be hearing anything; she trudged along, sullen and withdrawn in another of her confusing mood shifts.

"My lord," Idisio said at last, hoping to take his mind off the whispers echoing in the back of his head, "you said you'd be teaching me. When are you going to start?"

Scratha glanced at Riss. "I'd intended. . . ." He paused and shook his head. "Well, Riss may as well hear. It will help her to understand what you're going through, and you'll need that."

"Well, thanks for that kindness," Riss snapped.

Scratha stopped, turned, and gave the girl a ferocious glare that actually made her flinch.

She dropped her gaze. "Sorry," she said in a small voice.

Scratha resumed walking, his face grim. "Obligations. Every ha'ra'ha has certain obligations. I've been . . . instructed on what to tell you." His lips pressed together and a twitch passed across his face. "I'll start with the one you won't like most, and get it out of the way. You have to father at least one child."

Idisio stopped cold, his legs refusing to move another step. As if he'd expected the pause, Scratha shot a hand out, grabbed Idisio's elbow, and jerked him roughly into motion again.

"I don't make the rules," the desert lord said without looking at Idisio. "It's part of a very old agreement between the ha'reye and humans. Anyone with even a trace of the blood has to father or bear at least one child if they're able. Quite a few of mixed blood are sterile; they can't reproduce. So the burden falls on those who can, to give at least one and preferably more."

He didn't loose his iron grip on Idisio's arm as he spoke, and Idisio gave up on the idea of stopping to catch his breath after that incredible statement.

"You can let me go, my lord," he said. "I swear I won't run."

Scratha stumbled a half-step and shot Idisio a dark stare. Idisio forced a smile, and after a moment Scratha released his grip and offered a wry smile of his own.

"It's a long way from the gardens of the Bright Bay palace, isn't it?" Scratha said.

Idisio nodded, relieved that the desert lord had picked up on the reminder and allowed the mood to lighten a bit. "It is."

"Who does he—?" Riss started.

"Let me finish explaining, Riss," Scratha said sharply. "Hold your peace for a moment."

Riss fell silent. Idisio glanced back at her and saw an odd expression on her face. She seemed badly rattled. He didn't get a chance to ask her about it; Scratha started talking again.

"It's best," the desert lord said, eyes straight ahead and a pronounced strain in his voice, "if you have a child with a full human. If you choose another ha'ra'ha, there's a greater chance the child will be sterile, or . . . deformed." He seemed to force the last word out. "And you'll have to take full responsibility for the child. It's *your* child, not the mother's. That reverses, of course," he added, "for a female ha'ra'ha." A pained expression crossed his face.

Idisio just kept walking, alternating between staring at his feet and staring straight ahead. He felt overwhelmed and almost numb with disbelief.

"You don't have to marry the woman you choose," Scratha went on after a moment of thick silence. "I'd advise telling her the truth beforehand, though, or she'll get upset when you come to take the child." His tone returned to dry neutrality.

"Really?" Riss said from behind them, heavily sarcastic.

Scratha ignored her. "You'll be expected to bring the child to your sworn ha'rethe for a . . . well, call it a blessing. That's close enough. It's more of an examination, to find out if the child is, ah. . . ." He cleared his throat again. "True blood, true bred. The ha'rethe will determine if you're really the father and whether the child has inherited any of the blood traits."

"Gods, you're cold!" Riss said. She sounded really angry. "We're not talking about some . . . some foal and its bloodline here! This is a child! What's the matter with you?"

"I don't make the rules," Scratha repeated.

"That's a dodge," Riss said.

Scratha sighed. "Trust me," he said, "the ha'reye are far from indifferent to their children. I don't have the skill to explain it more gently, that's all."

"You mean you don't have the stomach to mask what's ugly with pretty words," Riss said.

"My lord," Idisio said before the man could speak, "have you had to give a child?"

Complete silence followed that question for several moments. Idisio noticed, almost absently, that the passage had started to widen.

"Yes," Scratha said at last. "It's part of becoming a desert lord." His expression became closed and fierce. Idisio wished he hadn't asked, but Riss, heartless, jumped into the moment:

"Where are your children, then, my lord?" she said. "Do *you* have responsibility for them?"

Another long silence. Finally, Scratha let out a long, hard breath, and said, "Dead."

Idisio heard a faint, startled intake of breath from behind him, and knew Riss regretted her harsh questioning.

"I'm sorry, my lord," she said quietly.

"Done is done," Scratha said. After another pause, he went on, his voice steadying as he spoke: "Idisio, I'm not saying you have to do this right away. But when you do, choose a partner with care, and make sure she understands what she's bedding. And . . . before you do . . . you're going to have to learn from another ha'ra'ha or ha'rethe; there's . . . it's not as simple for you as just taking a woman to bed. I don't know . . . how to explain what's involved."

"So he can't get some girl pregnant accidentally?" Riss asked in pragmatic tones. "That ought to be a relief."

Scratha half snorted, half sighed, and said nothing. Idisio, feeling a hot flush spreading across his face, kept his gaze firmly ahead and his teeth in his tongue.

Ahead, the passageway spread further and ended in an opening that ten men could have marched through with ease. Scratha's steps slowed as they moved forward into the room beyond, and for a long moment they all stood on the threshold and simply stared.

Idisio had never seen such an enormous enclosure; the sloping floor of the vast cavern before them leveled out, towards the center, into an area large enough for a thousand men to camp on. Many openings of varying size punctuated the rim of the gigantic bowl, and ramps had been cut—no, *worn*, Idisio realized after another look—from the cavern floor up to wide ledges in front of each opening.

The same steady light that illuminated the passage filled the entire cavern, as though the ha'rethe had reached ahead in anticipation of their arrival and poured out its strange magic to prepare the scene. Idisio shivered again, wanting nothing more than to turn and run; but once again the only way out lay ahead, not behind.

As they stood staring, a sense of *presence* filled Idisio's throat with wool, thickening his breath in his chest. Scratha glanced at him, frowning, then tilted his head as though listening to something Idisio couldn't hear.

"We need to rest, I think," he said after a moment.

Scratha led them back into the tunnel a hefty stone's throw; the muzzy feeling left Idisio's throat, and he drew in a deep, grateful breath. Riss slid her pack off her shoulders and sat. They all followed her lead, Idisio between Riss and Scratha, resting their shoulders against the sloping walls. In spite of the abundance of space, they huddled together, shoulders almost touching, as if they all shared a need in this strange place for human contact.

Scratha passed around chunks of dried fruit, cheese, and trail jerky. They ate in silence, sipping sparingly from their water skins.

"How much further do we have to go?" Riss finally asked.

"I'm not entirely sure myself," Scratha admitted. "My sense of time is a bit odd down here." He looked as if he intended to say more, then shot Riss a sharp glance and shook his head instead. "A day or two, maybe three."

Idisio grimaced, not liking the thought of traveling these passages any longer than necessary. Scratha caught his expression and grinned, although it held no humor.

"Walking the desert above us," he said, "we'd take seven or eight days to reach Scratha Fortress, at best; the desert's not a flat plain. Hills, valleys, rough terrain, sandy patches all slow travel down. This way is a straight line and an easy walk in comparison. And taking this path means we don't have to stop for political games." He took a swig from his water skin.

"Political games?" Riss said.

Scratha ate a piece of dried fruit, seeming to consider. "The major Families are like little kings," he said. "They each claim jurisdiction over a certain amount of land, and they all have ancient, huge fortresses as the center of their power. The minor Families don't have as much land, as many people, and so they don't have as much political power. The more desert lords sworn to a Family, the more power it holds." He paused to take a bite of jerky and chewed steadily.

"Boundaries shift," he went on finally. "Sessin Family, for example, used to be a fairly minor Family, hundreds of years ago. When they figured out the secret to clear, flat glass, they gained more power, more wealth, and expanded their holdings to match. Last I heard they're supporting seven full desert lords. Tereph is a fairly new Family in terms of centuries. They've been established for about two, three hundred years at best. They were granted some land at the edge of Sessin's southern boundary, and support three full lords."

"Granted by who?" Idisio asked, proud that he'd snuck a question in ahead of Riss.

"A Conclave."

"What's a Conclave?" Riss asked, frowning.

Scratha looked at her, eyes distant, for a moment, as if still lost in thought, then he shook himself sharply and said, "A gathering of desert lords. Any time ten full lords representing at least seven different Families are gathered, it can be considered a Conclave. Decisions made in Conclave are binding on all of the southlands. Every desert Family has to be notified and given a chance to attend."

"Wait," Riss said, squinting at him. "Ten lords, but only seven Families? Doesn't that slant things a bit?"

Scratha smiled. "It can," he admitted. "There used to be more Families, so having fifteen or even thirty lords show up to a Conclave wasn't uncommon. These days, it's a little trickier, and that's where the between-Conclave political games come in. Deals and alliances made out of Conclave are starting to affect votes within Conclave."

His tone became musing. "Pieas threatened to call a Conclave. He can't—only a full lord can, and his own Family wouldn't back such a notion—but he's developed allies in odd places, and one of them might just be fool enough to try it."

"Why would Pieas want to call a Conclave?" Idisio said, bewildered. "To challenge you over his sister? That seems a bit extreme."

Scratha blinked and seemed mildly startled, as if just realizing he had said that aloud.

"No," he said. "I don't think I have anything to do with that, actually. I think he wanted to challenge Oruen's appointment of Lady Alyea to hold my lands while I'm gone. I don't think it's a bad reason, at that. She's too young, and doesn't have the faintest idea what she's walking into. If I'd realized what a botch he'd make of the grant, I wouldn't have done it." He glared at the far wall as though it held the blame.

"So *do* you think Pieas is going to try to call a Conclave?" Riss said.

"He can't," Scratha said, and smiled unpleasantly. "I already did. Guests should be setting up camp outside the walls of Scratha Fortress as we speak."

Chapter Twenty-Two

Voices and a scratchy feeling of tension jerked Alyea from a dream in which yellow-eyed creatures glared at her from pools of deep shadow. Deiq crouched at the entrance to the *shall*, looking out.

He cast a tight-mouthed glance over his shoulder as she stirred.

"Trouble," he said. "Get yourself all the way awake." He went back to studying the uproar.

"What's going on?" She ran her hands through her hair, trying to rake out the worst of the tangles.

"Company," he said without turning. "Pieas Sessin, and others. Sounds like someone called a Conclave, and the first guests just arrived."

Alyea's stomach rolled and rumbled. She scrubbed her hands over her face, trying to decide if the sensation came from hunger or fear.

"Eat," Deiq said. "Bread next to you."

"Thanks," she said absently, reaching for the bread. She hardly noticed taste or texture as she bolted the food, her thoughts even more agitated than her stomach.

Pieas! Why? Had he convinced his Family to call a Conclave, as he'd threatened? If Sessin Family had decided to back Pieas, and stand against her, what would that do to their relationship with Oruen? Or did those two issues have no relation?

"Whatever the reason for this Conclave," Deiq said, as if sensing her thoughts, "it seems to involve you."

Alyea wiped her mouth free of crumbs. "I'm ready."

Deiq half-turned and looked at her critically. "Remember you're more than halfway to being a desert lord already. Don't let anyone push you around. You'll lose credibility."

She swallowed hard and nodded. He rose from his crouch, moving out of the *shall* as he did so, and pulled the flap aside for her. Outside, she swept the scene with a rapid, assessing glance. Several teyanain stood in a rough circle around her *shall*; she saw the small man with the blue tattoos standing to one side. Seeing her step out of his *shall*, he nodded neutral greeting, then looked towards Chac as though to direct Alyea's own gaze in that direction.

Chac seemed to be arguing with a tall, dark man whose face was marked with a sinuous white line from the corner of his left eye to the left corner of his mouth. Chac looked furious, the stranger uninterested. As Alyea watched, the tall man made a dismissive gesture, his numerous wide bracelets jingling with the motion, then turned his back on the sputtering old man and walked away, passing Micru, Gria, and Sela without a glance.

Alyea realized that her two slaves and the Hidden all sat together as they had been last night: even in the same spot. That worried her. She thought about walking over to them, but decided against it. Not understanding the situation meant not knowing what message her attending to them might send to watchers; safer to stay clear for now.

Altogether, the number of people in front of Scratha Fortress had easily doubled, and the tension had quadrupled. Chac, denied his argument with the tall man, turned, spotted Alyea and started towards her, scowling. The teyanain stiffened, looking to the tattooed one as though for directions; he nodded, and they allowed Chac though their line without protest.

Chac didn't even seem to notice the brief exchange, his attention—and his anger—focused on Alyea alone.

"Chac," she said as soon as he came within earshot. She straightened her back and did her best to look imposing instead of terrified. *You're more than halfway . . .* She felt her fear dissolving. Chac couldn't possibly do anything more dreadful than the events she'd already lived through.

The tattooed teyanin moved to stand nearby. He now displayed his own set of bracelets; small, flattened beads of semiprecious stones interspersed with even tinier silver and gold squares. She had no idea what that meant, but Chac's gaze fastened on them and stuck as though in horrified fascination.

"Lady," the tattooed man said, smiling. "*Teth hanaa silayha*; you grace us."

Chac, still staring at the bracelets, shivered as though abruptly terrified; a moment later his scowl reappeared and he seemed to regain control of himself.

"The grace is in your presence," Alyea said after a moment, and stared hard at Chac. "You seem unhappy about something, Chacerly."

"I'm not happy about *that* one being here," Chac snapped, pointing at Deiq. The ha'ra'ha stood slightly behind her, at her right shoulder. "Send him away!"

About to say: *I can't*, she stopped herself.

"No," she said instead. "He's my advisor now, Chacerly. He stays."

"You can't trust him!" Chac said.

"I trust him more than I trust you at the moment," she said. "You have a lot to explain, old man, and I have a feeling I won't be believing any of it." Chac had been more rattled by the teyanin's bracelets than by Deiq's presence; once again, Alyea wished she understood the secret language which seemed to be passing to all sides of her.

Smiling, the tattooed man bowed slightly and drifted away as though to allow them relative privacy for their quarrel.

"Deiq's just using you," Chac said. "You'll find that out. That's all he does, use people for his own aims. He lies, Alyea, he *lies*."

Those words held truth, an undeniable passion, and pain; but Alyea knew better than to ask for the history behind that. Not only would Chac probably lie again, it would divert the conversation from the most important point: his own betrayal of her.

"You haven't been honest, yourself," Alyea said.

"I've done what was needed," he said. "What I was ordered to do."

"I won't believe Oruen ordered me kidnapped."

"You weren't kidnapped!" Chac protested. "Not by my orders, certainly. I left instructions for you to be brought here while I diverted the teyanain from your trail. They want you dead! I was trying to save your life." He pointed at Deiq again, his hand shaking. "He's the one who interfered and had you taken to the Qisani. That's the most dangerous—"

"And the most respected," Deiq interrupted. "The Qisani produces the strongest lords."

Before Chac could answer, the tall man with the white line on his face approached and bowed to her. His bracelets, mainly thin strands of silver and gold twisted into narrow braids, glittered and jingled; none seemed to hold any beads, of any material.

Alyea despaired of ever understanding what any of it meant.

"Lady," he said. "*Teth hanaa silayha*." The words held a flat, broad accent that she had never heard before.

"The grace is in your presence," Alyea responded automatically.

"Let me introduce myself," the tall man went on. "I'm Lord Irrio Darden. My grandfather is the Head of Darden. And you would be Lady Alyea." He smiled. "Quite a fuss you have started, my lady."

Alyea grinned at him, knowing the expression held little true humor. "You give me far too much credit, my lord."

He studied her for a moment, his own smile widening. "I rather doubt that."

"My lord," Chac started.

The tall man looked down at him and said curtly, "There is nothing from your mouth that I want to hear at this moment."

Alyea clamped her jaw tight to avoid gaping like an idiot. Chac's eyes seemed to glitter with a cold fury she'd never seen in him before.

"She's under blood trial law, my lord," Chac said. "I've agreed to test her under the auspices of the sun-lord. That gives me rights—"

"As I've already told you, that gives you nothing," Lord Irrio said, "until your status is determined. That's been made a matter for the Conclave; her blood trial will have to wait until then."

Deiq made a soft humming sound of amusement. Chac turned a murderous glare on the ha'ra'ha, received nothing but a faint smile in response, and stormed away, muttering to himself.

"He's a fool," Deiq said amiably, "and a dangerous one, Lord Irrio."

"He's a snake with one tooth, and that about to be broken," the desert lord answered, and made a dismissive gesture with one hand. "My lady, will you join us in a morning meal? I think we may have a great deal to discuss."

The simple meal consisted of slices of desert flatbread rolled around a warm, spicy filling of beans and rice. The company and conversation proved considerably more complicated.

Three more desert lords introduced themselves to Alyea before they began to eat: Lord Rest of Ehrrat Family, Lord Faer of Toscin Family, and Lord Salo, also of Darden Family. Deiq studied the men.

"All western Families," he noted. "I hope the east will find itself represented fairly."

He made no move to take any food; Alyea followed his lead.

"If they stir themselves to show up," Lord Rest said sourly. A short man as southerners went, he stood no taller than Alyea herself, and his dark hair looked thick and oily. He studied her critically, like a fighter assessing his opponent's strength.

"If they've been notified, they'll come," Deiq said.

"Desert law requires that all Families be notified in the event of a Conclave," Lord Faer said. His voice emerged as a deep, rumbling bass that suited his bulk; not a fat man, but sturdily built and carrying a few extra pounds with it.

Lord Rest snorted contemptuously, but Lord Irrio said, "They've been notified. Scratha's always held by the law."

"Scratha!" Alyea said, startled, and found herself the target of multiple hard stares. "I . . . I thought perhaps Pieas Sessin. . . ." she faltered, looking around. She still didn't see him anywhere. "He was threatening to, last I saw him."

"Pieas Sessin doesn't have the authority," Lord Faer said.

"And Scratha does?" Lord Rest said. He wiped crumbs and rice from the corner of his mouth.

"Scratha was granted Head of Family status a long time ago," Lord Faer said, frowning. "That's not up for challenge!"

A movement nearby made Alyea turn her head sharply; the tattooed teyanin sat on her other side now.

"It is," he said.

Silence fell as the teyanin leaned forward and scooped rice onto a piece of flatbread. Nobody looked surprised, except for Lord Faer. Lord Irrio looked thoughtful, Lord Salo offended, Lord Rest amused.

"Who's challenging Scratha's status?" Lord Faer demanded.

"I," the teyanin said complacently. "Lord Evkit." He held out his arm and shook it so the bracelet clicked loudly.

"*You're*—" Lord Irrio blurted, clearly startled. The others stared at the bracelet with expressions similar to the one Chac had developed on seeing it clearly.

The tattooed man grinned at them. "I," he nodded.

Alyea's breath caught in her throat as she remembered what Juric had told her: *Cida Scratha ran off with a commoner the night after the announcement of her engagement to Lord Evkit. Her desertion was a mortal insult.*

Could this actually be the same man?

Deiq made an odd, pained sound. "Lord Evkit. I'm honored."

The other lords hastily chorused similar sentiments. "What brings the head of the teyanain to the deep desert?" Lord Irrio asked.

Lord Evkit turned slightly and pointed. They followed his gaze, and Alyea felt her chest tighten painfully; he was indicating the two northern women.

"Mine," he said, and looked at Alyea. "Stolen."

"Bought fairly," Deiq said, leaning forward slightly to look at the small man. "Legal under all laws."

"Mine," Lord Evkit repeated stubbornly. "Blood honor claim."

Lord Rest let out a low whistle. "You're a fool if you're going to challenge that, Deiq. None of us have that much power. Not even you."

"None of you have that much courage," Deiq retorted.

Lord Evkit laughed. That cooled the brewing argument, as everyone stared at the chuckling man, their anger visibly fading into bewilderment.

"He is right," the head of the teyanain said cheerfully. "You all know what happen if teyanain upset." He glanced at the ruins of the fortress and grinned.

"You'd punish a child for the fault of its parent?" Alyea demanded. "You're no better than the northern s'iopes!"

He stopped laughing. "Punish?" he said, his face wrinkling in apparent bewilderment.

Deiq put a hand on Alyea's arm, his expression intent as if he had just glimpsed the answer to a complex puzzle.

"What did you intend to do with the girl, my lord?" he asked.

"Fill contract," Lord Evkit said, as if it should have been obvious. "Get honor back."

"What contract?" Deiq pressed.

"Cida Scratha made contract," Lord Evkit said. "We have not forget." He spoke patiently, as if explaining to a child. "Cida go, have child elsewhere, child still bound to contract."

Everyone gaped at him in stunned silence.

"You just want . . . to marry her? You're not going to kill her?" Alyea said at last, almost dizzy with relief.

Lord Evkit shook his head, his expression opaque. "Dead, no contract. Dead, no use to us."

"But you killed. . . ." Alyea started. Deiq's hand clamped hard on her arm, cutting her off.

Lord Evkit looked at the ruined fortress again.

"You think we did this?" he asked. "You think teyanain do this?"

"You practically admitted it just now!" Lord Rest said. "What happens when teyanain are upset, you said, and looked at the fortress."

"We do nothing," Lord Evkit said, shaking his head again. "We not help, when contract broken; we withdraw support. Other Family follow us, their choice. We not tell them to turn back on Scratha."

The expressions around the circle suggested everyone had heard the strange edge to those words. To Alyea, Lord Evkit sounded like a man carefully dancing a thin line of truth.

The tattooed man took in the combined skepticism around him and shrugged. "I lord of teyanain. We judges. We neutral."

"But marrying into Scratha would have given you an alliance," Lord Irrio protested. "You wouldn't have been neutral any longer."

"Not," Lord Evkit said, shaking his head. "Teyanain carry male line. Cida agree become teyanain, no more Scratha. No upset balance."

"Let's wait on the rest of this discussion," Lord Irrio said suddenly. "Scratha's not even here yet, and we don't have the full ten. We're getting into an area that should be handled in full Conclave."

The others seemed displeased, but nodded agreement.

"Messy," Deiq muttered, and rose. "With your pardon, lords, we'll withdraw until the Conclave begins."

Alyea stood, bowed, and followed Deiq as he strode away.

"Damn messy," he said, just audible as they walked. "Damn, damn, damn."

"How long until the Conclave?" Alyea asked.

"It starts when Scratha and at least four more full desert lords arrive," Deiq said. "And the challenge to Scratha's status is going to have to be the first thing handled. Whoever calls the Conclave has certain rights and responsibilities." He shook his head. "Messy," he repeated.

"It could be weeks before everyone gets here!"

He slanted her an amused glance. "Desert lords have ways of getting places in a hurry," he said. "I expect it won't take more than a day or two to have the full ten. Conclave draws the politicians of the desert like a corpse draws flies."

She made a face at the comparison. He laughed, his good humor seemingly restored, and said, "Let's walk through the fortress."

"Can we?" she said, startled. "Everyone is camped outside—"

"And they'll stay outside," Deiq said. "They haven't the right to go inside, unless you invite them, and I advise you not to do that just now. But you have the key and the right; nobody can stop you from going in."

"I. . . ." Alyea stopped walking, horrified. "A key?"

"You don't have. . . ." Deiq stopped too, his face an open mixture of astonishment and gathering suspicion. "How were you going to get inside?"

Without conscious thought, she turned and stared back the way they had come, trying to pick Chac out of the crowd. She couldn't see him.

Deiq cursed again, in several languages this time. "Your king is a fool."

"I'm the idiot," she said ruefully. "I can't believe I never even thought of that."

He pursed his lips, as if restraining himself from agreeing with her, and finally said, "Well, done is done."

"Will Chac try to get into the fortress?" she said, suddenly anxious.

Deiq looked thoughtful, then shook his head. "The fortress wouldn't let him in."

Alyea frowned at the odd phrasing. "What—?"

"You have to get inside before Scratha arrives," Deiq said, as if he hadn't even noticed her attempt to speak. "Otherwise your claim is in dispute. And there's more chance of a snowstorm at noon today than there is of Chacerly giving you that key." He shook his head, his gaze distant. "This is a mess."

"What claim can I have against the rightful lord?" she demanded.

"You weren't listening," he said. "Cafad Scratha's status is going to be challenged. If the teyanain win that challenge, and there's no valid alternative, Evkit can claim the fortress."

She stared at him, shocked. "Is that what this is about? He wants the fortress?"

"Yes. Marrying the girl to Lord Evkit nullifies her Scratha blood-right, but her children still have the claim; so on the birth of that first child, Lord Evkit gains control of Scratha lands as guardian until they come of age. Stripping Lord Scratha of his Head of Family title would nullify *his* claim, now that there's a direct female descendant available. And if you don't get into the fortress before Scratha arrives, *your* claim is dead. But you need that last blood trial first." He shook his head, rubbing his large hands over his face.

"Why now?" she said. "All this time since the original slaughter, why now? And why does Lord Evkit want a fortress so far from the Horn? It doesn't make sense."

Deiq shook his head again and didn't answer. They stood silent for a while, staring at the gathering heat-glare over the sand. Alyea took advantage of the quiet to arrange her thoughts, picking out common threads and possible links. Slowly, a pattern emerged from the seemingly random events.

She took a deep breath, let it out; allowed all the frustration and anxiety to leave her body. Then she turned and started back towards the camp.

Deiq followed, frowning. "What are you doing?"

"I'm going to talk to Lord Irrio."

An enormous red sun-tent had been put up, large enough to shelter fifty people at once; and almost that many crowded beneath it. Under another, smaller sun-tent nearby rested four goats and two mules, and a large enclosure for a half dozen chickens had appeared.

Alyea stared, astonished; Deiq chuckled and said, "Desert folk tend to travel with their food if they expect to stay a while. You'll see a small city camped out here by the time everyone arrives. And most of it's intended as a gift to the host, so they'll leave lighter than they came."

Lord Irrio sat in the shade of the main tent, watching his surroundings with a bland expression which shifted to a smile as Alyea approached.

"Greetings, my lady," he said. "You grace me with your presence."

"Do you know, my lord," she said without preamble, lowering herself to sit in front of him, "I learned a valuable lesson, growing up during Ninnic's reign."

"And what would that have been?" he said, tilting his head a little to one side. He flicked the briefest of glances at Deiq as the ha'ra'ha settled beside Alyea.

"That the most courteous people are either servants or looking to use you."

Lord Irrio's expression went completely blank, but his eyes warned her she'd leapt onto dangerous ground with both feet.

"I doubt you're interested in serving me," she went on, disregarding the tension she could feel in Deiq and the dangerous glitter in the desert lord's eyes. "So what do you want from me, *my lord*?"

After a moment, he smiled, but she saw no humor in his eyes. "I might ask the same, as you came to speak to me, not I to you."

Alyea said nothing. She waited, locking stares with the man, and finally some real amusement twitched the corners of his mouth.

"It's been commented," Irrio said, "that there are as many plots and plans in the desert as there are grains of sand on the ground. You've simply stepped into several at once, and have them tangled around you. I'd prefer you to step aside, out of the way." He glanced at Deiq. "If you'd held to the original plan, you'd be quietly sitting at your needlework in there—" he pointed at the fortress, "and we'd all be happily maneuvering around each other without you."

"I'm terrible at needlework," Alyea said dryly. "I would have used the guards for pincushions and run away the first day."

He grinned. "I see that now. The *hask* miscalculated badly."

"You're not the first person to say that," she said. "What does that word mean, anyway?"

"*Hask*?" he said. "Traitor. Someone who breaks a sacred oath. It's unforgivable."

She nodded, not at all surprised. "Chac broke his oath to Datda," she said. "He set aside his status as Callen when he came to Bright Bay, and now he's trying to claim it again. Am I right?"

Deiq made a small, choking noise, and Lord Irrio's eyebrows rose.

"You are correct," the desert lord said. "How did you—"

"I never knew he was Callen," she said, "never heard the slightest whisper in Bright Bay of any disgrace on his name. Once into the Horn, everything changed—his behavior, the way people treated him. Now you're arguing over his status, and calling him a traitor; it's not all that difficult to set the pieces together for a whole."

"Very much miscalculated," Irrio said after a moment.

"And I would guess," she went on, "that one reason he misjudged me is because he's either Shakain or from some other community that believes women are lackwits, and he can't help having that color all his actions. Even though he's known me for years, once we came back into the southlands, old habits were too hard to shake."

"It's a blindness common to men of the lower western coastlines," Lord Irrio agreed, seeming thoroughly amused now. Deiq still sat tense and silent by her side, his evident worry not at all relieved by the desert lord's good humor; she nodded to herself and went on ignoring him for the moment.

"What I'm not so sure of," she said, "is why you're dropping him. He's been a useful spy all these years, hasn't he?"

All ease drained from the desert lord's face. "I wouldn't say spy."

"Say contact, then. Resource, if you like. Advisor to the king is a powerful position, especially if that advisor helped put that king on the throne in the first place. And whoever helped that advisor set up the plans to topple the previous king would have a fairly strong hold on both men." She paused, then added, "Ninnic wasn't very friendly to the desert Families, was he?"

"No," Lord Irrio said, watching her with a hooded stare. "Oruen is much easier to deal with."

"I remember being amazed at how perfectly everything worked out," she said. "Practically the day after Chac said he'd taught Oruen everything he could, Ninnic died. And nobody at all, not even the priests, argued against Oruen stepping up, although his dislike of the Northern Church was no secret." She lifted an eyebrow questioningly and stared at Irrio.

After a moment, he raised a hand in a surrendering gesture and laughed. "Yes, my Family, and others, helped . . . transfer . . . the throne to a better candidate. We'll do the same with Oruen, if he shows signs of madness."

"So why did you drop Chac?" she said, ignoring the obvious hook to draw her off track. "I'm guessing he went to Bright Bay on Darden orders. He set aside his Callen status for your sake. Why are you treating him badly now?"

"Because he blundered," Lord Irrio said, and the coldness returned to his face and tone. "A Callen of the sun-lord who can't kill is no longer a Callen. He is useless."

She stared at him, stunned. Beside her, Deiq sat very still, his breathing even.

"You wanted me dead?" she said.

He shrugged. "I wanted you safely set aside, doing needlework. When he knew he couldn't control you, he should have killed you."

She turned her head very slowly and looked at Deiq's grim profile. He stared straight ahead and didn't return her gaze. A muscle twitched briefly in his cheek.

"You knew this, didn't you?" she said.

His head dipped in the slightest nod. He still didn't look at her.

Lord Irrio seemed amused again. "Ask him why he intervened. Ask him the real reason he stepped in the way. Believe me, it wasn't love."

"I never said it was," Deiq said tonelessly.

"At least you were that honest," Lord Irrio said, and moved as if to stand.

"Wait," Alyea said, putting out a hand. She took a deep breath and forced herself to set aside her simmering anger at the ha'ra'ha beside her; things had finally begun to make sense. "I have more to ask you, my lord, if you would indulge me for another moment."

"Ah, courtesy," he said, and relaxed back to a sitting position. "Now, what is it you want from me?"

She managed to keep her gaze on the desert lord and her voice level as she said: "I don't believe Chac is the only Callen of the sun-lord in this gathering. I want to take the last blood trial. Now."

Lord Irrio's eyes narrowed thoughtfully.

"You're far to smart to pin your plans on one man alone," she said, aiming her words carefully, "and far too cynical. You're the type to cover yourself in all directions. You have another Callen within reach, and I'll bet you were going to hold that over my head to make me dance your tune."

"Good gods," he said, looking honestly startled, "you've got a devious mind, haven't you?"

"You're wrong," Deiq said, breaking his silence at last. "He doesn't. I do."

She smiled, keeping her stare on Lord Irrio. The desert lord's face split in a wide, astonished grin of his own. "Gods, girl, you just twisted a ha'ra'ha around your finger!"

Deiq sighed. "Acana was right," he muttered.

Lord Irrio laughed. "I will leave you alone to talk." He stood, bowed, and walked away. Alyea transferred her stare to Deiq.

The ha'ra'ha sat quietly, not looking at her, for several breaths. At last he sighed again and said, "Once a Callen starts a blood trial, nothing is allowed to stop it. I knew Chacerly's status would be challenged sooner or later, but I also knew he'd be sitting on Scratha land waiting for you to arrive, so it seemed unlikely that those most likely to challenge would track him down before we showed up. But you took longer to heal than I expected, and I didn't realize a Conclave had been called; and so it's too late for that now."

"Tell me this isn't just some game for you!"

He shook his head, still not looking at her. "You have no idea," he said, "how complicated desert politics get. That bit was relatively straightforward."

"But you arranged a backup," she said. "Why didn't you tell me? What were you waiting for?"

"It's not that simple. It wasn't entirely my doing for the backup to be here, and I haven't had a chance to speak to him yet, to gain his aid. He's not aware that he's known to anyone here as a Callen of the sun-lord; it's the sort of thing most *dathedain* don't advertise."

Alyea stood. His carefully ambiguous wording had clarified a suspicion into certainty. He scrambled to his feet, his expression turning anxious.

"Let's go ask this backup Callen, then." She turned and started threading her way through the crowd under the sun-tent.

"You don't even know who—"

"There's only one other person it could possibly be," she said.

After a moment he sighed and followed her without argument.

Gria, Sela, and Micru sat in a silent, sullen huddle near one edge of the tent; a handful of teyanain stood in a rough circle around the three. As Alyea approached, the teyanain watched her with wary interest.

She spared the guards a brief nod and passed them by, squatting in front of Micru. The two women lifted their heads, seeming vaguely relieved to see her, then sagged back into apathetic misery; every bit of their exposed skin showed the beginnings of sunburn, and the heat had clearly sapped their energy.

Micru straightened with considerably more vitality, seemingly unaffected by sun and heat; he met her gaze, his dark eyes unreadable.

"Are you a prisoner or a guard?" she asked.

One dark eyebrow quirked; he regarded her with considerably more interest. "You've grown up," he said. "Wouldn't have thought to ask that, back in Bright Bay."

"Prisoner or guard?" she repeated.

"Guard," he said, with a gesture towards the two women beside him.

"And these—" Alyea pointed to the teyanain around them, "are keeping an eye on *you*."

He nodded slowly, cocking his head to one side. "Someone's been teaching you the way of things," he said. "About time."

"She's passed the blood trials of Comos and Ishrai," Deiq said from behind her.

"So I heard. Congratulations."

"I want to take the third," Alyea said. Micru's expression smoothed into blankness again. Gria lifted her head, showing an awakening interest in the conversation.

"You'll have to find a Callen for that," Micru said.

"I already have," she said.

"You found out about Chacerly, then," he said, and shrugged. "Well, go talk to him."

"His status is in question," she told him. "He's not allowed to accept supplicants until that's cleared. I need *my* status cleared right now."

Micru shrugged and opened his mouth to speak.

"If you'd named yourself a prisoner," she said, "I'd have called you a fool and moved on. But you're not a fool, and you're not just one of the King's Hidden Cadre. You're a Callen of the Sun-Lord, and Sessin Family hired you as Darden Family hired Chacerly, to keep an eye and hand behind the scenes for them."

She kept her voice low, barely audible, but Gria apparently heard the words: her eyes steadily widened into a look of horror as Alyea spoke.

"You're accusing me of treason," Micru said evenly.

"I'm accusing you of politics," she said, and won a smile from him at last.

"Callen are above politics," he said.

"You're right in the middle of this mess, like it or not," she said, "and you were from the moment you accepted the job from Sessin."

He studied her for a few moments, cocking his head to one side and squinting one eye almost shut as he considered.

"True enough," he said finally, and added something else, sharply, in the desert tongue. The teyanain glanced at him, their expressions startled, and shifted aside to allow a wide, clear space around the small man. "Sit down."

Nothing mild or amused remained in Micru's manner now. He sat up straight, his hands resting on his narrow thighs, and watched her with the intent stare of a professional assassin sizing up his opponent. She'd never seen that look in his eye before; he'd always kept his expression placid.

She could sense Deiq retreating a few steps as she sank to the sand to sit, desert style, in front of Micru. She heard the faint sound of Deiq sitting as well, and a gathering murmur of attention being drawn their way.

She ignored it all, as did Micru. She studied him as he studied her, and kept her silence, waiting for him to speak.

He nodded after a few breaths and said, abruptly, "Have you ever killed a man?"

"No," she said.

"Have you ever honestly wanted to?"

She didn't hesitate. "Yes." She'd *dreamed* about being able to kill some of the s'iopes; and Ninnic had been on that list. She hadn't regretted his *accident* one bit.

"Why didn't you do it?"

"I didn't have the resources or skills."

"Meaning what? You would have botched it, or you would have been caught?"

She took a moment to choose her answer carefully. "Both."

"Which was more important to you at that time?"

She allowed herself to grin, knowing there would be no real amusement in the expression. "Botching it."

"And if you had the skills today, would you kill that man, whether or not you could get away with it undetected?"

"Yes," she said without reservation. "Absolutely, and without regrets."

"What if he has led a pious life without sin or evil since that earlier time?" Micru pressed.

"There is nothing in the way of grace," Alyea said flatly, "that can make up for what this man did. If he were before me right now, I would kill him."

He nodded. "I will accept you for the blood trial of Datda."

Behind her, she heard Deiq sigh; a moment later sand scraped and shifted as several people rapidly approached.

"Alyea," Chacerly said, his voice taut, "what are you doing?"

"Taking the final blood trial," she said without turning, and heard a ripple of shocked murmurs go through the crowd gathering behind her.

"You can't possibly be serious!" another voice sputtered. It sounded like Lord Rest.

Micru looked up and over Alyea's shoulder, his expression serene. "I am a sworn Callen of Datda, and bear his mark," he said. "I have accepted this supplicant for the blood trial of the sun-lord."

"You *can't!*" Chac said, sounding panicked now.

"I have," Micru said.

Someone laughed. Lord Irrio said, "You're too late, it seems. Pity you were off sulking, isn't it?"

Chac let out a low growl, and a scuffle erupted; Alyea leapt to her feet and turned to face the commotion. Chac lay face down on the ground, his arms twisted cruelly behind him. Lord Irrio, grinning ferociously, had a knee in the old man's back and held both skinny wrists in one of his large hands.

Lord Rest bent and picked up a thin knife with a worn dark hilt from the sand nearby. He handled it with unusual care, and held it well away from him as he studied it.

"Clean," he said after a moment.

"You attacked a desert lord," Lord Faer said, as if he couldn't quite believe what he'd just seen. "Are you insane?"

Chac writhed, cursing, and howled as Lord Irrio yanked his arms further back.

"Let him up," Alyea said, astonished at how cold her voice sounded. "He's not going anywhere."

Lord Irrio stood and stepped away, the grin still on his face, and watched as the old man staggered to his feet.

"Your life and honor are forfeit twice over now," he said cheerfully. "Only one way out of that, hask."

Chac spat on the ground at the desert lord's feet. Lord Irrio's fist lashed out before Alyea could protest, and Chac sprawled to the ground. He didn't get up, but huddled, glaring, and cursed them all in several languages.

Alyea tightened her mouth against speaking. Chac was being maneuvered, and she had no way to stop it. She had a fairly good idea what *one way out* meant, and suspected Chac had another knife hidden for the purpose.

Something tugged at her memory. Acana's face rose in her mind, a vision of the ishrait speaking, saying something important:

Once you begin the blood trials, you cannot stop . . . but there are two exceptions. . . .

Yes, Alyea thought, relieved. *That's how to get this knot unwound.*

Alyea stepped forward until she stood in front of the old man. She crouched to meet his bright, furious stare straight on. "There's more than one way out of this, Chac."

"*Alyea,*" Deiq said, sounding alarmed.

She ignored him. "Do you want your honor and your life back, Chac, or are you too much a coward to reach for that prize?"

He stared at her, face dark with anger and suspicion. "You have no way to grant me that. Not if you were a desert lord in full could you offer me that."

"But another Callen can, during a blood trial," she said, and watched his expression change.

Deiq hissed. "Alyea," he said again, urgently.

Chac lifted his gaze to Micru, who had moved to stand beside Alyea. The muscles of his throat worked as he swallowed convulsively.

"Micru," he said. That one word somehow held an entire speech: acknowledgment of years of mutual antagonism, a desperate apology, a plea; but little hope.

A taut silence hung in the air for just a moment; then Micru said, without emotion, "Accepted. You may play a part in this blood trial."

Deiq let out a hard breath, his dark brows drawn into a sharply wrinkled *V*, but held his peace.

Micru turned and gestured to the two northern women, both of whom now watched events with intense interest.

"Stand," he said.

Gria helped her adopted mother to her feet. The teyanain guards moved aside a little more, effectively forcing the gathered crowd back. Chac stepped into line beside the women.

Micru scanned the gathered crowd, his dark gaze thoughtful, and finally shook his head. He turned back to face Alyea.

"The trial of Comos," he said, "teaches you to set your will aside for the larger good."

Lord Faer made a faint, protesting noise.

"You can't interfere," someone muttered. "He has the right to do this any way he wants."

"But it never *starts* with—"

"*Shhhh.*"

Micru smiled, his gaze never leaving Alyea. "The trial of Ishrai teaches you to value your own life for the larger good."

Alyea wished they could have done this more privately; the stares around her felt like a hundred horseflies chewing on her skin.

Micru paused, watching her, then said, "The trial of Datda teaches you that there are times when you must kill for the larger good." His smile made a mockery of the words: in the back of her mind, she wondered if he believed his own teachings, or if he killed because he *enjoyed* it.

If the latter, she wouldn't walk out of this trial alive.

The silence became absolute. The heat beyond the shaded area warped the air into strange shimmers.

"I tell you this," Micru said, "every one of these three is, in some way, a threat to you personally and to the larger good as well. Choose which is to die, and kill that one yourself. That is the blood trial of Datda."

Gria and Sela's sunburned faces turned splotchy; they both looked as though they might faint. Chac, bizarrely, grinned as though pleased.

Alyea licked her lips. She'd suspected something like this lay ahead, but hadn't been prepared to choose among these three particular people.

Her mind seemed mired in disbelief and fear for a moment; then, like lifting a foot from deep mud into running water, everything unstuck and came clear.

"May I ask them questions?" she said.

"One to each, and one to all."

She drew a deep breath.

"Sela," she said, noting the way the woman's hands shook. "What is the worst thing you have ever done in your life, the thing of which you are the most ashamed?"

"You must speak truth," Micru said before the northern woman could answer. "I will know if you lie, and your life will be forfeit for it, whether she chooses you or not."

Oddly, that seemed to restore the woman's courage. High color flared across her cheekbones, replacing the pale blotching with a redder pattern; she straightened, glaring at the small man. "I'm an honest woman! But . . . there is a lie I've been carrying for years, and it's haunted me."

She looked at Gria. "Your mother wasn't some stranger who died on our doorstep bearing you. She's my half-sister, and she's still alive. Her name is Gaillin, and her mother was named Bela." Sela rolled a quick, haunted stare around the watching crowd. "And Bela's mother was named Cida."

Against the murmurs from the crowd, sharp and clear, came the sound of Deiq laughing.

Gria stared at her aunt. "You lied about my mother's death?" Years of pain and frustration rang through the question.

Sela winced but met the girl's fury steadily. "Yes. It's what she wanted. She said you were safer with me, and not to tell you anything about her. I only saw your grandmother's name when the s'iopes gave me the papers to sign. And they all swore the list of names only served as proof that you had enough southern blood to be allowed to marry into a desert Family. They swore your ancestors weren't anyone noble, or important. One of many things they apparently lied about," she added bitterly.

"Where is my mother?" Gria shrieked, her hands tightly fisted. She looked ready to pummel the answer out of the woman.

"I don't know," Sela said. "That's honest truth."

Alyea shook her head slightly, her thoughts knocked out of order by the revelation. It took her a few moments to gather herself again.

"Stop," she said as Gria began to speak again. "Gria. My next question is for you."

"I'm not playing your stupid game!" Gria said hotly. "I want to know where my mother is!"

"This isn't a game," Alyea said.

Gria stared at her, seemingly caught by Alyea's tone of voice; slowly, her temper faded. "You'd really kill me?"

Alyea stopped herself before the words *I don't know* came out of her mouth. "Answer this question: are you virgin?"

The teyanain all tautened into full alertness, and someone in the crowd made a soft, thoughtful noise. Alyea thought she heard Deiq mutter, "*Gods*, girl!"

Gria's face darkened. "I'm not going to answer that!"

Alyea wished she could rub the tension from her forehead and eyes; but that would show weakness at a very bad time.

"I'll take that as a no," she said. It explained the last bit that had puzzled her: why a northern of any rank would be interested in his daughter wedding a distant desert lord. It would have been far enough that nobody would carry news of the scandal to the wedding.

"The Church would have—" Sela started.

"You don't answer," Micru cut in sharply. "Speak again and I'll have you gagged."

Sela swallowed, cast Alyea a beseeching look, and shut her eyes.

"Answer the question," Micru said evenly. "Yes or no. Are you virgin?"

"No," Gria spat. "And I'm in disgrace. Nobody at home would take me now, since some *kind* people saw fit to spread the word about what I'd been caught doing. Not that it was any of their business in the first place, or yours; I'm old enough! Boys younger than I am aren't called whores for bedding a girl; why should I suffer for enjoying myself with someone I liked?"

Sela pressed her lips so tight they almost disappeared.

"Chac," Alyea said, focusing all her willpower on keeping her voice steady and emotionless, her expression impassive. "Who hired the machago Ierie to take Gria and Sela south?"

He grinned at her, as if pleased she'd asked that question. "I did."

Gria and Sela stared, open-mouthed, at the old man. He went on, unprompted, his words filling the silence. "Oruen wanted to secure an alliance with the teyanain. I needed something of value to offer; a chance informant gave me a lead on a female of pure Scratha descent. When Scratha put himself in disgrace, I convinced the king to send him out of the way. The timing got a little tricky in spots, but it worked out in the end. I chose Water's End for the exchange. The ugren cuffs surprised me; I didn't think they'd put permanent slave cuffs on a woman destined to be Lord Evkit's wife."

He glanced at Lord Evkit, but the teyanin lord's face remained expressionless, his attention focused on Gria as if he'd hardly heard the last few words. Chac licked his lips and raised an eyebrow, affecting a confidence Alyea didn't think he really felt.

"Micru," she said, hoping she'd put the pieces together correctly, "what happens to the honor of the one I choose for death?"

"It is restored in full," Micru said readily.

"What about those who live?"

"The same."

"And if any are slaves?"

"Freed," Micru said.

"Even from ugren cuffs?"

He nodded. "In this one instance alone, yes. The teyanain must remove them, by ancient law they themselves set down before the Split."

Sela sucked in a hard, gasping breath, her expression suddenly hopeful.

"Then I ask," Alyea said, turning to the three people in front of her, "that each of you think hard on what you've said, and what you've heard, and choose for yourself whether you deserve to live or to die for your actions." She paused, then said, "Sela?"

"I think I deserve to live," Sela said, straightening. "I've done nothing but protect my niece; my worst crime is believing Ierie's good intent. That's not an offense to kill over."

Alyea kept her mouth shut on her opinion of what the woman's stupidity deserved, and looked at the girl beside her. "Gria?"

"I haven't done anything wrong!" Gria said. "I believed people who said they loved me." She shot her aunt another sharp look, but this time Sela shrugged it aside without becoming rattled. "I've done nothing worth dying for."

Alyea looked at Chac, already knowing his answer.

He grinned at her, reached into his shirt, and drew another knife. He held it out to her, hilt first.

"Kill me," he said simply.

As she took the knife, she saw the faintest of dark stains on the lower edge of the blade. Poison, more than likely; fast or slow, she had no idea.

"The choice is made," she said, and drew a deep breath. "Gria and Sela are free to go."

The two women reached out and clasped hands, their stares wide and disbelieving. Gria's earlier resentment no longer evident, they fell into each other's arms, trembling.

"Take them away," Alyea said, her mouth dry. The teyanain, moving not as prison guards but as honor escort now, led the two shaken women towards the other side of the shaded area. She watched them go safely out of hearing range; looked at Micru, at Deiq, and finally back to Chac.

The hysterical sobs of the two reprieved women echoed through the taut silence.

"I won't do this for the amusement of an audience," Alyea said. "Let's go for a walk, old man."

Chapter Twenty-Three

They stood at the lip of the great cavern bowl, looking at tunnels that led like spokes on a wheel in all directions. Scratha's frown worried Idisio.

"Which way do we go, my lord?" Idisio ventured, hoping for a clear answer.

"I don't know," Scratha admitted. "I thought the ha'rethe would tell me, but it isn't saying anything."

"Why don't you just read the signs?" Riss said in a practical tone of voice.

"The. . . ." Idisio looked where she pointed, and saw, crudely etched into the nearby wall, a single word:

WALL

The last 'L' sat at an odd, drunken slant to the rest of the letters.

Scratha's frown deepened.

"Wall," he repeated softly to himself. "Wall." He finally looked away as if forcing himself to move. "Let's walk around and see what the other passages say."

Many had no label, or an obscure pictograph, or a word in some language Idisio didn't know. The desert lord paused in front of one, however, and traced the outline of two words, roughly etched as the first had been, with his fingertips. Idisio, peering around the man's elbow, didn't need this one translated.

BRIGHT BAY

The last letters of each word slanted at the same odd angle as the one for the Wall had displayed.

Scratha repeated that one, too, very quietly, and they moved on. A dangerous edge emerged in the desert lord's manner, a brittle searching quality in his movements. Idisio hung back another pace and urgently waved Riss to give the man more room as well. She obeyed, her gaze anxious and puzzled.

Almost back to the spot they had started from, Scratha stopped at another tunnel entrance. He stood very still, his fists clenching and unclenching rhythmically. Idisio edged forward, motioning Riss to stay well back, and squinted at the word beside the tunnel opening.

SCRATHA

Here again, the last 'A' was slanted.

Idisio had never seen anything like it. Shivers ran up and down his arms. The silence became oppressive. He caught himself just before saying something idiotic, like *Well, good, we'll just trot on up this one and be at your home in no time, right?*

The look in Cafad Scratha's eyes could have melted sand.

"I never realized," the desert lord whispered, as if completely unaware he had a frightened audience watching him. "All these years, and the answer was that simple."

He shook himself, rather like an asp-jacau after an unexpected rainstorm, and strode forward into the tunnel. Idisio scrambled to follow, afraid of being left behind. Scratha seemed to have forgotten about his dependants. His old madness had full hold on him, and Idisio wasn't sure how long it would take the man to snap out of it.

Ten steps into the tunnel, Idisio glanced back to check on Riss; she hurried close on his heels, her eyes huge and her face pale. He turned forward again, not wanting to miss a step and stumble.

Scratha was gone.

The tunnel continued straight, well-lit, and utterly empty ahead of them for a goodly distance. Idisio, unable to stop himself, broke into a run for a few hopeless strides, opening his mouth to yell—

—and found himself falling through blackness, with a feeling similar to emerging from the ha'rethe's den; from faint chill through intense cold into a blazing dry heat. As before, he fell forward onto his hands and knees, astonished as he felt sand giving way under him.

A hard hand hooked under his armpit and yanked him to his feet.

"I'm sorry," Scratha said, sounding more impatient than contrite. "I forgot about you for a moment. Is Riss—"

A thud and yelp cut him off.

"Apparently she is," the desert lord said dryly, and moved to help her up as well.

"What just happened?" Riss said in a high, strained voice as she stumbled to her feet.

Idisio took a moment to be sure Riss hadn't been hurt by the unexpected fall, then turned his attention to their new surroundings.

"Welcome," Cafad Scratha said with a proprietary, proud, and distinctly tired edge, "to Scratha Family Fortress."

They stood in the center of an enormous, roofless space, much of it paved with wide, sun-bleached brick tiles. White stone walls towered high above them to four sides, each broken at ground level by a single, centered archway. A series of small, connected stone fountain-troughs sat silent, worn, and cracked. Dry sticks, decaying trunks, and a heap of desiccated leaves were all that remained of what might have once been magnificent desert palms or sand-reeds.

Idisio's skin crawled with the uneasy feeling of being watched, but except for the sounds of their own small motions and breathing, the silence and stillness lay thick and absolute.

"How did we get here?" Riss shrilled. Her voice echoed around the empty, dead space. "What is this place?"

Scratha, who had been staring at a dry, cracked fountain, started and looked around.

"Hm?" he said. "Oh, this is the central gathering-yard—at least, it was. I haven't been in this part of the fortress for a long time. I used to play here; there were great desert palms. . . ." He pointed at the piles of dry-rotted sticks and broken trunks, his expression distant, and sighed. "Long gone. There's been no water; the well dried up. . . ."

"How did we get here?" Riss demanded, the fear in her voice no less sharp for being tinged with anger now.

Scratha turned and studied her thoughtfully, as if deciding how to answer. "I don't know," he said at last. The answer clearly didn't satisfy Riss, and the desert lord added, "I learned a long time ago not to ask *how* when the ha'reye are involved. I've seen much stranger things, Riss, than instant transport from one spot to another."

"But you're a desert lord," Riss said.

"That doesn't mean I know everything about the ha'reye," Scratha said. "I suspect what I know about them wouldn't fill the average thimble." He pointed to one of the archways. "Let's get out of the heat."

They moved from scorching, stifling midafternoon heat into a distinctly cooler, shaded passageway lined with dull grey tiles on each curving wall. The rough brick from the courtyard continued underfoot. Their footsteps scraped on patches of windblown sand for the first few steps, then became almost silent, as if the brick absorbed sound.

Scratha led them past several archways, some of which opened to more courtyards, smaller than the first but similar in style. Others had the remains of wooden doors blocking the views of what lay beyond, and two actually had fine metal latticework doors. At the second of the metal doors, the desert lord paused, put out a hand, and pushed gently against the edge of the door. It swung, noiseless, and stayed wide open, as if waiting patiently for them to enter.

Scratha sighed. "These were my rooms," he said, staring through the doorway.

Peering around him, Idisio saw a short passage, opening into what looked like a larger room littered with dust-covered furniture.

"Why is everything so quiet?" Riss said. "Where is everyone?"

Scratha turned and looked at her in what seemed genuine surprise.

Idisio searched his memory hastily, came up blank, and said, "You never told her anything about your family, my lord, and she's not from Bright Bay; she probably never heard the name Scratha before she met us."

"I didn't, other than Karic and Baylor talking about you being on their trail," Riss said. "What happened?"

Scratha reached out and tugged the metal lattice shut again. It closed with the faintest *clank*.

"My family was murdered," he said, "slaughtered in the middle of the night with no warning. Nobody knows who was responsible, or if they do, they're not telling." He ran his fingers lightly over the door. "I was walking the sands outside when it happened, as a preliminary test to see if I was fit to become a desert lord."

"How old were you?" Riss said, looking horrified.

"Ten," Scratha said. He started down the passageway again.

"Isn't that a little young?" Riss said.

"A little," Scratha admitted. "But things were going on that . . . well. It would take too long to explain."

Idisio blinked as he worked through the numbers. "You're only . . . twenty-five?"

"Twenty-eight," Scratha corrected.

"You look twice that," Riss said tactlessly.

Idisio glared at her; Scratha ignored them both.

They walked along empty, silent corridors, turning apparently at random into different passages. Idisio began to suspect Scratha simply wandered without direction, and tried to think of a tactful way to ask just where they were going.

"Here," Scratha said at last, and pushed open another wrought-metal door. They filed into a huge room, lined from floor to high ceiling with wide shelves of books: large and small tomes, racks of slender or thick rolls of parchment and vellum. Sunlight slanted from high windows to spread distorted squares of brightness against the dusty shelves. A heavy layer of dust coated a table in the center of the room.

Idisio sneezed. The room felt heavy, solemn, and old; above all, it felt neglected, as if lonely for human company. He seemed to hear a faint murmur in his head, as if the books spoke to welcome them. He shook his head sharply to dispel the frightening notion.

Cafad Scratha stood for a moment looking around the room, his expression slowly becoming grim. Riss's gaze lingered over each shelf as if she longed to reach out and sweep all the books into her arms at once.

"Sit down," Scratha said finally. "This might take a little while." He moved forward and squatted before one of the shelves. He began to examine the bound volumes, lightly pushing each aside to see another before shaking his head and shifting to his right.

They watched him without moving, stuck in mutual bewilderment.

"Er. . . ." Riss said after Scratha had searched through perhaps ten feet of the shelf. "What are you doing, my lord?"

"There's a book," Scratha said without looking back at her, "with a brief passage which never made sense to me before. But now I think it might lead me to the answer of how my family was slaughtered with no witnesses."

Riss and Idisio exchanged a long look; their shared, silent question *What are* we *supposed to do now?* hung in the air between them.

"Er . . . can we help you look?" Riss said, moving a tentative half-step forward.

"I can't describe it," Scratha muttered, studying a book spine intently, then shaking his head and moving on. "It's been so long since I've read it, I don't even remember what it looks like. I'm hoping I'll know it when I see it."

"Er," Idisio said, swallowing hard. The murmuring of the books seemed to be growing both louder and clearer. He could almost make out the words: not that he *wanted* to. "Er, my lord?"

"What is it, Idisio?"

"Um." Idisio looked at his feet, wishing he'd kept silent.

Scratha didn't look up from his study of the shelves, but he snapped his fingers impatiently. "Say it already!"

"Well," Idisio said, "if . . . what if you could . . . sort of . . . ask where the book is?"

Scratha stopped his search and turned to stare at him. Idisio could tell he hadn't said that clearly enough.

"I mean, the . . . the fortress would know," he went on, and heard an astonished snort from Riss.

"You've lost your mind," Riss said. "The heat's wiping your brain out.

Ask *who*?" She swept her hands out to indicate the room. "The air?"

"Um, yes," Idisio said. "More or less the air, yes. It's . . . it feels like that tunnel. Like something's trying to talk to us."

Riss opened her mouth as if to argue, then shut it again without speaking. Her eyebrows drew down in a thoughtful squint, and she looked around the room with far more suspicion than she had a few minutes previously.

Scratha cocked his head as if listening for something, then shook his head. "I can't hear anything," he said, "but I think you may be more sensitive than I am, Idisio. Why don't you try asking?"

Idisio took a deep breath and shut his eyes. *Lord Cafad Scratha wants a book,* he thought, trying to form the words as clearly in his mind as he could, but not sure where to aim them.

Who was he trying to talk to? The room? The fortress? He wasn't sure, and somehow it seemed important. He couldn't just talk to empty space. There had to be something to talk *to*. He hesitated, wavering, wondering if this whole idea was absurd.

The silence continued unbroken, with no feeling of a response. Idisio decided to give it one more try. He found himself imagining the fortress as a large, friendly beast—he carefully kept *lizard* from his mental picture—curled into a huge circle around them. He addressed his thought-speech to the head of the giant creature, which seemed to rest somewhere in the center of the fortress.

Lord Cafad Scratha is looking for a book, he thought again. *Please help him find it.*

The image in his mind abruptly clarified and shifted into something much more alien and less friendly. Huge golden eyes opened and seemed to stare at him from inches away. Idisio stood frozen, unable to move under that overwhelming scrutiny. He heard a faint whimpering and realized, distantly, that the noise came from his own throat.

Se'thiss t'akarnain, a voice said in his head. *Welcome.*

He heard a gasp and a thud. The image in Idisio's head vanished abruptly. He felt his knees giving way; a moment later his body connected gracelessly with the floor.

His eyes opened at the jarring impact. Riss knelt beside him, her face a ghastly white and her eyes huge.

"Are you all right?" she shrilled.

He blinked, shook his head tentatively, and sat up. The room seemed to spin around him for a moment; Riss's hands, gripping his shoulders, brought everything back into focus.

"Yeah," he muttered. "I think so, anyway."

Scratha, several feet away, had a thick tome in his hands and a strange expression on his face as he stared at Idisio.

"It just fell," he said. "I've never seen anything like it. It fell flat, and open to the page I wanted."

"Maybe I'm not all right after all," Idisio muttered, and shut his eyes again. His stomach seemed ready to turn itself inside out, and a headache started to pound behind his eyes.

"I felt—" Scratha hesitated, as if unsure of himself. "I felt, for a moment, as if there was a ha'rethe in the area. But that's not *possible!*"

"Why not?" Riss said sharply.

"Because if there were a ha'rethe in this fortress, my family would never have been slaughtered. They won't allow the people they protect to be harmed. And I've *never* seen or heard a single hint of one being here."

"The one by the Wall said it had just woken up," Idisio said, rubbing at his temples. "What if this one was asleep?"

"A protector would have woken," Scratha said, but a note of doubt threaded through his voice. "It wouldn't have slept through the attack. . . ."

Idisio had a sense of those great golden eyes opening again. They seemed amused. *We protect those you call desert lords,* the voice said softly. *If there is no desert lord present, there is no obligation.*

Idisio leaned forward and put his head between his knees.

"It said something," Scratha said, his voice hard and excited. "There *is* one here! *Gods!* I couldn't hear it clearly. What did it say? How long has it been here?"

Seeing no safe way to refuse an answer, Idisio repeated the words, lifting his head just enough to be clearly heard, and kept his eyes shut tight.

"Oh, gods." Scratha sounded sick. "The attack came within days of Lord Scratha's passing—But what about Orde? What about. . . ." He fell silent for a moment, then added, plaintively, "Why hasn't it ever spoken to me?"

This desert lord has never been bound to this place, the voice said. *I only allowed him passage as was his right.* With a sense of awakening interest, the beast stirred and raised its great head. *He never called my notice properly.*

Idisio repeated the words again, watching Scratha's face take on the darkness of sudden anger.

"Nobody ever told me there was a ritual involved," the desert lord said, almost spitting the words out. "I thought that if there was a ha'rethe here, it would know me."

I saw him as a desert lord, not as one bound to me, the voice said, indifferent now, and lowered its huge head, closing its eyes.

"How does he get bound to you, then?" Idisio said. "And how is it you notice me?" Speaking out loud seemed as effective as silent thought, and the hungry look on Scratha's face demanded to hear at least half the conversation.

One golden eye opened, regarding him lazily. *He must give his blood and seed, and swear himself bound to me, while within this fortress. And you are blood kin; how could I not see you?*

Idisio swallowed hard and wished he could get away with an edited version of that reply; but Scratha's dark stare bored into him. He repeated the words, trying not to look at anyone as he did.

After an awkward silence, Scratha cleared his throat. "I was afraid it would be something like that," he said. He shut the book, holding his place on the page with a finger, and sighed. "Let's go sit and eat. And think a bit."

Idisio started to nod—his queasy stomach might settle down with some food—and found his mind filled with that golden stare again.

You may want to know, young se'thiss t'akarnain, *there are others outside these walls. An elder—from your point of view—ha'ra'ha and several desert lords. They seem very agitated, and there are several with thoughts of claiming this fortress for themselves. There are thoughts of challenging this desert lord's claim to be head of Scratha. They know he is not bound to the fortress. They do not know he is here.*

Idisio stood frozen again, his mouth opening and closing like a fish out of water.

I do not care who binds themselves to this fortress. That is a human concern, and none of mine. I care only for the pact. But you are ha'ra'ha and seem to care about their world, and so I tell you. Do as you will with the knowledge.

The presence faded, and Idisio put his hands over his face.

"What now?" Scratha demanded, and Idisio told him.

"Those would be the lords I called for the Conclave." Scratha's expression turned ugly. "So they're wanting to challenge my right, are they? Because I haven't taken this ritual of blood and seed? I assume that means. . . ." His gaze settled on Riss, and his eyes narrowed.

"Don't touch me!" Riss snapped, backing away.

Scratha's upper lip actually lifted away from his teeth in a silent snarl. He pressed his lips tight and turned his back on them.

Idisio, caught between sympathy for the girl's obvious fear and Scratha's equally evident frustration, stood halfway between the two sides, feeling unable to move.

"Come on," he said, his voice coming out thin and raw. "Don't. This isn't . . . Riss, he won't. You know that. And, my lord, she wasn't saying you would. Just . . . just stop being so. . . ." He shook his head, at a loss for more words. The headache seemed to engulf him, streaking red-yellow-green lines behind his eyes.

With the faintest feather-touch of sensation, like a gentle hand stroking his hair, the headache faded away completely. The ha'rethe said, *The ritual he needs to complete is not one the human girl would be any use for. Tell him to go to the temple in the center of this fortress.*

Idisio let out a gasping breath of relief.

"Thank you," he said aloud, and looked up at Scratha. "Go to the temple in the center of the—"

Scratha's face lit with excited hope. He sprinted from the room before Idisio could finish speaking.

"—fortress," Idisio ended lamely. He sighed. "I guess we wait here."

Follow him.

Idisio swallowed hard. "Um," he said, waving his hands apologetically, "I mean, I guess, you wait here . . . please?" He tossed the last word over his shoulder as he hurried after the desert lord.

He thought he heard Riss say something, but a glimpse of Scratha rounding a corner far ahead distracted him from understanding it clearly. He put on his best speed and ran. A moment later he knew his weren't the only footsteps echoing from the stone walls; a glance over his shoulder confirmed his fears. "Go back and wait!"

"I *don't* think so!" Riss hollered back at him.

Idisio mouthed a silent curse and saved his breath for running. He'd never imagined that Scratha could run so fast; when they rounded the corner, the desert lord was further ahead than Idisio had expected.

In the background, behind his panting breath and the thudding of their feet, he sensed vast, ancient amusement. The faintest sense of a chuckle wove through his mind.

It took all his willpower and self-control not to fling a curse at the creature for laughing at him, now of all times. He saw absolutely *nothing* funny about this situation.

As if in reply, he saw a brief image of fluffy, ungainly baby chickens toddling frantically after one another as if their pursuit were the most serious thing in the whole world; and he had to laugh. It came out sounding manic and sharp, and he cut it off as soon as he could. Was that how the ha'reye saw humans? Small, preening life forms with no brain to speak of, with no thought for anything larger than themselves?

Sometimes, the ha'rethe said mildly. *Turn left up ahead. You'll get there before he does.*

Trusting the voice, although Scratha could still be seen in the distance, Idisio dove into the next left-hand passage that appeared, vaguely registering as he went through that a metal lattice door stood open. He heard the sound of Riss's footsteps still following him. She wasn't letting him out of her sight, for some reason.

Don't you understand why yet? the ha'rethe said. *She's in love with you.*

Idisio almost staggered to a stop at that concept.

"You're wrong," he muttered under his breath, and forced his legs to keep moving. "You're *wrong*."

Somehow the creature managed to deliver a mental shrug. *Turn left again. Now turn right. And you might want to slow down—*

Idisio managed to stagger to a stop just before he plowed straight into a heavy wooden door. Riss squawked as she rounded the corner behind him and bounced herself against a wall to avoid slamming into Idisio.

"You *could* have said," she complained, entirely unfairly, and rubbed her shoulder as she glared at Idisio.

He shook his head, still rattled by the ha'rethe's comment, and pushed the heavy door open. It swung, easy and silent, as if it had been oiled yesterday. Idisio took a deep breath and stepped into the room beyond.

It was round, and moist, and silent in a deep, profound way that felt more alive than the rest of the fortress. The sun streaming into the room had a different quality as well, a more filtered feel. Looking around, awestruck, Idisio realized living trees graced this room, great towering desert palms that stretched to the high ceiling and feathery sand-bushes that stood taller than Scratha.

"Gods," Idisio breathed. "I thought the well went dry!"

A huge pool in the center of the room, easily fifteen feet across, was clear enough to see white sand at the bottom.

The well did not go dry, the ha'rethe said. *It was blocked, and there was not a lord present, so I left it alone, and slept. Now I am awake, and you are here; you and this desert lord will need the water. So I have repaired it, and replaced the growing things.*

"That's pretty heartless," Idisio said, looking back at the pool. "People died here because they didn't have water." He moved forward a few steps.

To their right, another door opened and Scratha came in. He stared around the room, his expression dumbfounded. Astonishment turned to a sharp frown when he saw Idisio and Riss.

"What—" he started, then stopped, his gaze on the door they had come in through. The amazement returned. "How did you—" He stopped again, and shook his head, evidently caught between wonder and anger.

"That's the door the Callen use," he said finally. "Their quarters are sealed. I've never been able to get into that part of the fortress." He shook his head once more, slowly, and waved a hand as if dismissing the issue. His gaze traveled around the room again, drinking it in as if he had been craving water for days and found himself unexpectedly presented with a lake.

He never had a need, the ha'rethe observed dryly. *Or the right. You are ha'ra'ha; you can go anywhere you like.*

Scratha didn't seem to hear the voice.

"This room," he went on, moving forward, "was—Last time I saw it, it was *dead*. There was a dry pit where that pool is now, and these trees . . . they were little more than dry, dead husks. I remember wondering what kept them from crumbling like all the others in the fortress."

Humans, the ha'rethe sighed. *No understanding of the deep ways of the world at all.*

Idisio found himself grinning. This ha'rethe was nothing like the one he'd encountered near the Wall. He actually found himself liking this one. Remembering the dry well, he stopped smiling. Likable or not, this creature had a ruthless streak to be wary of.

The ha'rethe seemed puzzled. *You say "ruthless" and "heartless." We hold to the Agreement. We do not concern ourselves beyond that. We have never pretended to.*

Scratha paced around the room. He laid a tentative hand on the trunk of a giant desert palm, as if afraid it would crumble at his touch.

"Amazing," he muttered several times as he walked, and finally moved to stand in front of the pool. "You'll need to leave," he said over his shoulder.

Now why would you have to leave when I summoned you?

Idisio choked back a hysterical laugh. "Er . . . my lord," he said awkwardly, "the ha'rethe wants . . . me at least . . . here. It told me to follow you, and which way to turn to get here before you did."

Riss gave a snort of annoyance and muttered, "You're *not* sending me away."

Scratha turned and stared at them. For the first time, he seemed nervous.

"I don't understand why," he said a bit peevishly.

Idisio shrugged, spreading his hands.

"We should at least send Riss away."

No, the ha'rethe said. *She may stay as well, if she wishes.*

Scratha seemed to read Idisio's expression. "She's to stay too?"

Riss gave a satisfied "Hah!"

Move out of the doorway, the ha'rethe said patiently. Idisio jerked, startled, and motioned Riss forward into the room. As soon as they were clear, the doors swung shut, latching with a thin clang.

Do you care for the northern girl? the ha'rethe said unexpectedly.

"Um. . . ." Idisio said out loud, and coughed to hide the uncertain noise as the others looked round at him.

I see the answer, the ha'rethe said before he could figure out a response. *You need not reply.*

Idisio swallowed hard, not entirely sure what the ha'rethe saw in his mind. Care for Riss? She was all right as a traveling companion, but he wasn't sure that qualified as caring for her.

Riss stared at Idisio, then made a dismissive gesture and said, "What do we do now, Lord Scratha?"

Scratha seemed to consider for a moment. "Sit before the pool. Leave yourself some space. This isn't anything like what I've been through before; I have no idea what's going to happen."

With those less-than-reassuring words, he moved forward and lowered himself to the ground in front of the pool. Idisio took up a position on the desert lord's right; Riss settled to Scratha's left.

Riss squared her own shoulders and put her gaze on the pool.

Take a knife and prick your finger, the ha'rethe instructed gently.

"What, all of us?" Idisio said aloud, then realized that Scratha and Riss were already moving to obey. So they heard the ha'rethe for themselves now; he found that something of a relief. He'd hated relaying the creature's messages.

It may benefit you as well, little ha'ra'ha. You must decide for yourself.

Idisio swallowed hard and pulled out his belt knife, hoping Riss and Scratha hadn't heard "little ha'ra'ha." He'd never live that designation down.

Shake a drop of blood onto the sand before you.

Idisio obeyed, then stared at the tiny dark spot on the sand in front of him, feeling a sense of unreality. He heard Scratha murmur something that sounded like, "I offer the gift of blood to prove my honorable intent and dedication of my life to this place."

Idisio kept his mouth firmly shut. He couldn't bring himself to say that. Riss seemed to have chosen silence as well.

Abruptly, he felt a wrenching sensation somewhere in the center of his forehead. His surroundings faded into a hazy mist, and a distant wailing sound advanced towards him. The wail resolved into words:

"How can you do this to me?" a woman screamed. "How can you do this to my child?"

"Demon-spawn!" a male voice shouted, heavy with anger. "Burn it! Drown it!"

"It's a child!" the woman protested. "How can you harm a child?"

"It's a damned creature!" the male voice replied, still loud and furious. "You'll be joining it, woman, never fear!"

"The hells you say!" the woman cried with sudden, spitting passion. "No! You won't lay a hand on either one of us!"

Another wrenching feeling: a scream echoed in Idisio's head. The internal noise faded, although the fog remained.

Great golden eyes opened in the mist and regarded Idisio.

Interesting, the ha'rethe of Scratha Fortress said. *Your mother was a very strong woman.*

Idisio found himself shaking uncontrollably. *That was my mother?*

Of course. There is something odd about this Ghost Lake area. I would like you to go investigate this. I cannot travel so far any longer. Will you do this for me?

Idisio nodded, still dazed. *I will,* he said, not sure why he agreed. *How did my mother escape?*

I believe her ha'rethe helped her. The creature seemed to frown, emanating displeasure. *From what I see in your memory, it may have harmed some of those holding her captive in order to allow her to escape. I do not like that.*

What should it have done? Idisio demanded. *Let us die?*

There are many ways to do a thing, the ha'rethe said peacefully, *and not all of them require violence to a lesser form of life.*

You're responsible for the death of this entire fortress! Idisio shot back, suddenly angry again. *You let everyone be murdered!*

Idisio had the sense that the creature sighed. *You have been among humans too much, little ha'ra'ha. You do not understand. But enough. I am fin-*

ished with the Scratha lord.

Warm water splashed onto his face, just a few drops that speckled his forehead and cheeks. Realizing his eyes had been shut for some time, he opened them and wiped the moisture away, blinking hard.

Scratha knelt beside him, his face almost glowing with happiness. "Thank you, Idisio. I would never have known this was even possible without you."

Idisio, staring at the sopping-wet desert lord, couldn't help noticing that Scratha's clothes seemed to have disappeared somewhere along the way.

"Uhm," he said uncertainly.

Cafad Scratha glanced down at himself and grimaced ruefully.

"Damn," he said, pushing straggles of long hair from his face. "Didn't expect that. Well. . . ."

Idisio hastily pulled off his own shirt and tossed it to Cafad. The tall desert lord wrapped it around his waist.

"Did it work?" Idisio said. "Are you bound?"

Cafad smiled. "Yes," he said. "I'm bound to Scratha Fortress as rightful lord now. I never knew contact with one of the ha'reye could feel like that. It's always been painful before. That was *wonderful*." He seemed to bask in the memory for a moment, then grew serious again. "I can feel the fortress around me. I can hear the sound of everything that happens within these walls. It's incredible. I've always felt a strong connection to this place, but now I feel as if I've been living half-blind all my life."

Idisio found himself grinning. "That's good."

Turning his head to look at Riss, he stopped smiling; she lay sprawled on the sand, limp and unmoving. He scrambled over to her, but Cafad pulled him back.

"Leave her alone," he said. "She's only tranced. She'll come out of it when she's ready. Being in the presence of a ha'rethe can be a bit overwhelming. She'll be fine. I have to get some proper clothes and attend to my *guests*; go get our packs from the library and bring them back here, sit with her until she wakes up. The doors are open, and in any case I think you could probably open any door in this fortress if you wanted to." His speech rattled faster than usual.

About to shake his head in denial of Scratha's last comment, Idisio remembered what the ha'rethe had said: *You are ha'ra'ha; you can go anywhere you like.*

"Yes," he said slowly, "I could."

The vision of his mother had made it all *real*. He was a ha'ra'ha. He had status of his own, almost as though he'd been born of a royal line, and nobody could take that away from him. He didn't even have to be afraid of Cafad Scratha's moods any longer.

The ha'rethe by the Wall had been right. Cafad wasn't going to be able to teach him what he needed to know past a certain point. The idea of working with a ha'rethe or another ha'ra'ha didn't scare Idisio any longer; it seemed perfectly logical and right.

Nobody could hurt him anymore. Not the bullies of Bright Bay, not Cafad Scratha, not even the king or the desert lords gathered outside; and when he went back north, nobody was going to lay a *hand* on him. He found himself grinning as he turned towards the door, and broke into an easy jog as he went to fetch the packs.

Chapter Twenty-Four

"I should have killed you," Chac said without heat. "When Scratha handed over his lands to the king, I suggested your name."

Aleya nodded, unsurprised.

"I thought you were inexperienced enough to let me set you aside. Before we were halfway down the Horn, I knew you were stronger than I'd expected. The night I decided to arrange an accident, you caught Deiq's eye. That made harming you too dangerous. Then he followed us; I couldn't lay hand on you until he was out of the way. I started to lay plans for Water's End, but again, before I could act Sela and Gria were dumped on us, with Deiq's name attached. I had to get you away from anywhere he had influence."

Alyea glanced over her shoulder. Deiq and Micru sat several yards behind them, relaxed but intent; Deiq seemed amused. He nodded to Alyea, and she turned her attention back to Chac.

The old man had followed her glance. "Of course he can hear me. He's ha'ra'ha. He can probably hear a bird fart at half a mile."

Alyea heard a faint answering chuckle behind her. "Go on."

"Lord Evkit wanted you dead for interfering with his plans. I bought myself time to negotiate by sending you away with Juric. Lord Evkit agreed to meet me at Scratha Fortress and allow me to put you through the Sun-Lord's blood trial. I had a trial in mind that you wouldn't have had a chance with."

"What was it?" Alyea asked.

"I planned to put you up against a teyanin in unarmed combat, not to the death, but until third blood was drawn," Chac said. "It's a test someone properly trained would have had a reasonable chance with, and it's traditional to have some form of combat in the trial." He glanced over his shoulder at Micru.

"The requirement," Micru said, "is that blood must be shed in this trial. That will be filled."

He obviously had hearing as sharp as Deiq's; Chac hadn't raised his voice.

Chac shrugged and turned back to Alyea. "True enough. A supplicant who fails a trial puts themselves under the control of their testing Callen. The tester can do anything they like with the supplicant at that point. Lifelong servitude, if desired."

"Nobody told me that!" Alyea said involuntarily.

Chac grinned unpleasantly. "No, I imagine there's a lot nobody told you. But it's true, although traditionally the Callen simply kill the supplicant. We don't like keeping slaves. Too burdensome. But I could have given you over to Evkit as a slave, and as slaves can't own slaves, ownership of Gria and Sela would have passed to me. I could have legally given them to Evkit as well. Nothing illegal involved." He paused and stared into the distance.

"Except that Deiq stepped in," Alyea said.

Chac nodded without looking at her. "He threw everything out of order when he put you through the other two trials first. And when the desert lords started arriving for the Conclave and my status was challenged, I lost all control of what was happening." He shook his head. "Darden should have trusted me. If Lord Irrio hadn't interfered at the last moment, I still could have pulled it off."

"And what would you have gotten out of it?" Alyea asked.

"They would have found my wife, and brought her to me," Chac said, but Alyea sensed no love in the words. "I would have regained my honor and cleared my name in full by killing her."

That surprised her; she stared at the old man, shocked by how calmly he'd said such a horrible thing.

"I thought you loved her," she said.

"I did, and I do," Chac said. "If she had stayed with me, I would have fully renounced my status as Callen and stayed north of the Horn the rest of my life. But she found out I was *dathedain* and chose to abandon me, though I'd never harmed her." He shot a glare over his shoulder at Deiq. "When she left, I decided my own life was more important than a faithless woman's. I've been searching for her ever since."

Alyea shook her head, unable to grasp how a man she'd known as an occasionally irascible but mostly gentle person could harbor such cold-blooded thoughts.

"Deiq wasn't the one who named you as *dathedain* to your wife," Micru said quietly.

Chac half-turned, his eyes widening. "*You?*"

Micru's implacable stare said more than words could.

"*Why?*"

"You can't just walk away from being a Callen and start a new life where nobody knows who you are," Micru said. His face tightened. "If it were that easy, I would have done it myself long ago."

The old man glared, his breath hissing through his teeth, for a few moments, then returned his attention to Alyea.

"I'm done talking," he said. "I won't answer anything else. Get this over with."

"You're right. It's time."

"Yes," Chacerly said with no visible regret or fear. "It's time."

"No," Deiq said, "it's not. It's too late."

Alyea turned and stared at him, bewildered by the odd statement. "What are you talking about?"

"When you're on the land of a fully named and bound desert lord," Deiq said, "any blood shed must be approved by that lord. Even a blood trial killing must have his blessing."

"But there's no—" Alyea stopped, seeing the humorless grin spread across Deiq's face.

"Someone has gotten into the fortress, called the ha'rethe's attention, and bound themselves to this place," Deiq said. "We're right up against the wall; further out I might not have noticed, but it's like ice water in my face at the moment. Can't you feel the difference in the air?"

Alyea looked up at the great stone walls behind them, then sniffed the air; it held the dusty scent of sand, rancid smoke from cookfires, and something else. She didn't have a name for it, but a richness tinged the air that hadn't been there before.

"I feel it," Micru said, forehead crinkling a little. "Chacerly, did you give the key to someone?"

"No," Chac said. He reached into a pouch at his waist and produced a thick silver band. "Here it is." He proffered it to Alyea.

Alyea took the heavy ring from the old man and weighed it dubiously in one hand, studying the family crest etched on the widest part of the band.

"Put it on," Chac suggested. "Left thumb."

She received a nod of agreement from both Deiq and Micru. The ring slid onto her thumb and hung loose.

"I'll have to bind it up," she said.

"I wouldn't worry about that," said a new voice. All four scrambled to their feet and turned to meet the newcomer, who had approached so silently that even Deiq seemed honestly taken by surprise.

A moment of shocked silence hung, still as the motionless air around them.

Chac broke first, with an incredulous: "*Lord Scratha?*"

The man grinned, showing very white teeth in a dark face and deadly cold eyes above an eagle's nose.

"I'll take that ring back now, if you don't mind," he said, holding out his hand.

Once the ring had been settled safely back on Scratha's hand and brief introductions made, the man focused a sharp stare on Alyea. With little prompting, she found herself explaining about the blood trials, which led to an explanation of how she'd wound up being named king's proxy in the first place, the flight of Pieas Sessin, and, somehow, the incident with Wian.

Scratha's face grew still on hearing Wian's name. His hard stare returned, and he looked at the old man beside her.

"You claim blood trial right to kill this man?" he said.

"I do," Alyea said.

"Do you think he deserves death?"

She didn't hesitate, although her anger at Chac had vanished. "Yes."

Scratha seemed to consider for a moment, then said, "As you are on my bound land, the trial falls under my jurisdiction. I have the right to override even a blood trial choice. I believe Pieas Sessin, if present, would be a more suitable choice. Do you agree?"

Deiq said, "That right hasn't been invoked since before you were born, Lord Scratha. Yes, it's a valid point in desert law, but as you're putting her up against a skilled fighter with no scruples, who certainly isn't going to sit still for her, I have to ask: are you just trying to get her out of the way?"

"No," Scratha said evenly. "I believe Pieas needs to be called out for his crimes."

"Why not Chacerly?" Deiq demanded. "He tried to have you ousted! And Pieas has done nothing to harm you directly."

"On my own land," Scratha said, the words clipped and tight, "on my *bound* land, I don't have to answer to *anyone, s'e* Deiq. Not even to you."

Deiq squinted sharply, studying the Scratha lord as though both annoyed and puzzled, then shook his head and made a dismissive gesture with one hand. Alyea had a sudden sense of words passing her by without sound; a chill shiver tickled her spine as she remembered a disembodied voice, speaking in the darkness of the ishell without pause for breath.

More than the hidden language of bead-patterns seemed to be passing her by of late.

She moved a step forward; the motion brought everyone's attention back to her as she said, "Lord Scratha, I will gladly allow Pieas Sessin to step into Chacerly's place, if Micru will allow the switch; and if Chac regains his honor as he would have by completing this trial as planned."

Deiq made a displeased sound, but Micru nodded slowly, his expression unreadable as he studied Scratha.

"I advise against it," Micru said, "but I'll allow the switch."

Chac let out a long sigh. He and Micru locked stares for a moment; then the old man nodded slightly and lowered his gaze submissively. Alyea's skin prickled, and she looked away, biting her lower lip and wondering if she had just made a dreadful mistake. Deiq's dark, sour stare did nothing to help her nerves.

"Let's go find out if Pieas is here," Lord Scratha said.

"We will wait here," Micru said, still staring at Chac. "Bring him to us when and if you find him. If you do not find him, Chacerly remains the chosen of this trial."

Scratha nodded curtly and strode away, Alyea and Deiq trailing behind.

"Big damn mistake," Deiq muttered as they walked.

"Why?" she said through her teeth.

He shook his head without answering.

"If all you're going to do is moan empty warnings, then shut up," she said tartly, and increased her pace.

As they rounded the corner of the fortress and approached the camp, heads turned and people began to stand up. By the time the group reached the edge of the sun-tent, a wide path appeared through the crowd, as if nobody wanted to be in their way.

Alyea's whole body ached with the desire for food and sleep. Her stomach felt queasy and her hands shook; she didn't feel ready to face a child wielding a stick, let alone Pieas Sessin.

Scratha moved to the center of the sun tent and stopped, turning in place to scan the crowd with his dark, grim stare.

"I'm lord of this fortress and guardian of these lands," he said, his voice carrying, without apparent effort, to the furthest listener. "I called this Conclave. Are there nine other full lords here?"

"No," Lord Irrio said, stepping forward. "Myself, Lords Faer, Evkit, Salo, and Rest are present. Lords Halin and Obis of the eastern coast are within an hour's journey, and a bird just came in with word that Lords Azaniari and Rowe are on their way as well."

Scratha let out a soft grunt, as though he'd just been kicked in the stomach. "*Lord* Azaniari?"

Lord Irrio smiled without humor. "She didn't tell you, Scratha? Goodness, imagine her keeping secrets from her darling. The sands may just swallow us all."

"I certainly wouldn't grieve if it swallowed *you*," Scratha said, recovering his composure. "You're as much an ass as you've ever been, Irrio."

"And you're just as simple-minded," Irrio shot back. "What brought you back? We thought you were safely out of the way."

"I wonder how much of that was your doing," Scratha said, and a smoldering danger flared in his eyes. "Take my fortress from me, would you? Not while I have breath to fight it with!"

"That wouldn't have been a problem," Irrio snapped, "if the boys hadn't lost their nerve."

"The boys?" Scratha said, his eyes narrowing.

Lord Irrio pursed his lips and looked away loftily.

Lord Faer pushed his way to the front of the gathered crowd, his plump face damp with sweat and pale with excitement. "Lord Scratha!"

Scratha's stern expression softened for a moment. He looked at the stout lord almost affectionately.

"Lord Faer," he said. "Greetings, and welcome to my home. I'm glad to see you finally took up my invitation to visit."

Lord Faer beamed, then sobered and looked worried again. "There's a challenge to your status, Scratha," he said. "You'll need to settle it with Lord Evkit of the teyanain."

Scratha's expression changed with astonishing speed: from amiably welcoming to taut and murderous.

"Where is he?" Scratha said through his teeth. "I'll gladly give him an answer he's been owed for some years now."

"Here," a voice said, and the crowd parted again to let the small, dark teyanin lord through.

The two lords faced each other. Scratha's glare sent shivers up Alyea's back, but Evkit seemed unruffled.

"You challenge my status?" Scratha said.

"No," Evkit said. "Not now. Before, yes. Now, you are bound. Challenge withdrawn." He shrugged.

"Then I'll challenge *you*," Scratha said, "on the matter of my family's death."

Evkit shook his head. "No. We not kill."

"You didn't have to, you three-headed, snake-mouthed son of a dasta whore!" Scratha roared. He emanated a terrifying rage; the crowd around them hastily moved back a few more steps, clearing a wider circle around the two men. "You *led* them to my family! You told them where to go and when to strike, and you gave them the means to do it! There's blood on your hands, Evkit, and by all the gods as witness, I'll bathe in your Family's blood before I'm done with the retribution for it!"

"Good gods," someone muttered. "He's declaring blood feud with the teyanain? He *is* insane!"

"Not I," Evkit insisted, seeming unaffected by the threatening words. "I say nothing."

"Someone did," Scratha said grimly, "and that person had to be teyanain. Your family were the first guardians of the secret ways; your marks are all over the central eastern chamber. Three of the passages are freshly labeled in the common northern tongue, and all three have the slant-mark that only the teyanain use." He paused, his gaze locked on the small man, then added, slowly, "They read as follows: 'Wall,' 'Bright Bay,' and 'Scratha.'"

As he spoke, more than one of the desert lords made distressed noises.

Alyea didn't look to see who protested; her attention stayed riveted on the two men arguing.

Evkit's eyes widened.

"You could not have come through there!" he said, and his voice rose, distinctly high and shaken. "You do not have permission! You are lying!"

Scratha's grin reminded Alyea of the snarl just before an asp-jacau snapped its sharp teeth into flesh. "*Ish-tchiki, ha'rethe esse chaka.* I paid the price to the watcher of the eastern Wall passage, and was granted entry to its underground ways."

"Damn it, Scratha!" Lord Irrio said, and pushed forward urgently. "Don't speak of this here! Are you mad?"

Scratha's eyes held a bright and feral light. "When a secret is used to kill those it should protect, I no longer consider it sacred."

"You'll damn us all for the folly of one?" Lord Irrio demanded. "Save this for Conclave!"

"The damage is done," Lord Faer said, his face unusually stern. He glanced over the crowd, assessing, and shook his head. "Close the camp, and we'll hold the rest of this discussion in private. Scratha, not another word on this topic until then!"

"While you're closing the camp," Scratha said, "would someone be so good as to bring Pieas Sessin to me?"

Lord Faer, who had begun to turn away, swung back to face Scratha. "Why?"

Irrio turned away to mutter in the ear of a lean, scarred man dressed in Darden Family colors. The man nodded and hurried away. The other lords, Alyea noticed, were motioning to their own assistants and sending them off on hasty errands.

"I have words for him," Scratha said, and his mouth twitched as though with brief amusement. "He may have none for me, but it's my damn land and he'll have to listen, at the least. Is he in your tents, Lord Faer?"

"Yes. He came to me for shelter. He claims the young lady here—Alyea, isn't it?—laid unfair accusations against him, and wanted his chance to be heard in Conclave."

Scratha's mouth stretched in a thin smile. "Bring him here."

"I promised him my protection, Lord Scratha," Lord Faer said coldly.

"I won't hurt him," Scratha said, without a flicker in his expression.

Lord Faer frowned. "I want to know your intentions, Scratha."

"I've invoked my right to change the supplicant's choice in the sun-lord's blood trial. If Pieas agrees, he will switch places with Chacerly."

Lord Faer blinked, his eyebrows arching, and stared at Alyea, then back to Scratha. "You've lost your mind!" he said. "Pieas would be agreeing to his own death!"

"But an honorable one," Scratha said mildly. "In any case, my lord, it's not a request. So go get him before *I* do."

Lord Faer shook his head, his lips tightening, and seemed about to refuse again.

"You promised him the chance to clear his name," Deiq said. Everyone turned to look at him as if they had forgotten he stood there. "What better way to do that than to let him confront his accuser? Does that really have to be in full Conclave?"

Lord Faer started to speak, then hesitated, rubbing his forehead fretfully.

"How's this," he said. "I'll grant you a meeting with him. If he convinces the majority of the full lords present that he's innocent, then I'll release him from my protection and you can pursue the matter of the blood trial with him without my interference. If he's guilty of the charges, you can do as you like with him."

"Agreed," Scratha said promptly. "Now will you go *get* the boy already?"

Lord Faer sighed and hurried away without looking back.

Deiq moved to stand beside Alyea, his expression somber and a little worried.

"That man," he said in her ear, "is a lunatic."

"Lord Faer?" she said, keeping her voice as low as his. The crowd around them buzzed with whispers and muttering; even the desert lords nearby probably wouldn't hear her through the noise.

"No," he said. "Scratha. He just talked openly about one of the most sacred secrets the desert lords hold. If he had spoken those words so publicly anywhere else but his bound land, he'd be dead right now, desert lord or not, along with every servant present who isn't bound under the Threefold Oath. But they can't kill him here, not now."

"The—"

"I'll explain later. As it is, most of the servants who heard him are likely dead as soon as they leave his land. The camp's being closed to keep the smart ones from bolting."

"Does he know that?" Alyea said, shocked.

"Oh, yes," Deiq said. He went back to watching the crowd, eyes narrow and thoughtful, and only shook his head to further questions.

Lanterns and torches flared into life as the afternoon sunlight faded. Scratha seemed content to wait, blinking almost placidly in the uncertain light. Lord Evkit made no move to withdraw; Alyea had the sense that he knew better than to test Scratha's volatile temper further.

At last, the camp was declared secured and Lord Faer returned, Pieas Sessin glowering sullenly at his side.

"Let's move away a bit for this discussion," Lord Scratha said. He lifted two long-necked torches and their holders and motioned for the assembled lords to follow him. Scratha led them around the side of the fortress, back to the place where he had first surprised Alyea. Chac and Micru, dim shadows in the growing twilight, stood up as the group approached. The light from the torches in Scratha's hands wreathed his face in shifting, demonic light.

"I'll beg your pardon, my lords," Scratha said, "that I'm not inclined to invite you inside my home until I resolve a few issues, given you were plotting to take it from me." He drove the torches into the sand, one to either side of him. The flaring, sputtering light threw shadows into disarray among the assembled group.

Lord Rest said, "You've changed, Lord Scratha, since I last saw you."

"I've learned a lot since the last time you saw me, Lord Rest." His dark stare swept over the group again. "I only wonder why you haven't tried to kill me before, since I'm such an inconvenience to your little plots and plans."

"We don't want you dead," Lord Faer said, appearing deeply shocked.

Scratha grinned fiercely. "Dead or safely out of the way in the northlands, what would be the difference?"

"You'd have been happier wandering the north," Lord Irrio said, prompting a startled, dismayed look from Lord Faer. "You were only ever granted desert lord status as a courtesy, Scratha. Last of a dead line? You didn't have a chance."

"*What?*" Lord Faer gasped. They ignored him.

"Except that I'm not the last," Scratha said. "Sons and daughters of the line are still living, and one of them is less than two hundred yards from where we stand now." His gaze went to Lord Evkit, and what little humor he had been displaying faded.

"We didn't know that then," Lord Irrio said carefully.

"Oh?" Scratha said, not taking his stare from the teyanin lord. "Imagine, Lord Evkit keeping secrets from his darling. The sands may swallow us all."

A dark flush spread across Lord Irrio's face. For a moment, he looked ready to launch an attack on Scratha. Alyea found herself tensing, unsure whether to back away or to intervene. Deiq's pressure on her elbow tightened briefly.

Lord Irrio drew a deep breath, seeming to gain control of himself.

Lord Evkit watched everything with a bland detachment that seemed almost eerie in the midst of the raging tempers around him.

"It's not worth arguing," Lord Faer said abruptly. "Scratha's a full lord, bound to his lands, and with a true female line open he'll be rebuilding his family within a few years. You're never going to be able to leave your lands again, Scratha, and neither will the girl—her name's Gria, isn't it? She'll never leave the southlands."

Lord Evkit opened his mouth as if to speak, then shook his head and subsided, a faint smile on his face. Alyea suspected he had been about to mention his previous claim on Gria, and had thought better of it for some reason. More than likely, the fact that the poor girl wasn't a virgin any longer had been enough to kill his interest. And what would Scratha do when he found that out?

"She'll never leave the walls of my *fortress*, if I have anything to say about it," Scratha said. "I want her to stay alive." His glare went to Lord Evkit, then back to the gathered lords.

"I want this held aside," Lord Faer said sternly. "Your accusations against Lord Evkit and the teyanain should be aired in Conclave. Just because you're on your bound land, my lord, does not mean you can side-step the laws of the desert."

Scratha stared at the plump desert lord as if considering arguing the point, then shrugged. "I'll agree," he said, "if you'll hold him here for that time."

For the first time, Lord Evkit showed anger. "You think I would *run?*"

Scratha looked down at the small man from the whole of his towering height, managing to convey a sense of utter scorn.

"Enough," Lord Faer said hastily, and stepped between the two men as the teyanin lord visibly stiffened with rage. "Hold it for Conclave, the both of you! I'll vouch for Evkit's honor, Scratha. You two stay apart until this is brought up formally!"

Lord Evkit hissed, his glare pure venom, and turned away, his shoulders and lips tight.

"I have other business this night which is *not* a matter for Conclave," Lord Scratha said, turning his stare on Pieas Sessin.

Pieas lifted his chin and sneered at Scratha, but a livid bruise on the side of his face and a haggard puffiness under his eyes detracted from the attempt at arrogance.

"You asked for a chance to clear your name," Lord Faer said before Pieas could speak. "Here is your accuser, and several desert lords to hear your defense."

"You promised me a hearing in Conclave!" Pieas said. His hands knotted into fists.

"I promised you a chance to defend yourself against the charges," Lord Faer said with no trace of uncertainty. "That doesn't have to be in Conclave. Tell your story."

"I was being set up!" Pieas cried. "Lies, my lord, and manipulations. She had no basis for a challenge, but nobody would believe me!"

"What were the charges, and what is your defense?"

Pieas wet his lips and glanced around at the faces watching him.

"I was accused of rape," he said, "unfairly. The servant girl was a slut and threw herself at me. Lady Alyea came around the corner, the girl started to fight, and the lady decided I was raping her. I believe it was set up from the beginning, to put a bad name against me. The girl was a former servant of the lady; how can you view her actions without suspicion?"

"Lady Alyea?" Faer said without a flicker of emotion in his voice or face. "How do you respond to that?"

Alyea had to admit that Pieas seemed utterly sincere, even to her newly sharp senses.

"I had no idea they were around that corner," she said carefully. "I saw a struggle and separated them, and the girl claimed he had been forcing her. She had marks of rough handling, and I know her character; she's no slut. Pieas himself, when accused, did little more than sneer and swagger away, without the least guilt or remorse. I brought the matter before the king, with Pieas and Lord Eredion Sessin in attendance, and backed my charge with personal experience—"

"More lies!" Pieas cried, but his gaze darted away from Alyea as he spoke. "I never touched you!"

"*That* is a lie," Lord Faer said immediately, a deep scowl forming on his face. "Don't be a fool. You're not good enough to lie in front of this many desert lords."

Pieas wet his lips again and glanced around.

"Running now would be exceptionally stupid," Lord Rest rumbled. "Hold still, boy."

Alyea stared. Lord Faer hadn't challenged Pieas's earlier statement about Wian; did that mean it had been true? She considered that for a moment, forcing herself to be fair, then said slowly, "I can speak to Pieas Sessin's actions regarding myself, but on the other matter, I only know what I saw when I came around that corner. I believed Wian when she told me it was rape. I still have a hard time believing she could have acted as Pieas claims she did."

"The girl came at me as I was returning to my rooms," Pieas said. "She told me she found me handsome and had long wished for my attentions. She was attractive; I wasn't inclined to put her aside if she was so desperate to throw herself in my path. As soon as we were alone and I was roused, she sought to leave. I'll admit I was losing my temper when Lady Alyea came round the corner, and I'd hit the whore once already. She tried to claw at my eyes! I was defending myself."

Alyea drew a deep breath, hearing absolute truth in Pieas' voice.

Lord Scratha's face remained stony. "And you had no knowledge of her previous to this?"

Pieas shook his head. He looked at Alyea directly and went on, his voice wavering: "I admit to and apologize for my earlier offense. I used to experiment with—ah—*exotic* substances." He looked away and lifted his chin, straightening to a stiff posture. "I've made mistakes. I'll do what I can to make amends."

"When you fled from us at Sandsplit Village," Lord Scratha said unexpectedly, "you left Wian behind. Are you claiming you're not responsible for the state she was in?"

"Sandsplit!" Alyea said before she could stop herself. "She should be safe in Bright Bay!"

"She is now," Scratha said without taking his attention from Pieas.

"Answer the question!"

Pieas's lips thinned. "No," he said at last, "I won't say that." He swallowed and shifted in place. When he went on, his voice had dropped to a near-whisper. "The people I used to deal with weren't pleased when I decided to distance myself from them. I believe they sent the girl after me to cause a scene, and when it wasn't as public as I think they wanted, they went looking for the girl . . . and left her in my apartments. I woke in the middle of the night. . . ." He made a vague gesture with both hands. "She'd been badly beaten. I knew nobody would believe I hadn't done anything to her. I couldn't leave her behind. I decided to follow Scratha and convince the girl to tell him the truth. But she fought me the whole way, screaming and clawing, and I had to restrain her with drugs and rope to make any speed." He drew a deep breath and rubbed at his face with his hands. "It wasn't pleasant."

"You'll have us believe this entire accusation comes from the manipulations of a disgruntled potions dealer?" Lord Rest said skeptically.

Pieas made a despairing motion with both hands. "It's the *truth.* I know I haven't been the most admirable person, my lords, but I've been trying to get free of my poor choices for months now. It's harder than I expected."

"Why did you decide to distance yourself from your former friends?" Lord Faer asked.

Pieas looked as if he'd rather sink beneath the sand than answer that question. After a long, flushed moment, he said, barely audible, "My sister, Nissa." He swallowed hard. "We've always been close. I could never refuse her anything if she leaned on me hard enough. She said she'd found someone she wanted to marry, if he'd have her, and if he knew who she was . . . that she was related to me . . . I had such a name that she didn't believe he would even look at her. She said she was going to have to lie about who she was, just to get his attention. She begged me to clear my name, so that when her lie was finally revealed, as she knew it would be, she could at least not have the shame of my behavior held against her."

Scratha's face held a grey tinge in the uncertain light.

"She swore to me that if I cost her this chance," Pieas said, "she'd never speak to me again, and do her damnedest to get me thrown from the family as a disgrace. I wouldn't have taken that from a single other person walking this earth, but she's my *sister.* I'd die to keep her happy." He raised a ferocious glare to Scratha. The two stared at each other; and for the first time, Alyea thought Pieas looked the stronger man.

Scratha looked away first, visibly shaken, but said nothing. Alyea didn't know what to believe. Everything she remembered of Wian said the girl couldn't have been involved in any such scheme to disgrace the son of a desert family, but she had heard no false notes in Pieas's voice. None of the desert lords seemed to doubt his word, and even Deiq offered no objection.

She didn't envy Scratha his new knowledge, either. Nissa was obviously naive about politics. She had apparently assumed Scratha's legendary hatred of Sessin Family came from her brother's disgraceful antics, and sought no deeper for a reason.

Alyea met Pieas's gaze squarely. He almost quivered with tension and seemed more than a little sullen, like an asp-jacau that had been kicked too many times by its master; but his stare ran clear and honest.

"I won't fight you, if you want to punish me for . . . for hurting you," he said. "My mistakes are going to follow me all my life, and damage those around me on the way. At least I've had a chance to clear my name of the lies. That's all I wanted, for Nissa's sake."

"Why did you run?" she demanded.

He grinned bitterly. "My own uncle was going to kill me. Nobody else would have defended me, once that was said. I didn't want Nissa thinking that I'd broken my promise. Once I knew Scratha wasn't going to listen to me, I decided to try my luck in the desert."

"Did Eredion know you were telling the truth?" Alyea asked.

"He must have," Pieas said, "he's a desert lord. You can't lie to a desert lord, can you?"

The silence that followed hung uncomfortably long.

"*You* can't," Lord Scratha said at last, a subtle inflection aiming the words at Pieas. Alyea shot the tall man a sharp look.

Pieas frowned, then shook his head. "Well, then, he must have known. But he chose to call me a liar, and turn against me. I saw no option but to run and try to clear my name along the way."

"How did you know I was headed east?" Scratha said. "The king told everyone I was going west, to the Stone Islands."

Pieas snorted. "I knew before you cleared the perimeter of Bright Bay which way you were going, and under what name."

"I didn't put any of that in the note to the steward," Scratha said. "Or speak to any but the king about it."

"You didn't have to," Alyea said. "Some of the King's Hidden have dual allegiances. Some are to Sessin."

Pieas grinned sourly. "I wasn't far behind you," he said. "But that stupid girl slowed me down with her kicking and wailing. I'd have caught up earlier if I hadn't been trying to convince her I wasn't the one who attacked her. I never did succeed. Whatever they used on her drove her half out of her head, and I had no way of curing it."

Scratha shook his head, brooding, and said, "Apparently I should have waited to see if Yuer could get sense out of her after all."

Pieas grimaced. "I hope you didn't leave the girl with Yuer, Lord Scratha. That's like dropping a baby chicken into a nest of hungry snakes."

The silence hung for a moment, then Scratha, avoiding Alyea's glare, said, "Done is done. You're innocent of the one charge and guilty of the other, it seems. You have a choice, Pieas. Alyea is in the middle of the Sun-Lord's blood trial. You can wait until she completes this trial and face her under the original blood challenge she issued, which means if you fall, you fall to a desert lord and your name goes into permanent disgrace. Or you can step up to be the blood-sacrifice of the trial, and regain all honor."

Alyea drew a deep breath, but Pieas, smiling strangely, spoke first. "I deserve death. Several times over—and that's only for what I remember of past years. It would be a mercy. I'll never be free of my mistakes, and at least this way my name will be clear. I'll only ask one thing in return." His gaze went to Scratha. "My lord . . . give my sister another chance. I've never seen Nissa so heartbroken before. Don't hold her blame for my sins."

"It never had anything to do with you," Scratha said in a strangled voice.

Pieas looked honestly puzzled. "Then what?"

They all stared at him in silence for a moment. Lord Faer finally said, "Pieas, Scratha Family was slaughtered, and Sessin refused aid. Every other desert family held out a hand save yours. You don't know that?"

Pieas's face flushed. "I was told that Scratha refused our aid, alone of all the desert families—that we weren't good enough for him to ally with."

"I was *ten*," Scratha said into the astonished silence, "and grieving. Lord Sessin offered me help if I agreed to conditions which would have given him control of my lands in all but name; of course I refused! After that he had nothing for me."

Alyea blinked, looking at Cafad Scratha more closely; she'd been assuming he was in his late thirties, possibly even early forties. But as Scratha Fortress had been attacked somewhat less than twenty years ago, if he'd been ten at the time, then he couldn't be above thirty.

Pieas shook his head slowly, his expression clearing. "I'm sorry, Lord Scratha. I never knew that, but it sounds like something Lord Arit would do. He was always looking to gain Sessin more power. But to pressure a grieving child—that was wrong."

"The sands are about to swallow us all," Alyea said without meaning to put the thought into actual speech. She covered her mouth with one hand, appalled at her timing.

Pieas turned, gave her a hard look, then shrugged and grinned ruefully. "I deserved that, I suppose. Which brings me back to the point." He reached to his belt, drew two long, slim daggers out, and dropped them on the sand. He pulled two more from his boots and tossed them to the ground, then another from a neck-sheath. Stepping away from the small pile of knives, he spread his hands and looked at Alyea.

She stared back at him, feeling oddly paralyzed.

"Do it," he said, and dropped gracefully to his knees, keeping his stare locked on her face.

"I don't. . . ." she started, not sure what to say.

"Gods know," he said, "my life won't be any loss to the world."

She drew a deep breath and looked around. The other lords had backed away a few steps, leaving a clear ring of space around her; clearly, none of them intended to interfere. Even Deiq had stepped away and watched her with absolutely no expression.

Pieas dropped his hands to his sides, curling them into fists.

"Out of all the people in this camp," he said hoarsely, "I'm the most deserving of death right now."

His clenched hands trembled.

A humorless, strained bark of laughter came from her throat. "I never thought I'd have any respect for you."

His grin looked forced. "Funny you should say that. I've always thought the same about myself. Best not give me a chance to ruin it, don't you think?"

She drew another, long, steadying breath, and bent to pick up one of his knives.

Chapter Twenty-Five

Cafad had been gone for a long time when Riss opened her eyes and slowly pushed herself into a sitting position. She stared at nothing for a while, seeming dazed. Eventually her gaze focused on the world around her, and then on Idisio.

"That was . . . interesting," she said hoarsely, and shut her eyes again.

"Water?" Idisio offered, holding out a flask. She took it and drained the contents in one long steady swig.

"How long was I out?" she asked, handing him back the empty flask.

"I don't know," Idisio said. He glanced up at the high windows, long since dark. A strange, steady glow had filled the room at dusk; it rose from several alcoves along each wall and reminded Idisio of the odd lighting in the Bright Bay palace dining hall.

He had prowled the room earlier, examining the alcoves, and found them hot enough at close range as to discourage close inspection; but the alcoves seemed to be thin shafts cut down into the walls, and the light came from beneath. Idisio guessed at a fire, somehow reflected upwards into the room, and amused himself by thinking out possible ways that could be done.

"It's probably almost midnight by now."

"Oh," she said, looking relieved. "It's only been hours? That's good."

He stared at her, astonished at the odd reply.

"Never mind," Riss said. She rubbed her eyes. "Idisio. . . ."

The tone of her voice would have terrified him in the recent past. Now he found himself evaluating it, calculating possibilities, comparing the tone to the motion of her hand and how her gaze slid awkwardly away from him. He considered responses, decided on patient silence as the best path, and waited.

She drew a deep breath, another, and finally said, "I'm pregnant."

"I never," he said involuntarily.

She grinned, coughed half-laughter, and said, "No, stupid. Not yours. It's from when . . . back north. Before I met you."

"Oh," he said, then, "*Oh.*"

"Yes. Oh." She regarded him steadily, her expression sober but somehow content. "I thought I might be. I hadn't had a chance to . . . prepare." She looked away, a faint flush coming to her cheeks. "And by the time I woke up . . . anyway, the ha'rethe confirmed it."

"Oh," Idisio said again, unable to come up with anything more coherent.

She shrugged a little, sighed, and looked up at him. "Do you think I'm a whore?"

"No," he said, astonished. "No, nothing like that."

"Do you—"

"Wait." Idisio cut her off with a gesture and tilted his head, listening to distant sounds. "Someone's coming. Cafad. And he's not alone. Two others."

She rubbed at her face with both hands and raked her hair into a semblance of order. Idisio watched, mulling over what she'd told him, and found himself glad of the interruption. He didn't know what to say to her, didn't know the right response to make. He had an uncomfortable feeling that she wanted to hear that he liked her, or thought she was beautiful, or something equally soppy.

Words bounced from the stone walls, muddied into incoherence by the echoes, then clarified as they moved into the passageway outside the room; one voice held a female timbre, and the third set Idisio's arms into gooseflesh. He stood up just as the door swung open.

Cafad strode into the room, followed by a man and a woman. The woman stood almost as tall as the desert lord, with glossy dark hair that hung, unbound, well past her shoulders. Dark eyes, olive-tan skin, and the stern pride in her carriage marked her as having at least some measure of noble blood, although it probably came from a Bright Bay, not a desert Family, line. At a second glance, Idisio read tremendous weariness and a deep grief beneath the surface. She seemed ready to drop where she stood. Only willpower kept her on her feet.

The man whose voice worried Idisio stood slightly taller than the woman, with a darker skin and broader face. His expression, at the moment, held as much bleak and powerful bitterness as Cafad's madness had ever produced. Idisio suspected that he never wanted to see this man upset, not even a little; but here, too, a second glance showed more. Something weirdly familiar and at the same time frighteningly alien glittered in those dark eyes. Idisio found himself backing away.

"It's all right, Idisio," Cafad said. "This is—"

I am named De'sta'haiq, a quiet voice said, just audible.

"—Deiq, and Lord Alyea—" Cafad's voice echoed over the words in Idisio's head.

Deiq is simpler, the voice agreed, and the man smiled.

"Gah," Idisio said, and backed up again.

"—Idisio?" Cafad stepped forward, stretching out a reassuring hand. "What's the matter?"

"He's never met another ha'ra'ha before," the man said easily, still smiling.

"Of course not," Cafad said, looking thoroughly chagrined. "I should have remembered that. Idisio, I'm sorry, it's been . . . a bit hectic the last few hours."

"I would like to pay my respects, if I may," Deiq said, "and Lord Alyea needs to rest."

"Of course," Cafad said. "Riss, come with us; you'll be attending to Lord Alyea. Idisio, guide Deiq wherever he wishes to go. He has full access to the fortress; no door is closed to a ha'ra'ha."

"Gods," the woman said, wearily sardonic, "you're letting me out of your sight, Deiq?"

"You're safe here," the dark man said. "Go get some rest. If you need me, just call my name. I'll hear you."

She quirked an eyebrow, shook her head, and followed Cafad from the room, Riss trailing behind. Idisio wanted nothing *less* than to be alone in a room with Deiq, but Cafad swept out of the room too fast for protest. Idisio tried to think of an excuse to leave, and came up blank.

Deiq watched him with an amused expression. "Most of us grow up knowing what we are, in the company of our own kind and kin," he said. "You seem to have had an unusual life."

Idisio felt his face flare into bright, mortified color.

"Scratha didn't tell me details," Deiq said. "He said you needed instruction, nothing more. Excuse me."

He walked to within an arm's length of the pool and sank to his knees. He sat that way, head bowed, for several minutes. Idisio watched, fascinated, as a faint mist formed above the surface of the water. As if subject to a localized breeze, the mist swirled into patterns that looked almost like writing for a few moments, then slowly dissipated.

Deiq drew a deep breath and stood, turning to face Idisio; incredibly, tears streaked down that imposing, dark face.

"Scratha has no idea," Deiq said, "how lucky he is. Neither do you." He shook his head and walked away from the now-quiet pool, motioning Idisio to follow him.

Deiq moved through the silent passageways as though entirely familiar with the fortress. At that thought, Idisio realized *he* knew the halls they walked, knew when a door or turn in the passage lay ahead. He could have found his way to the kitchens, storerooms, main hall, and more: as if he had lived here all his life.

He stopped and rubbed at his eyes, feeling disoriented. Deiq paused, waiting patiently. After a moment Idisio said, "I . . . feel like I know this place. It's weird."

"You'll never be lost," Deiq said, "with a friendly ha'rethe around." He smiled and started walking again. Abruptly aware he had no value as a guide, Idisio grimaced and followed. He wondered if Cafad had known that Deiq didn't need a guide and, if not, whether he should say anything about it.

"Friendly?" Idisio said after a few steps.

Deiq made a humming noise in the back of his throat. "One of the great myths about them is that they're all the same: emotionless, interested only in their own survival, and without personality or preferences. It's an understandable mistake, given how little contact even the desert lords have with them."

Idisio felt a burst of excitement. "Is that why I couldn't stand being around that one at the Wall," he said, "but the one here was all right?"

Deiq paused again and looked at Idisio with a curiously intent expression on his face.

"The one at the Wall?" he repeated.

Idisio told him the story, cutting it to a brief and relatively dry account.

"Ah," Deiq said, and resumed walking. "That's another mistake humans make, one that I think is rather less forgivable than the first. They assume that every voice in a dark place is a ha'rethe."

Idisio had been walking slightly behind Deiq; now he moved to walk beside him. "It wasn't? Then what was it?"

Deqi's expression remained serene as he said, "It's been over a thousand years since the original Agreement, and the ha'reye were old then. How many do you think are still alive?"

"Good gods," Idisio breathed, stunned. "I never thought about that."

"Most people don't," Deiq said. "There were about a hundred ha'reye left when the first Agreement was made. Today, I'm guessing there are probably fewer than twenty still alive. One of those lives under this fortress. Most of the Families think they have ha'rethe but what they actually have protecting them is a first generation ha'ra'ha. Sometimes it's even a second generation ha'ra'ha. Nobody lower than that could pull it off—they're too weak. Too human."

"So what I met at the Wall was a ha'ra'ha?" Idisio said, intensely relieved and not sure why.

"More than likely," Deiq said. "Probably first generation." He paused and cleared his throat. "I'd advise against you going anywhere near the Wall again until you're fully trained, Idisio. Some of the first ha'ra'hain . . .

it's complicated."

He turned into a side corridor, sharply, as if he'd made the decision to do so at the last second. Idisio almost bumped into him.

"We both ought to rest. I'll have to finish talking to you later. Go find your friend Riss. She needs you right now."

"She *what*?" Idisio said involuntarily.

Deiq increased his pace until Idisio had to jog to keep up. "Trust me. Go."

They came to a cross-passage which Idisio instantly knew led to the honored guest quarters. Deiq took it without pause or farewell. Idisio stood silent, watching the tall man hurry down the passage, and chewed on his tongue. He'd finally started getting some of the answers he needed. Deiq's abrupt departure felt like a splash of winter-cold water on a hot day.

You'll have time to talk, the ha'rethe said unexpectedly. *He's right. Go see her.*

"Is she all right?" Idisio said out loud, suddenly worried, and started jogging again. He realized he could feel her presence in the servant's quarters. Cafad must have assigned her a room; she was probably unpacking or resting there. What could be wrong with that?

Go see her, the ha'rethe repeated.

"For what?" Idisio said, still speaking out loud; stubbornly reluctant to use any form of telepathy.

Humans, the ha'rethe sighed, and fell silent.

Riss was crying. He could feel her distress. He hesitated, considering whether to knock. As he dithered, the thin door seemed to shift slightly; now it hung open just a little.

"You don't have to push," Idisio muttered under his breath. He received no answer.

He nudged the door just enough to slip through, and shut it behind him without making a noise. He didn't know if that silence came from his own skill, the light weight of the door, or the ha'rethe.

Riss lay curled up on the low bed, hugging a large red pillow; her thin body shook with muffled sobs. Idisio watched her for a moment, uncertain whether to retreat or advance, and finally moved forward. He sat gingerly on the edge of the bed, half-expecting her to lash out.

Instead, he wound up, as he had once before, with her arms around his neck and her head on his shoulder. At least she wasn't entirely on top of him this time. He shifted awkwardly, trying to get her elbow out of his ribs, and somehow the movement ended with his back against the headboard and Riss firmly in his lap again.

He grimaced ruefully, eased her into a comfortable position, and stroked her hair lightly as she cried herself out.

"What's the matter?" he said when her sobbing hiccups had slowed.

"Let's see," she said in a thick voice, not lifting her head from his shoulder. "I'm hundreds of miles from home, disgraced, pregnant, alone, terrified, surrounded by more strangers than I've met in my entire life, and I have no idea what's going to happen to me. There's a weird creature that spent several days talking to me, but it was really only hours, and some of the things it told me scared me about to pissing myself. Nothing's wrong. Why would you think anything's wrong?"

Idisio, at first taken aback, found himself grinning by the time she finished. If Riss could be that sharp, she'd be all right.

"Let's see," he said into her hair. "You're on a grand adventure, earning respect from everyone you meet and learning lots of new things. And, yes, you're pregnant, with a desert lord ready and willing to support every need you and the child might have. You've met and befriended one of the oldest and most sacred creatures in the world, and it shared some amazing secrets with you. You're right; I don't think anything's wrong."

She lifted her head and glared at him. "You're impossible."

He shrugged, still smiling. "My version is as valid as yours."

She wiped her face with a shaky hand and sat up a little straighter. "I keep thinking Karic's going to show up around some corner unexpectedly and laugh at me, and tell everybody that I'm a whore. . . ."

Idisio abruptly felt a phantom surge of thick, salty water filling his throat, and an almost overwhelming, thrashing panic. It passed in moments, and he coughed hard to clear his throat.

"I don't think . . . you need to worry about that," he muttered, his stomach churning. "Damn, this is going to take some getting used to."

"What is?"

He shook his head, unwilling to share his vision of Karic's death. "Nothing. I guess I'm a little rattled by everything too. Look, you're the servant of a desert lord now. If they even show up, Cafad's liable to have them strung up for what they did to you. Don't worry about them any more."

She sighed. "Thank you. I've been so scared. . . ."

The words trailed off into silence. When her breathing evened into true sleep, Idisio carefully eased her back down onto the bed and slipped out the door with an immense sense of relief.

Chapter Twenty-Six

The fortress seemed to breathe around Alyea; the air currents moved in strange patterns here. Sometimes it felt as though an invisible eye watched everything that went on within the walls. Alyea couldn't decide whether that comforted or terrified her.

She lay on the wide, low bed, staring up at the ceiling, unable to sleep. Lord Scratha's servant had shown her to a room and withdrawn with hardly a word; there seemed something tremendously strained in the girl's manner. Alyea hadn't felt up to handling someone else's troubles, so she had let Riss go without pressing her to talk. Now she wondered if she had made the right decision.

Blood darkening the sand at her feet. . . .

She shut her eyes and covered them with her hands, wishing that could erase the image. Her stomach rolled heavily. She moaned, more miserable than she could remember ever having been in her life. Even the horror of Ethu's death paled before the bleak fact of having become a murderer herself.

Exhaustion dragged at every muscle and nerve; she'd expected to be asleep as soon as she lay down. But every time she relaxed that moment came back to her, destroying her peace of mind more effectively than a physical attack.

It should have been easy. It should have been simple. He'd said himself that he deserved death. Nobody had moved to stop her, not even Scratha.

But it *hadn't* been easy, or simple, and the silence from the watching lords had been oppressive, not friendly. Had she made the right choice? What if the opportunity to kill Pieas had really been a test to see if she could *refuse* to take a life? What if, after all, she had failed? What if she'd missed some vital clue, some way to get out of the situation without killing anyone?

Nobody had spoken afterwards. Scratha gathered the body into his arms and disappeared around the far side of the fortress without a word, and everyone just waited, silent and expressionless. Not looking at each other; not looking at her.

The surrounding darkness seemed like a live thing, writhing to attack her, held back only by the torchlight. Alyea had broken into a cold sweat by the time Scratha returned.

Discussion remained minimal even then: Scratha formally invited Alyea and Deiq into the fortress. The other lords bowed, excused themselves, and returned to the camp. Pieas's death hadn't been referred to again, as if, once over, it had never happened; as if Pieas had never actually existed in the first place.

The room swayed gently around her. Alyea sat up and curled forward, hugging her knees to stop the trembling in her hands. None of this had gone as expected. Not that she'd had any clear idea of what *would* happen once the last blood trial ended, but she'd never expected this wrenching, dizzying nausea, this unsteady balancing on the edge of a bottomless chasm of guilt.

She felt a faint movement nearby, and then Deiq sat down beside her.

"Alyea," he said. "Look at me. Please."

She kept her face pressed into her knees, afraid to face him, sure he meant to tell her she'd made a dreadful mistake. If she looked at him, met those dark eyes, she'd see it, she'd know he'd lost all respect for her and thought of her as nothing more than a vengeful whore.

"*No*," he said sharply, and gripped her upper arms hard. "Stop that!"

Of course; as a ha'ra'ha, he could probably read her mind. He'd likely been doing it all along, using Alyea's weakness to manipulate her into doing what he wanted. She'd been a tool, a toy, pushed this way by one and that way by another, and she'd be discarded soon; she'd become only an inconvenience now, but one too strong to be tolerated.

Deiq cursed softly, tangled his hands in her hair, and hauled her head up. The pain of her hair being pulled that hard forced her eyes open. She reached up to bat his hands away just as he released her hair and splayed his hands on either side of her face, thumbs under her chin to keep her still. Unable to move her head, she found herself staring directly into his eyes.

"Alyea, *stop it*."

She inhaled sharply, shocked at his tone as much as at the mad glitter in his eyes. The gentle, amused veneer had vanished completely; the visage in front of her, at the moment, would give the strongest desert lord pause.

"Good," he said, although his tautness didn't relax in the least. "I'd rather have you scared. That's easier to deal with. Take another breath, a good deep one."

She drew in another breath, and another, her gaze locked helplessly on his unyielding expression; and abruptly burst into tears.

"That's better," he said, sounding relieved, and his hands softened. She found herself leaning forward against him. He pulled her into his arms, cradling her like a child, and said nothing while she sobbed helplessly.

When her breath started to hitch painfully, he pressed a large hand gently between her breasts and held it there. A sense of warmth spread through her chest; the sobs eased and her breathing slowly evened again.

"I shouldn't have left you alone," Deiq said quietly. "I'm sorry."

She moved her head side to side in faint negation, not understanding the apology.

"You need to rest, Alyea."

"Can't sleep," she mumbled. "Blood on the sand. . . ."

He drew in a hard breath, as if he'd seen the image in her mind. "Damn," he said, "I *am* an idiot sometimes. Listen to me, Alyea: you shed blood on a ha'rethe's land, and you're not comfortable in your own mind that you did right. Even though the bound lord approved, the protector of the land is going to make you accept what you've done before it lets you rest. Your agonizing is aggravating the ha'rethe. Do you understand? Alyea?"

"Tired. . . ." she whispered, closing her eyes. "So tired."

"I know," he said. "Do you think you did right?"

"I don't know," she said. "Do you?"

"I can't answer that."

"More stupid rules," she muttered, and forced her eyes open. "I don't know. Yes. No. I don't know that I had a choice. No, there's always a choice, isn't there?" She sighed, letting the words trail off into a half-coherent mumble, then made herself go on. "I wish I hadn't. But that won't change anything; it's done. And I'd do the same thing again, if I had the same choice in front of me."

Her eyelids slid shut.

"I *would* do't 'gain," she mumbled. "Di'righ."

The bloody sand image wavered and faded like smoke on a strong wind.

"I think that's good enough," Deiq said. "You can rest now."

"Oh, good," she said, or thought she did; words faded away into a thick softness.

Emptiness eased into form, and consciousness slid in around the edges of her vision. She lay still, eyes closed, and became nobody for a time. Memory intruded; she allowed it reluctantly and watched, still hazy, as pieces of her life built themselves back into structures of behavior and personality.

Alyea sighed and opened her eyes, grateful that the dizzy, numb feeling had faded into simple exhaustion. She still felt tired, but it wasn't the overwhelming sensation it had been.

A broad band of sunlight lay across the far side of the room; she had no idea whether it signified morning or afternoon. The room held the cool of early morning, but that might be deceptive.

Deiq lay sprawled on the wide bed beside her. She'd never seen him so relaxed before; his breathing held the deep hoarseness of complete exhaustion. Alyea realized for the first time that he'd been pushing himself even harder than he'd pushed her. She admitted to herself that she hadn't wanted to see any weakness in Deiq, but decided he'd also probably concealed his weariness; Deiq's pride would never let him sag and yawn in public.

As she studied Deiq's slack face, Alyea wondered *why* he had taken such an interest in her. Whatever their relationship, Eredion Sessin couldn't possibly be so concerned about one person's welfare as to ask a ha'ra'ha to follow her around. And Deiq tended to present himself as hard-edged and manipulative, but someone like that wouldn't have agreed to Eredion's request—or fallen so trustingly asleep beside her. More questions; no answers in sight. She'd have to be patient, which had always been her least favorite activity.

Careful not to disturb him, she sat up and edged back to lean against the wall. With nowhere in particular she wanted to go and nobody she cared to speak with at the moment, there seemed little point in getting up. She'd certainly be notified of dinner, or the start of Conclave, or anything else of importance which concerned her.

Alyea rested her shoulders against smooth, cool stone and contented herself with watching a ha'ra'ha sleep.

The band of sunlight shifted as she sat, moving, little by little, away from the far wall and towards the bed. She'd never studied how long it took for that to happen, but she guessed at least an hour, maybe two, had passed by the time the warm golden light lapped at the foot of the bed and Deiq woke up.

Before he even opened his eyes, he put out a hand to the place where she had been, and found only empty space; she'd long since drawn her legs up close to her. With a startled grunt, he rolled to his side, his eyes wide. Seeing her, he relaxed and drew a deep, shuddering breath.

"I'm not going anywhere," she said.

Deiq propped himself up on one elbow and looked up at her, pushing his long hair out of his face. He didn't speak for a long moment, seemingly content just to study her.

"How do you feel?" he said at last.

"Much better," she said. "Did you get enough rest?"

"For the moment," he said. "I'll need to rest some more after the Conclave is over. Lord Scratha has offered us unlimited hospitality—a rare gift."

She decided, rather coldly, to take advantage of his lingering vulnerability and press for answers. "Your merchanting business won't suffer from the time you're spending away from it?"

He winced a little, his gaze sharpening. "I have good managers. They handle most of the work already; I'm almost a figurehead."

"How old are you?"

He blinked at her, a frown forming, and didn't answer.

"I'm guessing over a hundred years," she said.

His mouth quirked. "That's a conservative guess. Leave it at that."

"And in all that time," she said, "how many times before this have you fallen in love?"

"*Damn it*," he said, and rolled onto his back.

She waited, studying the dust motes whirling through the sunbeams.

"None," he said finally.

She looked down at his bleak expression. "You weren't supposed to help me this much, were you?"

"No." He sat up. After running his large hands through his hair for a few moments, he said, "I was only supposed to make sure you got to the fortress safely. To kill Chac if he threatened your safety."

"Why didn't you?"

He made a vague, helpless gesture, still not meeting her gaze. "I just . . . couldn't."

"You couldn't kill Chac?"

"I'm not a Callen of the Sun-Lord," he said. "I don't consider killing a good way to handle most problems. I thought I could do better by rearranging your trials to help you survive what he had planned." He made another vague gesture and offered her a pained smile. "It's worked out, in the end."

She drew a deep breath. "No. It hasn't, actually. You've made me a desert lord without a family," she said, her throat tight. The words came out hoarse and more than a little bitter. "I doubt Lord Scratha will stretch so far as to name me honorary family, and I don't think I'd want that. You've given me power with no way to use it, Deiq. What am I supposed to do now? I can't go home; they'd never take me back. Do you think I'll follow you around the southlands like some baby bird and share your bed? You can't be that stupid."

As she spoke, his face slowly became a hard, expressionless mask.

"No," he said. "I wasn't . . . thinking, I suppose. I didn't see it quite that way."

Alyea hesitated, then said, "I'm not saying I don't like you, Deiq. But you've pushed me around to suit yourself with never a thought for the ending, and now I'm stuck between two worlds with no bridge between. It's not a comfortable spot."

"This isn't quite the way I wanted events to happen," he said, staring at his hands.

"I'm sure you had a wonderfully romantic ending in mind," she said, and found herself laughing.

He glanced up at her, frowning, plainly hurt. She waved her hands in the air and shook her head.

"I'm not making fun of you," she said when she had her breath back. "This is all so absurd, Deiq—it's like something out of a bard song. And it's just so silly, thinking of you with candles and roses and romance; that's not how you are at all. It certainly wouldn't have impressed me a bit."

His frown slowly lifted and changed to a rueful look.

Sensing an opportunity for an unguarded answer, she asked, "How true are the rumors about you bedding your way to power?"

He hesitated, then said, "I started most of those rumors myself. It was something humans could understand, something that turned their eyes from any other explanation for my influence."

"But not all," she said.

"Any good rumor has to have a grain of truth to it."

"Chac said once," Alyea said, not at all sure she should bring this up, "that rumor called Pieas your son."

Deiq shook his head. "No truth to that one. Lady Sessin started that one herself, I think, to see if she could tweak her husband's temper a bit. She's a strange one."

Alyea let out a breath of relief. "What's that grain of truth you mentioned?"

He let out a hard, frustrated breath, obviously wishing he'd never said that aloud. For a moment, she thought he wouldn't answer, but then he shrugged and said, "One of the first problems new desert lords usually have to face, and ha'ra'hain live with all their lives, is the . . . there are changes in . . . in your . . . drive. Your desires." He made a brief gesture near his lap. "It's higher than in normal humans. You're not feeling it yet, because you're still healing. That's why you have to be in a safely sequestered place after the trial of Ishrai. To avoid . . . problems." He shook his head and rubbed his hands over his face. "I didn't want that to influence your decision. I made Acana promise not to tell you. She said I was being a fool."

"She was right," Alyea said tartly. "How *could* you have held that back?" Not giving him a chance to answer, she swung her legs over the side of the bed. She didn't want to be anywhere near him at the moment. "I'm going for a walk. Leave me alone."

The door was too light to slam properly, but she did her best.

She could still feel the eerie breathing sensation around her as she stormed through the passages of the fortress. It didn't frighten her any longer; at the moment, she doubted a nest of sand-asps in her path would have slowed her stride.

Obviously, he'd hoped for her to fall easily into his bed and never question it as anything other than true attraction to him. She never should have thought of trusting him.

That's not true, said a voice in her head. It sounded old, and oddly accented; and although nobody had mentioned this possibility, she knew the voice came from a ha'rethe.

She let her pace slow to half of what it had been, to avoid crashing into a wall while she sorted out how to talk to this thing. Tentatively, she focused a thought: *How do you know?*

It doesn't actually take much effort to speak to me, the creature said. *If you shout, someone else might hear you. There are several sensitive people here now. And I know because he asked me what to do. He's very attached to you; I find that surprising. Ha'ra'hain do not normally hold any human in high regard. This one prefers spending time among humans, and being involved in your politics and problems, which is admirable from a human point of view and rather useless from ours.*

A thoughtful pause followed. Alyea didn't try to speak, sensing it would be an interruption.

At last the voice resumed: *I have asked the young ha'ra'ha you call Idisio to look into some problems in the northlands. If you are willing to travel, I would like you to go with him. He is still very young, and needs guidance.*

Alyea stopped in the middle of a stride and stood balancing on one foot for a moment, her mouth hanging open. "Why me?"

You are, as you recently said, a desert lord without a family. You have no ties holding you to any lands. You are strong, and learn quickly, and can give the young one good guidance.

Alyea slowly lowered her foot to the ground and stood still, frowning at nothing. *I'm bound to Deiq for a year,* she said. *Does that mean he has to come along too?*

A young ha'ra'ha must have the guidance of an elder, either ha'rethe or ha'ra'ha. He will serve two purposes: teaching you, and teaching the young one. The arrangement has been paid for, and cannot be undone.

"Paid for?" she said aloud, startled.

The one you call Deiq paid the price for changing the arrangement. You cannot go to the Qisani or any other source of learning; you must learn from him.

"What was the price?" Speaking aloud seemed to work perfectly well; and at least this way she didn't worry about someone "sensitive" overhearing.

That is a question you must ask him. I will not answer.

She drew a deep breath. "All right. I'll go with Idisio to the northlands."

Thank you.

"You're welcome." She sighed and turned around to head back to her rooms.

Deiq stood several yards back, leaning against one wall, arms crossed. He watched her with an unapologetic, dark stare as she marched towards him.

"I told you to leave me alone," she said when she drew close.

"I did," he said. "I moved quietly and didn't speak to you. You didn't know I was here until you turned around."

"You said this place was safe. You could have let me walk unsupervised."

"No," he said without visible emotion. "My duty is to stay with you at all times. I shouldn't have let you be alone before, and I won't make that mistake again. When the ha'rethe was trying to talk to you about what happened with Pieas, you could have gone mad if I hadn't gotten there in time to explain what was happening. I neglected my responsibility. I won't do that twice."

She nodded, conceding the point.

"Do you want to keep walking?" he said. "I'll stay back out of your way, if you'd like to go on stomping around the halls."

She stiffened, started to snap at him, then once again found herself laughing. "It is a bit silly, isn't it?"

He nodded, a faint smile twitching the corners of his mouth.

"Is there somewhere to sit and talk?"

"There's a courtyard not far away," he said, and led the way.

The sweet scent of desert roses and the dry, dusty smell of desert palms filled the air. Gravel and sand crunched quietly underfoot. A cactus warbler fled from its shelter in a flowering shrub as they walked by.

The sun laid a dappled pattern on the ground, screened by the wide leaves arching far overhead; the only solid patch of light glittered on a shallow pool of water in the center of the courtyard. Alyea chose a bench by the pool and sat, Deiq settling down beside her without a word. She stared at the placid water for a while: remembering a cool, stone cavern and flickering oil-lamps, contrasting it with the warm, peaceful atmosphere here.

"What was the price for you to be my mentor instead of the Qisani ha'rethe?" she said finally.

Deiq made a small, pained noise. "I had to swear under the binding oaths of blood and fire to stay with you until your training was complete," he said. "*Only* with you. Do you understand?"

"Whether I share your bed or not?"

He snorted. "I should remember by now that tact isn't your strong point."

"We're well matched, then," she said, "because you can't seem to say anything straight out unless I twist your arm round twice." She couldn't help prodding that sore spot. "So you're willing to be celibate for a year?"

"You still don't understand," Deiq said. He picked up a small piece of gravel, rolled it into his palm, and clenched his fist around it. Alyea heard a faint crunching noise. Deiq slowly opened his hand to reveal several fragments.

Alyea realized she'd been holding her breath. She let it out in a long hiss.

Deiq tilted his hand and let the pieces fall to the ground. "You're still human," he told her. "You'll never get that strong—but bone's a lot softer than rock. And *you* won't be able to hold celibate for a year, once you heal."

Alyea shut her eyes, feeling ill.

"Restraint has to become as much a part of you as breathing," he said. "You have to *learn* that kind of restraint. Do I really need to explain further?"

"No," she said after a moment. "No, I don't think so." She stood and slowly paced around the courtyard. Deiq stayed on the bench and watched her, his expression pained.

"I know it won't help," he said, "but I'm sorry. I realized at the Qisani that I'd made a very bad mistake, pushing you into this. I let the politics of the human world and my own . . . feelings override the safety of a potential desert lord, and that's unforgivable."

She stopped at the edge of the pool and stared into the clear water for some time without speaking. A few wide-leafed water plants floated on the surface, and insects buzzed on translucent wings from flower to flower. No fish appeared, and she wondered absently if Scratha would be stocking the pool any time soon.

"The ha'rethe wants me to go north with Idisio," she said at last. "It wants to find out why the ha'ra'hain are meddling in human affairs. I agreed to go. You'll be teaching both of us."

"Thanks for consulting me before you made that decision," he said.

"As much as you ever consulted me," she shot back. She turned to face him. "Are you going or not?"

"I don't have much choice, if you've already agreed to a ha'rethe's task," he said. "It won't take kindly to my trying to refuse now."

She found herself grinning at him with no real amusement behind the expression. "Think of the trip as penance for your many mistakes. After all, if it weren't for you I wouldn't even be a desert lord, and you wouldn't have to tag my heels for the next year."

Deiq opened his mouth, looking indignant; then rose and moved to stand in front of her. "Alyea, you're stuck with me at your side, like it or not."

His tone turned harsh and cold. Alyea forced herself not to flinch at the change.

"Done is done. Let go of what was and look at right now. I can't teach you anything if you're fighting me. If you want to walk away after I'm done, I won't stop you. But damned if I'll let you walk without properly training you. Let me do my job, even the parts you may not like."

He paused, studying her. She stared back at him, caught between anger and astonishment.

"And if I'm lucky," he went on more softly, "you'll forgive me when I'm through, and think more kindly of me. But if not, at least I'll have trained another desert lord, and a damned good one at that. I'll consider that enough."

Her anger had drained away by the time he finished speaking, and she felt a surge of compassion for him. In love for the first time in a long life, but forced by his own errors in judgment to hold himself at an emotional distance; he would be miserable no matter what she did.

She suddenly found herself with a new awareness and respect for Deiq's willpower. Accepting Oruen's rejection had been terribly difficult for her, and she'd never questioned her subordinate status. How much worse must the coming months look to the proud ha'ra'ha? By agreeing to travel north without consulting Deiq on the matter, she'd just forced him to follow *her* lead, not the other way around.

"I'm sorry," she said, and meant it.

He nodded. With a brisk gesture as though to say: *let's move on to more important things*, he said, "There's a banquet tonight. I've asked for us to be seated at the lower end of the table, away from Lord Scratha."

She considered that. The placement made a certain amount of sense. Lord Scratha wouldn't want her near his hand to remind him that his guests had tried to put an easily controlled usurper in his place.

"Lords Evkit and Rowe of Sessin," Deiq said, "will be seated below us, at the very end."

Alyea nodded slowly. That made sense, too, although she didn't look forward to conversing with either one.

"I suggest," Deiq said, stressing the word only slightly, "that you avoid antagonizing either man. I think Lord Scratha would appreciate that."

"I was thinking the same thing," Alyea said.

"Lord Evkit respects you," Deiq said. "I suggest you cultivate that. Lord Rowe will follow Evkit's lead."

"How?"

"You're resourceful, creative, and strong-willed," Deiq said with only the faintest trace of irony. "I'm sure you'll find a way."

Chapter Twenty-Seven

"Riss is pregnant."

Cafad shrugged and turned another page. Someone had carefully wiped the table and shelves of the library free of dust, and the room felt indefinably more awake, more alive; a faint smell of oranges and cinnamon hung in the air.

The book Cafad studied didn't look like the same one Idisio had "found" for him; this one bulked twice as thick and much broader across, occupying a good third of the large table. Idisio eyed the book with respectful envy, knowing the words within likely stood far beyond his still-developing skills to interpret.

There hadn't been much chance to practice of late.

"You knew?" Idisio said, looking back to Cafad.

"Of course I knew," Cafad said. "I told her it was likely, given the timing." He sighed and straightened, rubbing his neck.

"What timing?"

Cafad gave Idisio a long, level stare. "Her moon cycle, Idisio."

Idisio felt his face heat rapidly to crimson embarrassment. "Oh. You asked her about—? I mean. . . ." He bit his tongue to stop more inanities from emerging.

The desert lord shook his head, looking amused.

"I'm going north," Idisio blurted, suddenly desperate to change the subject.

Cafad tilted an eyebrow expressively.

"—oh. You know that too?"

"Yes. Lord Alyea and Deiq will be traveling with you."

"Oh."

"Riss will stay here."

Idisio opened and closed his mouth a few times, finally managing: "Oh. Good." The last word came out sounding far too much like a question.

"I have a favor to ask." Cafad pointed to a nearby chair. "Please. Sit."

Idisio pulled the chair around and sat, then tried to duplicate the eyebrow twitch the desert lord used when waiting for someone to speak. Cafad smiled. Many of the wear lines on the man's face seemed to have smoothed out over the past few hours, as if a tremendous strain had been released. Now he *looked* twenty-eight, instead of forty-eight.

"I want you to take a letter to the king when you leave."

"All right." Idisio didn't relish the thought of facing King Oruen again, without Scratha's direct presence as backing. He chewed the inside of one cheek and tried to tell himself he'd handle that audience with dignity and confidence.

He almost had himself convinced when Scratha said, "I also want you to take over as King's Researcher."

Idisio's jaw dropped open. "You *what?*"

"I can't leave the grounds any longer," Cafad said. "Being fully bound apparently has a drawback: since the ha'rethe can't protect me from a distance, it won't let me leave the area. The research assignment, even though it was meant to get me out of the way, actually does need doing. I'd be grateful if you'd carry it through for me. You can even take the name I chose to travel under if you like, to keep the appearance of obedience alive. No reason to annoy the king by making him look a fool."

Idisio stared at the desert lord, unable to think of anything coherent to say. "I can't even write," he said finally.

"You're learning fast," Cafad said. "Deiq and Alyea can continue teaching you."

"But," Idisio started, then shook his head helplessly.

"Will you do it?"

Idisio couldn't think of any reason to refuse. "Yes," he said, wishing he could justify a *no*.

"Thank you." Cafad looked back at the book. "Is there anything else you want to talk to me about?"

"Um," Idisio said. "Riss is staying?"

"She's pregnant," Cafad said without looking up. "It's not safe for her to travel with you."

"Does she know that she's staying?"

"Not yet," Cafad said. "She doesn't know you're leaving, either. Do you want me to tell her?"

Idisio really wished he could say *yes* to that question. "No. I'd better do it. Thanks for offering."

"Mm-hnn." Cafad glanced up, his expression politely blank. "Anything else?"

Idisio shook his head, sighed, and left the room.

"You're *what*?" Riss said not long after that. "I'm going."

"No," Idisio said, forcing himself to meet her eyes directly. "You're staying. Lord Scratha's orders."

"I'm not his slave! He can't tell me what to—" She stopped, her gaze suddenly unfocused. "Why?"

She seemed to be addressing the air around her. Idisio shut his eyes and grimaced.

"But," she said after a few moments. "He can't. . . ." She fell silent again, frowning. "Oh, all right." She looked at Idisio.

"The ha'rethe?" he guessed.

"Yes." She stood and paced the room, her steps jerky and restless, then moved to stand in front of him. "All right. I'll stay, and you'll go. But you'll come back."

It sounded like an order.

"Yes," he said. "As soon as I can."

"Fine." She turned her back on him. "Go away. I want to be alone."

Idisio stood, drew a deep breath, and walked towards her instead. He put his hands on her taut shoulders from behind.

"Riss," he said into her ear. She didn't move.

He summoned all his courage, heart pounding in his throat, and put his arms around her waist. He let his hands rest over her stomach and his forehead against the back of her head.

She didn't push him away, but she didn't move, either.

"I didn't want this," she said after a while.

This could have meant anything. Idisio said nothing, hoping she'd clarify without a prompt.

"I wanted to go traveling," she went on. "I wanted to see the world. Now I'm stuck. Just like I was always afraid of."

She shifted her weight; he let go, not wanting her to feel trapped. She turned to face him.

"You're not stuck," he said.

"I can't travel."

"Just because you're not going with me doesn't mean you're not allowed to go anywhere," Idisio said. "Lord Scratha needs to arrange alliances with the other desert families."

"Lord Alyea would be better at that than I would."

"She's going to Arason with Deiq."

Her eyes narrowed. "And with you."

"Well, yes." He squinted at her, baffled by why that should matter.

She considered, then shook her head as though to let that issue go and said, "You really think Lord Scratha will let me travel locally?"

"I think he'll make you his ambassador," Idisio said, "and train you up to the job. He doesn't have many people with your kind of brains right now."

He felt rather proud of himself for sneaking in the compliment. He hadn't even stuttered.

"True," she said, and smiled.

It abruptly occurred to him that he stood far too close to that smile, with no obscuring door between them. He swallowed words that would have sounded inane and backed away a step, his stomach tightening.

She reached out and grabbed his upper arms. He froze, caught between impulses, not sure whether to run or move forward. She solved the impasse by putting herself right up against him.

"I want you to come back," she said.

"I will—"

"I'm going to make sure you do."

"Isn't that a little dramat—"

One of her hands shifted distinctly downward.

"*Uh.*"

She smiled and pressed herself even closer, sliding her other hand down his back. "What were you going to say?"

With the last of his coherency, he managed to gasp, "Never mind."

"Thought so."

The great hall of Scratha Fortress echoed with the chatter and movement of the guests and servants. A caravan had arrived, to Idisio's surprise, with a large load of supplies; but as Cafad hadn't been at all startled, Idisio decided that the caravan had been part of the "arrangements" the desert lord made during their travels.

Even so, the feast had been drawn mainly from the supplies of the visitors rather than those of Scratha Fortress, and the dining-hall servants wore the colors and symbols of several different Families, not one; but the gathering turned out no less festive for those small details.

Idisio sat, rather uncomfortably, by Lord Scratha's left hand. He hadn't expected to be placed at the seat of highest honor. Gria smiled at him across the table, seeming perfectly content with her secondary status at the desert lord's right hand, and went on talking to Riss, who had been seated beside her.

Riss, for her part, was happier than Idisio could ever recall seeing her before. Her pale hair had been expertly braided into a ring on top of her head; Idisio had always thought that style silly, but somehow it looked just right on her. Someone had given her a dress of light blue fabric that almost slithered across the curves of her body when she moved.

Several servants had turned to stare already, and Idisio watched, out of the corner of one eye, the occasional quiet argument over who brought Riss her dishes and refilled her water cup.

Idisio couldn't help remembering the sweaty, irritable stable hand she'd been not so long ago, and shook his head at the contrast between then and now. He found himself wishing she'd remained that hard-edged person. It would have been easier to leave her behind.

Lady Azaniari—she refused to allow anyone to call her *Lord*—patted his hand. "You seem unhappy about something," she said.

He searched hastily for a reason that wouldn't be too humiliating to admit. "You should be sitting here. Not me."

"I had to twist her arm," Cafad said, "to get her that close. And she only agreed because I said she could sit next to you."

"That's not polite, Cafad," Azni chided him, leaning forward slightly to look around Idisio at the desert lord. "Idisio wasn't speaking to you."

"Would you have said anything different?"

"No," she said, and laughed. "Not really."

He grinned and turned his attention to the girls at his right. Idisio watched as the tall man deftly slid into their conversation, pulled their attention away from chattering only to each other, and maneuvered them into talking to people further down the table.

"Amazing," he said under his breath.

"It's in his blood," Azni said quietly, her expression more pensive now. "You should have met the previous Lord Scratha; the man could make a stick agree to jump into fire—and the fire not to burn it."

"Lord Scratha—this one, I mean—didn't show any of that when I first met him," Idisio said.

"Call him Cafad," Azni advised. "You've certainly earned the right, even in most public situations. And I certainly won't be offended by it." She paused, seeming lost in thought for a moment, then went on, "But you're right: he's been a very bitter, angry man for a long time." She dropped her voice, leaning in closer to Idisio. "It's difficult to be charming when you've been hurt as badly as he has. I think Nissa was the first person who ever really touched his heart."

"I'm surprised she's not here," he murmured with a glance down to the end of the table, where Lord Rowe of Sessin Family sat across from Lord Evkit. Not places of honor, exactly, but at least they both sat at the main table. Neither seemed displeased, although Idisio noted that Lord Evkit tended to avoid looking in Cafad's direction.

"A Conclave isn't the place to sort that out," she told him. "It's enough that he's allowed a Sessin onto the grounds. More would be pushing tolerance right now. And Gria has to come first, in any case."

Idisio watched the girls across from him for a few moments, covering his silence with several bites of roast vegetables. Cafad had managed to start Riss talking to others and pulled Gria's attention to himself; he mostly listened, his dark eyes intent on her thin face as she rattled on. Now and again, when she gestured, Idisio could see the thick bandages on her wrists, mostly hidden beneath the long, dark sleeves of her dress.

"She'll always have the scars," Lady Azaniari said very quietly. "I'm surprised she's even on her feet. She must be in tremendous pain; the cuffs only came off hours ago."

Gria's eyes did have a vaguely fevered sparkle to them, now that Idisio looked for it, and her face shaded towards ash-pale at times. A quick glance around showed no sign of Sela.

"She's Scratha, all right," Azni sighed. "She's got that stubborn blood. Well, at least he's keeping an eye on her. He won't let her faint at the table."

Servants began clearing away dinner plates. One reached for Riss's plate; she thanked him with a bright smile. The servant beamed, then almost dropped the dish as he hastily retreated. She hardly seemed to notice, turning her attention back to her interrupted conversation.

"Riss will make a good ambassador," Azni said, following his gaze. "I'll have my hands full training her, but she'll do well in the end."

"You're staying?"

She nodded, her gaze still on Riss. "Cafad asked me to train Riss. And I'll be setting up a proper staff to take care of the place again." She sighed and looked around the room. "I've missed the desert more than I thought I would."

"Why did you leave?" Idisio asked, unable to resist. "I mean, you're a desert lord. If you don't mind saying."

Servers threaded around the tables, distributing small plates of fruit. Azni smiled at her server and thanked him in a low voice; he grinned, winked, and slid an extra piece of fruit onto her plate.

Azni waited until the servers had moved further down the table before answering Idisio's question.

"I was very young when I decided to become a desert lord," she said finally. "I chose that path for a bad reason: a broken heart."

Her gaze misted. Idisio began to wish he hadn't asked; he suspected this tale would turn out maudlin or soppy.

"I was very young," she repeated, and sighed. "I came up second on a random draw for the trials that year; the first supplicant. . . . didn't make it." She looked down at the fruit on her plate, nudging it absently with one finger. "He was the boy I'd been in love with."

Idisio stared at his plate, ashamed of his initial, condescending expectations. Under the haze of embarrassment, the fruit didn't look nearly as appetizing as it had a moment ago.

"I'm sorry," he said.

"Oh, it was a lifetime ago," Azni said. She shook her head, long metal earrings chinkling, and offered him a wry smile. "A lifetime, and yesterday. I fell in love again, of course, with Lord Regav Darden. We were both young, and idealistic, and decided to heal the breach between the northlands and the southlands. It didn't work very well."

She sighed. "We probably made everything worse, in fact, with our attempts to force order onto chaos. Regav died. . . ." She shook her head, her gaze distant again. "I couldn't stand being around the memories, so I moved north, hoping to gain some peace. That didn't work very well, either, but I'm not as angry as I used to be. I see my own mistakes now."

"It's hard to believe you were ever angry," Idisio said.

She smiled and picked up a piece of melon. "Cafad's been a welcome distraction from my brooding over the past few years. Mm, this is good."

Idisio allowed himself to be steered into a discussion of the food and from there into general talk of trade. That subject quickly involved people further down the table, and he didn't have much to contribute at that point, so he mostly watched Riss. She had quieted down and seemed to be doing more listening than talking now. Every so often she glanced up and met his eyes for a moment, adding a smile that caught his breath.

Servants cleared away the fruit plates and distributed small cups filled with a black liquid. The smell had an unfamiliar, acrid tang; Idisio stared at his cup doubtfully, then glanced to Azni for guidance. She lifted her cup, grinned at him merrily, and drained it in one gulp.

Idisio raised his cup; Cafad's strong fingers closed around his wrist.

"You've never had desert coffee before, have you?"

"No," Idisio admitted.

"I'd rather not have Riss and Gria covered in spray. Take a sip first."

Idisio glanced at the two girls, who watched him with open amusement and displayed their empty cups.

"Trust me," Cafad said, and released his grip. "Slow sip."

Idisio sipped cautiously. The bitter, hot liquid tasted like a mouthful of liquid ash.

Cafad reached to a nearby bowl of suka crystals and dumped a large spoonful into the small cup. The liquid inside almost overflowed at the addition.

"Stir that for a moment," Cafad said, "and try it again."

Now the coffee tasted like sweet liquid ash. Idisio shook his head and set the small cup aside. "I'm sorry," he said, "I think I'll pass."

Cafad shook his head, grinning. "You can't. It's traditional courtesy. Everyone has to drink the whole cup. Go on, toss it down."

Idisio shut his eyes and gulped the two mouthfuls in the cup. It took all his willpower to keep his mouth shut instead of spitting the harsh liquid back out.

A cheer went up, and several people started banging their cups on the table.

"What's going on now?" Idisio muttered to Azni. She rapped the table sharply with her cup and grinned at him.

"Tradition," she said, so he followed suit, a bit uncomfortable with the clamor.

Servants returned and began filling cups again. He tried to pull his away; Azni trapped his hand.

"Oh, no," she said, still grinning like a maniac. "You hit the table with your cup! That means you want more."

"Oh, gods, no," he said, his eyes widening. "One was plenty!"

"Well, it's full now," she said as the servant moved away, "so you have to drink it. It's rude to refuse a full cup."

By one strategy or another, his cup was refilled four more times. Each time it tasted less bitter, and seemed to pick up a new flavor. The second cup tasted of oranges, the third like roasted nuts. The fourth had a distinctly minty taste, and the fifth reminded him of berries.

"This issn' so bad," Idisio said finally, and stared as Cafad let out a roar of laughter.

"Whazzo funny?" He couldn't understand why he'd slurred such a simple sentence: *slurring a simple sentence,* he thought, and let out a braying snort of laughter at the way the words tangled together in his mind.

"It's a drinking contest. Each cup has more hard liquor and less coffee," Azni said in his ear. "I expect you'll be hitting the floor soon."

"Huh?" He began to form the protest: *Why would I hit the floor, it hasn't done anything to me*; realized he couldn't even slur such a complicated sentence right now; and slid out of his chair with another loud, snorting laugh at his own incompetence. A moment after that, the world went sharply away.

Just before everything blacked out completely, he thought he heard a tiny voice sigh, *Humans*.

"That was mean," Idisio moaned the next day, when the headache had faded enough to allow him to open his eyes and glare accusingly.

Riss draped a cool cloth over his face, ruining the effect. She didn't say anything, but she'd been smiling before the cloth blocked his vision.

"Why didn't you say anything?" he demanded, pushing the damp towel away.

She pulled it back into place. "I thought you knew the game. Gods, I grew up with it. We used strong tea, not coffee, but the notion's the same. I figured you understood what they were doing."

"I didn't," he said.

"Well, now you do," she said prosaically. "You've got a surprising tolerance, you know. By the time you went down there were only three other people left: Lord Alyea, Lord Evkit, and Lord Irrio."

"Who won?"

"Lord Alyea, actually. At seven cups, Lord Evkit was the last challenger. He went down and she was still smiling. I think Deiq was keeping her in a straight line on their way out, though."

"Surprised Deiq didn't win," Idisio muttered.

"Deiq wasn't drinking," she told him. "Neither was Lord Scratha, past the first two cups."

"Of course he was," Idisio said, and pushed the cloth away. He squinted at her. "I saw him!"

"He faked it, to keep you going," Riss said patiently. "You weren't seeing too clearly past the third cup, anyway."

He shut his eyes and groaned as the headache returned.

"You need to rest. Conclave starts at nightfall, and you're expected to attend. It's just past dawn now. Cafad said to make you spend most of today in bed." Riss took the cloth; the sound of her dunking it in a nearby bucket of water crackled in his hyper-sensitive ears. She wrung it out and draped the cool towel over his face again.

"If it's any consolation, I think you earned some respect, lasting through five cups."

"It's not."

"I didn't really think it would be."

Chapter Twenty-Eight

"A *drinking contest?*"

Alyea shrugged and took another sip of hot coffee. Unlike the harsh, black brew from the night before, this had been sweetened and milk of some sort added, making this cup much more palatable than the after-dinner version. She tried not to think about where the milk had come from, given the distinct lack of cows anywhere nearby and the goats penned outside the fortress.

Alyea knew southerners considered goat milk an everyday staple, but her mother had pronounced it "filthy" and refused to allow it into her household. Alyea had never questioned that belief before, and the notion of drinking it roiled her stomach.

Then again, my stomach upset might come from last night, she admitted to herself, and took another sip of coffee.

"A drinking contest!"

She gave up trying to ignore him. "It worked."

Deiq shook his head and took another turn around the room, which began to seem far too small to contain his nervous energy. "It's my own fault. I shouldn't have told you to be creative. And gods, Scratha's a lunatic, getting Idisio drunk! At least that sort of madness I expect from humans. But *you*—I didn't think you'd try to outdrink Lord Evkit!"

"Stop fussing so much," she said, and shut her eyes. The mug felt warm against her palms; she turned it gently, the rough clay scratching lightly across her skin. "Like I said, it worked. I don't even have a hangover."

Which wasn't strictly true; a nasty, tingly pain shot temple-to-temple every so often, and she really wished he'd lower his voice. But compared to what she'd seen of other people's day-afters, the headache hardly qualified as a hangover.

She idly wondered if Idisio had woken in better—or worse—shape.

"Did you expect to win?" Deiq demanded.

She opened her eyes and found him standing in front of her, scowling.

"No," she admitted. "I thought I'd manage a decent showing, enough to gain points for trying."

He stared at her. "You don't have any idea, do you? *Nobody* has put Lord Evkit under the table in more years than you've been alive."

"Well, now the record's broken." She couldn't understand what had him so upset.

"Is it?" he said. "How much help did you have?"

She blinked at him, startled. "What?"

"The ha'rethe of this place," he said. "How much did it help you?"

"It *didn't*," she said, offended. "Do you think I'd cheat?"

"I think *it* would, if it saw a good advantage. What I don't understand is why." He went back to pacing.

"As far as I know," she said, frowning at him, "I didn't have any help. I certainly didn't ask for it!"

"Lord Evkit is teyanin. He could have tossed down twice that much desert lightning without folding," he said, turning to face her again. "You've never had it before. You're not a big drinker, from what I've seen. How is it possible that you won that contest?"

"Desert lightning? Same thing as what Bright Bay calls 'white lightning'?"

He made an impatient gesture.

"I'm a desert lord," she said, taking that as agreement. "You said yourself I'm changing."

"So is Evkit. He should have been good for another several rounds."

She shrugged, exasperated. "I don't know, Deiq. Quit hammering at me already, would you? Go ask the man yourself. Maybe *he* faked the fold. Gods only know why he would," she added, cutting off his next words. "Go bother him about it, if it worries you so much. I'll stay right here and drink my coffee and finish waking up in *peace*."

They glared at each other.

"You're going to make this a very long year," Alyea said levelly over the rim of her cup, "if you don't loosen up a bit."

Deiq's scowl deepened for a moment, then slowly eased just a little. "Consider it penance for all your sins."

Alyea sighed, seeing only one possible answer to that.

"I will," she said, and went back to ignoring him.

Chapter Twenty-Nine

"You sent for me—" Idisio discovered he couldn't say 'Cafad' as though they'd become equals. Not just yet. He stuttered a moment, then finished, "—my lord?"

"Call me Cafad," Scratha said, waving Idisio into the library. "I'm not your lord any longer. You're earned the right."

Idisio let out a long breath, not sure whether to feel relieved, proud, or nervous. He settled on vague apprehension. From street thief to noble: he'd long dreamed of such a transition but still couldn't consistently grasp the reality of his new life. He often found himself strutting as confidently as as a chachad bird, then falling sharply into a fit of nervous tremors, terrified that this would all turn out to be a lie, or a joke, or a terrible misunderstanding.

"I thought you'd like to see this," Cafad said, holding out a rolled piece of parchment. "Bird just came in."

Idisio sat on the edge of a chair and unrolled the message, flattening it carefully on the wide table. He absently pulled a large book from a nearby stack to pin down the top edge of the parchment, and frowned, lips moving, as he struggled to decipher the crabbed writing. The writer seemed to have intended to cram twenty letters to the inch, and very nearly succeeded.

He read aloud: "To Lord Scratha of Scratha Fortress, greetings and—"

"You can skip the first four lines," Cafad interrupted. "It's all formal nonsense. Scribes always add in a lot of silly wording if any rank is involved."

"Oh." Idisio counted down carefully and squinted at the fifth line. ". . . in regards to the inquiries you sent me on, to investigate and determine. . . ." Idisio paused as Cafad gave a dry snort.

"The scribe again," Cafad said. "I imagine he actually said something like: *Thanks for the tip, I found what I was looking for.*"

"Who?" Idisio said, bewildered, and glanced at the end of the letter. His heart skipped a beat as he made out the scrawled, sloppy signature at the same time Cafad answered.

"Red, of course. He's found his son."

"That's great!" Idisio said, grinning broadly.

"Yes. Why don't you read the rest of the letter? It ought to give you some good practice." He returned his attention to the book he'd been reading.

Idisio hesitated. "My lord?"

"Mm?" Cafad didn't look up.

"Why are you in the library reading? I mean . . . there's Conclave tonight, and a lot of desert lords waiting around, and . . . I just thought you'd be. . . ." He shrugged.

"Socializing?" Cafad put a long finger on the page, marking his place, and looked up. "Lady Azni is handling the hosting duties for me at the moment. I have research I need to do before Conclave starts."

Idisio eyed the stack of books at Cafad's left hand. "That's a lot of reading."

"Good thing I'm a fast reader, then," the desert lord said, and resumed reading.

Idisio watched the man scanning lines for a moment, then let out a very quiet sigh and returned his own attention to the letter.

After a while he said, "Um . . . my lord?"

"Yes?"

"Do I understand this right? Red's son was taken in by. . . ." He squinted at the writing, which now looked as if the scribe, in a sudden spasm of excitement, had tried to cram thirty letters into an inch.

"The Aerthraim," Cafad said without looking up. "Yes."

"Lady Azaniari's Family?"

"Yes."

Idisio read on, frowning now. "They've *adopted* him?"

"Yes."

He worked his way through a few more sentences, sorting out the sailor's "voice" underneath the scribe's posturing.

"And Red's all right with that," he said under his breath.

"It's a far better life than he could ever give the boy," Scratha said.

"But. . . ." Idisio reread two lines to make sure he understood them. "He doesn't even know his father went hunting for him! Shouldn't he at least know that, and have the choice?"

"No."

"But—"

Cafad looked up, not bothering to mark his place this time. He met Idisio's gaze directly and said, "Idisio, understand this: Red is a randy northern sailor with a lady in every port, and if those women are as dense as his Yhaine, more children as well. He has no home, no family, no life outside the ship's ways. He's old enough to be set in his habits and smart enough to know that. Having the Aerthraim find his son first and adopt the boy as one of their own was a pure blessing from all the gods you care to name. Red probably went out after sending that letter and got himself smashingly drunk out of relief."

Idisio said nothing. He stared down at the letter, not really seeing it. "He should at least know his father *tried*," he muttered.

Cafad sighed. "What difference would it really make? Would it erase the years he spent in dark places? Would it make them hurt less—or more? Think about it. His father probably passed through the port where his son was born many times over the last years, and never . . . once . . . thought . . . about . . . Yhaine. Never once tried to see her. Forgot all about her, in fact, until his chance encounter with an old friend. You tell me what would hurt the boy more; not knowing that his father tried—or knowing that his father never tried?"

Idisio wiped at his damp eyes. "All right. I see what you're saying. All right."

"Red's not a bad man," Cafad went on. "He was genuinely upset about his son when I spoke to him. But he's no father."

They sat in silence for a few moments.

"Idisio," Cafad said, "when you get to Arason—"

"I know. My father." He swallowed and looked away. "I've thought about it already."

"I'm not surprised."

"You were talking about me just now, too, weren't you?" Idisio said, still staring at a bookshelf to his left.

"Arason was a very troubled place back then, and still is, I think."

Idisio scrunched his eyes tightly shut. He didn't want to see Cafad's expression, even out of the corner of his eye. "Can you imagine Deiq ever letting Lady Alyea run away with their child?"

Cafad's chair creaked as he leaned back.

"Idisio," he said, "learn from Deiq. Don't idolize him. And don't judge your . . . father until you hear his story. The world isn't a simple place, and people are complicated. If anything, ha'reye are even more so." He paused, then added, "And for all the gods' sakes, *don't* repeat that thought about Deiq and Alyea to *anyone*, do you hear me? You *have* to learn to guard your thoughts. You're among people now who will hear those as clearly as spoken words if you're careless."

"Yes, my lord," Idisio said reflexively.

"Stop that. I'm not your lord any more. Feelings like love are a vulnerability that first-generation ha'ra'hain do *not* have," Cafad said. "Ever. For anyone. Understood?"

Idisio looked into the desert lord's fierce, worried stare and nodded without speaking.

"Good," Cafad said, seeming to relax. He looked down at his book and turned the page. "Now leave me, please. I have a lot of reading to do."

Idisio rose, then hesitated.

"Lord Scratha, thank you," he said in a rush. "I owe you—"

"Nothing," the desert lord cut in, not looking up. "Absolutely nothing. You're a ha'ra'ha. Gratitude to a human is beneath you."

Idisio stood still, shocked.

"Gods, I hope not," he said without thinking.

Cafad sat back, looking at Idisio steadily, and pursed his lips. At last he said, "Welcome to your new world, Idisio. Now please go, and let me get used to mine."

The desert lord flicked a hand in clear dismissal, and Idisio left the room. As he walked through the empty hallways, he listened to the sound of his own footsteps; and in the echoes, he thought he heard a sound, soft but distinct: *shass-shass-shass*.

The warning shout of servants clearing a path for their noble masters.

"Clear the road," Idisio muttered, and sighed. "But what do you do once it's clear?"

After thinking about it for some time, he decided to go ask Riss.

Secrets of the Sands

Glossary and Pronunciation Guide

A number of the words in the southern language include the glottal-stop, which is rendered here as ^. A glottal stop involves closing, to some degree, the back of the throat, resulting in a near-coughing sound when released. Sometimes this sounds as though a hard "H" has been inserted.

Aqeyva (ack-**ee**-vah, alt. ahh-**keh**-vah): A combination of martial-arts training and meditation disciplines. The combat training is often referred to as a 'dance' as it involves smooth, flowing motions that have no apparent resemblance to any fighting mode.

Asp-jacau (**asp**-jack-**how**): A slender canine with long, thin snout and legs. Its short-haired coat tends toward fawn or brindle coloring. Its excellent sense of smell is primarily used to detect dangerous snakes and (in some cases) drugs. In Bright Bay, only royalty or King's Guard patrols may own an asp-jacau, but below the Horn the asp-jacau is a common companion animal.

Callen (**call**-en): One sworn to the service of a southern god.

Comisti (cohm-**mist**-ee): Criminal working out his/her punishment through service to the god Comos.

Comos (**Cohm**-ohs): One of three gods honored in the southlands. Represents the neutrality/balance/questioning energies; also linked to the season of winter, the colors white and brown, and curiosity. Callen of Comos, if male, must be castrated; women must be past menopause to be allowed out in the world at large.

Datda (**Dat**-dah): One of three gods honored in the southlands, Datda represents the negative/death/change energies; also linked to the season of high summer, the colors red and black, and the emotion of anger. Commonly called "the Sun Lord"; saying the name aloud is held to be bad luck. Only Datda's Callen may safely pronounce the holy name, but they tend to be reluctant to advertise their affiliation; everyone knows that most Callen of Datda have trained extensively as assassins and spies.

Dathedain (**dath**-heh-**dane**): Followers of the god Datda.

Dista (**diss**-tah): Southern term for *mistress;* implying a dishonorable arrangement or a woman without honor.

Esthit (**ess**-thitt): A drug.

Ferahd (fheh-**rahhd**): Illegitimate child, implications of dishonor on the part of the mother.

Ha'ra'ha (hah-**^rah**-^hah); plural **ha'ra'hain** (hah-^rah-^**hayn**): Person of mixed blood (human and ha'rethe).

Ha'ra'hain (hah-^rah-^**hayn**): Plural of **ha'ra'ha**.

Ha'rai'nain (hah-^ray-^**nayn**): Plural of **ha'rai'nin**.

Ha'rai'nin (hah-**^ray-^**nin); plural **ha'rai'nain** (hah-^ray-^**nayn**): One who has dedicated his or her life to serving the ha'reye.

Ha'rethe (hah-**^reth-**ay); plural **ha'reye** (hah-**^ray**): Lit. translation: *golden eyes*. An ancient race, predating humanity.

Ha'reye (hah-**^ray**): Plural of **ha'rethe**.

Hayrar (**hay**-rahr): Southern term for *judge*.

Hee-ay, hee-ay (**hee**-ayyy): Lit. translation: *Hey! Water! Hey! Water!* Common water-seller's cry.

Iiii, iii-sass, iii-sass (**eeee, eeee**-sahhhh, **eeee**-sahhhh): Rough translation: *My woman would castrate me!* A typical exaggerated protest by a merchant about lowering the price of his wares.

Ish (**isshh**): Prefix indicating feminine/female aspects.

Ish-tchiki, ha'rethe esse chaka (issh-**chick**-ee, hah-**^reth-**hay esss **chack**-ka): Lit. translation: *I gave of myself to a ha'rethe and it granted me a boon.*

Ishai-s'a (ishh-**ai**-ss-**^ah**): Lit. translation: *sister under Ishrai;* implies shared service to or understanding of the god Ishrai.

Ishell (ishh-**ell**): A room in which women worship.

Ishrai (**Ish**-wry): One of the three gods honored in the southlands; represents the positive/feminine/birth energies. She is also connected to the season of spring, the color green, and the emotion of love.

Ishraidain (ishh-wry-**dane**): Women serving penance for various crimes, under the protection of Ishrai.

Ishrait (ishh-**rate**): High priestess of Ishrai.

Justice-right: The right of a desert lord to intervene in a situation and see it resolved according to his own opinion of justice.

Ka (**kah**): Honored (generic term).

Ka-s'a (**kah**-ss-**^ah**): Honored lady (generic term).

Ka-s'eias (**kah**-ss-**^ey**-as): Honored (mixed gender) group (generic term).

Kaen (**kay-en**): Honored leader/supreme authority.

Ke (**keh**): Prefix or suffix indicating masculine/male aspects.

Ketarch (**kee**-tarsch): Organized groups of healers in the south who focus on preserving old healing lore and researching new ways of healing.

Mac'egas (mack-**^ayy**-gahs): Slaves.

Machago (mah-**chahh**-go): Slavemaster.

Micru (mick-**rue**): Rough translation: *small death;* a small, black and tan striped viper found in rocky desert areas, whose poison is instantly fatal to large animals. Also the call-name of a member of the Hidden Cadre.

Nu-s'e (**noo**-ss-**^eh**): Honored man of the south; generic honorific in the absence of specific indicators.

Perroc-s'etta (**pay**-roke-ss-**^et**-tah): Fermented cactus "milk".

Perocce (pay-**roach**-ay): A kind of cactus, one that is used as a source of water by desert travelers.

Qisani (key-**sahn**-nee): A rocky cavern in the southern desert, which was given, under a Conclave decision, to the Callen of Ishrai many years ago as a haven of their own. All the desert Families contribute to supporting the Qisani. The followers of Datda and Comos also have central havens, but they are more secretive about the locations. Blood trials conducted at any of the havens are considered the hardest of all possible.

S'a / S'e / S'ieas / S'ii: Respectful address designators, analogous to *sir* and *madam*; specific to gender, and frequently parts of complex and highly specific expressions of relationship between the speaker and the person being addressed.

> **S'a** (ss-^**ah**): feminine
>
> **S'e** (ss-^**eh**): masculine
>
> **S'ieas** (ss-^**eh**-ahs): a group of mixed gender
>
> **S'ii** (ss-^**ee**): neuter; generally used to address a eunuch.

S'a-ke (ss-**^ah**-kay): Familiar *mother's-brother*.

S'ai-keia (ss-**^ayy**-key-ah): Roughly, *sister's-child;* used only to address children less than a year old. Used against adults as an insult to suggest the person addressed is behaving like a child.

S'e deaneat (ss-**^eh** day-**ah**-nit): Lit. translation: *male of a desert family.* Usually inferred as 'son of'.

S'e-ketan / S'a-ketan (ss-**^eh**-keh-tan / ss-**^ah**-keh-tan): A complex relationship designation. The rough translation is *uncle: father's side/mother's side*, but depending on inflection and surrounding modifiers, it can indicate status, legitimacy, and even bloodline. *Aunt* would be *s'e-katan* (father's side) or *s'a-katan* (mother's side). To add a little more confusion, the casual use or slang cuts the last few letters off, resulting in *s'a-ke, s'a-ka,* and so on.

S'a-nashan-kai (ss^**eh-**nah-shan-kai): Mother's-side cousin, twice removed.

S'e-netan / S'a-netan (ss-**^ehh**-neh-tan, ss-**^ahh**-neh-tan): Another complex relationship designation. The rough translation is *grandfather*, but depending on inflection and surrounding modifiers, it can indicate status, legitimacy, and even bloodline.

S'iope (s-**^igh-o**-pay): Lit. translation: *beloved of the gods;* implications of being neuter, all energy devoted to the gods. Term used to refer to the priests of the Northern Church. Disrespectful nickname: soapy.

Sa'adenit (sah-**^ad**-den-nit): Rough translation: *blood of the sand*. Some sages claim it should read *blood* ***on*** *the sand*. It comes from a very old song about blood-feud and vengeance.

Saishe-pais (**say**-shh-**paws**; alt. **say**-she-**pays**): An expression of heartfelt gratitude, indicating that the one so addressed has shown great honor in his/her actions.

Sessii ta-karne, I shha (sessy tah-**carney**, ee shh-**ha**): Rough translation: *You noxious, useless (castrated) little prick*!

Se'thiss, t'a-karnain (sehh-^this, tah-**^ah**-kar-**nayn**): Rough translation: *beloved child of the northern relatives.*

Shall (shawl): A temporary, portable desert shelter.

Shass-shass (shaass-shaass): Lit. translation: *move, move!* Used by superiors to inferiors.

Sheth-hinn (shethh-**hnn**): Assassin.

Su-s'a (sue-ss-**^ah**): Northern lady.

Ta (tah): Prefix implying masculine aspects; usually involved in insults (see ta'karne).

Ta-karne (tah-**carn**-ay): Insult. Rough translation: *asshole.*

Taishell te s'a-lalien (tie-shell **teh** ss-**^ah-lahh**-lee-en): Lit. translation: *This woman has emptied herself/has no more to give you now.*

Taishell te s'a-naila (tie-shell **teh** ss-**^ah-nail**-ah): Lit. translation: *This woman offers her blood to you/opens herself to you now.*

Tas-shadata (tahz-shah-**dah**-ta): Rough translation: *fool, coward, idiot.*

Taska (task-ah; alt. **tah**-skah): Courier and guide.

Te (teh): Prefix indicating formality and honor; no gender.

Teth hanaa silayha (tehth hah-**nah** sill-**igh**-ah): Lit. translation: *You* (female) *grace us* (male or mixed company).

Teth-kavit (tehth-**kah**-vitt): Lit. translation: *Gods hold you, and blessings to your strength.*

Teyanin (tay-ah-nin); plural: **teyanain** (tay-ah-**nayn**): A very old, small tribe which retreated to the mountains of the Horn after the Split. Originally the judges and law determiners of the desert, they're now considered the guardians of the Horn.

Thass (tass; alt. **thass**): A person with great status, beyond even noble rank.

Thio (thee-oh): Status.

Toi, te hoethra (toy, teh hoe-thrah): Lit. translation: *I swear to you I am speaking truth.*

Ugren (oo-ghren): a very rare universal bonding mixture; also used in the southlands to imply unbreakable permanence in an arrangement or situation.

Appendix A:

Desert Families

Aerthraim Family

Desert Family specializing in technology, engineering, and science; they keep themselves isolated from the other Families and do not hold to the Agreement.

Family symbol: Feathers, signifying freedom and the ability to soar above others.

Succession: Hereditary, matrilineal

Leadership: The leader of the Aerthraim is given the title of *mahadrae*; which translates, roughly, as "chosen mother of the free people."

Political: Alliances with each Family, based mainly on mercantile interests; reluctant to "side with" anyone in a dispute.

Current Family leader: Mahadrae Kallaisin

Aerthraim of note in ***Secrets of the Sands****:*

Lord Azaniari Aerthraim-Darden (**Adzh**-ah-knee-airy **Ayer**-thraym **Dar**-den; prefers to be called Azni [**Adzh**-knee]): For her own reasons, she long ago left the southlands in favor of in a modest home some distance north and east of Bright Bay.

Genealogy Notes:

Lord Azaniari Aerthraim-Darden is descended in unbroken matrilineal line from the past five generations of Aerthraim mahadrae. When Azaniari disqualified herself from leadership of the Aerthraim by choosing to become a desert lord, the leader-line was forced over to Pauca's branch and resulted in Kallaisin taking over as mahadrae. There remains to this day a great deal of ill-feeling towards Azaniari over this situation, especially among the Aerthraim loremasters.

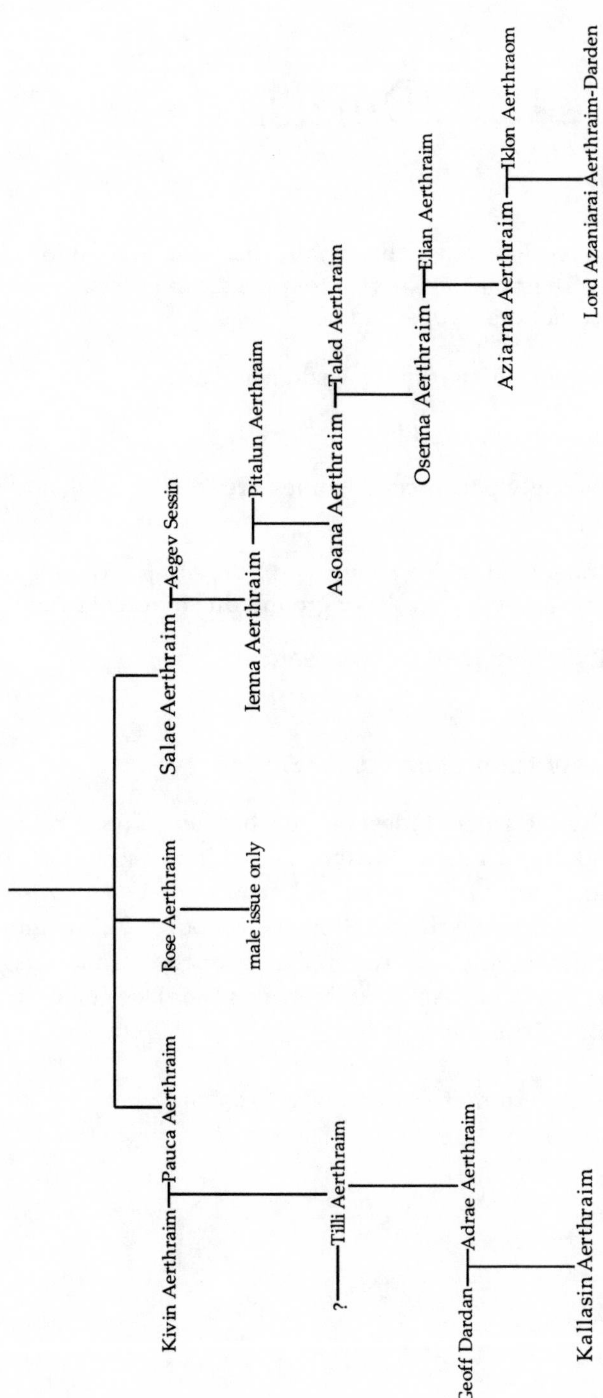

Aerthraim Genealogy

Darden

Located on the western coast, this Family has a reputation for treachery and deception. Their major exports are trained asp-jacaus, excellent (and strong) distilled liquors, drugs, and herbal teas.

Family symbol: Snake, signifying wisdom and alchemy

Succession: Hereditary, patrilineal

Leadership: Strongly patriarchal; women are seen as weak and unfit to rule.

Political: Ongoing feud with F'Heing, and Darden's trade agreements with Aerthraim Family are on shaky ground due to recent events.

Current Family leader: Lord Emmon Darden

Dardens of note in ***Secrets of the Sands***

Lord Irrio Darden: Eldest of three brothers, Lord Irrio is the son of Tecky and Ferra Darden; Tecky is the youngest of Lord Emmon Darden's three sons. Lord Emmon's eldest son, Geff, married into the Aerthraim line and renounced his Family status, while the middle son, Amlin, has not produced any legitimate children as of yet; Amlin still remains Heir Designate, and at this time Lord Irrio is next in line.

Azaniari Aerthraim-Darden: see *Aerthraim*

A subfamily of F'Heing, known for their colorful and color-fast dyes, excellent fine cloth, and coffee (a slightly lesser grade than the famous F'Heing Ridge, but still excellent).

Family symbol: Desert porcupine, signifying strength in submission

Succession: Assigned by F'Heing

Leadership: Decided by F'Heing

Political: Allies with and supports F'Heing in all matters.

Current Family leader: Lord Wiltin Eshan

F'Heing

West coast desert Family which produces drugs and dyes, loves power-grabs, and has a long and bloody history of treachery. Their "enclave" area used to be home to another, smaller desert Family; F'Heing annexed it for the fertile land and even more importantly, the sea access. F'Heing used their new port to send ships north, building the "independent" (read: F'Heing controlled) city of Kismo before the Northern Church had time to explore that far.

Family symbol: Mountain lion, signifying decisiveness and dominance

Succession: Hereditary; patrilineal

Leadership: Strongly male-dominated; women are seen as weak and unfit to rule.

Political: Ongoing feud with Darden Family; almost as xenophobic as the teyanain.

Current Family leader: Lord Rimmel F'Heing

Scratha

This line traditionally served as the premier diplomats of the desert, able to achieve a truce where others failed. But nearly the entire Family was mysteriously wiped out some years ago, leaving only Cafad Scratha to rebuild from the disaster; and Scratha has not inherited his family skill at charming combatants into peaceful negotiations.

Family symbol: Groundhogs, signifying community and shared resources.

> Ginger plants, a secondary Family motif, signify matters of the heart and spirit.

Succession: Hereditary, matriarchal

Leadership: Technically matriarchal, but in practice a team effort between the female Head of Family and a male desert lord bound to the Fortress; they are generally either related or married.

Political: Traditionally neutral; keeps alliances evenly balanced. The slaughter of the residents of Scratha Fortress, and Cafad's own actions, have thrown that entire equation into chaos.

Current Family leader: Lord Cafad Scratha

Scrathas of note in ***Secrets of the Sands****:*

Lord Cafad Scratha: Last survivor of Scratha Family; a brooding man with a quick temper and the obsession that Sessin Family was involved in the death of his entire Family.

Sessin

A desert family whose specialty is glasscraft of all sorts. They are the only ones who know the secret of casting clear, unflawed glass in large sheets.

Family symbol: Lizard, signifying sharp perception and a subtle, quick wit.

Succession: Hereditary; usually patrilineal

Leadership: Patriarchal but not averse to allowing smart, strong women to take positions of command—just not the very highest spots.

Political: Strong ties to the northern kingdom, strong influence in two major east coast port cities; tend to think of themselves as people to ally with, not people who need to seek allies.

Current Family leader: Lord Antouin Sessin

Sessins of note in ***Secrets of the Sands****:*

Lord Antouin Sessin: Current leader of Sessin Family; a much more open-minded man than his predecessor, Lord Arit Sessin.

Lord Arit Sessin: The leader of Sessin Family during Cafad Scratha's youth; a hard and intolerant man who thought only of advancing his own Family's power.

Lord Eredion Sessin: A desert lord of Sessin Family; Sessin Family's ambassador to the northern kingdom. Great-grandson of Lord Arit Sessin; uncle (see also: *s'e-ketan*) of Pieas Sessin and Nissa Sessin.

Nissa Sessin: A daughter of Sessin Family, and sister to Pieas Sessin; when King Oruen calls her "Lady" he is making a common northerner's mistake on ranking. Nissa Sessin has no rank title beyond her last name.

Pieas Sessin: A hotheaded, wastrel son of Sessin Family; brother of Nissa Sessin.

Genealogy notes:

Pieas and Nissa Sessin are the children of Lord Antouin Sessin by his second wife, Tashaye Sessin. Tashaye Sessin is Lord Eredion Sessin's sister. Lord Antouin's first wife died giving birth to a son, Dorsil Sessin, who is currently Heir to Sessin. Eredion Sessin's father, Chidor Sessin, was the only male offspring of Sashea Sessin, Lord Arit Sessin's daughter. Lord Arit Sessin had three children: Jonnui, the original Heir, Sashea, and Forus. Jonnui died during the Purge, turning Forus's line primary; and Forus fathered Antouin Sessin. Thus, Eredion is Pieas and Nissa's uncle, and at some remove, cousin as well; but he is not in line to lead Sessin unless Antouin's children fail to produce any legitimate heirs.

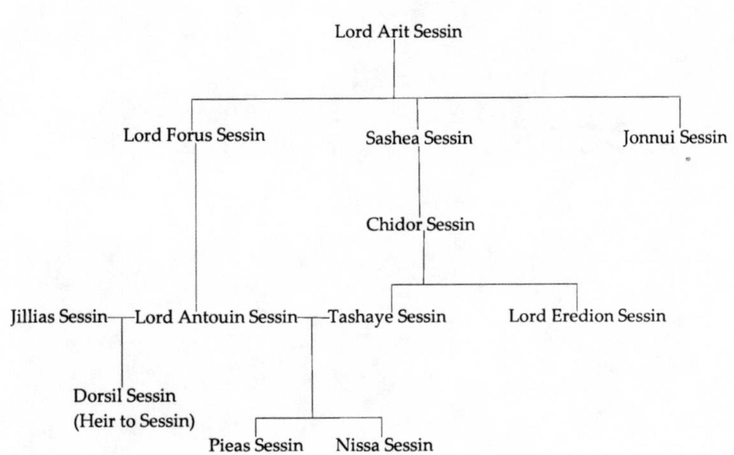

Tereph

A subfamily of Sessin; they do a large amount of the work for Sessin and have almost no real independence; essentially slaves to the larger Family.

Succession: Decided by Sessin

Leadership: Largely patriarchal, but wholly dictated by Sessin

Political: Follow Sessin's lead on all matters.

Current Family leader: Lord Hail Tereph

Family no longer exists; the head of Tehay got himself so far into debt with his gambling addictions that he had to give his lands and everything on them to F'Heing Family; residents had the choice of converting to F'Heing Family or going with their lord out into the deep sands to die in shame. The acquisition turned F'Heing into a formidable name and erased Tehay Family from existence, as well as sparking a number of still-unresolved questions on whether F'Heing had 'loaded the dice' to put Tehay in that situation.

Teyanain

A very old, small tribe which retreated to the mountains of the Horn after the Split. Originally the judges and law determiners of the desert, they're now considered the guardians of the Horn.

Family symbol: Owls, especially the great horned owl, signifying ferocity and adaptability.

Succession: Normally hereditary, but exceptional circumstances and individuals have occurred in the past.

Leadership: Teyanain leaders are called "Calcen", which literally translates to "Master"; they have absolute authority over all teyanain.

Political: Keep to themselves and ally with nobody, although some Families are under the mistaken impression that they have formed an alliance of convenience with the teyanain. Extremely xenophobic.

Current Family leader: Lord Evkit

Teyanain of note in ***Secrets of the Sands****:* Lord Evkit (leader of the teyanain)

Genealogy Notes: There are no publicly accessible records dealing with the genealogy of the teyanain at this time.

Toscin

A subfamily of Darden, with the most independence of any subfamily. Given complete latitude in their actions and alliances; generally turn matters around to benefit Darden in the end. Almost completely self-supporting; train "diplomatic and research services" (i.e., spies and secret alliance negotiators).

Succession: By merit

Leadership: Semi-hereditary; a wide range of bloodlines are considered valid for leadership, regardless of gender, and the Toscin Council selects a new leader as they see fit. Members of the Toscin Council are selected by a majority vote of the other members of the Toscin Council.

Political: Bias towards keeping Darden happy, but ostensibly neutral.

Current Family leader: Lord Quill Toscin

Appendix B:

The Bead Language of the Southlands

Bead codes in the south range from incredibly complex to very simple. A few general guidelines apply:

The more rows in the bracelet/beadwork, the more important the wearer.

The material, color, shape, size, and surrounding colors, and even the string material for the beadwork, can influence the conveyed message. Therefore, the simpler the arrangement, the simpler the message.

General Meanings of Colors

Aquamarine/blue-green: (lightest shades) Family ties, travel toward the sea, the sea (darkest shades).

Black: Absence and endings.

Blue: Depending on hue, this color can indicate: male or night (indigo); foretelling/prescience or eyewitness (medium hues); the direction north, the direction up, or the sky (lighter hues).

Brown: One of the colors of Comos; also signifies winter or an ending.

Gold (color)**:** Used in decorations to signify endings or money changing hands (not necessarily wealth—could mean the bearer is a merchant or accountant, for example).

Green: Can signify, depending on hue: new beginnings or safety (lighter green); sanctuary or political shift (darker green); wealth or travel out of dry lands to more fertile areas (emerald green); family ties or travel towards an ocean/large body of water (blue-green).

Red: Blood, violence, or death.

White: One of the colors of Comos; can also indicate female, daytime, or 'a day' (as a measure of time).

Yellow: Depending on the hue and placement: death, the sun, extremes, the Sun-Lord, or deceit.

Sample Combinations:

Red combined with yellow – violent death or transition
Red combined with white – death of a female or (paradoxically) a birth
Red combined with indigo – death of a male or change of ruler

Specific Pieces Explained:

Pieas Sessin's bracelet (during the audience of Alyea Peysimun, Eredion Sessin, and Pieas Sessin with King Oruen): "a thin bracelet of gold and green beads on his left arm, arranged asymmetrically on fine silver wire". This signifies that Pieas, while a member of an important southern Family and thus under its protection, is actually little more than a child in official terms, and holds no rank a king need recognize. It's a humiliating piece of jewelry, and one Eredion almost certainly forced Pieas to wear, as the proud young man never would have sported such an admission willingly.

Eredion Sessin's arm-band (during Eredion's audience in open court with King Oruen): "A wide, beaded band covered the man's right forearm from the wrist nearly to the elbow." This very likely was in the Sessin Family colors of emerald-green and sand-tan, and composed of hundreds of small round beads. The width indicates that Eredion is claiming contextually preeminent Sessin status; he could never wear this arm band within Sessin Fortress, for example, because his relative status there is much lower. But as Sessin ambassador to the northern court, this armband indicates that he outranks any other Sessin Family member who might be present. It's a slightly audacious statement, but not one likely to be challenged. Patterns within the beadwork itself probably also indicated, to the experienced eye, items such as Eredion's parentage, marital status, and whether he has any children.

Alyea's bracelet (which Chac gives her at the first way-stop): "small, round pieces of some dark green gemstone interspersed with squared off, unevenly sized pieces of thick white shell, threaded on a thin golden wire". This indicates a female under political protection by a major name, but not someone important in her own right: Chac's version of "hands off, she's mine". When Deiq sees it, he understands exactly what Chac meant, and knowing what he does of the overall situation and how he intends to manipulate events in the near future, finds it extremely funny.

The dining-hall attendant's bracelet (at the first way-stop dinner): "A bracelet on his right wrist ran through a gamut of grey hues, in three rows of precisely-matched beads." This indicates a servant of rank or status sufficient to wait on those of noble blood. In the south, even the servants have an internal ranking system, and this particular waystop is very sensitive to those nuances. Most likely, there were actually only three shades of grey, one for each row; the beads were of flawed glass or clay, and they were at least the size of a cherry pit. Alyea can perhaps be forgiven for not noticing such small details in a moment of stress.

***Note about the use of silver/gold 'wire'**: Metal wire, at a thread-thin width, breaks far too easily to be used for heavy beads; what Alyea sees is either at least a rigid frame of at least an eighth-inch diameter, or braided strands of a stiffened fiber dipped in a thin coating of silver or gold.*

Miscellaneous Symbols

Not all of these are used, directly, within this novel, but may help flesh out understanding of the Families and customs involved.

Feathers are the Aerthraim Family symbol, signifying freedom and the ability to soar above others.

Owls are the symbol of the teyanain, especially the great horned owl, signifying ferocity and adaptability.

Lizards, the symbol of Sessin Family, signify sharp perception and a subtle, quick wit.

Groundhogs, the symbol of Scratha Family, signify community and shared resources.

Ginger plants, also often seen on Scratha tapestries, signify matters of the heart and spirit.

Badgers, often used by loremasters, signify keepers of stories and deep secrets.

Brickroot plants represent tenacity and strength, but also imply a strong resistance to change.

Appendix C:

An Examination

by Loremaster Council no. 1576

of Gerau Sa'adenit's

A History of Places

This book, which was only recently made available to the Council of Loremasters, is a detailed and mostly accurate, if unauthorized, examination of the kingdom and its relation to the southlands. It must be stressed that King Oruen commissioned this study without the knowledge or approval of this Council, and thus this History must be examined with great care and appropriate corrections submitted to the King with the greatest possible speed. . . .

The kingdom and the southlands are generally considered completely separate entities from a political standpoint, and their interdependence is often overlooked. But even a brief examination shows that the one could not, throughout our shared history, have flourished without the other.

The southlands came first. That is undisputed. Civilization began in the once-fertile lands south of the Horn; in fact, oral history insists that once the entire southlands was as lush as Water's End, and not much higher in elevation. The abrupt rise into a mountain-high desert was due, according to various legends, to natural cataclysm, the anger of the gods at humanity's presumption, or an even stranger explanation involving an ancient race with godlike powers.

Whatever the cause, the changing land forced the tribal structure into closer and larger groups, and led directly to permanent settlements and the first towns. Dialects unified and merged, as did bloodlines long held separate; loremasters gather in great numbers to sort out frustrating questions over ancient genealogy when an important inheritance is at issue. . . .

The text of this thick book is notable for two things: one, its comprehensive nature, and two, the odd changes in the 'voice', as though it had actually been written by two separate people. The first is stiff and formal, as one would expect a highly educated noble to write; the second is rather more *common. . .*

Place-names in the kingdom sound simple, but a little digging reveals deep roots. The word "king", for instance. The original word for "honored tribal leader/supreme authority" was Kaen (Kaena for females), and the northern kingdom, in the old books, is called Kaenoz. Those names have since shifted to our modern "king" and "kingdom". Attempts to give the kingdom a proper name have run into strong resistance from the Northern Church and its followers, who believe that their founder, Wezel, should be in some way honored in the chosen name. Their suggestions have tended towards names like Wezeldom and Fourgodsland, and have generally been rejected out of hand; although Ninnic and Mezarak apparently worried the court deeply at one point by seriously considering making those names official. Fortunately, both men were easily distracted and the issue soon faded from their minds. . . .

The simplistic approach displayed in the above excerpt turns an important subject into near-mockery, a sharp contrast to the more learned approach of the first section. Repeated inquiries as to the true identity of the author or authors meet no answer from King Oruen or any of his court, staff, or scribes; whatever hand transcribed this entire volume, no doubt from a collection of notes, is not admitting to the act. . . .

As language changes, the origin of names is lost to all but the loremasters who dedicate their lives to preserving the past; but a better understanding of our beginnings is vital to a firm comprehension of our present, and furthers planning for the future. A word as simple as s'a, *"honored woman", can be traced back hundreds of years to the original* saaera, *a woman of status; likewise the mascu-*

line form, s'e, *was once* seere, *which indicated not only an honored man but could, with a slightly different inflection, indicate that the subject possessed predictive powers. The implication that the ancients believed that women could not be seers is undeniable.*

Place names proved as fluid: the mountain area known today as the Horn was, when initially settled by the teyanain, called the Teychek-haiz, "Horns of Justice". As the teyanain became more insular and less involved with the general population, that name fell out of favor and was replaced with the more neutral "Horn". The king's home city was once Iliaye-Ayrq, "Bright Triumph of Ayrq", in reference to King Ayrq's astonishing achievement of pulling all the squabbling factions together into a relatively unified settlement; the fast-growing town's success as a port altered the name, over time, to "Bright Bay". . . .

The author goes on, with a fair degree of accuracy, to detail the history behind every significant name in the southlands and the kingdom. This section is largely in the more formal voice, but now and again the common tone raises its head again. . . .

The names given on maps and the names used by ordinary people are often very different. The large swamp to the east of Bright Bay is a perfect example. Maps in the royal library assign the incredible name Optsch t'a Kella Wezel; literally, "The Wealth and Divinity of Wezel". A shorter version, on less official maps, is Optakazel Swamp, which translates to "Madman's Swamp." Some local commoners even call the area "Ugly Salt Swamp", referring to its main export, a cloudy, lumpy grey salt which tastes exceptionally bitter and is for some reason in high demand at noble tables (under its official name of optschalz, or "rich man's salt", rather than the common moniker of "ugly salt" or "madman's salt", of course). . . .

There is a distinct and reprehensible slant to the overall History, in that the author or authors are clearly disposed against the Northern Church. Historians must needs remain neutral to accurately convey facts, and considering the many good works the Northern Church has to its name (one of the few names not traced in this volume, another example of bias) it is improper to base all perceptions on the recent difficult times.

Appendix D:

Excerpted Notes from Loremaster Council Records

Transcribed shortly after the slaughter at Scratha Fortress:

While Cafad Scratha does not hold a true leadership line, his unusual circumstances dictate that his claim to Head of Family status be upheld. The alternatives are even further removed from the true bloodline than the boy himself, or are unacceptably tainted in their associations . . . Should a true-line survivor ever be discovered, of course, his status as Head of Family is to be stripped immediately and the proper line reinstated. . . .

Azaniari's status, unusual though it may be, and against the duly recorded objections of her own Family loremaster, must be upheld due to taking the trials through Darden and her current known association with Regav Darden. She is hereby confirmed in these Records as an Aerthraim desert lord, and her children are to be watched with great care and steered into choosing partners outside the Aerthraim bloodline. . . .

Transcribed shortly after Ninnic's death and the ascension of Oruen to the throne of Bright Bay:

The child given through Cafad Scratha's blood trial turned out deformed and has not survived; the bastard child produced in the adjustment period after his third trial turned out deformed and has not survived; there are no further traceable offspring after that point. It must be considered, at this point, that Cafad Scratha was so damaged by the emotional trauma of losing his family as to render him effectively sterile. A close watch shall be kept to ensure that any deformed offspring are duly destroyed to avoid introducing undesirable variables into what may remain of the Scratha line, and a new attention is being paid to the previously dismissed alternates . . .

The children of Azaniari Aerthraim and Regav Darden did not survive long enough to beget children of their own, and as Regav may now be presumed dead and events have altered Azaniari such that she may no longer bear children, that line is to be considered, regrettably, closed. However, Azaniari's twin brother, Allonin, must be given closer scrutiny despite his multiple offenses; his viable fertility is proven beyond question, as are his wits, strength, and ingenuity . . .

Pieas Sessin is moving in a thoroughly undesirable direction. Those of his illegitimate children we have confirmed are being removed and placed in more appropriate surroundings . . .

Lord Oruen's fertility is proven, and his illegitimate children are being watched closely; but he has, as yet, shown no interest in an official match. Until his sanity is established as utterly secure, this Council declines to press the issue further . . .

About the Author

Photo: Earl Harris

Leona Wisoker got her start as a writer when she was eight, with a story about all the vacuum cleaners in the world breaking down at the same time. Ever since then she has successfully used the excuse of writing to avoid housework, even going so far as writing poetry (which is then safely locked away in a lead-lined box) when nothing else will save her from chores.

Leona's work is fueled equally by coffee and conviction; she has been known to take over the entire dining room to deconstruct a difficult novel-in-progress. Addicted to eclectic research and reading since childhood, she often chooses reading material alphabetically rather than by subject or author. This has led her to read about aardvarks, birds, child-warriors, dragons, eggs, faeries, ghosts, horses, and many other random subjects.

Her short stories have appeared in *Futures: Fire to Fly* and *Anotherealm*; she is a regular reviewer for *Green Man Review*. She has lived in Florida, Connecticut, Oregon, New Hampshire, Nevada, Alaska, California, and Virginia; has experienced the alternate realities of Georgia, North Carolina, Arizona, New York, Long Island, and Italy; and believes that "home is wherever my coffee cup is filled."

She currently lives in Virginia with an extraordinarily patient husband and two large dogs, and she almost never vacuums.

Read more about Leona Wisoker and her work at

http://www.leonawisoker.com

Free eBook

Whether you're traveling across the desert or just taking the train to work, sometimes you want the convenience of reading electronically. At the Mercury Retrograde Press website, readers who purchase the book in Trade Paper format can download the eBook version of *Secrets of the Sands*—for free. Just enter the code GERAU on this form:

http://www.MercuryRetrogradePress.com/eBookform.asp

and we will email you a download link for *Secrets of the Sands*, in whatever eBook format you choose.

Want More?

Visit the Children of the Desert page on the Mercury Retrograde Press website:

http://www.MercuryRetrogradePress.com/Worlds/ChildrenoftheDesert.asp

for even more background on the world of *Secrets of the Sands*—and a sneak peek at the first chapter of Leona Wisoker's next novel, *Bells of the Kingdom*.